"**D**o you s[...]
"I'd die first."

He flinched at the cold statement. Keeping her wrists locked in one hand, he reached back and slid his silver knife free of the holster. *Don't cut her, don't cut her.* He repeated the mantra as he brought up the knife and laid the flat of the silver blade against her bare shoulder.

Her body jerked at the kiss of cold silver against her skin. But she didn't scream in pain.

Lifting the blade, he looked at the spot. Her skin stayed clear. Relief poured through him like water. If she had been a demon witch, the silver would have burned her. But the real shocker was that he didn't want her to be a demon witch. What was going on? He forced his hand to slide the knife back into the holster. "Don't summon your magic." He slowly let go of her hands, shoved off her, and pushed back to his knees.

She sat up, scooting back on her butt, and rose. "It didn't work anyway. You don't stink of sulfur like a possessed human would, and if you were possessed, my magic would have banished the demon. You're too fast and strong to be a mortal. What the hell are you, and why are you here?"

By Jennifer Lyon

BLOOD MAGIC
SOUL MAGIC
NIGHT MAGIC

A WINGSLAYER NOVEL

NIGHT MAGIC

JENNIFER LYON

BALLANTINE BOOKS • NEW YORK

Night Magic is a work of fiction. Names, characters, places, and incidents are the products of the author's imagination or are used fictiously. Any resemblance to actual events, locales, or persons, living or dead, is entirely coincidental.

2011 Ballantine Books Mass Market Original

Copyright © 2011 by Jennifer Apodaca

Published in the United States by Ballantine Books, an imprint of The Random House Publishing Group, a division of Random House, Inc., New York.

BALLANTINE and colophon are registered trademarks of Random House, Inc.

ISBN 978-0-345-52006-7
eBook ISBN 978-0-345-52007-4

Cover design: Jae Song

Printed in the United States of America

www.ballantinebooks.com

9 8 7 6 5 4 3 2 1

In memory of my father.

You taught me passion and imagination by sharing your love of flying through your funny, tragic, and beautiful stories of being a fighter pilot.

You taught me love with your devotion to Mom.

You taught me how to work hard by example.

We lost you much too soon, but I look up and imagine you soaring across the endless blue skies, whole and free.

Love you and keep flying, Dad!

I'll see you when I get my wings . . .

ACKNOWLEDGMENTS

I could not have written this book without my truly amazing editor, Shauna Summers. It was during the revision process that Phoenix and Ailish took shape, and the story that emerged surprised even me. It wouldn't have happened without you, Shauna!

I'd also like to thank Jessica Sebor, another fabulous editor at Random House, for her hard work on the book. Nothing gets by you, Jessie, and the book is stronger for your diligence!

My agent, Karen Solem, read the original idea and was very enthusiastic. That initial excitement kept me going through the long days of writing and nights of worrying. Thank you, Karen!

To my friends who never let me give up, I couldn't have done it without you. I want to say a special thanks to Marianne Donley—though she now lives across the country from me, she did emergency email plotting during revisions that helped me take this book to the next level. And so many more friends who were there every single time I needed them for plotting, encouragement, butt-kicking, laughter, and commiseration: Maureen Child, Kate Carlisle, Laura Wright, Michele Cwiertny, Silver (Penny) James and so many more! I wish I could name you all!

To my family: My husband who is the hero of my world, my three sons who are the center of my world, and my sister who shared her passion for reading with me and got me hooked at an early age. You all put up with my strange deadline behavior and continue to love me anyway. I love you all!

And to all my friends who hang out at Jennifer lyonbooks.com—you all rock! A tip of the Appletini to you! You all know the question: Is Phoenix Wing Slayer worthy?

The Birth of a Siren

TWENTY-THREE YEARS,
ELEVEN MONTHS, AND TWO WEEKS AGO

The phoenix soared across the sky, his blue-and-purple wings sweeping up and down. He was waiting.

Then he heard it, the siren's cry that signaled the first breath of life in the newborn. It was a sound of such aching beauty, it drenched his eyes with tears and reverberated down his feathers, muscles, and bones until it filled his soul.

It was too much. Each time, it was always too much.

He erupted into flames, the heat bursting from his very cells in an agonizing explosion. The fire snapped and roared, eating his feathers, melting his muscles, and pulverizing his bones in endless torture.

Ending only when he was reduced to ash, burned and gone.

Until he was called by the siren to rise from the flames once more.

1

Ailish Donovan was home for the family reunion from hell.

She stood at the French doors of the small house she'd rented as the sun sank into the horizon. It had been nearly eight years since she'd seen a sunset or anything else. As a witch she was connected to the earth elements that fed her powers, so she could feel the day slipping away and the long fingers of darkness spreading across Glassbreakers, California. The darkness fed her mood, her tightly controlled anger, her determination.

With her right hand, she touched the binding around her left wrist. It was about an inch wide with a rounded shape that felt like a snug plastic bracelet, but it was indestructible. Once it had been plain rope that had been twisted by dark magic into a handfast binding. Nothing broke through it, no magic, no knife, no bolt cutters, not even fire. She'd tried every possible way, but nothing worked.

Thanks to her mother's betrayal and trickery, she was handfasted to the demon Asmodeus. If the handfast was completed, Ailish would become a demon witch. Asmodeus would own her soul in exchange for dark powers. No way was she giving her soul to a demon. She had no intention of spending eternity in the Underworld as a minion.

All this added up to Ailish being one pissed-off witch. But she'd learned how to channel her anger into action, and she'd trained her body into a weapon. She was one of the top professional women kickboxers in the country. Being blind got her noticed, but her skills, speed, and power won her titles.

And now she'd come home, back to where it all started eight years ago, to win the most crucial battle of her life—break the handfast and face down her mother. Knowing her mother, she was sure it would be a fierce battle. Maeve Donovan was the high witch of the Deus'Donovan coven. She was a determined and dangerous demon witch who had never loved Ailish, only used her to gain more power.

Ailish might have run away a scared little girl, but she'd come home ready to fight. That meant she'd use every advantage, including the magic in her voice. When she sang, all magic was enhanced. She didn't know how far her power reached, but she sensed it radiated for miles. It was the same power that had led to her blindness, but this time she intended to get control of it.

She would find the way to control her voice power. She had to.

"Ailish, here's the knife," Haley Ryan said from behind her.

She shut and locked the French doors, then turned and held out her hand. "It's all silver?"

"Yes," Haley answered. "I got it from some witch hunter friends. They always carry silver knives."

The knife was cool in her palm, about eight inches in length. She felt the smooth hilt, then ran her fingers along the flat side of the blade. "Thanks, Haley. You've been a huge help. But you need to go." Worry for her friend edged along her spine. Haley had insisted on helping Ailish get settled before flying out to Washington, D.C., where she was lobbying for more funding for her homeless shelter. But the woman was mortal and all too vulnerable; she needed to leave.

"My car won't be here for a half hour or so." Haley moved into the kitchen, then came back and set two glasses on the table. "Iced tea. How long do you think it'll be before the coven knows you're here?"

Ailish sat, placed the knife carefully on the table, then found her tea glass and took a sip. All she could see of Haley was a gray shadow across the table. Did she still wear her hair in a thick blond bob? When Ailish had seen her last, Haley had been slim, with an athletic build. She'd had piercing blue eyes that saw right through bullshit. Bringing her thoughts back to the question, she lifted her wrist. "Since I'm wearing the ultimate tracking device, the demon knows, and he's told the coven. Tonight, they'll summon Asmodeus into a mortal's body and try to seduce me into the Claiming Rite that will finish the binding." And turn her into a demon witch. She shivered at the thought. The handfast binding created a link between her and the demon that not only allowed him to track her, but could also ramp up her lust until just a simple touch from a man would create a painful hunger in her.

Haley set her glass down with a determined thump. "I'm canceling this trip."

"Hell, no. My mother tried to kill you to get to me." She wouldn't let her. Ailish would use magic if necessary to force Haley to get on that plane.

"What's your plan, Ailish? Why come back now? What's the knife for?" Worry and frustration underlined her short, sharp questions.

Ailish reached out and touched the knife. "Silver conducts magic. Since my voice enhances all power when I sing, I should be able to focus enough of it into the silver knife and cut the binding."

Haley sucked in her breath. "Can you open your fifth

chakra? You'll need it to control that magic. If you can't control it . . ."

"I know, Haley," she said dryly, reaching up to touch the thin, spidery scars around her eyes. Right after she ran away at sixteen, her mother had found her with Haley. Furious, Maeve Donovan had used her dark magic to strangle Haley in retaliation. Ailish had panicked and begun to sing, sending out the waves of uncontrolled enhancement. The car windshield had exploded, hitting her mother in the eyes.

The witch-karma backlash blinded Ailish. In doing her mother an injury, she'd lost her own sight. In one life-changing moment, she had learned the brutal price of using her powers to cause harm.

Shaking off the memory, she said, "I'm physically much stronger now." She had to be. She couldn't use her powers to protect herself because of witch karma, so she'd honed her body into a weapon with kickboxing. The beauty of all that training was the added strength in her mind-body connection, giving her more control of her first four chakras.

"That's good, but you need more than your elemental magic in your first four chakras to control the power. Have you been able to open your fifth chakra?"

"No." The failure tasted bitter. Without a familiar, few witches could open their fifth, sixth, or seventh chakra. A curse three decades ago had broken the witches' bonds with their familiars.

"Then what makes you think you'll be able to use your voice to cut the binding?"

"I've been using it. When I get stuck in the dreams"— she tried not to shudder as the memories tormented her, memories of the nights Asmodeus had used the link between them to force sex dreams on her that took her to the edge of desperation—"I can wake myself by singing. If my voice can break the demon's hold on my dreams, then it should work when I'm awake." It had to, it was her only hope.

"I still think you're taking too big a risk by being in Glassbreakers, where the coven is. Why now, Ailish?"

She wished she could see Haley's face. All those years ago, after her mother's attack, Ailish had expected Haley to revile her, to hate her because she was the daughter of a demon witch. But Haley hadn't. Instead, she'd thought Ailish to be some kind of hero for fighting her mom. *Hero* . . . the idea was laughable. She was handfasted to a demon! She'd lived for sixteen years with her mother and the coven without grasping what they were doing, how they were hurting people. Haley had known the terrible things demon witches did, like stealing homeless girls for sacrifices. Yet in Ailish, Haley saw something . . . worthy.

It had been Haley who used her connections with homeless shelters across the state of California to get Ailish out of Glassbreakers and away from her mother.

But Ailish had never told Haley this part. In fact, over the years, she'd kept their contact minimal so her mother wouldn't try to use Haley to get to her. She'd waited until just before Haley had to leave to tell her. "The handfast binding contract is for eight years. It ends on my twenty-fourth birthday in two weeks."

Haley set her glass down sharply. "What does that mean? You'll be free if you don't submit to the Claiming Rite?"

"No. Not if I still have the binding on." She lifted her wrist.

"But then what . . . Oh God, no." Haley's voice rose in horror. "You'll die?"

Maybe it was better that she couldn't see Haley's expression. "Yes." Then she forced a smile she didn't quite feel. "But at least I won't be a demon witch. Even better, my mother and her coven will die with me."

*   *   *

Later that night, Ailish dreamed of the only boy she'd ever loved, Kyle Whaling. They had met in high school when she'd longed to be just a normal girl. In her dream, she could see him clearly. He had sea-blue eyes in a boyish face, with high cheekbones and a full mouth. He smiled at her, his eyes crinkling. "Ailish, I knew you'd come back to me," he said, his fingers trailing down her neck and sliding over her collarbone.

Fire traveled through her veins, heating her skin and making her nipples swell and ache. Her womb contracted and throbbed. The painful hunger gripped her until she couldn't lie still.

Kyle leaned his mouth close to hers and said, "Ailish, let me touch you, kiss you, claim you. Let me in. Get up, open the door, and I'll give you what you need."

Get up, open the door? She realized then that she was dreaming. Of course she was dreaming, she could only see in her dreams. She began to sing, *Light of the moon, rain down your power. Bring me strength, carved in stone.* As her voice rose, energy began to swirl softly in her pelvis, then rise like water flowing through her first four chakras, the pure light pushing the dream back.

She woke to her dark and shadowy world. Her tank top and shorts were twisted around her body, the sheet beneath her was wrinkled. She sat up and swung her legs over the side of the bed, then reached over to press a button on her phone.

A mechanical voice said, "One twenty-four A.M."

"Ailish, open the door, sweetheart. I've waited a long time to see you." The seductive male voice floated from outside the front of the house and reached deep into her memories, the memories of a young girl desperate for love, desperate to belong. That pissed her off. She knew the voice was a trick.

Oh yeah, she'd open the door, she thought as she shoved

off the bed. Walking the path she'd memorized, she headed out of the bedroom of the tiny house she'd rented. She crossed the hallway into the small living room. Through practice, she knew how to memorize her surroundings. There was a TV on her right, a couch and coffee table on her left. She counted off the steps automatically, turning left at eleven. She held out her hand until her fingers brushed the door. Undoing the double locks, she inhaled and smelled the scent of sulfur.

Fury pounded in her head. The Deus'Donovan coven had kidnapped another man, then summoned Asmodeus into him. The poor bastard's real self was held prisoner deep in his subconscious while the demon had control of his body.

"Ailish, hurry!" His voice was slightly tinny, as if being forced through a cylinder, yet it still had traces of that painful familiarity. "You ran away eight years ago before I could make you understand. I loved you, I still love you. How could you think I'd harm you?"

Because she wasn't a painfully naïve sixteen-year-old girl anymore, that's how. She pulled open the door. With the porch light on, she could just make out the shadow of a man.

"I came back for you. To make you mine and—"

Careful not to pull on her powers, she used a hopping side kick and slammed her foot into the blurry shadow's midsection. She had to stun the mortal man's body in order to banish the demon.

"Ooof!" He flew off the two steps, landing on his back on the grass.

She followed, the cement cool on her bare feet. As she stepped down onto the damp grass, she summoned her power, funneling the earth's energy up from her chakras and through her hands toward the groaning man on the grass. "Never, Asmodeus, I will never submit to you!" She had to control her fury to keep her witchcraft going.

The smell of sulfur grew.

The handfast binding on her left wrist began to throw off sparks, causing electrical pulses that fired her nerve endings until her nipples ached and it was all she could do not to squeeze her thighs together and sob. Aching, desperate need coiled tight inside her, and a small part of her mind pleaded for the release the demon offered, even though she knew she would damn herself forever if she surrendered.

Gathering her strength, she silenced that beseeching voice within and stood still under the onslaught, keeping her powers flowing from the earth through her to banish Asmodeus back to the Underworld and free the spirit of the mortal man the demon had possessed. Her head pounded, sweat coated her skin, and her hands shook.

The mortal on the ground thrashed and muttered in a guttural language.

Then the scent of sulfur bloomed thick and heavy, almost stealing her breath. It felt as though the battle went on forever, Ailish matching her powers against a demon lord. Five seconds later, she had won and the stench vanished.

"What happened?" a confused male voice asked.

Drained, tired, and still aching for the touch she could never have, Ailish realized that now this voice sounded nothing like the Kyle Whaling of her dreams. That had been a trick of Asmodeus. Another reason to hate that three-headed bastard. "Maybe you had too much to drink and the cab dropped you off at the wrong house?"

He climbed to his feet. "I don't remember. . . ."

The man sounded confused and disoriented. "How about I call you another cab?" she suggested.

"But my car is here," he said, as if trying to understand what was happening and coming up empty. "Right here in front of your house. I guess I drove it here?"

Wonderful, he drove under the influence of a demon. Never mind the drugs given to him by the demon witches before they did their summoning. But the upside was that her magic should have cleared the toxins from his body. Using a magical push behind her words, she said, "Go straight home and to bed." He'd wake up tomorrow and be fine, if a little vague about what had happened.

She heard him turn and walk away. Her damaged eyes could make out the shadow moving across the grass toward another, dimmer shadow at the curb. Finally, she heard the car start up and pull away.

She was alone. Slowly, she turned and walked up the two steps, the four steps across the porch, and inside the house. She closed the door and locked it. Leaning back against the door, she shuddered.

She'd won this round. With the demon freshly banished, she should have a window of time. It would be very dangerous if she used her voice power when the demon was near her in a mortal's body. It had been risky enough to sing to escape the dream. When she sang, her voice enhanced all magic regardless of its source. If she used that power again while Asmodeus was nearby in a mortal's body, she might enhance his power enough that he could gain control of her will and make her submit to the Claiming Rite.

She wasn't willing to take that chance.

She would try using her voice power to break the handfast binding now, while Asmodeus was recently banished.

Phoenix Torq downed the whiskey in his glass, swung around on the stool in the dive biker bar, and zeroed in on the two rogues he was tracking. Their rank copper stink had led him right to them. They'd slaughtered a witch just an hour ago. He'd found her husk of a body drained of blood.

Damn, that pissed him off. A witch alone, without pro-

Axel's square jaw twitched. "Carla wants to talk to you."

"Need sex, not a shrink or a witch." He could sure as hell use a soul mirror, though. Only two hunters so far had found that single witch that was the other half of their soul. The soul-mirror bond broke the curse for the witch and the hunter. Would it also chase out this voice in his head?

Oh yeah, because in his life, good things like a soul-mirror witch happened.

Fuck that, he knew how to survive. Sex was survival. He shifted to walk around his hawk. Sex first, then he'd find the source of that voice and silence it forever.

Axel blocked him. "You're going to see her."

He narrowed his gaze. "Got other plans."

"To die?" Axel's voice dipped to anger. "Ram's report said you were seconds from your last breath tonight."

He growled out, "Not your problem, Locke. Step off my balls."

Axel didn't move. "Wrong answer."

Phoenix liked violence, but right now he needed sex more. "Try this. I'm so close to the edge that it's either sex or going hunting for a witch to butcher for her blood."

Axel stepped aside. "Go."

He walked to the woman he'd eyed earlier, the need climbing and swelling in him. The music cut, the strobes died, and the house lights came up in a signal that the club was closing.

The sudden silence echoed in the bright glare.

Then singing surged in his head and cut off his thoughts. *Not again.* He froze to the floor, clenching his fists and jaw in an effort to will it away. He would not allow a repeat performance of losing control to a voice. Forcing his jaw to relax, he stepped up to the woman and said, "Name's Phoenix. Looking for company?"

"Iris."

He barely heard her over the insistent singing. Sweat prickled his neck, back, and pits while his biceps burned. The voice circled his brain, the singing intense and commanding. Heart-pounding urgency rode over the hot, desperate need for sex, turning into a compulsion to find the source of that voice. Problem was, Axel would see him leave, assume he'd gone after some witch blood, and try to stop him.

He reached out and snagged Iris's warm hand. She followed him toward the stairs that led to the second-floor condos. Phoenix looked around, saw that Axel had noted where he was heading, then turned his attention to closing the club.

The pitch of the singing vibrated his brain, and his muscles jumped and twitched. Stopping, he turned to the woman and muttered, "Sorry." Then he let go of her hand and broke into a ground-eating stride to go out the back way.

Had to leave.

Find the voice.

Now.

He headed out to his Yamaha R6. Straddling the machine, he fired it up and then screamed off into the velvety darkness.

The compulsion to find the voice grew with every mile he covered. His brain echoed with the ups and downs, the smooth slide of notes that resonated with power pumping through his bloodstream in an ever-growing urge to find it. The growl of his motorcycle didn't matter, nothing dimmed the sound. He kept following the voice.

To where? End of the fucking rainbow? Or maybe a trip to the morgue?

Key's words came back to him. *This how you want to die? Like your mom?*

He'd been hearing distant singing in his head for two months. Being a witch hunter prevented him from developing the schizophrenia that had tortured his mother, so he'd simply ignored it. Figured it was his superenhanced hearing picking up a radio station or something. But tonight the voice had demanded he acknowledge it and damn near killed him in the process. He would hunt down the source and destroy it or die trying.

But his mother's death? That was at his feet. She'd died because of him. Because she had needed him and he'd failed her.

He'd spent every day since then paying for that. He'd pay forever, and it wouldn't ever be enough. He could hunt down every man who ever hurt a woman until all women were safe and protected, and his mom would still have died on that street because he hadn't helped her when she'd begged him to.

If this voice led him to his death, he deserved it. No big loss. But what he couldn't stomach was this voice interfering in his life and causing him to *fail*. What if he failed while rescuing a witch from a rogue, or a woman from an abuser?

Unacceptable. He couldn't live with failure like that. Not again.

Leaning into a turn as he left the main road to enter an older neighborhood, he realized that the voice was no longer inside his head. Instead, he could actually hear the woman singing somewhere nearby. He pulled the bike over to the curb and shut it off. The song flowed around him, like water over rocks in a stream.

Earth, water, air, and flames ascend to the sound of my voice.

With the flow of my blood, enhance this knife.

No longer shall this binding rule, deny the handfast in blood and truth. Cut the shackle of lies and deceit, wings of freedom come for me!

Before he could feel relief at tracking the source or worry about what it meant, urgency shot through him, making his muscles jerk and twitch with the need to track the sound. He threw his leg over the bike, stood, and walked silently up the street. Several large trees cast shadows from the moon and streetlights, while the roots buckled the sidewalks and driveways. He followed the soft voice to a home at the end of the street.

It was a small yellow house with the garage on the left, a patch of grass out front, a little porch, and a front window. The sound came from behind the house. He ignored the door and went around the two-car garage to the five-foot fence that surrounded the backyard.

No longer shall this binding rule, deny the handfast in blood and truth. Cut the shackle of lies and deceit, wings of freedom come for me!

Witchcraft. He felt the power tremble through his insides, and his blood began to burn in his veins. He caught the scent of spicy witch blood, and his gut cramped with need. The craving of the curse hit him harder than he'd expected. Never had he smelled any blood this alluring, thick and tangy with a cadence all its own—something familiar—coconut.

How was her voice in his head? Suspicion slowed him enough to consider the possibility that she was a demon witch. It had been demon witches and their demon lord Asmodeus who caused the blood and sex curse a generation ago. The demon witches had captured three witch hunters and tried to bind them as familiars. The spell went wrong, ending up cursing them all. Maybe a demon witch was trying it again?

He fought to stay in control even as sweat broke out on his skin. The pull to get to her was irresistible, and he put his hand on top of the fence, bent his knees, then sprang up and over to land in a crouch on the other side. He didn't pause but hurried along the side of the garage. It was darker back here, which was no problem for his hunter vision.

The tiny backyard came into view. The scent of blood hit him again, filling his nostrils, rushing down his throat, and making him burn to capture the coconut-scented power. He swept his gaze over the empty patio and across the yard until he came to the woman sitting on a towel in the middle of the square of overgrown grass. Moonlight poured over her, revealing choppy black hair skimming her shoulders. Her face was tilted down, and a black tank top exposed her toned arms. Her left wrist lay on her lap, and bright red blood trailed over her bare thighs. Hovering in the air above her hands was a silver knife with a wicked-sharp blade.

Her voice soared again.

Cut the shackle of lies and deceit.

The knife jiggled and danced in the air, then suddenly sliced the skin of her forearm. "No, damn it," she said, and the knife dropped to the towel. She picked up the knife and edged the tip of the blade against her wrist.

His gut clenched at the sight. She was using magic and cutting herself, but it didn't look like a ritual. It looked lonely and desperate. The call of her blood was too strong, too powerful. He tried to tell himself to freeze, to hold and not . . .

But he was already striding across the patio, over the grass, until he was one step away from her. He had to stop the witch from cutting herself and reached for her arm.

The woman jerked, dropped the knife, rolled to the left, and came up to a standing position.

Phoenix blinked in shock as his hand closed around empty air. Then a foot caught him in the solar plexus and knocked him on his ass. Before he could get his breath back, a current of magic ripped through his guts. "Don't!" he shouted at the witch standing there with her hands up.

"Leave, demon!" she ordered, and released her power.

A wave of pure witch energy hit him in the chest, sucking the breath from him. The curse screamed through him, hot agony racing through his veins like Drano. Only witch blood would cool the pain. He fought his brain's demand that he grab his knife and cut her. Instead he rolled to his feet and slammed into the witch, shoving her to the ground. Pinning her with his body, he dragged her hands over her head and secured them in his grip.

Instantly he felt the blood from her wrist touch the skin of his hand. The kick of power bowed his back and locked his muscles. He groaned at the rush of pleasure blasting through him, like some kind of internal orgasm. Finally his vision cleared, and he dragged in a breath.

And smelled her, smelled the mango of her skin mixing with the coconut of her blood. She was like a damned tropical drink, and his veins begged for more.

She bucked and fought. "Get off me! I won't submit, I refuse!"

The more contact he had with her body, the more the bloodlust drained. Or her magic had just knocked him senseless. Trying to gather his wits, he looked down into her angular face, full lips pulled back in a snarl. Her black hair spread beneath her. He lifted his gaze to her eyes and froze in the grip of another shock. There was a fine webbing of scars, almost like spider cracks in safety glass around her eyes. The color of her irises was a blue so light as to appear silver, and her gaze wasn't on him. She wasn't looking at anything.

The witch beneath him was blind. Swear to the Wing Slayer, he thought he felt the winged tattoos on his arms tremble.

"Get off! You can't rape me, demon. I have to submit, and I refuse!"

Fury throbbed in her voice. Not fear, but rage. He had to get control of the situation. "I'm not going to hurt you. Stop squirming." He could feel the sinew of her muscles as she writhed beneath him, and her movements ignited a whole different kind of lust inside him. Every slide of her body made him hotter and harder. Damn it, he'd only pinned her to stop her from pounding him with her magic before he killed her in response. He'd been so close to palming his knife and cutting her. But now the feel of her, the scent of her, the sensation of her body against his, heated him until his cock grew hard and heavy with the ache to bury himself inside her.

"I don't care what you do, I'll never give in! No matter how much it hurts . . ."

He was hurting her? He hadn't meant to, damn it. He eased back from her, waiting warily for the blind witch to take another swing at him. Then Phoenix looked around for her knife. It was on the towel where she'd left it when she rolled. He shifted his gaze to her sightless eyes, and his stomach tightened. He had to get control! "I'll let you up if you swear you won't use your magic."

"Screw you, demon."

"I'm not a demon, witch." Phoenix couldn't stop looking at her. Her face was so strong, a slightly squared chin that screamed stubbornness, full mouth, blade-sharp cheekbones, black hair, all framing her damaged eyes. How had her blindness happened? Who had hurt her? Another witch hunter? The demon she seemed so worried about? The idea of it infuriated him. What coward had hurt this witch? Earth witches . . .

But he didn't know for sure if she was an earth witch. He'd caught her in the middle of a possible ritual. The knife she used looked silver, but maybe that was a trick. What had she been doing? Damn, she had him so tied up, he nearly forgot it was her voice that pulled him to her. That didn't sound like the power of an earth witch. "Do you serve a demon, little witch?"

"I'd die first."

He flinched at the cold statement. Keeping her wrists

locked in one hand, he reached back and slid his silver knife free of the holster. *Don't cut her, don't cut her.* He repeated the mantra as he brought up the knife and laid the flat of the silver blade against her bare shoulder.

Her body jerked at the kiss of cold silver against her skin. But she didn't scream in pain.

Lifting the blade, he looked at the spot. Her skin stayed clear. Relief poured through him like water. If she had been a demon witch, the silver would have burned her. But the real shocker was that he didn't want her to be a demon witch. What was going on? He forced his hand to slide the knife back into the holster. "Don't summon your magic." He slowly let go of her hands, shoved off her, and pushed back to his knees.

She sat up, scooting back on her butt, and rose. "It didn't work anyway. You don't stink of sulfur like a possessed human would, and if you were possessed, my magic would have banished the demon. You're too fast and strong to be a mortal. What the hell are you, and why are you here?"

He stood up, his gaze traveling over her long legs displayed nicely in the tiny black shorts she wore. She had slender hips, a tucked-in waist, and small breasts. She was sleek, like a fast car. Her witch-shimmer was sheer gold, making her skin glow in the moonlight.

She put her hands on her hips and waited for his answer.

"I'm a witch hunter. My name is Phoenix. Your voice has been haunting me," he told her.

"You hear me?" Her tone was sharp. "How long?"

"A month or two, but it's gotten louder and more intrusive in the last couple weeks. Tonight it was unbearable, and I had to find you. What kind of magic is that?" Whatever it was, he needed to make it stop.

She crossed her arms and rubbed her palms over the bare skin. "Shit, that can't be good."

"You think?" he snapped at her. The smell of her drying blood was torturing him. His veins were beginning to swell and pulse beneath his skin. He'd touched her blood, and now his body wanted more. Wanted it all. "Hell, woman, your singing damn near got me killed tonight!"

She sighed and scrubbed her hands up and down her arms.

Getting a tight rein on his temper, he muttered, "What were you doing cutting up your wrist and singing like that?"

She lifted her left arm. "I was trying to get this off."

He saw the band around her left wrist, and his heart sped up in some visceral, instinctive dislike of the thing. He moved closer until he was one step away from her. The bracelet was an inch wide, chalk colored, and just wrong somehow. He reached out to rub his index finger over the surface but couldn't place it. It wasn't plastic, or glass, or any metal he'd ever felt. It made him think of old bone worried smooth and creepy as hell. He looked up to her face. "What is it?" He scraped his fingers over the circumference, looking for a clasp, but there wasn't one.

She jerked her hand from him and moved back another step. "It's a handfast binding from a demon."

Shock punched him and totally pissed him off. "Bullshit. I touched you with a silver blade and you didn't burn. You can't be a demon witch."

"I'm not!"

"But you sold yourself to a demon, then reneged on the deal?" Disgust and anger brewed up an ugly mix inside of him. "Was your voice one of the powers you got from the demon? And why are you using it to screw with me?" Did she and Asmodeus plan to force him to go rogue? His hatred of demon witches buzzed in his head until he could only hear the roar of his rage.

She crossed her arms over her chest. "I didn't even know about you. My voice didn't come from the demon. The power is mine. Asmodeus wants my power and is trying to force me into becoming a demon witch so he can control it. I'll never give in to him!"

Her voice rang with the truth of that statement. So what the fuck was going on here? "What are you talking about? You had to agree to the handfast."

Her mouth pulled tight, the faint silvery scars around her eyes standing out against her skin. "I did *not* agree."

He didn't believe that. For a second there, when he first saw her damaged eyes, he'd felt . . . what . . . pity? Tenderness? Admiration? For this witch. She dealt with a demon! Now she was trying to renege and, surprise, the demon wasn't taking rejection well. He had to get away from her. "I don't believe you. And I don't give a shit about you or Asmodeus. Just keep your voice out of my head!" He turned to leave.

"Tough shit, witch hunter. I'm using my voice to break this handfast. Stay out of my way." She turned and strode over the small patio toward the house while adding, "Don't let the gate hit you in the ass on your way out."

Phoenix moved fast enough to create a breeze, getting around her to block her before she got to the house.

She slammed right into his chest and started to fall back.

He grabbed her arms. "Do not fuck with me, little witch. If you keep taunting me with your demon magic voice—"

Her head snapped up. Her gaze seemed to find his shape. "It's not demon magic. God, are all witch hunters as dense as you? It's my power, *mine*." Her body was tight with her quiet fierceness.

The controlled anger emanating from her rattled him on a level he didn't understand. Gentling his hold on her arms, he looked down at her upturned face. Her skin colored with her fury, her gold shimmer darkened almost to a bronze as it shifted over her skin. Her silvery blue eyes shone. She was . . . breathtaking. Fighting the dual urges strangling him, to either touch her or cut her, he said, "Exactly what power is in your voice, then? What is this power that Asmodeus wants from you?" And why, he wondered furiously, was it affecting him?

She blinked, lowered her chin, and said, "I just call it my voice power. It's rare, so rare I can't find out much about it. What I do know is that when I unleash my magic into my voice, I can enhance all magic."

Phoenix felt his throat tighten as the words sank in. "All magic? Even demon magic?"

She said softly, "Yes."

He stared at her. "Are you out of your mind?" He ground out the words as he realized she could be helping other demon witches with her voice. "You're unleashing dangerous magic."

"I'm working to get control of the power to break the handfast. I can't let the demon get hold of my voice power." She jerked out of his hands and crossed her arms protectively over her chest.

He saw that goose bumps had broken out over her skin, her nipples pebbled to delectable little points beneath her tank, and when he inhaled, he caught more than just the scent of her skin and drying blood. He smelled desire, the buttery scent of lust in her. How was that possible? She should be terrified of him. All earth witches were afraid of hunters since the curse.

But he didn't smell the thick, too-sweet scent of fear. Could she be reacting to his pheromones? Hunters had them to draw women to them for sex, but as far as they knew, it worked only on mortals.

Was she on the level and really trying to keep Asmodeus from getting control of her power? Or had she cut some deal with the demon and was working with demon witches to destroy him? Maybe her desire was another trick to get control of him. How did he find out? Softening his tone, he asked, "What's your name?"

"Ailish."

"Ailish." Her name was strong and sexy. "Your voice is dangerous."

"Not if I learn to control it. I've only started working on it the last two months."

He was losing his tight hold on himself. "That's how long I've been hearing you in my head. It's getting stronger. You must know witch hunters are cursed. If you keep this up . . ." He sucked in a breath.

She went still, shifting her weight slightly.

He felt the sudden intensity in her, the gathering of her muscles to react. But he needed her to stop this shit, so he told her the truth: "I'm going to end up killing you." Too late, he smelled her burst of adrenaline, that pungent spike of fight-or-flight hormone. His body responded on a cellular level. "Don't run!" he warned.

She whipped around and ran for the door.

The cursed predator in him broke free and sprinted after her.

The French doors that led to the house flew open from magic.

Her magic goaded the predator, and he exploded into a bring-down-his-prey run. Her power sang through his veins, and he wanted it. Needed it. *Witch blood! Get her!* He reached out, locking both hands around her upper arms.

He fought it, fought the raging beast that wanted to cut her, bleed her, get her power. He shouted, "No!" in an effort to stop himself.

She went still, freezing in place.

Then he felt her skin beneath his palms, so soft and smooth over lean muscles. He pulled her back to his chest and pressed his swollen cock against her back. He grunted out, "Don't run. Don't. When you run it brings out the predator in me." But was he going after her for her blood or sex? Christ, he couldn't sort out the hungers exploding in him.

She tensed but didn't move. "You threatened to kill me. I'm fighting to stay alive, while not submitting to the Claiming Rite. I'm not going to let a witch hunter with questionable self-control kill me."

Her skin smelled of warm mangoes with only a lingering scent of the coconut-blood aroma. But it was the buttery-cream scent that told him her desire was growing as fast as his. The bloodlust receded under a possessive sexual lust that had him tighten his hands around her. "That's what you were trying to do with your magic. You thought I was a human possessed by the demon to finish the handfast with sex, and you were trying to banish the demon." His voice dropped to a growl as his heart pounded with anger. It was irrational and dangerous, this sudden compulsion to have her, mark her, take her, and kill anything that got in the way.

"Yes. Let go of me, I don't like being touched."

He leaned his head down to the curve of her neck. "You're lying. I can scent your desire." He had to stop. Now. He didn't know what her game was, what deal she'd made with Asmodeus.

She shivered more and shook her head in denial. "It can't be real. The demon forces lust on me through the handfast binding. Even if this feels different, it's just another of his tricks to ramp up my lust."

"So he can seduce you." That knowledge splashed cold water on him, and he released her. He had to leave, get the hell away from her. Figure out what to do next. "Go inside. Shut the door. And don't sing."   •

She straightened her back and walked inside the house. He watched her close and lock the door. What the hell was he going to do? She wasn't a demon witch, at least not yet. But that voice of hers could destroy him.

3

Phoenix let himself into the condo over the club that he and Key used, sometimes for sex, sometimes for convenience. No lights were on, but he could see perfectly well. The furniture was black leather with chrome-and-glass tables.

He strode over the black-and-white marble floor to the wet bar, poured out a measure of Glenfiddich into a heavy crystal glass, and took a drink. He sank onto the couch, the leathers of his pants and couch meeting with barely a whisper. He leaned his head back and closed his eyes.

His veins burned as if they were laced with acid. The witch Ailish, her blood was in him now, *she* was in him. He drained his glass, tried to drown out the bloodlust.

He heard Key walk out of one of the two bedrooms and across the marble in his bare feet. Opening his eyes, Phoenix saw the hunter wore a pair of sweats, the massive dragon inked across his chest visible even in the dark. "Alone tonight, huh?" He didn't hear a woman in the other room.

Key went to the wet bar and came back with the bottle of Scotch and a glass for himself. Refilling Phoenix's glass, he said, "She went home. Why, you looking for leftovers?" He went to the chair on the right and sat down.

Sex made him think of Ailish. Her lean body, her in-his-face attitude, and the way she moved as though she owned the whole damned world, blind or not. Just the memory got him half-hard. "Shit."

"I smell a trace of witch blood. You'd better have your lifelines."

Phoenix held up his hand, palm out. He knew Key could see the lines that meant he still had his soul. But if Ailish kept singing, would he keep his soul? Or would the power in her voice drive him to kill her? Then he'd have baby-butt-smooth palms, no soul, and an ironclad promise of eternity as a pain-racked shade trapped in the between-worlds.

Key breathed out a sigh of relief and said, "What the hell happened tonight? Axel said you were off getting laid, but you weren't here in the condo."

He leaned his head on the back of the couch and stared at the ceiling. "I tracked the source of the voice."

"Finally," Key snapped. "That denial shit was going to get you dead."

"Before tonight, wasn't enough there to track," he pointed out.

"Carla thought she could help you find the source with her magic."

He stared at the blank TV. "I don't do shrinks." Too many years of the county head docs doping his mom, but nothing helped her. Sheri had started hearing voices telling her to run when Phoenix had been four years old. Up till then, she'd held a job as a nurse and been a great mom. Then everything changed. The voices destroyed their lives, and they ended up homeless and living on the streets. He jerked his mind from the past and shifted his gaze back to Key to drop his bombshell. "Doesn't matter anyway. I found the source. An earth witch hand-fasted to a demon."

Key dropped his feet and sat up. "The hell you say? Did you test to see if she's gone demon?"

"Silver didn't burn her. And it gets better." He told Key about her voice power that enhanced all magic.

Key drained his glass of Scotch. The single-malt wasn't

getting any respect tonight. "This is so totally screwed up. She could be working with Asmodeus to destroy you." The green-and-blue dragon seemed to ripple across his chest. "What did you do?"

Phoenix shrugged. "She's still an earth witch so I can't kill her." He took another deep swallow of the whiskey and said, "Chuck Norris—"

Key groaned.

Phoenix ignored him. He'd grown up watching Chuck Norris movies and that cheesy TV show whenever he got the opportunity. Norris never met a problem he couldn't solve with a roundhouse kick. Phoenix had honed a killer roundhouse kick. He continued, "Chuck Norris never retreats, he just attacks from another direction."

"You retreated."

"For now. Seemed better than roundhouse kicking her. Trust me, this chick kicks back." Okay, he couldn't help a small grin at that memory.

"There's a first, you walking away from violence."

Phoenix reached for the bottle on the table. "Says the man who draws some really freaky shit." Key's comic books were dark, violent, and brilliant.

Key leveled his gaze on him. "Freaky? Dude, you've got a witch voice in your head that nearly got you killed tonight, but you can't kill the witch doing it."

Restless and agitated, he stood up and walked to a window looking out of the front over the club. It was early morning, the club was shut down, and the surrounding neighborhood was barren. He stared at the dirty buildings and thought about the days they'd lived on the streets. His father was killed before Phoenix was born, and Sheri's family wanted nothing to do with her as long as she kept her bastard kid. Only twenty-two years old, pregnant, and left with no help. Then, when she'd been twenty-six and the voices started in her head, she'd had nowhere to turn. As he got older, Phoenix tried to be her hero.

He failed.

He didn't need a PhD in psychology to know that's why he'd gone into bounty hunting—looking to be the hero he'd failed to be for his mom. He'd helped women who had nowhere else to turn. Ironically, now it was a woman destroying him, a blind witch who brought out his protective instincts. Yeah, talk about freaky. . . .

A raised voice outside the condo jerked him from his ruminations. He turned from the window and frowned as he recognized the voice. "That's Joe." He put down his glass and strode to the door.

Key got up and went to the security panel. "Nothing's been disturbed in the building."

Phoenix grabbed his knife from the holster, opened the door, and stepped out. Looking right, he saw Joe MacAlister with a very pregnant woman in his arms. He was kicking Axel's door. "Hurry! It's Morgan." Joe wore barely buttoned jeans and no shoes, his dark hair was matted, and his voice thundered.

Phoenix hurried the length of the hallway. Axel and Darcy had the largest corner condo. Morgan and Joe were next to them. Joe was Darcy's cousin, a mortal who'd protected Darcy when she was a kid and had no idea she was a witch. Then when Joe discovered the truth a few months ago—nothing changed. She was still the cousin he treated like a little sister.

Phoenix holstered his knife. "Joe, is it the baby?"

The man whirled, his blue eyes nearly wild. Joe had spent six years in the Special Forces, barely blinked when he found out Darcy was a witch, and fought rogue witch hunters almost to the death. Nothing rattled the mortal. But something sure as hell had tonight. "I don't know." His voice had a forced calm.

Axel yanked open the door, wearing pants and nothing else. "Bring her inside."

Phoenix and Key followed.

Darcy rushed out from the back room, dressed in jeans and a T-shirt, her hair a tangled mess around her face. "Contractions?"

Joe zeroed in on Darcy. "Don't think that's it. But she's in pain and swears there's blood on her stomach. There's nothing there."

Phoenix moved closer. Morgan was wearing shorts that settled below her swollen belly and a T-shirt. Her blue eyes were wide and unfocused. "Hurts. It's Eric, he's cutting me, trying to get the baby!"

Phoenix felt a wet chill slither down his back. Eric Reed was dead; Phoenix had been there when Axel killed him. Eric had been a rogue and married an unsuspecting Morgan. He'd shifted her memory while using his knife to cut her, torturing her and causing brain damage. Morgan had been a fighter, struggling to survive and protect her unborn child. Eric had wanted their child, that much was true.

Darcy laid her hand on the woman's shoulder. "What hurts, Morgan?" She flinched suddenly.

Axel moved in a blur, putting his hand over Darcy's. "What is it?"

"Her stomach. The pain is real to her."

"Darcy, do something," Joe hissed.

Phoenix felt Darcy's magic rise and simmer in the room as she drew the pain from Morgan and sent calming energy to her. He glanced at Axel, who was helping Darcy focus her powers while taking the pain from her through their soul-mirror bond.

Morgan relaxed visibly in Joe's arms.

The hawk met his gaze and said, "We need to see if there's any blood."

Phoenix nodded and said, "Morgan . . ." He shifted his gaze to her face. She was pale and sweaty, with strands of blond hair sticking to her skin. "I'm going to lift your shirt so we can see what's happening."

She nodded.

Phoenix took the edge of the navy-colored shirt and gently peeled it up. The mound of her stomach was marked by two rows of silvery scars that had been caused by Eric Reed's knife. His veins caught fire at the sight of the healed wounds. "Morgan," he said gently, "there're no open cuts, no blood."

"I saw them, felt them. They were there. Darcy must have healed them with her magic," Morgan insisted, her voice rising as tension stiffened her muscles. "I'm not crazy."

Eric Reed had told everyone that his wife was a mentally disturbed cutter. The brain damage he'd inflicted on Morgan should have made her believe it, too, but she had a strong mind and her subconscious resisted.

"Morgan, we're trying to help you," Joe said gently, then he looked up to Axel, Darcy, Key, and Phoenix. "She was restless all night, then woke up in a panic. She was convinced her stomach was bleeding."

Morgan's eyes widened. "It's Eric, he's back. He's trying to get the baby. He's trying to cut the baby out of me."

"What the hell is happening to her?" Joe demanded, his arms pulling her tighter against him.

Darcy lifted her gaze to her cousin. "Not sure. I'm going to get Carla on the computer and see if the two of us can figure it out." She dropped her gaze to the woman. "Morgan, you have to help us and fight this. Focus on your baby. He needs you to stay calm."

Tears welled in Morgan's eyes, but she nodded. She shifted her gaze back to Phoenix. "Eric's not here, right?"

Phoenix took her hand and looked into her eyes. "No.

Axel killed him. I saw him die." Joe had been protecting
Morgan and Carla, but the rogues had managed to get
all three of them. As lethal as Joe was, he was still mortal and couldn't win against half a dozen rogues. But it
still rankled the man that he hadn't protected Morgan
and Carla. That's why they lived in the condo with the
witch hunters, where they could all keep Morgan safe.
Rogues would love to get their hands on her baby since he
was a boy and would therefore be a witch hunter. They'd
find a way to get the kid and turn him rogue around the
age of fourteen and add him to their army. They kept
building the Rogue Cadre with the goal of killing all
witches.

"You're safe, Morgan," Joe said tightly. "No rogue can
get through us."

She closed her eyes and turned her face into Joe's chest.
"I don't want to be crazy."

Joe bent his head, putting his face close to hers. "You're
not crazy, you're a fighter. We won't let him win."

Darcy said, "Joe, take Morgan into the guest room.
Morgan, you need to rest, and I'm going to get Carla so
we can both help you."

Joe walked off, leaving the four of them.

Key had hung back by the door, probably to not crowd
Morgan or maybe to keep watch. Now he walked up. "Is
the baby okay?"

The question hung there for a few seconds. Morgan
was seven months along. While a mortal baby could survive if born early, a witch hunter baby needed to go full
term. Their enhanced biology required every minute in
the womb for their lungs to be able to support them. If
born even two weeks early, they often didn't survive. Before the curse, witches always helped women pregnant
with witch hunter babies. But since the curse, there'd
been more deaths than live births.

Darcy looked tired as she drew in a breath and said, "For now, he feels okay as far as I can tell."

"And Morgan?" Phoenix asked.

"If she loses this baby, it'll destroy her. She loves Joe, but she's holding back with him, afraid that somehow Eric's going to come back and kill Joe for being with her. The brain damage that bastard inflicted on her was so brutal. . . ." Her witch-shimmer, normally a beautiful gold, tinged with a slight red pain. Not physical pain, but the pain earth witches felt when others suffered.

"Damn it." Fury rolled through him. That asshole Eric Reed was still reaching from the grave and torturing Morgan. This wasn't a flesh-and-blood problem he could kill. He looked at Darcy. "Anything you need, anything I can do, you just name it."

Darcy reached out and touched his forearm, just a comforting touch, then she hurried after Joe and Morgan.

Phoenix felt so fucking helpless. He ran his hand through his hair. Not only was Joe his friend, but Morgan, she was a tough chick who fought back against the bastard rogue torturing her. She loved her baby, even knowing he was a witch hunter who could one day turn into the monster his father had been.

Axel moved fast, stepping in front of him. Even dressed only in jeans, he looked the part of the menacing leader. "I smell witch blood on you."

Key said, "Going back to the condo." He slid out silently.

It was just him and Axel. Phoenix forced his shoulders to stay relaxed and raised his hand. "Got my lifelines, so back off."

Axel didn't look at his palm but stared him down. "If you were rogue, your blood would be staining my floors. Don't jack with me, Phoenix."

Dropping his hand, he waged an internal struggle. Axel was the leader and needed to know about Ailish and her voice power. Yet part of him wanted to protect the witch. But from what? Axel wouldn't hurt an earth witch. Taking a breath, he quickly outlined tracking the source of the voice in his head.

Axel's mouth compressed and his shoulders bunched into piles of pure muscle. "Demon?"

The tension crawled up his spine and his muscles coiled in defensive mode. He always felt protective of women, but this was more ferocious and very focused on the witch. "No." His jaw tried to lock, tried to stop him from explaining. Refusing to let this overwhelming protectiveness control him, he added, "She's handfasted to a demon."

Axel's green eyes went from intense to lethal. "Where is she?"

His palm itched to reach for his knife. It occurred to him that this reaction might be not the voice, but the fact that he'd touched her blood. Ailish was in him now, and he didn't want any other hunter near her or her powerful blood. Keeping still, he said, "You can't kill her. She's still an earth witch. I tested her."

Days Remaining on Handfast Contract: Thirteen

Ailish felt the way she did the morning after a kick-boxing match, sore and tired. Her head hurt from the uncontrollable power surges and hormone rushes.

Last night, she'd failed to make progress on getting the binding off. And worse, her voice was somehow reaching out to a witch hunter.

Phoenix. His voice, scent, and touch were burned into her memory. That encounter had left her restless and needy all night. What was going on?

Dressed in jeans and her customary black shirt, she

left her hair wet and headed for the kitchen. She walked over the cool tile of the kitchen floor. Grabbing a mug from the cupboard, she opened her chakras to summon her favorite chai tea.

The cup filled, and gentle steam wafted up. She inhaled the scent and thought about what she would do today and how she'd attempt to break the handfast. She reached into the pantry for a bag of dried fruit and nuts, then carried both her tea and breakfast into the living room. She switched on the TV to a local news channel, then settled onto the couch. While commercials droned on, she put her tea on the coffee table and opened the Ziploc bag to grab a handful of dried cranberries and almonds. Then the morning anchor's voice caught her attention.

"Paramedic Kyle Whaling was taken to the emergency room, where he was treated and released. He and his partner were on a call with full lights and sirens when a tire blew and they hit a tree." The reporter added, "There's some confusion about the call. We're trying to get the nine-one-one tape to confirm there was a call."

"Oh shit!" She dropped the bag and jumped to her feet. Fear-laced adrenaline dumped into her bloodstream. Her heart raced and her muscles twitched. Forgetting the tea and nuts, she hurried into the bedroom and grabbed her phone, then hit the speed dial for the driver Haley had hired for her. "Dee, I need you here ASAP."

She had to get to Kyle. This was no accident. They weren't going to find that 911 call because it didn't exist.

Her mother had done it.

Ailish yanked on some socks, then her boots. Next she picked up a couple packets of ground-up silver shavings that had the consistency of heavy glitter and put one in her boot and one in a jeans pocket. She slung her small backpack purse over her shoulder and headed to the front of the house, then stopped and went back to the bedroom.

She picked up her sunglasses. She didn't usually hide her eyes, didn't really give a rat's ass what people thought.

Usually.

But she needed Kyle to focus on what she was going to tell him, not her eyes. She slipped on the shades and went to wait by the door for the car.

Ailish had thought Kyle would be safe. She hadn't contacted him since the night of the handfast ceremony eight years ago. Her mother had used Kyle to trick Ailish back then, using her desperate love for him. But today he was just a memory, and she hadn't thought her mom would try to use Kyle now. It was one thing to lure a seventeen-year-old boy to a handfasting and drug him. Hell, that was almost too easy.

But a twenty-five-year-old paramedic wasn't going to be led so effortlessly, especially one who had been possessed before. The human body was pretty amazing and built up antibodies to the foreign invader, making it harder for a demon to possess the same person repeatedly. She could only surmise that her mom thought she could grab Kyle at some point when he was injured and his resistance weakened by painkillers. Then the demon witches could get control of him and summon Asmodeus into Kyle's body.

Ailish heard the car pulling onto her street, but she waited until there was a knock on her door. "Yes?"

"Hi, Ailish, it's Dee."

She recognized the voice. Even so, as she opened the door, she used her air chakra to feel for any unusual disturbance like demon magic. But the woman on the porch was fully human and free of magic residue. Ailish went out, then shut and locked the dead bolt on her door. She followed the vague shape of the driver to the car.

Dee went to the passenger door and opened it. "Where to this morning?"

"I need to see a friend." She rattled off the address

Haley had given her for Kyle, then reached out and touched the top of the doorframe to guide her into the seat on the passenger side.

"No problem. That's down by the beach." Dee shut the door and went around to her side, and they took off.

Ailish clenched her fists in her lap to control her impatience.

"Hey, so I've seen some of your matches. How do you, umm, well . . ."

"Fight blind?" She got the question a lot.

"Well, yeah."

"I use my other senses. It took years to learn, but being blind forces me to be sharper than if I was still sighted." She also used her chakras to guide her. They had become more sensitized since she'd gone blind and could feel the disturbance in the air as the opponent began a move. That told Ailish how to block or counter the action. Over time, it all became second nature. She added, "When I first started kickboxing, I got my ass handed to me every single day. And it really pissed me off."

Dee laughed. "You don't seem to like losing."

"Who does?" But her motivation ran deeper. She had to be strong and fast enough, even blind, to drop a mortal man and keep him still for the length of time it takes to magically force Asmodeus out.

And she had to learn to tolerate pain.

Because Ailish would never be what her mother was— a woman who gave her soul to a demon in exchange for dark powers and then sold her daughter to a demon for more power. Maeve had ascended to high witch of the coven shortly after Ailish was born and Maeve learned of Ailish's rare power. In exchange, for the promise of delivering her daughter to the demon when she was of age, Maeve was made high witch, and Ailish became the princess to be protected and sheltered until Asmodeus claimed her. But of course, Ailish knew none of this . . . not until the night of the handfast.

So, no, she didn't like to lose. Because every loss meant she had a weakness, and just one flaw in her skills could let the demon too close.

They'd tricked her once with her own vulnerability—love for a boy.

"We're here."

Kyle's house. What did it look like? she wondered as she turned toward Dee. "Just tell me where the front door is."

"I'll show you."

"No—" She stopped talking, since she heard Dee open the door and get out. Ailish stepped out of the car.

"Follow me," Dee said.

At least the woman didn't touch her. She followed the shadow figure of her driver while using her air chakra to "feel" for any sort of bump, rock, or curb in front of her. It was similar to using a cane, she assumed, and usually kept her from falling flat on her face. She could hear the waves in the distance and smelled the faint scent of the ocean.

"The door is a couple feet in front of us. Do you want me to knock?"

She fought down a flare of irritation. The woman was only trying to do her job. "I can manage to knock on a door. You're free to leave, go get some coffee or do whatever. I'll call you to pick me up when I need you."

Dee replied cheerfully, "I'll wait in the car. I've got a book to read, so I'm good."

Ailish nodded, impressed that Dee didn't get offended. She listened until she heard the car door shut. Seeing Kyle again hadn't been in her plans. But now, here she was at his house. She heard a TV from somewhere inside, so he was home. Was someone else here? A buddy or girlfriend? That would make it harder to talk him into leaving town. She'd heard that his parents had retired to the warmer, drier climate of Arizona. She was going to convince Kyle to go recover with them. He had to get out of Glassbreakers.

After touching the door with her fingertips, she raised her hand and knocked.

"Come in."

Oh hell. He just invited people into his house? What if it had been her mother or one of the other witches from the coven? She felt along the door until she came to a door handle. Opening it, she quickly reached out with her chakras for any traces of sulfur or the cold, oily sensation of dark magic, but it was clean. She closed the door, hearing what sounded like sports on the TV. "Kyle? It's Ailish, Ailish Donovan."

Silence, then some rustling, as if he were trying to sit up. "No shit? Ailish? What are you doing here?"

His voice stirred memories, but she refused to let them surface. "I just got back in town. I heard about your accident and wanted to see if you're okay." She stood there just inside the door. Sweeping the room with her air chakra, she had a sense of a wall on her left and various pieces of furniture on her right. The TV sounded as if it were across the room. Kyle was closer, just ahead at two o'clock.

"How'd you know where I live?"

His voice cooled just a tad. Not exactly suspicious, but not entirely trusting. "A friend looked up your address for me. Kyle, I know this seems weird, but I need you to listen to what I have to say." Ailish couldn't hear anyone else in the house, nor did she feel any other energy vibrating her chakras.

"Okay, sit down."

"I'm fine here." Moving around an unfamiliar house was a challenge.

"So it's true? You really are blind. It's not just a gimmick? You know, the blind kickboxer."

She should have realized the shades were useless. She pulled them off and said, "More like an inconvenience than a gimmick."

"Oh," he said, like a verbal wince. Then he added, "There's a chair a couple feet to your right. Sit down, you're making me tense just standing there."

Turning her head, she saw the vague shadow. She reached out to feel the fabric, then sat down. "How bad are you hurt?"

"Couple cracked ribs, stitches in my face and right arm, and some bruising here and there." He took a breath and said, "I've seen you, you know, on TV. It's hard to believe you're a kickboxer." He paused, then asked, "How did you lose your sight?"

She had to ease into telling him that magic and witches were real, and he was in danger. The truth about her blindness would be too much, too soon. She answered simply, "Car accident."

"Sounds like you had it rough." His sympathy rolled into confusion as he asked, "What happened? Why did you run away? The rumor was that you had some kind of breakdown."

Being around Kyle was ripping away the years of discipline to expose the vulnerable young girl who had loved him. But she was no longer that girl and hadn't been in years. "Lies. I never had a breakdown." She heard the ice in her voice, took a breath, and softened her tone. "Kyle, do you remember the last time we saw each other?"

He paused, then said slowly, "Uh, you had run away and your mom asked me to help look for you. But, wait, I didn't see you that night because we never found you."

Somewhere in his subconscious, he remembered seeing her, and that's why he was slightly confused. Her mother must have told Kyle she ran away to get him to go with her. Then she'd drugged him and the coven had summoned the demon into his body. By the time Ailish saw him at the handfasting ceremony, he had already been possessed by Asmodeus, although she hadn't realized it until almost too late. "You saw me that night, Kyle. See this binding on my wrist?" She lifted her left hand. "Look at it and try to remember."

"Remember what? I didn't see you. You ran away and I never saw you again. Except on TV, but—"

Damn it, she wasn't going to convince him by trying to get him to remember. She never told mortals that she was a witch, but Kyle was in danger. "Stop, Kyle, just stop and pay attention." She waved her hand at the TV, cutting the power supply.

The TV went silent.

"What did you do? I have the remote, but it's not going back on."

"I'm a witch, Kyle." She released the hold she had on the power supply and the TV burst back to life.

"Cute trick, but I was watching that game."

"It's not a trick." He'd told her where the remote was, so she held out her hand. The hard plastic rectangle appeared in her palm. She held it up. "I'm a witch and so is my mother."

Silence. Then he laughed. "Sure, a witch. Why not? So are you changing careers? Giving up kickboxing to be a magician?"

She leaned forward. "What magicians do isn't real magic. This is." She focused her powers, using the remote as a channel, and sent her memory of the handfasting to the television.

"How . . . That's me. And you . . ." His voice trailed off as he watched.

Ailish couldn't see the image on the screen, but she could see it in her mind.

Her mother had given her a black silk robe to wear. Her instructions had been clear: This was important magic,

*and she had to wear nothing under the robe. She was
making a promise to the boy she loved, and she would
seal the promise by joining . . . she had to be ready under
her robe. They went to the Infernal Grounds the coven
used. There was a crumbling old clapboard, one-room
chapel said to be haunted. The truth was the grounds
were heavily warded and protected by hellhounds. Mortals who tried to approach the grounds heard screams of
the dead and growls of the hellhounds and were driven
off. Ailish had never been there. She had always been
kept away.*

*They bypassed the crumbling chapel and went in-
stead to a cleared area outlined in black candles. Kyle
was led from inside the chapel by one of the other
witches, and they stood together before her mother, with
the coven witches behind them.*

*The scent of incense grew thick, while the air seemed
magically charged. The hairs on Ailish's skin stood up.
But she was so excited. Kyle was there! He did care about
her! Her mother had done just as she had promised!*

*As high witch, her mother began by raising her hand.
A gold goblet encrusted with three heads appeared. "Ailish Donovan, you have reached the age of consent. You
are sixteen and no longer a child, but now a full-grown
witch, responsible and answerable for all that you pledge.
To symbolize this, drink deeply now from the Goblet of
Choice."*

*Feeling Kyle's gaze on her, she took the chalice in her
hands and brought it to her mouth. The first sip was
sweet and tangy, so she kept drinking as she had been
instructed. When she had swallowed the last of it, the
goblet vanished from her hands.*

"So be it," the coven said as one.

Kyle said, "Enough. You paid someone to dub my
picture into that scene. I wasn't there, I would remember
it. It's just another trick."

She froze the scene on the TV. "Not a trick, it's magic. I told you, I'm a witch, an earth witch. But my mother is a demon witch, and she's more dangerous than you can imagine. That night you believe I ran away, my mother kidnapped and drugged you to use in the ceremony to handfast me to a demon." She was glad she didn't have to see his expression, didn't have to look at the disgust or distrust or whatever he felt. "You were possessed by the demon. I realized what was happening and used my power to get the demon out of you. Then I ran away."

He gave a short laugh, but she heard the tension in the bark of sound. "You're crazy. Do you hear yourself? Demons, witches . . . Maybe it's me. Maybe it's all the painkillers and I'm dreaming or hallucinating."

"No, this is real, it's happening." She leaned forward. "The crash this morning wasn't an accident. I'm sure they will never find the nine-one-one call you were supposedly responding to. My mother did it. She used her witchcraft to radio a fake call to you. Then once you were responding, she used magic to blow your tire."

He moved something on his lap, maybe a pillow, and said harshly, "Okay, this is getting out of hand. You need to get help, Ailish."

Frustration boiled up, but she stayed in control. "Did they find the nine-one-one call? Does the dispatcher remember calling it to you?"

"Not yet, but there was a malfunction." His voice thinned with less certainty.

She kept pushing, trying to make him see that something wasn't right. "What about your partner?"

"He said the call was garbled, like static, but I heard it, damn it! And I was driving, so I just took off. He was just reaching to call for clarification when the tire blew and we rolled. He's still in the hospital with a concussion."

His partner was probably safer there. She rose and moved toward Kyle's voice. She went around an obstacle, probably a coffee table, and sat on the couch. Holding out the remote, she said, "What if I'm right?"

"I haven't seen you in eight years. Why would you suddenly show up now? Maybe you're holding a monster grudge."

"Grudge? Against you?" She was baffled.

He sighed, his words heavy as he finally took the remote from her. "I didn't call you or really even talk to you after, well, after we had sex."

She was unwillingly yanked back across the years, remembering the dates of movies, going to the beach, parties, and then that night when she'd finally said yes. She and Kyle had had sex when his parents were out. Kyle had made her feel important and valuable for herself, not her magical power.

Ailish had grown up protected and sheltered, warned never to use her special voice power because earth witches would find her and kidnap her. Over time, she began to see that she was nothing more than a pawn in some kind of witch war she wasn't interested in or even allowed to participate in. She was put on the sidelines and told to stay there, just existing.

But what she had wanted, longed for, was love and family. Like she saw on TV or at her friends' houses.

And then she'd met Kyle at school, and he liked her. They went out, and she became part of his group. She belonged. She felt safe. Safe enough to give her body to him as well as her heart. It had been awkward and embarrassing and sweet, and Kyle had been nice.

Then he'd stopped calling, stopped answering her calls, and ducked her at school.

"Ailish?"

She pulled herself from the past. She wasn't that lonely, desperate girl anymore, and she had to make Kyle understand the danger he was in. She was there to keep him alive, not to reminisce about old times. "Get over yourself,

Kyle. I've been over you for years. I'm only here because you're in danger. Didn't I hear your parents moved? Couldn't you go see them while you heal?"

"Right. I'm going to pack up, get on a plane with cracked ribs, and leave because you just showed up with a few clever tricks and said you're a witch. Not gonna happen. We're done with this little reunion."

Shit, his voice throbbed with anger and uneasiness. Mortals couldn't deal with the idea of witches; they never could, as evidenced by all the witch hunts. But Kyle's denial went deeper, it had a magical root. Plus they'd used drugs to gain control of him and further confused the memory. Ailish knew it was a risk, but she reached out, touched Kyle's arm, and began to hum. Just barely, a sound so soft, it was only a whisper. If she could use just a little of her voice power, maybe she could break through.

The couch began to shake and the windows rattled.

Kyle jerked his arm away. "Earthquake or something," he said.

Ailish pulled her hand back and closed off her power. She didn't have enough control, and she could hurt Kyle. Badly. Shit. Her head throbbed from the worry.

"Kyle—"

He ignored her, rising slowly from the couch and shuffling over to the TV. After a few seconds, he said, "There's nothing in the DVD player. How'd you get this scene onto my TV?"

She'd left it frozen on his set. She sighed. "I told you—"

He walked back, his shadow bent as though he were protecting his ribs. "You're a witch. Yeah, heard you." He sat down slowly.

"But you don't believe me," she said flatly. "It's easier to believe the story my mom spread about me having a breakdown. Easier to believe I rigged your TV, and that an earthquake happened at the exact moment I touched you." She knew he just couldn't digest it. The magical block had been in place for eight years, she couldn't undo it in a half hour. Instead, she fished a business card out of her backpack and put it on the table. "This is my cell number. I'm staying at 334 Maple Street. If anything strange happens, call me."

"What about my TV?"

She stood, lifted one hand, and cleared her magic so that he could control the TV with his remote again. Then she looked toward Kyle, and suddenly she wondered, What did he look like now? Hell, she didn't even know what she looked like, and she didn't care. This little trip down memory lane had been a mistake. But she would at least give him a fighting chance. "Silver burns demon witches. Anything silver." She reached into her pocket and pulled out one of her packets. "This is basically a heavy silver glitter. If anything you can't believe comes at you, throw it in their eyes and run like hell." She dropped it next to her card and walked out the door.

4

Phoenix slept a couple hours at the condo rather than drive to his house and was downing his first cup of coffee when the security panel started beeping. He pulled out his BlackBerry and hit the key to see what the hell was interrupting his coffee.

Once he saw the screen, he shot up off the bar stool and hauled ass out of the condo. Key slammed shut his laptop and fell into step behind him. Axel tore out of his door with Joe racing out behind him. They all pounded down the stairs and into the club. Joe hit the lights.

Phoenix never paused, he skirted the bar and got to the front door just as Axel yanked it open. Phoenix caught Ram as he fell, covered in blood.

Ram sputtered, "It was Tully and Chaz."

Phoenix picked up the six-foot-five hunter and took him to one of the red leather couches. "Two of our recruits? They've gone rogue?" he said, to verify whom he was going to kill.

"They said they just killed some rogues and were coming to report in. I smelled copper and thought it was the dead rogues. A couple yards from me, they both pulled guns and started firing. I think . . . Shit." He closed his eyes and sucked in a breath that rattled.

"Darcy's on her way down," Axel said. "Joe, go up and stay with Morgan. Darcy doesn't want her alone."

Joe turned and strode away, his posture frustrated and angry that one of theirs had been attacked.

Key ripped open Ram's shirt and said, "Two gunshots. One to his stomach, second to his shoulder."

Axel put pressure on the wounds using folded white bar towels.

Key moved lower and ripped open the blood-soaked pants at Ram's upper right thigh. "Damn it, third shot hit the artery." Key stuck his hand into the bloody mess to clamp down on the spewing vein.

Fury dumped adrenaline into Phoenix's bloodstream. Only the fact that Ram was a witch hunter and healed fast was keeping him from bleeding out. Ram was a god-damned machine, never stopping for injuries. He never missed a workout. Never gave up a hunt because he'd been cut or caught a bullet. That's why when Ram tripped the club security and they'd seen the picture of him injured, they'd all snapped into action. "Ram"— Phoenix leaned over the man—"tell me what I need to know."

The injured man opened his fierce steel blue eyes. His normally olive-colored skin paled to a sickly white. "Still hearing that voice in your head?"

Phoenix's chest burned and his throat tightened. Even down and bleeding, Ram was the military leader, assessing and judging the men he sent out. Phoenix had been six kinds of furious at Ram last night, but he'd never doubted his motives. "Just the one screaming for revenge. Only voice I'm listening to."

Ram took a breath. "The blood on them wasn't just witch blood. I think they killed other recruits. Find them, kill them." His voice was soft, but the anger came through loud and clear. Ram didn't yell or make threats, he struck. All the men, both Wing Slayer Hunters and recruits, respected him.

If Ram had been able to stand at all, he'd be after them. But since he couldn't do it, Phoenix would. He reached down and gripped the man's forearm. "This isn't on you.

It's on Tully and Chaz. I'll find them and kill them. You hear me? It's not on you. You couldn't have known they'd go rogue."

Darcy hurried in. "Ram," she said softly, her hand going to his face. "You just do this to piss off Axel, yeah?"

Ram's mouth twitched. "Make him share his witch."

Axel said, "Heal him, Darce, so I can kick his ass."

Key said, "Got a bleeder here, Darcy."

"Okay, let's do this. Axel, I need your knife and blood."

Axel handed her the knife and looked at Phoenix and Key. "Go. Find them."

"We're on it," Phoenix said.

"Shit," Phoenix said as they entered the house of a recruit. "Copper and witch blood."

"Dead witch blood." Key came in from the back of the house. They found the recruit in his bedroom on his bed. The witch was dumped on the floor.

Both were dead.

"Second one," Key said, his gray-eyed gaze sweeping over the room as if it were a painting. "This is a statement. A murderous rendering of what will happen to witch hunters who don't go rogue and join the Rogue Cadre—they will be killed."

Phoenix paid attention. Key's artistic nature was deeply embedded in violence. He could read a scene of violence better than any cop. At just a hair over six feet, with his short, spiky blond hair, dimples, and loose-jointed movement, he looked as though he belonged on a surfboard, not ankle-deep in blood. Phoenix knew better. After Key ran away from home, his father had sent a rogue to kill him.

Key had killed the man, sketched the carnage, and sent the drawing to his father, along with sketches of their deaths if they kept coming after him.

"They are trying to turn them with the witch blood."

Key spoke in a voice devoid of interest as he pointed to the witch on the floor, drained of blood.

So many cuts . . . and worse. Phoenix's blood ran a little hot at the sight. His skin tingled, wanting all that powerful blood. Disgust at himself just added to the mixture brewing in his gut.

Key went on, "The hunter on the bed was shot in the legs and crippled so he couldn't escape. Then witch blood was dumped on him."

Phoenix moved over to the bed and studied the knife sticking out of his chest. He recognized it. "The blade belongs to him. He killed himself rather than go rogue." He stood up and turned to find Key staring down at the dead witch. His hands opened and closed reflexively. His black muscle shirt shifted over his chest as if the dragon tattoo were moving. "Key . . ." Phoenix walked closer.

The man looked up. "If I killed witches, would I draw with their blood?" He dropped his gaze back to the witch. "I think I would."

Key was caught, the curse working him like a seduction. Phoenix moved fast and shoved him hard, knocking him a couple steps toward the door. Following, he roared, "Can't draw if you're dead. You kill a witch and I'll kill you myself and cut off your hands just to make sure." Key had a dread of losing his ability to draw. His art helped him vent the internal rage.

The haze of lust receded in his eyes, and the shifting of the dragon beneath his shirt stopped. He sucked in a breath and said, "That'd make a statement. Hell, that'd be downright artistic."

Relief eased his chest. "Fuck you, I'm no pansy artist." Phoenix got back to work as he looked around the room, careful to keep his body between Key and the dead witch. "This is organized. Planned. Efficient. The rogues killed the four recruits that had the outlines of their wings and were waiting for their test to be accepted by the Wing Slayer."

"And they went after Ram, the one who oversees their training."

Phoenix snapped his gaze around. "Where will they go next?"

Key jerked with the realization. "Eli. I'm going to outline his wings as soon as he chooses what he wants."

Phoenix turned and launched into high speed to reach his motorcycle. He could get there faster on his bike, and Key would catch up in his truck. He knew where Eli lived. He fired up the R6 and whipped through the city, winding around cars and pedestrians until he got into the neighborhood where Eli lived with his sister.

Christ, his sister!

Phoenix parked his bike a few houses down. The street was quiet; most people had gone to work. Going invisible, he ran toward the house. It was surrounded by a wrought-iron fence and shrubs. He grabbed the top of the fence and leaped over.

He heard the deep roar of an angry male. Inhaling, he caught the scent of copper, indicating a rogue was nearby. He went to the front window, but the living room was empty. He made his way into the back, leaping over another fence.

He passed a kitchen window and stopped at a sliding glass door.

Inside was a nightmare. Eli was on a chair, both legs bleeding. He wore shorts and athletic shoes, as though he'd been out running. Now both massive thighs had ugly gunshot holes in them and blood pouring out.

His chest had smears of blood.

On the floor at his feet lay a witch. Her mouth was taped, her clothes torn off, and there were cuts everywhere. Her witch-shimmer had huge red holes burning in it. Pity, rage, and bloodlust mixed in his gut.

Tully stood over her, holding out the dripping knife to Eli. "Kill her."

Eli's powerful chest rippled, his biceps twisted, and he had his hands clenched around the sides of the chair. "Let Ginny go."

Shifting his gaze to the right, Phoenix saw Ginny with her back to the refrigerator, her arms pulled tight behind her. She was either cuffed or tied to the door handles. Her mouth was taped, her eyes red and leaking tears. She had on a green tank top, jeans, and tennis shoes. Chaz, who towered over her by almost a foot, sliced her tank top up the front. "Take your time deciding, Eli. Your sister is hot." The slimy prick then shoved the tip of the knife under the front clasp of her bra.

Blood welled up and trailed down between her ribs.

Chaz sliced the bra.

The impossible choice enraged him: If Eli killed the witch, he'd lose his soul and go rogue. If he didn't kill her, they'd rape and kill his sister. Phoenix wasn't going to let that happen. He tested the sliding glass door, found it unlocked, then palmed his knife in his right hand and coiled the long chain around his left.

Eli bellowed, "Get away from her! I'll kill you, I'll cut your balls off and—"

Phoenix shoved open the sliding glass door with his knife hand. He materialized to fight, and as Chaz turned away from Ginny, he threw the knife.

It hit the center of his chest. The blond man sputtered, dropping his knife to grab the hilt of the blade in his chest. Phoenix figured he'd be dead in seconds and turned to the other rogue.

Tully had his gun up and fired.

He dived forward, feeling the bullet slice the air by his ear. As soon as he hit the tiled floor with his shoulder, he tucked into a front roll. He snatched his second knife from his boot as he came up to his feet.

Tully turned the gun on him.

Phoenix snapped his chain, and the thick links coiled around the rogue's gun hand so hard that it caused the weapon to drop from his nerveless fingers.

"Behind you!" Eli screamed.

Holding the chain, he spun around. Chaz lay on the floor with the knife in his chest and a two-handed grip on a small gun. What the hell? Direct hits to the heart killed witch hunters. He should be dead. Phoenix threw his remaining knife, hitting the bastard in the throat. The gun clattered to the floor.

He whirled back around in time to see that the witch had put her hand over the gun that had fallen from Tully. The rogue kicked her in the side so hard, it lifted her body off the ground. She made horrible gagging sounds behind the tape.

Tully scooped the gun off the floor, brought it up with a dead perfect aim to Phoenix's heart, and fired.

There was a hollow click. Nothing happened. In that second, Phoenix felt the magic. The witch had jammed the gun.

Phoenix smiled. Then he dropped the chain and spun into a roundhouse kick to the bastard's face. As the rogue flew into a wall, Phoenix grabbed a knife off the ground, stalked after the murderous traitor, and stabbed him straight through to the heart.

Tully blinked in shock, then said, "Won't die. Won't. Young swore the witch blood was enhanced. . . ."

A strange chill raced down Phoenix's spine, and he twisted the knife hard until he was sure the heart was shredded and the rogue was on his way to eternity as a shade.

Phoenix had showered, scrubbing off the lingering scent of witch blood. But the craving was there, slithering through his veins, making him more and more edgy. He strode down the stairs and into the cavernous warehouse located next to Axel's club. The Wing Slayer Hunters used it as a headquarters.

It smelled like wet concrete, sweat, coffee, and musky pheromones. His boots rang out on the cement floor. Just ahead was the pool table that sat in the center. On the left was a high-end computer about the size of a small bedroom. The corner wall had security monitors showing them the surrounding area outside, the interior of the club, and anything else they desired. There were several flat-paneled computer screens and all the equipment any tech geek could want. Sutton sat in his customary roller chair, doing his electronic wizard stuff.

Axel leaned against the L-shaped desk, drinking coffee as he watched.

Next to that was their sitting area, which comprised a leather couch and chairs. Phoenix went to the coffeepot sitting on the table next to the small fridge and poured some java for himself. He preferred his fresh-ground coffee, but this wasn't bad.

He glanced up to see Key at his drafting table. He'd showered, put on a muscle shirt and jeans. His hand was flying over paper, his face shadowed as he worked. Pinned on the wall over his board were drawings by his favorite little girl, Hannah. She was Axel's four-year-old sister. But right now, Key was in his zone, in the place where no one dared interrupt him when he was drawing out his rage, the killing violence that lived inside him.

Phoenix poured a second cup of coffee, added some sugar, and walked to Key's area. He set the coffee into the holder at the top of the drawing board and moved away. Key heard them, but he needed to draw. Needed to spill out the venom inside him.

Across from Key was the partitioned-off weight room. That was empty right now.

"Sutton."

Phoenix recognized Linc's voice. He was their newest Wing Slayer Hunter.

Sutton answered, "You're on the screen, Linc. Axel, Phoenix, and Key are here with me."

Phoenix walked over to the screen. Lincoln Dillinger reminded him of a feral lion hiding in a man's skin. He was cut and styled to perfection, draped in expensive clothes, lived for his next high-stakes bet, and could charm a nun out of her robe. But there was one thing he couldn't hide—his keen gold eyes, as though a lion lived in that man ready to burst out in a ferocious attack.

Linc said, "Eli's sleeping. Told him I'd stay while he rests and heals. Don't want to leave Ginny unprotected."

Phoenix tasted the hot rage in his throat. The memory of her tied to the fridge, being tormented to force Eli to go rogue. That was the kind of animals rogues were— they used women like Ginny. If he hadn't gotten there in time, Eli would have given up his soul for his sister.

"Stay there, just keep in touch," Axel said, his voice harsh with the same anger.

Sutton added, "I've activated all the alarms and the security cameras on the place."

Linc said, "Axel, was this Eli's test?"

The question surprised them all. Linc was the first of the new recruits to get his wings and join the original five of Axel, Sutton, Phoenix, Key, and Ram. Key had tattooed the outline of wings, signaling to their Wing Slayer god that this was their candidate. Then there would be a test. No one knew what it would be until it happened. When it happened, Axel, as the hawk, recognized it. If the candidate pleased the Wing Slayer, then they had the Induction Ceremony. It hadn't occurred to Phoenix that this could be Eli's test.

Axel broke the thick silence with his answer. "No. He doesn't have the outline of his wings yet."

Linc's eyes heated, but all he said was "You know where I am. Later."

"Wait," Phoenix said. "You should hear this, too. Something one of the rogues, Tully, said as he died: *Young swore the witch blood was enhanced.*" He saw Darcy and Carla walk in as he added, "He seemed to think he couldn't die."

Carla stopped by Sutton. "Because of the witch blood? Like it was stronger, enhanced, and if he absorbed enough, he wouldn't die?"

"That's the impression I got. He was shocked that I could kill him. I had to work at it." He explained how both rogues had been harder than usual to kill.

Carla looked at Darcy. "We haven't heard anything about this."

Darcy sat in one of the chairs, her eyes thoughtful. "We were tied up with Morgan and Ram, so I had Axel take the witch Tully and Chad had cut up to some other witches. They thought they would need extra power from the Circle Witches to heal her, but it turned out to be easier than they thought."

Phoenix felt that deep in his chest. "They had more power than usual."

Carla said, "But they also had the will and desire, too. They saw how badly she was hurt. Could be their chakras responded just from their sympathy."

He had to tell them. "I don't think so."

Axel moved to sit on the arm of Darcy's chair. "This have something to do with the witch voice in your head?"

Phoenix explained as much as he knew about Ailish. "She calls it her voice power," he added, dropping into the chair across from Darcy.

Axel looked down at Darcy. "Have you felt like you have more power?"

"It's harder for Carla and me to judge because our power has grown so quickly since we completed the soul-mirror bond. Now that you and Sutton act as our familiars and we can access our high magic in our top three chakras, our magic isn't finite or measurable."

"You were able to heal Ram."

She put her hand on his thigh. "Yeah, but that was pretty straightforward, and his enhanced witch hunter biology helped, too. We're having a harder time helping Morgan."

Phoenix straightened and set his coffee cup on a nearby table. "What is happening with her? She'd been doing great before this. I thought the pregnancy hormones were helping her in spite of what Eric did to her."

"She's remarkable," Carla said, her hazel eyes sincere but troubled. "But given the extreme reactions she's having, I think that Eric may have buried some orders deep in her brain and they are trying to surface." Carla specialized in helping mortal women who'd been indoctrinated into cults, so she understood brainwashing.

Key strode up, holding his coffee. The dark violence was banked now, his eyes more blue than gray, his face relaxed. "Can you find the buried orders and do whatever you do?"

"Morgan seems to be fighting to keep the order from surfacing. I've tried straight hypnosis, but I can't get to it."

Sutton rolled his chair over to the group. "What about the astral plane, Carly? Can you take her there? She'd feel safer."

Carla shook her head. "She's too far along in her pregnancy. The baby's spirit is beginning to separate from his mom. If I pull Morgan from her body, and the baby doesn't come, he may panic and send her body into labor. That's just one scenario."

Linc had been quietly listening on the screen, but now he said, "Wait, Morgan will actually leave her body? I thought it was just a state of mind, like meditation."

Carla turned to look up at the screen. "The astral plane is another realm of existence. It's real. To go there, Morgan's spirit will leave her body and then form a doppelgänger body on the astral plane. While she's there, she won't know what's happening to her body here on this plane. Her baby will know she's gone."

"So what can you do to help Morgan?" Phoenix liked the woman, admired her. He and Joe were friends. Even though Joe wasn't the father of the baby, the man loved Morgan and would be devastated if she lost her child. The grief would kill Morgan.

Darcy said, "We're surrounding her with calming energy, and we're gently prodding, looking for the buried order in her memories. But it's not enough." She looked tired. Axel settled his arm around her shoulders and stroked her upper arm. Darcy added, "We're going to have to try something more invasive and risky if we can't find the order this way."

"What?" Key leaned against the pool table.

"I'll try to reach the baby's spirit and keep him calm, while Carla takes Morgan to the astral plane and finds the memory. It'll be traumatic, and take a lot of power to try and keep the baby feeling safe without his mom."

"Can the Circle Witches help?" Phoenix asked.

"They are split on the idea. We're working on it," Carla said.

Darcy's brown eyes glittered with anger. "Silver, that bitch. She's so furious that the Ancestors chose Carla as the Moon Witch Advisor that she's doing everything she can to undermine her."

"To be fair," Carla broke in. "Silver created the Circle Witches, and she feels like she's losing control to us soul-mirror witches. She desperately wanted the Moon Witch Advisor position to reestablish some of her authority. And we can't forget that she still has significant influence with many of the witches in the group."

"Don't you dare defend her." Darcy shifted her gaze to the others. "Silver actually said that since we know the baby is a boy and a witch hunter, and that his father was a rogue, Carla is trying to help a future rogue."

Sutton stood up so fast, his chair shot backward.

Key reached out and caught the chair.

"Sutton, it's okay," Carla said gently. "We're handling this. And before you starting yelling, my mother already did enough of that."

Sutton's massive shoulders lowered an inch. "Okay, yeah. Your mom won't let that bitch get away with saying shit about you."

Carla covered up a grin by saying, "Mom and a few other witches have agreed to help if we have no other choice. Maybe"—she turned to Phoenix—"if this power thing in Ailish's voice is true, we will have enough strength between us."

"If it is true," Key asked, "then how did Quinn Young know about it, but not you witches?"

Phoenix's biceps began to burn around his tat. Quinn Young had Asmodeus's Immortal Death Dagger burned on his forearm. They weren't exactly sure what powers he had, but that Death Dagger gave him the ability to kill immortals like Axel and Sutton for sure. They assumed he was in contact with the demon as well. Young was the leader of the Rogue Cadre whose mission it was to kill off all earth witches so that Asmodeus could have free rein on earth. So yeah, it was strange that Young knew, but he defended Ailish by saying, "Ailish swore the power is hers, that she was born with it."

"She handfasted to a demon, Phoenix," Axel said. "She could be working with Asmodeus, using her voice to enhance witch blood and making the rogues stronger to kill off the earth witches. If she is, it's clever because we can't kill her while she's still an earth witch."

The burning sensation grew worse on his arms.

"I sent out a query to the Circle Witches . . ."

Carla's words faded out beneath a strange cracking noise that echoed in Phoenix's head, followed by a vivid memory of a bird soaring across the sky. Then he heard the beautiful cry of the newborn child, and as if that cry were a detonator, flames roared to life around him, burning and consuming him. He could smell his feathers burning, feel the flames eating his flesh, until finally, he was gone.

Phoenix realized his eyes were closed, and branding hot pain seared his biceps. He opened his eyes.

Axel, Darcy, and Key were on his left, Sutton and Carla on his right. They all stared at his arms.

Axel shifted his gaze to his face. "Did you hear the voice?"

"No." The burning faded on his arms, but he twisted his left arm and looked at his tat. "No fucking way." The original single wing had reshaped itself to a blue head, beak, neck, and top of a bent wing rising from an outline of red-and-gold flames.

Phoenix shoved up to his feet, and everyone moved back. "What the hell is going on?" His heart was pounding as though he'd just killed half a dozen rogues.

Axel responded, "The tat reacted to my comment about killing Ailish. It's coming out, trying to protect her." He glanced at the new markings, then added, "You touched the witch's blood last night. The tat must have recognized her. The soul-mirror bond requires an exchange of blood and then sex to seal it."

Ailish was his soul mirror? He'd envisioned his soul mirror being a witch like Darcy or Carla. Good, kind, willing to sacrifice to help others. His soul mirror would be a woman of courage, and together they'd be stronger. He'd have a mate he could protect and help to do her magic.

He wouldn't fail with a mate like that. A real partner.

A blind witch who had bargained with a demon? How the hell could he protect her from blindness? Or the handfast? He sure as hell hadn't been able to save his mom from the voices. It was a recipe for failure. He'd be forever trying to take care of her, to save her. . . . "Can't be her. She handfasted herself to a demon." In spite of that, his head throbbed. The tat pulled and itched, as though it wanted him to move. Go.

To her.

Shit, he didn't want this.

But his tat didn't have the same reservations. The markings vibrated in the skin over his biceps, quivering with the need to see her, be close to her. He rolled his neck and said, "Is it even possible to finish the soul-mirror bond if she's handfasted to a demon?"

Darcy answered first. "Not sure. We'll see if we can talk to the Ancestors and find out. We'll also try to find out about this voice power."

He had to be satisfied with that for now. The Ancestors should have some answers; they were witches who had reincarnated over and over until they completed their journey, learning all that they were meant to. At that point, they no longer reincarnated but stayed in Summerland to act as guides for witches. Summerland was the place of rest for both witches and witch hunters . . . if they still had their souls. Right now, he thought helplessly, the handfast binding on Ailish put her soul in limbo.

Axel broke into his thoughts. "We need to know more about her, and keep her from using her voice power until we know what it is and what it's doing."

The need to get moving was building to an unbearable pressure. "She was adamant that she had to use her power to break the handfast so that Asmodeus doesn't get control of it."

Carla said, "Make her a deal. Tell her we'll research

breaking the handfast if she'll cooperate and not use her voice."

A cautious hope forced its way into his roiling emotions. "Do you know how to break it?"

Both witches shook their heads, and Carla answered, "No, and if any witch in the Circle Witches has done it, they aren't going to want to admit to it."

He had no choice: He had to find Ailish and get answers.

5

Ailish sent Dee home and went into her house. Seeing Kyle had brought back memories of being young and in love. That left her annoyed and restless. She hadn't really expected Kyle to believe her. But it still was irritating. How did she protect him now? She didn't know how to get past the magical block shielding his memory.

Using her voice power was too dangerous. She had only hummed in an effort to release a small amount, and it had shaken the windows. Ailish remembered all too well what had happened when she'd unleashed her power to save Haley—she'd hurt her mother. Not to mention blinding herself from witch karma. Damn it, she had to get control of that power.

She dumped her backpack on the table by the front door, then headed over to the coffee table to pick up her cold tea and the bag of dried fruit and nuts she'd left there. She'd get something to eat, then regroup.

She wasn't going to let her mother get her claws into Kyle again. So she'd find a way to protect him, while figuring out how to control her voice power to get the blasted binding off and break the handfast. After rinsing the mug, she put it in the dishwasher, stowed the nuts, and—

A sharp cry jerked her around. What was that? She held her breath, waiting.

Another whimper, then pitiful mewling.

It was coming from her backyard and sounded like a

hurt or scared animal. Maybe a cat? She walked across the room to the French doors.

There it was again. Definitely from her backyard. It reached right through to her heart. Maybe a kitten had wandered away from its mother?

Could it be a demon trick?

The critter cried out again, a thin, pitiful sound that made her head ache in sympathy. The little guy must be really hurt. She reached for the door handle, unlocked the door, and eased it open a couple inches. She didn't smell sulfur, so she stepped out onto the patio.

She followed the yelps and cries over her patio toward the grass. "What's wrong, little guy?" she said softly.

It whimpered.

She moved closer, then crouched and used her hand to pat the grass in front of her until she felt the bony back of a kitten. But it darted away from her and cried some more. She started to open her chakras to send calming energy to the poor thing. "It's—"

"Hello? . . . Ma'am?" a male voice called out.

Ailish jolted in surprise, turned, and stood up. The voice came from the other side of the fence by the gate. "Yes?"

"I think our kitten is back there. My daughter was playing with her and dropped her. The kitten ran under the fence."

"Uh . . ." She tried to think. He sounded young to middle-aged and a little harried. She caught the faint scent of paint fumes.

The kitten cried again.

The man said, "That's her. Is it all right if I come back there? Or could you bring her to me?"

His voice still sounded harried, but a little sheepish, too.

"Careful, though," he added. "She sounds hurt. She's only a couple months old."

The kitten was crying frantically now. Ailish knew it was in pain. She needed the man's eyes to help the poor animal. "Come on back," she said.

"Thanks."

She heard the gate open and the man walk toward her. "Name's Bruce, by the way. Took a couple days off work to paint the living room. Ah, there she is." He moved past her.

The kitten screeched.

Ailish winced. "What's wrong with her?"

"Ah, hell, it looks like her leg. Must have landed on it. I don't know . . . guess I'll take her to the vet or . . . She's in so much pain." He came back to stand by Ailish, shifting nervously.

The paint fumes were stronger, nearly burning her nose. She could make out his shadow, and he was big, under six feet but meaty. There was a heavy feel to him. She took that in, but her focus was on the kitten. "Which leg?" Reaching out, she felt the man's hand.

A flicker caught her nerves and raced through her body. The handfast link heated, forcing more excitement pulsing through her. It took her breath away for a second.

Bruce grabbed her arm. "I'm done playing with you, witch."

She stiffened as the sensations of forced pleasure raced up her arms and through her body, making her nipples harden, her skin heat, and her womb ache. The pain infuriated her. "The paint fumes," she snarled, "disguised the sulfur." She took stock. He had his left hand on her arm, while the right hand had the kitten. "Give me the kitten. At least—"

"In the house. Now." He shoved her.

"Hell, no, I'm not—"

The kitten screeched.

"Its leg is broken, want me to break another one?"

The ache of the painful forced lust throbbed in her, but the pure hatred howled in her head. "Bastard. Stop hurting her!" The poor kitten was whimpering.

"In the house."

It didn't matter. She wasn't giving in to him. She could take him down in the house, she just had to get him off his guard. Asmodeus had never shown this side in his possessions before . . . they had always been a kind of seduction, not this brutality. She turned and walked across the yard and patio, going through the doors. What if she didn't invite him in? Could he still . . .

He walked right in behind her, the animal still crying.

"Thought I had to invite you," she muttered.

"You did. You said, 'Come on in,' in the backyard."

Amusement snaked through his voice. She wondered if the man who was being possessed really did live next door.

She stalked past the table to the open area at the end of the kitchen/dining room. It was a little study with a desk and a reading chair and light. She whirled around.

He was three feet from her. "There's no escape. You will submit."

His voice was losing its human quality; a chilling growl vibrated beneath the words. Fear iced her spine, but the lust kept roiling inside her. She hated the way the bastard controlled her body and made her feel something artificial and revolting. Ailish couldn't even trust her own body.

"I'll kill the animal, first I'll finish breaking its legs and then I'll slice its throat."

Furious adrenaline whipped through her. She couldn't let the cat be killed. If she did, then she was as vicious and cruel as her mother. But if she gave in, she'd lose her soul.

"Next will be Kyle. My coven will torture him until you submit."

God, she hated all of them! She had to think. What should she do?

The kitten continued to cry.

She gritted her teeth, fighting to get control of her body, of the unnatural lust and hot, sick fury. "You win."

"Take off your clothes. Now."

"Just let me heal the kitten's leg. I can't stand the squalling." She zeroed in on the crying sounds, then snapped into action. She grabbed the kitten, jumped back, and tried a hopping side kick, attempting to drive her heel into his solar plexus.

He caught her foot and jerked up, and she landed hard on her back. Her head hit the ground so hard that she heard a roaring in her ears.

The kitten screamed in terror and crawled away.

The hand was still wrapped around her foot. He squeezed hard through her boot. "Done playing, witch. You're mine. Your power is mine. I'll shatter every bone in your body until you submit to the Claiming Rite."

It was the man's voice, but with a strange reverberation that sent chills down her spine and made her magic cringe. It was Asmodeus taking more control of the mortal.

The growling-roar in her head stopped, but more pain shot up the nerves in her leg. Sweat broke out under her arms, while the lust pulsed in her pelvis. Unbearable.

After yanking her across the carpet, he began to climb on top of her. She fought, twisting her body.

He slammed his elbow into the side of her breast.

Sharp pain seared through her, taking her breath away. Hot tears burned her eyes. But she'd trained to deal with pain and forced her mind past it. This guy was huge and trying to climb on top of her. Much as she didn't want to hurt the mortal, she was going to have to use a groin strike. Her power would heal it once she had banished the demon. She waited, feigning compliance as he loomed over her—

Her front door exploded open and slammed into the wall. A huge shadow filled her damaged vision, and before she could react, the man was jerked off her.

Someone else was in her house! Who? Was it real help or another trick? The vivid sounds of fighting and grunting seemed like help. She rolled to her feet, trying to get a read on what the hell was happening.

"Ailish, on the floor at two o'clock. Banish the demon!"

It was the witch hunter from last night! *Phoenix*. What the hell was he doing here? Did she dare trust him?

Did she have a choice?

Suddenly, Phoenix was behind her. "Hurry."

His voice blasted through her already raw nerves, but she focused past the pain to call the energy from her pelvis floor, funneled it up her spine and through her hands. And all the while, lust and desperate aching need pounded at her. Her stomach growled in hunger, her leg was half-numb, and her left breast was so sore that just holding up her arm was agony. In a sharp contrast, she could feel the hunter behind her, looming over her, and making her acutely aware of a horrible barren feeling of incompleteness that echoed inside her.

The man on the floor of her living room sputtered and spewed rough sounds.

Finally the cloying, sickening scent of sulfur exploded around them, then vanished. She dropped her arms. "He's gone."

The silence behind her felt heavy. The hunter's hot breath stirred her hair. She shuddered as tingles ran down her spine. Her head throbbed from a mean combination of hormones being forced through her, banging her head, the effort of controlling her magic, and the huge presence of Phoenix.

Wait, why was he here now? Just in time to save her?

What if Asmodeus hadn't been banished but had jumped to him? She whipped around, bringing up her arms and assuming her fight stance in spite of the pain.

"You're fucking kidding me," he snapped. "I just saved your ass and you want to attack me?"

"How do I know you can't be possessed?"

She felt him shift his weight. "Your bigger problem at the moment is my bloodlust. Your power is still zinging through me." He stalked past her.

His scent caught her. Leather, soap, and musk. No sulfur. She heard Phoenix pull the guy up from the floor.

"Hey!" the man said, his voice thick.

"Who is this guy?" the hunter asked.

She had to pull herself together. "Not sure. While possessed, he said he's Bruce and lives next door."

"I do, but why am I here?" His voice started firm, then slid into confusion. "Hey, that's my cat. She's hurt. What did you do to my cat?"

The kitten! Ailish bent down, ignoring the protest from her leg, and held out her hand. The crying little girl put her head in her hand. She scooped her up. She wasn't any bigger than a coffee mug. "Have to use more magic." She cradled the kitten to her middle, closer to her chakras, then opened the first four and sent healing energy into the cat. It took every last bit of strength she had to do it.

Finally, the crying stopped. Ailish breathed a sigh of relief. She was sore, dizzy, starved, and depleted with a lingering headache from the unnatural hormone rush.

"What the hell?" the neighbor said. "What's going on? How'd I get here? What are you doing to my cat?"

Ailish stood up and hissed at the hot stab of pain in her leg. She took a step toward them.

Phoenix's voice stopped her. "I've got this, Ailish. Just give him the cat."

She held out the animal, and Bruce took him while saying, "I don't understand. . . ."

"I'll explain," Phoenix said while moving to the door, obviously tugging the man with him. Once outside, she heard Phoenix say, "Your kitten got into the neighbor's house. You came over, got her, and went home."

A few seconds later, she heard the witch hunter striding back into her house. She asked, "What did you do?"

"Memory-shifting. He was confused as hell, I gave him an explanation. What do you usually do?" He shut the door.

His voice, his scent, they were touching her, stirring her magic into pleasant tingles. "Use magic to convince them to believe what I tell them."

"How bad did he hurt you?"

He was too close, right in front of her. She had the oddest sensation of feathers reaching out to brush over the bare skin of her arms. It was soothing and unsettling at the same time. She stepped back, trying to regain her senses. What had he asked her? Oh, right, how badly she was hurt. "That was new. Up till now, it's all been seduction. First time that bastard used someone to attack me. Or hurt an animal." Cold fury swirled in her emotional stew, and just to keep it all interesting, she pulled out her suspicion. "How did you happen to show up at just the right moment?"

"Didn't you hear my motorcycle?"

She pulled her lips in. Hell, she had heard a roar, but she'd thought it was from hitting her head. "I was a little busy." She wasn't ready to actually move, so she stood there and demanded, "Why should I believe that you can't be possessed?"

"Wing Slayer created us, and he's half demon and half god. He knows the tricks of a demon and made sure we couldn't be possessed and controlled the way a human can. He and Asmodeus have been enemies for a long time. We were created to hunt and kill the witches corrupted by the demon."

She frowned at that. Carefully, she tested her left leg and found it held her weight, so she walked into the kitchen. "I thought Wing Slayer was dead." She opened the refrigerator, reached for the waters she kept on the shelf, and sucked in her breath. Damn, her left breast hurt. She took a second, leaning on the door while breathing.

"That's what everyone thought but us. They were wrong. He's alive, and he's regaining his god power to fight back against Asmodeus."

He was there suddenly. Behind her. So close that she felt his body, felt the weight of him, the security. If she stood up, her back would touch his chest. A sizzle slipped into her skin and stirred gently. Not the harsh, fast, fake sizzle of the handfast, but a softer sensation that she wanted to just feel and enjoy. . . . Damn, just how hard had she hit her head? "What are you doing?"

"You're hurt. I can almost feel it."

His breath shifted her hair and traveled down her back. Soft waves of pleasure. She didn't understand it. "Move. I'm just getting water."

"Got it." He reached past her.

His arm slid by her face but didn't actually touch her. It was weird being surrounded by him, by his leather, soap, and tangy, thick musk scent that made her want to lean closer and inhale until her lungs were saturated. It was as if she could almost soak in his strength and feel safe. She frowned. Obviously she had a concussion and it was making her sappy and stupid. "Don't touch me."

He moved away, leaving her in the fog of cold air from the fridge. Ailish straightened, shut the door, and turned. He was right there in front of her. His huge body felt like some kind of shield. Protection. In fact, she could almost see his shadow spreading wings.

He handed her a bottle of water and asked, "Why didn't you heal yourself when you healed the kitten?"

She blinked and looked again. His shadow was just the vague outline of a huge man. Concussion, that's all. She took the bottle, opened it, and answered, "Didn't have enough juice."

"You ran out of power?"

For the first time, she noticed the edge in his voice. As though maybe he wasn't having the best day ever, either. "I'll be fine after I eat."

"How about pizza? Pepperoni?"

What was he doing? "Yeah," she heard herself answer. While he called in the pizza order, she wondered why she was being passive and not throwing him out of her house. Wait, why was he here to begin with?

He walked by her while rattling off her address on the phone.

She tilted her head, tracking him as he ended the call, watching as he bent over as if there were something on the floor. Then he rose and moved to the other side of the counter. What was he doing? "Why are you here?"

"To talk to you." She heard him slide onto a bar stool, then the sounds of him fiddling with something, probably his cell phone, as he said, "I Googled you last night. You're a professional kickboxer."

There was something unnerving about him being in her house. It wasn't the handfast link; that felt cold and dead on her wrist. He was causing the odd reactions in her. Like worrying that she wasn't measuring up to his standards or some bullshit like that. Annoyed, she said, "That's not a news flash, Slick."

"How does a witch get involved in something like that? Most witches are . . ."

Oh, this would be good. "Are what?"

"More gentle."

She snorted. "Well, maybe most witches don't have a demon stalking them. You get over that gentle shit real quick." She used to be gentle, sweet, naïve, and look where that had gotten her—handfasted to a demon. So if she didn't fit Phoenix's idea of what a witch should be, too bad. She picked up the bottle and drank some of the cool water to wash out the memories. "This little chitchat is special, but why are you really here?"

"Your voice is unleashing dangerous magic. This morning, a rogue I killed claimed that the enhanced witch blood made them stronger."

The implications stunned her. "My voice can do that?"

He kept playing with whatever was in his hands. "You told me it enhances all magic, so yeah, we think it's possible."

She tried to grasp what it meant. "But if that's true, it would make the witches stronger." Wasn't that good?

"They have no defense against rogues." His voice hardened. "They can't use their powers, no matter how strong, because of witch karma. They are sitting ducks, and if it's true the rogues think they've hit the mother lode of power in witch blood, they'll go after them with a vengeance to feed their addiction. We are the only defense the witches have."

His fury pounded at her, making her skin feel tight and her stomach churn. Worry set in. Was it possible? Could she be doing harm while trying to get control of her magic? If so, then she had to stop. But there hadn't been any witch-karma backlash, not like when she was blinded. She needed her voice power to break the handfast. Then she picked up on the one word he kept using. "Who is *we*?"

"Wing Slayer Hunters."

"Because you believe the Wing Slayer is alive." She wasn't sure about that. Her mother insisted the witches had killed the god with the curse.

"We're committed to him. We know he's alive. He's granted two of our hunters immortality."

Shocked, she set down her water bottle and leaned her

hands on the cool countertop. "How did he do that? Hunters lost their immortality with the curse."

"There's a loophole called soul mirrors."

She'd never heard that term. Could he be lying? Making shit up to manipulate her somehow? She wished she could see him, see his face. His eyes. Ailish wondered what he looked like. From tangling with him last night, she knew he stood a few inches over six feet and weighed about 110 pounds more than her 130 fighting weight. He was faster and stronger than anyone she'd ever encountered. But what stood out the most was when he'd pinned her and she'd felt his biceps.

Feathers.

For a second, she'd thought she felt feathers. Since that was last night, she couldn't blame that on a concussion.

It had to be her imagination, maybe some kind of hallucination from all the hormones or stress or even from nearing the end of her handfast contract.

"Soul mirrors are usually a good thing," he was saying. "They can break the curse for the hunter and the witch."

"What?" She'd been daydreaming. What the hell was wrong with her? "So this soul-mirror thing lets a witch bond with a familiar and access her high magic?" She would be able to control her voice power and break the handfast. "How do you get this soul mirror, is it magic?"

"A kind of magic," he said, his voice going to that edge again. He got off the bar stool and prowled the room. "When the demon witches cast the curse, they used the words, *We bind thee soul to soul; in the blooded power that you crave above all else; in sex to claim your descendants.* They were attempting to bind witch hunters to them, turning us into nothing more than mindless creatures to do their bidding."

She heard the hatred and revulsion in his voice as he

moved around. Knowing what she did now about demon witches, she couldn't blame him. He'd hate her, too, if he knew she was the daughter of not only a demon witch, but the high witch of the coven. "Go on."

He moved back to the bar. "It all turned into a clusterfuck. The souls were pulled out of the witches' and witch hunters' bodies, binding together as the curse decreed. The earth witches called the souls back, causing them to halve. In essence, we all have half a soul now."

Ailish felt a fission of recognition ring in that hollow place in her chest. The place that had always felt empty, not quite full.

Incomplete.

"That's why we can't bond with a familiar. An earth witch must have her soul to form that magical bond." It made sense. Her mother had only told her that the curse had been a power play by Wing Slayer and that he'd failed, getting himself killed and leaving his witch hunters without a god. Of course, her mother lied. But did that mean Phoenix was telling the truth?

In a dry voice, he said, "The curse left witch hunters with the unbearable craving for power in witch blood, as well as a craving for sex."

A whole different kind of soft tingles glided along her nerves at the mention of sex. She ignored that, however, and was thinking over the implications of what he'd told her when the doorbell rang. Pizza. "Wait here," she told him.

She walked into the living room, hooked a right, and had reached for her backpack purse when she heard the door open and Phoenix say, "How much?"

The pizza guy named the price. Ailish had the bills in her wallet folded to tell her the denomination. She pulled out a twenty and a five. "Here." She pushed the money toward the shape of Phoenix.

"Already got it." He stepped back and closed the door. "By the way, here's your cell phone. I found it on the floor." He pushed it into her hand and strode away.

It must have fallen out of her pants when she'd been struggling with the demon-possessed man. But then she remembered Phoenix fiddling with something while sitting at her counter. What had he done to her phone? And why?

The smell of yeasty bread, tomato sauce, and warm cheese filled the living room. Her stomach practically twisted in hunger.

"Got paper plates?" His voice floated back as he walked to the table.

Normally she'd force the money on him and toss his ass out of her house, but he'd intrigued her with the soul-mirror stuff. She tucked her phone into her pocket and went into the kitchen, snatched up a few plates and napkins, then took them to the table. She moved with confidence, pausing only at the table to find his shape already in a chair on the side of the kitchen bar. She sat on the patio side of the table. Rather than fumble for the box to get a slice, she summoned her powers to—

"Don't. No more magic. Bloodlust." His voice was low and rough, almost like a Rottweiler's warning bark.

With the threat of the demon looming over her, she'd forgotten about the bloodlust. Was that why the edge kept appearing in his voice? He was fighting the urge to cut her and get her blood? She should be afraid or worried. She didn't want to dwell on why she wasn't.

"Tell me more about the soul-mirror thing. How can I do it and get a familiar?" She put out her hand, found the box, and was able to get a slice onto her plate. As far as she knew, she didn't knock anything over. Refusing to care, she took a bite of the pizza.

"Your water is at two o'clock."

Swallowing, she looked at his shape, biting back a sharp comment. But he wasn't treating her like an idiot, he'd just told her where he put her water. She nodded in thanks. The truth was that her blindness didn't seem to bother him at all.

"Your soul mirror becomes your familiar."

She froze in surprise, then said, "What does that mean? Is a soul mirror a person or an animal?"

"Both, I guess. Witch hunters have wings tattooed somewhere on their bodies. When they bond with the witch who is the other half of their soul, the bird comes to life. That bird acts as the witch's familiar. You have to find the other half of your soul, then finish the bond."

She'd wolfed down almost her entire slice. She dropped the crust and wiped her greasy hands on a napkin. "Find the witch hunter who my soul was joined with, then halved. Is that what you're saying?"

"Yes. And then you exchange blood and sex to finish the bond."

She reached for her water, which was exactly where he'd said it would be. Yet alarm bells blared in her head. Sex finished the handfast with the demon, so she avoided it altogether. Just because Phoenix said he couldn't be possessed didn't mean it was true. Or hell, maybe her mother and the coven had found a way to control a witch hunter. Maybe he was gaining her trust and then Asmodeus would possess him. Setting down her water, she said, "I thought witch hunters craved our blood. Yet you're sitting there eating with me."

"I'm fighting the bloodlust. Right now, my veins are on fire. So don't push me, Ailish. How is it that you don't know any of this stuff?"

Was he a threat to her? "How would I know? Earth witches won't talk to me once they see this." She held up her left hand. "I avoid demon witches, and until last night, I'd never encountered a witch hunter."

"How? How the hell is that possible? What about your family? Your mother? Can't they help you?"

Depends on how you define help. Her mother was desperate to force Ailish to become a demon witch. But damned if she was going into the saga of her pitiful family history with him. "No."

She could feel him studying her. Then he said, "I don't see you wearing anything silver. Where's your witch book?"

Her what? She didn't think he meant a novel type of book. Thinking quickly, she guessed it was some kind of book witches had, one kept in silver, and one that she wouldn't need her sight to use. At a loss, she turned the question back on him. "What do you want with it?"

"What are you hiding?"

She smiled dryly. He was feeding her just enough information to keep her talking. "No more than you, I suspect. You're here to pump me for information. For who? Why?"

"For me. Because I might be your soul mirror."

6

Ailish couldn't quite take in the idea that she and this hunter could be soul mirrors. "You? But—" But what? Wasn't this what she wanted? A possible solution? But what if it was a trick? She'd believed the kitten story, and that had been a trick. She had to be careful, had to think.

She'd learned the hard way that her choices mattered, and they had consequences. Easy answers weren't always the way. Asking her mother to make Kyle love her again . . . yeah, there were consequences.

But what if this was real? Her thoughts kept circling, but it was obvious she needed more information. "How do you know it's me? That we're soul mirrors?"

He shifted as if trying to find the words. "I have the wings of a phoenix tattooed on both biceps. After touching your blood last night, the bird is coming to life. A head and part of the body showed up today."

She strained her eyes, struggling to see him, to see this man who claimed to be her soul mirror. But all she could make out was the shadowed outline. How could she check the tattoo? She couldn't. And yet hadn't she thought she'd felt feathers? Frustration bubbled up. "That doesn't help. I don't know what your tattoo looked like or if it changed."

She heard him move, a hush of sound, and then he stood on her left. He leaned over her then, placing one hand on the table and the other on the back of her chair.

The air shivered between them, and she couldn't get her breath. But she could feel his heavy stare on her.

In a low voice, he said, "Touch the wings, Ailish. Tell me what you feel."

Before she thought, before she considered her actions, she lifted both hands. Inside, deep against her spine, a burbling began, as if her powers were swirling and jumping in her chakras. She touched his forearms, feeling the hot skin over thick, bunched muscles.

"Higher," he said in a rough voice.

She skimmed her palms over his elbows and up the steep curves of his muscles. She hadn't felt a man in eight years. And never like this. Kyle had been a boy and she a girl. But Phoenix, she could feel the leashed strength of him in the flexed muscles of his arms. He felt . . . safe.

That was insane, she told herself. But her chakras slid open and her energy streamed out, bouncing and pinging inside her.

She skimmed higher and froze.

"Feathers."

Her powers slowed their pinging, almost as if they heard her. Then they joined together and forged a path straight to her fingers. She couldn't stop herself—she stroked over the hard curves of his thick arms, feeling the skin, then the feathers. The feathers lifted and caressed her palms as if they knew how much she needed that kind of connection.

His muscles twitched and tightened even more, feeling like hot marble. "I feel your powers, your magic. What do you feel, Ailish?"

His breath touched her face, and she shivered. More sensations rolled over her. Not the sudden, painful forced lust of the handfast, but a warm, liquid feeling that softened her muscles so that she found herself gripping his arms for support.

Trusting him.

"Feathers. I can feel . . ." She touched again, trying to explain it. "The sweep of a wing with a bend at the top. The feathers are soft, but the wing itself is strong. And higher up, here, I can feel the head of the bird."

"Believe me now?"

"I don't know." She couldn't stop stroking the bird, but she wanted to touch more of him. Wanted, needed, to see him with her fingers. "What do you feel?"

"You. Jesus, Ailish, from the second you touched me, I felt you. When I was sitting across from you, I burned with the curse, but once you touched me, hell . . ."

"What?" This scared the shit out of her. What was she doing? She, who never let anyone touch her. But she didn't feel the painful lust of the handfast. She felt . . . desire. Deep, growing desire. And that was some scary shit.

He groaned. "You're bringing out something in me. Breathing life into a part of me I didn't know was there."

She tilted her head, trying to see his face, but it wouldn't come into focus. Unable to stand it any longer, she released the feathers and lifted her hands to his face. First she laid her palms on both his cheeks. His face was wide and strong, with hollows between his protruding cheekbones and squared jaw. She could feel the stubble on his cheeks and chin. Then she brushed her fingers over his strong forehead and moved her thumbs over his slightly arched eyebrows.

"Keep going," he said, and closed his eyes.

A thrill danced through her. She gently felt his eyes, deep set and a bit wide, a nose with a bump slightly to one side. "Broken?"

"Few times."

She drifted her hands down to his cheeks, then used her thumbs and touched his lips. Full, firm lips, the bottom one bowed in the center. The top lip had a perfect little dent. "What color is your hair?" She was trying to form a picture of him.

"Black. Eyes almost black."

She slipped her fingers into his hair. The strands were thick, soft, and cut unevenly to fall to the middle of his neck. His features were strong, his skin smooth but for the beard stubble, his hair dark, a little choppy—in her mind, she saw him. Pictured him. Long, muscular, with a face like an outlaw, framed in that I-don't-give-a-shit hair.

"Damn, Ailish. Just . . . damn." Keeping his hands anchored on the chair and the table, he leaned toward her. "Dangerous, stupid, risky . . ."

Her hands slid to his shoulders. She was caged in her chair by him, surrounded by his scent, the scent that was all Phoenix and not a trace of demon sulfur. She knew the feel of his skin now and craved more . . . wanted to feel more. "What?"

He moved closer until she could all but feel his mouth on hers. "Kissing you."

No, she couldn't. Wouldn't. She couldn't be sure of him, didn't trust him. No. She hadn't kissed anyone since she'd been sixteen. She was a loner, and— "I live for risk and danger." *What? Why had she said—*

"Oh yeah." He closed the last fraction of space and brushed his lips over hers.

Desire swelled like a gently rising wave. The feel of his mouth was incredibly soft, and then he sucked in her bottom lip and caressed it with his tongue. Her powers began humming, causing a soft vibration inside of her. Her stomach flipped over, and she dug her fingers into his shoulders. She was being drawn into a rich sensuality that scared her. Yet she was desperate for more.

He released hold of her lip. "More, Ailish. Let me taste you."

His darkly beseeching voice compelled her. She wanted to taste him, taste what it was that made her body hum and shiver and yearn but not *hurt*. She shouldn't trust this, but then she moved her hand from his shoulder to touch the feathers, and they responded by stroking her fingers, holding her. Ailish opened her mouth, and Phoenix made a noise of approval as he sank his tongue into her. In seconds, he wrapped his other arm around her waist and pulled her up from the chair. Her feet dangled, but her mouth . . . He plunged in, tasting her, sliding his tongue along hers as tremors of pleasure raced down her spine and spread through her womb.

His chest swelled against her breasts. He shifted her until her hips pressed against his erection.

Her magic built into a lush waterfall of sensations, stirring a tingling ache in her breasts straight down to her groin, making her want to rub up against him as if he were slowly possessing her.

Possessing? The fear bloomed, followed by hot rage. *What the hell was she doing?* She jerked her head away. "Put me down."

He went utterly still, while continuing to hold her tight against him.

His superior strength slammed into her. He was holding her with little effort. "I said—"

"I'm trying. Can't . . . one second." He drew in a deep breath, then eased her down to her feet.

She stumbled, caught the back of her chair, and recaptured her balance. Her powers were swirling around her spine, her body felt . . . ready and willing. Not that sudden, painful lust; this was organic and real. "What was that?"

"Soul mirror." He paced away from her, grabbing stuff off the table.

She heard him go into the kitchen and open her fridge. What was he doing now? "Crazy," she muttered. "I have to think. Even if it's true, if this whole soul-mirror thing is true—"

He slammed something on the counter that sounded like the empty water bottles. "You can't possibly deny it. You felt it."

"I did." She wasn't going to lie, but she couldn't afford to be stupid, either. "Not denying it. I need to check it out. And besides, assuming it's true, it can't be that easy."

His voice shifted, going harder. "There are complications."

There it was. Again. The derision in his voice. Even suspicion. She kept her reaction flat, focused. "Because I'm handfasted to a demon."

"Yes." He walked around her, going to the table, then moved back to the kitchen. "That's one problem. Another is that your power is stirring up trouble, possibly driving rogues to slaughter even more witches."

She heard him open the cupboard under the sink, dumping in trash, but her stomach clenched at his words. "You don't trust me. You think I might be doing it on purpose."

He moved fast, stopping in front of her. "You handfasted with a demon, Ailish. You were willing to deal in dark magic once."

She was a fool. An idiot for forgetting how much he distrusted her. Softly, she answered him. "I was never willing."

He paused, lifting an arm, maybe to drag his hand through his hair. "If that's true, then you'll help us fight against whatever is happening. Don't use your voice power until we can figure this out."

He was trying to manipulate her. "So I'm supposed to just sit here and wait for the demon to win?" But she couldn't allow her power to harm others, either. It felt like a trap that was closing around her tighter and tighter.

"I'll make you a deal," he said tightly. "Don't use your voice power, and we'll try to help you find a way to break the handfast."

Now they were making deals? "We? How can witch hunters—"

"A couple of the hunters are mated to earth witches. They are connected to the Circle Witches, who are a group of witches that meet on the Internet to—"

Oh no, she wasn't going that route again. She'd asked, she'd all but begged those self-anointed witches for help. "I know who they are. They are a group of pretentious, self-righteous, judgmental prigs. I went to them a couple times and they turned their bitch backs on me. They won't help. They see this handfast binding and they close ranks."

The air between them nearly crackled. "What the hell do you expect, Ailish? You handfasted with a demon. Why would they trust you?"

She sucked in a breath, and her voice dropped to ice. "You don't know me. You don't know what it's been like. . . ." She felt the cut of his distrust, his disgust. She was trying to break the handfast and become a real earth witch. But no one believed her, believed in her. "Save your judgments for someone who cares."

He nearly vibrated with some internal force. "Ailish, damn it, I'm trying to help both you and the innocents out there, like the earth witch I managed to save today. All I'm asking is that you don't use your voice power."

Oh well, if that's all. Just don't use her last hope. She stayed quiet, fought down all the years of rage and anger.

He reached out, touched her face while softening his voice. "Don't forget, I'm your soul mirror. The answer to breaking your handfast might be in that. We just have to find out more."

Ailish pushed his hand from her. He was using this possible soul-mirror connection between them to control her. "I'm not promising you or your group anything. But I won't use the power unless I have to." It was all she could give him. She didn't want to hurt innocents, didn't want to hurt anybody. She just wanted to live . . . but short of that, she meant to protect those who were suffering because of her.

Like Kyle.

"We haven't found one." Phoenix slammed his palm against the dash of the truck. He couldn't sit still in the passenger seat as rage boiled inside him. "Not one! Where are the witches?" Darcy, Carla, and Sutton had set up a reporting system for missing witches. Tonight, all the hunters were out except Ram, who was coordinating from the warehouse.

"Gonna beat the info out of my truck?" Key turned a corner, and they moved through the sleek night.

"Truck fights better than you with all your I'm-a-tortured-artist bullshit."

"Can't help it if I'm getting laid and you're getting nada. Women like me. Probably because I'm not an asshole," he announced cheerfully.

He mimicked, "Let me draw you naked . . . oh, I work better if I draw you with my cock inside you."

"See, that right there is classic asshole behavior."

He was so tied up, so tense, so supremely horny, it felt as if his brain were going to explode. "I could get laid if I didn't keep getting interrupted." He'd had a hot woman with lonely eyes halfway up the stairs at the club earlier tonight when Ram tagged him about a missing witch.

"Your voice jealous? Keeping you all for herself? Maybe you can have voice sex in your head?"

"Maybe I can rip out your voice box and shove it up your ass. Then you can talk out of your ass for real." The cold truth was that he couldn't get the feel, scent, and taste of Ailish out of his memory. He'd told himself sex with the woman at the club would help. . . .

But he'd been partially relieved by the call from Ram. He was walking a dangerous line here. Feeding the sex part of the curse helped them battle back the bloodlust. By not doing that, he was letting the curse get too deep a hold on him. The craving for witch blood was slithering through him, just ready to explode. A mere splash of witch blood would send him over the edge.

He had just leaned his head back on the headrest when he heard the first scream. Jerking his head up, he heard a second scream and knew it was coming from his right. "Stop!" He shoved open the truck and jumped out while Key was still braking.

He smelled witch blood. "I got this!" he shouted, then turned and raced around the corner, one block over. The scent was stronger, filling his nostrils and throat. His veins warmed and swelled in anticipation. He ran faster.

Another scream came from the church up ahead. The streets in this section of Glassbreakers were barren this late at night. The church, school, and surrounding businesses were closed.

As he raced across the parking lot of the church, the smell of live witch blood was so potent that his skin began to itch in response.

"No!"

The choked cry jerked his head up. The witch stumbled out of the church and around the building. She trailed blood from multiple cuts, soaking her clothes.

Witch blood! His veins twisted in searing, agonizing demand. He wanted it, needed it. He changed his path, passing the church and running toward—

A man burst out of the church seconds later, chasing her, just as Key caught up. "Check inside, I'll get this!" he told Key.

Key didn't answer, just raced into the church.

Phoenix sprinted around the side of the building, followed the blood trail of the witch to a ladder on the side of the church, and started climbing.

It was an A-line roof two stories up. Damn, he wasn't

a fan of heights. Why couldn't people do their business on the ground? Hell. He grabbed the edge of the roof and silently hauled himself up to the wickedly slanted top. The tiles were slick, and he had to lie flat on the slope to keep from sliding off. He looked around while digging his fingers into the raised edges of the tiles. The witch was standing and clinging to the cross that stood proudly at the front tip of the roof. The scent of her blood was stronger. His gut cramped with need while the pores of his skin opened up, desperate to feel the warm relief of her blood. It made his skin so sensitive, every scrape hurt like a burn.

The man chasing her was directly between them, belly-inching his way closer and closer to his prey. Seeing that set off his fury. Oh hell, no.

The rogue was so crazed with the need to get to the witch's power-laced blood that he wasn't paying attention to what was coming up behind him.

The tile under Phoenix's left hand creaked and pulled up, causing him to lose his grip. Swearing silently, he slid down an inch, got another hold, and steadied himself. The copper-stinking rogue was a foot closer to the witch. Phoenix had had enough of this shit. He slipped his knife from the holster at his back and put the blade between his teeth. Then he army-crawled a few more feet, dug in his left hand for a strong hold on the tiles, and grabbed the rogue's calf.

Swear to all the gods and demons, he'd better not fall off this roof. It wasn't the heights he hated, but falling. Anytime he fell, he had a horrible feeling he was going to burst into flames. Plus landings were always a bitch. He yanked the rogue down so the bastard started sliding and scrabbling to catch himself.

Phoenix let go, and in a fast move, he took the knife from his mouth and stabbed it in the rogue's back as the man fought to keep from falling off the roof.

The witch belted out a piercing scream. He looked up, and the rogue slammed his elbow into Phoenix's face.

Grunting in pain, Phoenix twisted the knife in the other hunter's back, shredding the bastard's heart. Finally, the damned rogue quit fighting and had the decency to die.

He pulled out his knife, cleaned it on the back of the dead man's shirt, and holstered it. Then, after checking his hold on the roof, he rolled the body off to the ground below. He heard a satisfying thunk.

The witch was his. All that blood . . . all his. It smelled more alluring than ever! Using his boots, he pushed himself up a few more inches and hooked his hand over the top of the roof.

"No!" the witch screamed from her perch at the cross. "Stay back!"

Her piercing fear hit him and cleared the haze of lust. Sick disgust churned in his gut at what he'd been thinking. Yet his blood sizzled with need, and he realized the truth—Ailish's voice power was enhancing even the scent of the witch's blood, driving rogues to madness and testing hunters' willpower. But he wouldn't hurt her. He'd just get her down, then get his ass to the club and find some mortal woman to take to his bed.

"Easy there," he said soothingly as he pulled himself toward her. Women tended to respond to him, trust him. "I'm not going to hurt you. I'm going to get you down." He threw one leathered leg over the arch of the roof.

"Don't come any closer!" She had dark blond hair that had been torn loose from a clip, terrified brown eyes, and a death grip on the cross. She was bleeding from three places, her right arm, her left thigh, and a cut to her side. Crosscutting like that usually caused so much pain, a witch couldn't reach her powers.

He eased up to his feet, balancing where the sides of the roof sloped up to form a two-inch-wide edge. He focused on her pinched face and breathed through his mouth to avoid smelling her blood. "I can't leave you up here clinging to the cross." He took another step, intending to get close enough to show her the lifelines on his palm. Rogues had smooth, lineless palms, a sign that their souls were gone forever. "I'm going to—"

She lashed out with her foot.

The blow caught him behind his left knee, and he teetered on the edge, throwing out his arms to catch his balance.

The voice exploded in his head, and he had to listen. Needed to listen. Her voice was everything. . . .

Breath of life
In my cry

From the flames
Wings shall rise

Aching in beauty
Tears of healing

Wings of my soul
Soar to my call

Just as that last line filled his head, the witch kicked him again and he went ass over teakettle down the slope and flying off the edge of the roof.

He slammed into the ground, the impact rattling every cell in his body. But what hurt the most, what made him ache, was the absence of the voice. It felt as if he were missing some vital part of his chest now that it had stopped.

A shadow fell over him, and Key said, "Why are you on the ground again?"

He rolled to his feet, yanked his BlackBerry out of his

pocket, and checked on Ailish. She was at her house, hadn't moved.

But she had sung!

A shadow swept across the sky, then landed next to him and Key.

Axel had arrived. His brown-and-gold hawk wings lifted behind him as he asked, "Status?"

Key said, "Looks like a rogue snatched the witch and took her into this church. Another rogue found them and there was a fight, and the witch ran. One killed the other, then chased the witch up onto the roof. Phoenix killed that rogue, then the witch kicked Phoenix off the roof."

Axel looked up at the witch with the death grip on the cross, then lowered his stare to him. "Ailish?"

He could barely stand in one place. His muscles twitched with the need to get moving, to go to that voice.

To Ailish and her utterly compelling voice.

"Yes. Key, need your truck."

The hunter dug out his keys and tossed them. "You know what you're doing?"

Phoenix snatched them out of the air. "No."

7

Fifteen minutes later, he pulled up to Ailish's house. From the front, it looked quiet and dark. He got out of the truck and circled the house, jumping the fence in silence, but Ailish wasn't in the backyard.

He went back to the front where he'd parked the truck. The house was secure, and she was inside according to the tracking device. *Get in the truck and drive away.*

His boots were rooted to the ground. Uneasiness tightened the back of his neck. Why had she sung?

Earlier today, she'd been attacked. He'd seen her fighting off that demon-possessed man. What if she was in trouble and he just couldn't hear it? She was blind; anything could have happened. Maybe she got up and fell, was hurt, and used her voice to try to heal. Maybe . . .

"Fuck." He'd been down this road before with his mother. The constant worry and struggle about her. He hadn't been able to leave her for fear of what the voices in her head would tell her to do. And when he did leave her, all he did was worry. Years and years of that shit and it still hadn't been enough.

He didn't want to be this witch's caretaker. She wasn't crazy like his mom, but she was too damned vulnerable. She had too much baggage, she wasn't one of his "get in, do the job, and get out" bounty hunts. This witch was soul-destroying trouble, and he should just walk away.

But he couldn't leave. Not until he was sure she was okay. Quietly he opened the truck door, got out a case containing slim tools, and moved up to her door. He'd learned to pick locks on empty buildings, desperate to find him and his mom a warm, relatively safe place to sleep. Other times, when his mother wasn't in the grip of the voices but was fully with him, they'd get into empty buildings just to explore and find treasures. Those were the good times, the memories that were like bright, dazzling stars in his dark mind. He went to the door, dropped to one knee, and went to work on the dead bolt.

Using his witch hunter ability to bend sound waves, he muted the scrapes and clicks and opened the bolt. It all felt depressingly familiar. He'd worked and made a good amount of money, built a custom home, and he still felt like a street rat. Standing, he slid the tools into his pocket and then opened the door.

He would just check. If she was asleep, she never needed to know he'd been in her house. He closed the door and inhaled her mango scent. He ignored the living room, kitchen, and dining room, following his nose to the first bedroom across the hallway.

The scent was stronger. She smelled too damned good, too alluring. Just a hint of coconut blood, but enough to stir his bloodlust. The thought of slipping into her room, pulling his knife, and cutting her for the cooling relief of her warm blood splattered in his head.

Shit, he belonged in the gutter. Breaking into her house, then thinking about cutting her . . . Enough. He stepped into the room. He'd leave as soon as he knew she was okay.

Then he saw her. Ailish lay still, twisted up in tan-colored sheets, the burgundy comforter thrown back. Her body was tensed—he could see the definition of her biceps, the bulge of her jaw, and her clenched fists. But even though her lids were closed, her eyes were doing that rapid movement thing.

Something wasn't right. He didn't like this; he could

almost sense that she was trapped and hurting somehow.

He clenched his jaw. She was *asleep*. He was going to
leave.

But he walked toward her, dropping the shield that
muted the sounds he made. "Ailish?"

She made a desperate noise in her throat, her face screwing up as if she were in pain. Then he saw her hips rising,
her body curving as though she were arching for a lover. A
sex dream? He shifted his gaze back to her face and saw
one lone tear slide down and disappear into her hair.

A burnt butter smell was overtaking her scent. *She
was in pain!* He didn't think, just reacted, putting his
hand on her bare shoulder, his finger touching the strap
of her tank top. "Ailish, wake up."

"Can't!" she cried desperately.

Her tone set off a shriek of rage in his head. What the
fuck was this? He reached for the sheets beneath her
breasts and jerked them off her. Still not thinking, he
scooped her up, turned, and sat down with her on his
lap. "Come on, Ailish. Wake up."

She jerked in his arms. "No! I refuse!"

Refused to wake up? No, wait . . . when she'd thought
he was a demon last night, she'd told him she refused.
She started to fight him in earnest, one fist catching him
on his shoulder.

If she hit him with her magic . . .

"Ailish! Damn it, it's Phoenix. Stop!"

The fight drained out of her. "Phoenix?" Slowly she
opened her eyes. The pupils were dilated, her silvery
eyes damp. She tried to scramble out of his hold. "What
the hell are you doing here?"

He let her go, and as soon as she broke contact with
him, his skin felt as if it were being peeled back from his
nerves. Shit, the bloodlust hit hard. Rising, he snapped,
"You sang and called me to you like a damned dog.

Why, Ailish? You were asleep, so don't tell me you were trying to break the handfast."

She backed up to the wall and crossed her arms over herself in a protective gesture. "You can't break into my house!"

"Can and did. Answer the question." He should go, yet he couldn't seem to leave her alone in the house, blind, with no protection.

She rubbed her forehead. "The demon trapped me in a dream, and I sang to wake up. Once I woke, I remembered what you said, so the next time, I didn't use my voice." She dropped her hand. "I won't go back to sleep now. No reason for you to be here."

He tried to tell himself to just walk away. But the memory of her trapped, that single tear running down her face, the acid scent of burnt butter, battered the hell out of his chest. "What kind of dream?"

Her fingers dug into her crossed arms. "Sex dreams. Asmodeus amps up my lust, hoping to break me down so I give in to the next possessed man. But tonight, I think this was just about revenge for today."

That three-headed prick of a demon was hurting her with lust. Phoenix couldn't stand it, could not tolerate it. Her scent was torturing him. Mango heat, teasing coconut, but it was the burnt scent that was making his nose twitch. He took a step toward her, drawn to her, unable to stop.

Ailish snapped her head up. "I told you I'm not going to sing. I don't want you here."

It was like a slap. "You think I want this? Suddenly leashed to a blind witch who is handfasted to a demon?" He was so close to her, he could feel her breath, feel the warmth of her skin.

She flinched, her voice dropping to icy control. "No one's leashing you, hunter. No one asked you to be here. Get the hell out of my house."

He clenched his fists at his sides to keep from touching her. "Not like I had a choice! I got my ass tossed off a two-story building tonight when you started that singing shit. Then I was compelled to come here, had to check to make sure you were okay, like I'm a fucking babysitter." He knew he was being an asshole, but goddamn it, he'd fought to build his life. Nothing had caged him, not even the bloodlust. He'd controlled that by copious amounts of sex and taking out his rage on rogues. Now it was all being ripped apart and he was powerless to do anything about it.

She lifted her chest, her cheeks and neck darkening with angry color. "Lucky for you there's an expiration date on your *babysitting* job."

Her sarcasm cut through his roiling emotions. Forcing himself to calm down, to get control, he said, "What does that mean?"

Her silvery gaze settled on his face, as if she could almost see him. In a calm, talking-to-a-two-year-old voice, she said, "If I don't get this handfast off by my twenty-fourth birthday in less than two weeks, I'll die. Then you'll be free."

Die. The word clanged in his head, banging around like a pinball machine. She'd die. His soul mirror. The new tattoo began pulling at his skin, as if trying to reach out to her, to somehow get its wings around her and hold her safe. While Phoenix's chest felt like a heavy stone of failure.

First his mother.

Then his soul mirror.

Ailish walked past him, straight out of her bedroom.

It snapped him out of his shock, and he turned, following her. She moved with a surety and grace that was surprising in a woman who couldn't see, not pausing until she got to the front door. She yanked it open. Stood there, one hand on the door handle, the other on her hip, chin up, sightless eyes defiant. "Next time you get the urge to drop by and break in, don't."

He strode to her, jerked the door out of her hand, and slammed it. Then he backed her to the wall and pressed his hands against the plaster on either side of her head. "That's why you came back here, because time is running out. So here's the question: What are you going to do if you can't get the handfast off?" All kinds of thoughts rushed through his mind. Including the scenario that if he finished the bond with Ailish, his soul would become one with hers.

What would happen to his soul if she became a demon witch?

Her face was impassive. "Die. I've resisted for seven years, eleven and a half months. I'm never going to serve the demon."

The stone in his chest was crumbling into hot, possessive lava rocks. His biceps twitched with the need to hold her, to somehow stop death from touching her. Yet the bloodlust whispered to kill her now, slide his knife from the holster and cut her, bleed out all the power in her blood. And then there was the ache in his groin. It was all gathering, all pressing in on him. Yet she stood there with her shoulders pressed back against the wall, alone and self-contained, with no one to help her. It twisted his balls. Before he knew it, his hands slid to her face.

Her skin was hot against his palms, and the dark, bloody craving faded beneath a recognition when he touched her. Something he couldn't define, but a real, this-is-where-I-belong feeling that Phoenix had never had.

Ever.

As if he'd searched and searched for a century and finally found his home. Now he had to taste it, touch it, learn it. He leaned his head down. "I want to believe you, believe in you, Ailish. Believe that you will fight this demon even into death." But how could he believe she'd fight to the end when there was a way out by becoming a demon witch? Hadn't he found his mother bloodied and dead by her own hand, unwilling to fight the voices anymore? Not even for him.

She sucked in a breath.

He felt the swells of her magic wash over him in waves of velvet heat. The need in her was so vivid, his cock went hard and ready, while her mango-tropical scent saturated his lungs. No more acrid burn, only clean tropics with the lush, buttery desire. "Christ, I can feel your need. Even your magic is yearning for touch." It hurt him to feel it.

She put her hands on his chest. "I can handle it—"

"I can't." He cut her off by brushing his mouth over hers, back and forth in a plea. He could ease her. He wouldn't go too far, just feed some of her need, give her some pleasure.

She dug her fingers into his chest, her body twanging with desire.

Phoenix shifted, opening his mouth over hers, sliding his tongue into the damp heat that tasted like warm mango. He wrapped his arms around her, pulling her from the wall into his body. The feel of her breasts against his chest, his cock pressing into her stomach, her hips arching . . . He swept his hand down the curve of her back to cradle her hip.

More! She was so enticing, her hot body fitting against his, her magic shimmering over him, her tongue stroking his. More skin, more of Ailish. He snaked his hand under her shirt, sweeping his palm and fingers over the curve of her waist and up the bunching muscles of her back.

Lifting his mouth, he looked down into her flushed face. "You're strong." That enticed the shit out of him, the realization that she was strong enough to handle him, all 240 pounds of him thrusting into her, with nothing between them. He shuddered at the image. He slid his hand down her back, dipping his fingers into the waistband of the little shorts she wore.

Deeper.

Until he felt the globe of her ass in his hand. Felt exactly where she got the pure power behind her kicks. So sexy . . . Still watching her face, he said, "Let me take you back to your bed and . . ."

Her brilliant witch-shimmer dimmed, her magic pulled back, and he felt her muscles tense. "No. I . . . no." She pushed against his chest. "Let go of me."

Her voice rose slightly, an edge in there he couldn't pin down. Taking his hand from her sweet ass, he fought the raging need. He stepped back but kept one hand on her upper arm. He didn't dare let go, not when he was so fired up. The bloodlust would rush in like a geyser. "What's wrong?"

Her eyes tightened at the edges; even her neck was tense. "I'm not sleeping with you. Not with anyone. I'm not."

He couldn't get his head around her sudden shift. "Is this about the soul-mirror bond? That takes full-on intercourse, along with an exchange of blood. But we can do other things."

She shook her head, her gaze shifting around as if she couldn't focus. "No. I'm not . . . just no. You don't want this, either, you said you don't want this."

Shit, he'd been too long without sex. It was making him willing to drop to his knees and beg. But Phoenix didn't beg, and he'd never had a shortage of willing women. "Do us both a favor, then, Ailish, and don't sing." He turned, still holding her shoulder, and yanked open the door. Then he let go and hurried out.

The first wave of bloodlust hit him on the porch. "Lock the damned door!" he snarled. By the time he got to the truck, he was sweating, his guts were cramping, and his veins burned. He climbed in the truck, jammed the keys in the ignition, and told himself to drive. Get away from her and find a woman to help him ease the pain.

He couldn't bring himself to turn over the ignition.

Couldn't leave her there, alone, blind, and unprotected.

He slammed the steering wheel with his palm. "Idiot." But the battle was lost. He was right back where he'd been as a kid, trapped in the cage of a caretaker.

And his patient was slated to die. He was doomed to failure.

"Fucking perfect."

DAYS REMAINING ON HANDFAST CONTRACT: TWELVE

"You stayed here again?" Phoenix asked as he walked into the condo kitchen, inhaling the scent of freshly ground coffee beans.

Key had just finished working out. His hair was matted with sweat, and that weird-ass dragon on his chest seemed to watch Phoenix. "You had my truck until you dragged in an hour ago."

He'd slept in the truck, parked in front of Ailish's house. "My bike was here, and there're several vehicles parked in the garage. Something is eating you."

Key grabbed two mugs and poured out some coffee. He slid Phoenix's cup across the granite bar and spooned some sugar in his. "I've been drawing Liam again."

Phoenix snatched the spoon from him to stop the massive sugar dumping. Key's family considered him a puny runt and tried to kill him, as if he were the runt of the litter. At just a hair over six feet, Key was tall for a mortal, but not for a witch hunter. He'd escaped, running away and living on the streets. Through Haley Ryan, the woman who ran the homeless shelter, Key and Phoenix became friends since they were both witch hunters. And

Sheri took to Key, too, loving him nearly as much as she had Phoenix . . . when she wasn't caught up in the voices. "You sure Liam's even alive? He's rogue, went rogue at what, fifteen?"

"If I'm drawing him, my brother's alive." The muscles in his chest and shoulders rippled with his old rage. "I see him in the drawings, and that he's killing witches, but not where he is." He lifted his gaze. "He is alive. That bastard breathes while . . ." He snapped his mouth shut on the words.

Phoenix took a drink of coffee but tasted only bitter memories. Key's brother lived while the girl Liam had tortured and killed to find out where Key was hadn't breathed in over a decade. She had been Key's first love.

Key hadn't been able to find Liam to kill him as he'd killed all the others who came after him. At the time, Phoenix thought he'd go insane with the rage and grief inside him. He had felt so furious and helpless, and he hadn't known how to help Key.

But his reality-challenged mother had been there, stepping in and caring for Key, giving him a safe place to fall apart, then teaching him how to cope by spending his inner rage in drawings.

Key drained half his mug of java, then ran his hand over his face. "I have to find him and—"

Someone pounded on the front door. Loud and long.

Phoenix slid off the stool and stalked to the door, then jerked it open.

Joe paced in the hallway, his hands fisted, his hair looking as if it'd been combed by a shredder, his face pulled back in a grimace. He jerked to a stop, whipped his head around, and said, "Morgan thinks I'm working for Eric."

Phoenix couldn't be more shocked if Joe had said he'd started life as a woman. "She was there when her husband clamped you to a table to torture you for sleeping

with her. Morgan knows you love her." Joe did love her.
He was willing to take on another man's kid. Hell, the
kid was a witch hunter, not a mortal like Joe.

"It doesn't matter! She's not listening! Carla and Darcy
told me to leave, that I was upsetting her too much.
They're afraid she's going to start having contractions."

Phoenix narrowed his eyes, feeling the old anger rise.
At Morgan's dead rogue husband, and all rogues who
did this shit to women. But there was more . . . letting
the craziness in her head hurt Joe sent Phoenix off the
edge. "This is bullshit." He stormed out into the hallway, went right, then opened the door to Joe's condo.

Morgan sat on the couch, her hands clenched beneath
her belly. Her blond hair was pulled back in a clip, her
face was thinner, and she was rocking slightly. Carla sat
on the coffee table facing her, her hands on Morgan's
knees. Darcy sat next to her with the laptop open.

They all looked up in surprise. Morgan sucked in a
breath. "See! He's brought help! They'll take my baby!"
She jumped up, almost tripping over Darcy as she tried
to run to the hallway on the far side of the condo.

Phoenix moved at high speed, getting in front of
Morgan.

"Phoenix!" Darcy called out.

He ignored them, looking at the woman in front of
him. He could smell her too-sweet fear, and it tugged at
his chest.

"No!" She lifted her hands, pounded on his chest. "I
won't let you hurt my baby!"

His chest constricted, but Phoenix wasn't giving up.
"Blondie, listen to me!" He purposely used his nick-
name for her, trying to reinforce to her that they were
friends. He respected the hell out of the way she fought
Eric's brutal brainwashing to save her baby. "Your baby
needs you to fight back. Don't let Eric win. You know
Joe loves you. You know it."

"Phoenix . . ." Darcy laid her hand on his bunched arm. "She can't help—"

"Let him try," Carla broke in.

Morgan tilted her head back, staring up at him with white-ringed eyes. "I'm afraid. It feels like he's coming back, like he's going to cut the baby out of me and take him." She began to shake.

He didn't dare try to use his witch hunter ability to shift memories. She had enough brain damage from Eric. Instead, he just told her the truth. He always told the truth, and somewhere in her beleaguered brain, Morgan knew that. "He's dead, Morgan. I saw Axel kill him. But he's put some kind of orders or suggestions in your head, and that's what's doing this."

She closed her eyes. "Oh, God. I know Joe wouldn't help Eric. I know it, but it felt so real."

"Look at me, Blondie. You have to fight that, and you have to listen to Carla and Darcy. They are protecting your baby with their magic."

Opening her eyes, she said, "I'm trying." Her eyes were dry and tortured. "I don't want to lose my baby." She swallowed and added in a whisper, "Or Joe."

Joe put his arm around Morgan. "You're not going to lose me."

Phoenix dropped his hold on Morgan. "Blondie, go with Joe and get some rest. Those dark circles aren't your best look."

She reached out a hand. "Thanks, Phoenix." Then she let Joe lead her to the bedroom.

"How'd you do that?" Darcy asked. "We've been using magic, but we couldn't pull her out of the delusion."

He shrugged, feeling uncomfortable.

Carla rose and said, "She related to you, trusted you somehow. Maybe because you're struggling with a voice pulling you." She gathered her long hair in her hands, twisted it up, and it somehow just stayed, bunched up on her head. Wearing jeans and a button-down shirt, she looked a bit tired. "Axel said you heard the voice again last night."

Phoenix nodded, dropped into a chair, and gave Carla and Darcy the sanitized version of what happened. Then he dropped the bombshell. "She will die in twelve days if she doesn't get the handfast binding off or become a demon witch." The bird pulled and fretted in his skin, as if trying to move up and break free. His chest ached at the thought of Ailish dying. So vibrant and alive, she was strong, a fighter, but for how long? What would be her breaking point? He looked at both witches sitting on the couch to his right. "Have you gotten anything on breaking a handfast?"

Darcy shook her head. "Not yet. But Carla and I consulted the Ancestors about the soul-mirror bond and the handfast bond."

He stretched out his legs, looking down and seeing the custom-made motorcycle boots with the pockets for his backup knives. "If we finish the soul-mirror bond, our souls become one. If she becomes a demon witch . . ."

Carla said gently, "Your soul goes with her. Since you're not a witch but a hunter, you'll go rogue."

He noticed the scuffs and marks on his boots, much like his soul, he imagined. "I would literally be trusting Ailish, a witch handfasted to a demon, with my soul."

"Exactly," Darcy said.

He shoved up out of the chair and paced around the furniture, trying to sort out his feelings. "Can't the Ancestors help her break the handfast? Don't they want to help her?" Then he and Ailish would have time to figure this thing out, see if they wanted to bind themselves together in the soul-mirror bond.

Carla said, "They aren't gods, they are simply old souls and can only help earth witches. Ailish chose Asmodeus when she accepted his handfast and promised her soul to a demon. And she accepted his terms, which must have been demon witch or death after eight years." She rolled her neck in a sign of fatigue. "We have to keep searching for a solution. The Ancestors will tell us what they can. I have to believe they want her to break the handfast, but she has to make the right choices."

His chest burned with frustration. No way would he trust Ailish with his soul when she was facing an impossible choice. "We have to find a way to break the handfast. Maybe her voice power—"

"Siren. Ailish is a siren."

He turned, looking at Carla. "You know what it is? Her voice power?"

Carla said, "My mom made the connection. When your tattoo changed, forming into a phoenix rising from the flames, that tripped her memory. Before the curse, every hundred years a siren witch was born. At her birth, a phoenix flew overhead, and when the newborn siren witch cried with her first breath of life, the phoenix burst into flames and vanished. Until the witch called him forth with her voice, summoning her phoenix familiar to rise from the flames."

He froze to the spot, dizzy, sweating, his heart pounding his mouth dry . . . in ice-cold recognition. "Jesus, Buddha, and Wing Slayer, it was real." He went back to the chair, sat down, and leaned forward with his elbows on his thighs. The memory sharpened until he could hear the crackle of flames exploding around him, the fire eating his feathers, muscles, and very soul. The pain, the smoke, being burned to ash . . .

"Phoenix . . ." Darcy's hands cradled his, and he felt cool waves of calming energy.

"It happened. When I was four. I thought it was a nightmare kids get, but . . ." He heard the door open, knew it was Axel and Key. Darcy had probably called Axel through their soul-mirror bond, and Axel got Key.

He went on, "Ailish was born, I remember her cry, the flames, and dying. Then I woke up in my bed, a kid again. Is that possible?"

Her brown eyes flickered with compassion. "I believe it is. I believe you have the essence of the phoenix in your soul."

"That's what died? In those flames? It had felt real."

She nodded. "The witches all believed that since the curse destroyed the bond with their familiars, it would no longer be possible for a siren witch to exist because the power in her voice is linked to her familiar. The legend of the siren and the phoenix was pretty much forgotten. No living witch had ever experienced it. Until now, that is. Ailish has the voice of a Siren. When she was born, the bird in you must have flown over and then burst into flames."

Carla came over and added, "The way my mom explained the legend before the curse, it only happened every hundred years. Witches waited and waited, keeping track of the time between sirens calling their familiars because their siren voice was incredibly powerful. It enhanced magic, all magic. They performed important spells during that time."

Darcy squeezed his hands. "But once the phoenix rose and became the siren's familiar, she got control of her voice power and enhanced only the magic she chose. So the witches had only a small window of time to use that scatter enhancement of all magic."

Phoenix glanced up to see Axel standing behind Darcy, and Key next to him. Then he looked at his biceps where the tattoo had changed to the head, neck, and part of a wing rising from the outline of flames. "That's what's happening. Ailish's voice is calling and the phoenix is rising. And I'm powerless to stop it."

8

Ailish had gone for a run, come back, showered, and dressed. She was in the living room drinking her tea when the phone rang. "Hello."

"Ailish, it's Kyle."

She dropped her feet from the coffee table and sat up. "Kyle, you okay?" She had found Kyle's phone number, then, using her magic, she'd checked on him by listening in through his phone. Sort of the way a baby monitor might work. He'd evidently had to sleep with the TV on but otherwise seemed okay. She could summon enough power to check in periodically, but she couldn't hold the magic to keep the connection ongoing.

"I don't know . . . maybe it's the power of suggestion. Maybe you freaked me out. But last night, every time I slept, I thought I heard different women trying to get me to go outside. Or let them in." He sighed. "It could be the painkillers, they can cause weird dreams, but . . ."

"But what?"

His voice dropped, as though he didn't want anyone to hear what he said. "A couple times when I woke up, I was sure I heard someone outside my condo. I yelled out, 'I have silver.' And they left."

He was describing the methods of demon witches. They needed him *voluntarily* in order for Asmodeus to possess them. In other words, they couldn't break into his house and drag him off. They had to seduce, trick, and drug him into compliance. "Kyle, I'll come over, we'll talk." And she'd convince him to get out of town.

"Ailish, if you're a witch, why didn't you tell me when we were dating?"

That question caught her by surprise. "Because I didn't want to be a witch. I just wanted to be a normal girl." How did she explain it? She'd been so lonely and starved for affection, for the feeling of belonging. Ailish had either been treated with kid gloves or ignored in the coven. How many nights, as a very young girl, had she gone to sleep alone and scared? Her mother had coven business and had warded the house, raised hellhounds from dead animals to guard her, and told her she was safe.

But she hadn't felt safe. She'd felt alone and terrified. The dark always scared her, but the hellhounds were the worst. It was as though they knew they were hideous, having been put together from different parts of decaying animals, so they stayed in the shadows. She hated them, and they hadn't liked her, either. Now she knew it was because they sensed her earth witch powers. At the time, she had understood they were a part of demon magic, something she shouldn't touch. She knew because her chakras would cringe. She'd turn on every light in the house to keep them as far away from her as she could.

The irony now was that she lived in the dark.

Kyle finally answered, "I don't know if I really believe you. Believe any of this."

She stood up, anxious to get moving. "You don't have to believe. I just want to keep you safe. We'll figure something out, okay?"

"Tell me why. Why you're that concerned about me."

She paused a moment, then said, "It's a debt I owe you. I'm the reason you are in danger." His memory was magically blocked so he wouldn't recall her realizing he was possessed, banishing the demon, and then running away and leaving him at the mercy of the coven. But Ailish knew, she remembered, and she had to right that wrong. "Just stay in the house and don't let anyone else in." She hung up and called Dee.

Twenty minutes later, she was in the car with Dee, who was in a cheerful mood once again. "Where to?"

"Kyle's house again."

"Yeah?" Dee reversed out of the driveway, put the car in gear, and they took off. "You and Kyle have a thing?"

"No. Just helping him out. Might bring him back to my house to stay while he's healing from the accident." She was hoping she could get him to leave town, but her house was plan B.

"So you obviously know him."

"We went to high school together for a while."

"Dated?"

She reined in her annoyance. "It was a long time ago. I don't date now. Ever." Unless she counted Phoenix breaking and entering in the middle of the night as dating. Or counted kissing him. Twice. She still couldn't believe she'd done that. But touching him had ripped open her old desires, her need for affection, for contact. The damn hunter had made her feel safe. She'd woken from that torturous dream with his arms around her, and it had felt *right*. Twice when he'd kissed her, she'd experienced real desire, the kind that builds into mind-blowing passion—not the forced lust of the handfast binding.

"You have the look of a woman thinking about a man."

She whipped her head around, able to fix her gaze on the shadow. "Are you this nosy with all your clients?"

"You're my only client now. I'm on call night and day with strict orders to do whatever you need and to look out for you."

"Haley," Ailish muttered. Haley had hired Dee and evidently given her carte blanche to be annoying.

"Yep," she said cheerfully. "She obviously cares about you. And I'm nosy because you're interesting. Plus, it seems like you're capable of telling me to back off. So . . . who is the man on your mind?"

Ailish shook her head, amazed. "I intimidate most people into not prying."

"Yeah, one of my qualifications? Not easily intimidated. I'm also persistent, like wondering what man brought that pretty color to your face and made your mouth go all soft."

"What?" Horrified, she put on her match face. "I do not blush, and my lips . . . ewww." She couldn't believe this conversation. She'd rather be in the ring with a woman twice her size than in the small car with Dee. Sheesh.

"So it's not Kyle?"

God. "No." She snapped off the word, her voice an icicle, while her stomach grew warm. Kyle had never kissed her the way Phoenix had.

Dee turned another corner and said, "What does he look like?"

She sighed. "How would I know, I'm blind." Too late, she realized she'd slipped up. "Damn it."

Dee's laughter filled the car. "You fell for it. Come on, what does he look like? Feel like, if you'd rather."

She knew, just knew, she was blushing now, right down to her hair follicles. Hot and amused at the same time, she said, "Phoenix. He just showed up, and like you, annoys the shit out of me." She turned to look at Dee's outline. "He feels like a dangerous outlaw. Wears leathers, has major muscles, rides a motorcycle."

"Mmm. Sounds like your kind of man. Hell, he'd be my kind of man, but you saw him first." Dee chuckled and said, "Sorry, you felt him first."

Ailish was surprised when a laugh bubbled up and came out of her mouth. Then, even more shocking, she said, "You married, Dee?"

"Divorced. We had a nice limo service going, until I

found out he was screwing clients. Literally and figuratively. Sex and credit card fraud. The business is gone, we were sued up the ass, and I could use a man on a motorcycle to take me away."

Ailish's own problems went on the simmer burner. "Wow, Dee, I'm sorry—"

Dee cut her off. "Thanks. I'm okay, though. Surviving." Her voice bled determination. "I'm beginning to rebuild my life, and I'm happy." She turned into a driveway and stopped the car. "We're here. Do you want me to go to the door with you or wait here?"

Ailish smiled at the phrasing, noting that Dee was not giving her the option of being here alone. "You're tough, I like that. I'll find my own way to the door," she said, then she turned and got out of the car. She had pouches of ground silver in her pockets and boots in case any demon witches showed up. Walking up to the door, she couldn't feel the weight of cold, oily dark magic in the air, so it was probably safe for now. She didn't pause and take a breath but determinedly lifted her hand to knock. And that's when she smelled copper. The scent was so disturbing and out of place, she froze as she tried to identify it.

Then Dee screamed, a pitch of shock and pain.

Ailish whipped around. That put the garage on her right, the door behind her, leaving her front and left side open. The copper was stronger, and a sense of deep menace lifted the hairs on her arms and neck. Almost as a reflex, she snapped into her staggered stance and opened her chakras to feel around her.

There was something big directly in front of her, a man. Focusing on the shadow, she could see he was as big as Phoenix, but the smell was wrong. The copper scent was rushing down her throat and causing a sting of metallic fear that sent adrenaline coursing through her. She had the sense of a snake toying with her before striking.

She felt him move and jump back, felt something just miss her arm.

Then a sharp burn slashed her thigh. The pain was sudden and hot. Shit, it was a knife cut. The blade ripped through her jeans and into her skin. She could feel the wound bleeding, but her bigger concern was that she was trapped against the door.

And what about Dee? Worry for her strengthened Ailish. She didn't have room to do anything fancy, so she improvised with a side kick aimed high. She rammed her heel hard and felt it strike his chin and snap his head back.

He gagged and stumbled in surprise. She brought her foot down and broke into a run, desperation giving her more speed. She zoomed past him toward the car. Slapping her hand down onto the warm hood, she raced around to the driver's side and then hit the opened door. "Dee!" Where was she? Frantic, she edged around the car door and felt something slick under her foot.

Stomach jolting, she dropped to her knees and felt Dee's body curled into a ball. "Dee?" Brushing her hand over the woman's face and down her neck, she hit a gusher of warm blood. "Oh God." Her neck was cut. Flipping open chakras, she put her hand over the wound and struggled to pull up healing energy and pour it through her hand.

Dee's heart was slowing. She was dying. "No way. You're not dying!" She concentrated everything she had on the woman, willing her to live.

"She's doing magic!" a man snarled.

The voice came at her from the front of the car. Before she could react, a hand grabbed her, yanking her up.

Ailish got her feet under her, grabbed the guy's arms, and felt a second of shock. His skin was soft and smooth, like a girl's skin, but his muscles were huge. *Rogue,* she thought as she attempted a knee strike to his groin.

A second man wrapped a thick arm around her chest from behind and yanked her off the ground. She tried to kick out as panic and fear for Dee blasted through her head. "Let go! Dee's—argh." She bit off a scream as a knife slashed her right side below her ribs. The hot pain closed off her chakras.

The rogue holding her bent his head and said, "Want more? Keep fighting." He shoved his free hand against her wound and shuddered.

The pain bloomed hot and agonizing while the man behind her panted as he dug his hand in the wound. His excitement scared her and made her sick. Her fear and pain intensified the power in her blood, giving him a bigger kick as he absorbed it through his skin. She had to stop them, or at least find a way to save Dee.

"Enough," the other rogue snarled. "Young said she has to be alive."

They started dragging her away. Terror pounded in her head. Ailish could think of only one way to try to force her chakras open and help Dee. She began to sing:

> With the light of the sun
> The power of the moon
> The energy of the earth
> The wisdom of the Ancestors
> Bring forth the power to heal the wounded and
> restore the blood of life!

"Shit, what's she doing?" yelled the rogue dragging her.

Her chakras shot open, spilling out energy. Ailish had only seconds before the rogues cut her to ribbons. With the massive arm trapping her, all she could do was bend her arms at the elbows and try to control the sudden and thick power racing through her. She pointed her hands to where Dee lay fallen by the car, hoping enough healing energy would get to her.

Everything happened at once. Power ripped through her and exploded from her control. Magic crackled and streaked around them, creating a strong whirling wind. The second rogue slammed into her from the front, and all three of them hit the ground.

"Mine!" one of them screamed.

"I'll kill you!" the other yelled.

The rogues had turned on each other! Ailish had barely rolled away before she heard the clash of knives and pounding of fists. What the hell was going on?

"Ailish? What's happening?"

It was Kyle's voice. She got to her feet and made her way toward him. "Kyle, see if the woman by the car door is alive!" Her side hurt, but a quick feel told her the wound was closed. Same thing with her thigh. Her powers had healed her, but had they reached Dee? Or maybe even Kyle?

"Blood everywhere, but the wound is shallow and she's breathing," Kyle reported. "Hell, the wound is closing."

"Have to get her—" Something slammed into her, and she hit the back of the car.

"He has a knife!" Kyle shouted.

She tried to squirm, twist, and use her elbows, but the copper-smelling rogue's huge frame and weight had her pinned to the car. Then the blade slashed the outside of her right arm, from her shoulder to her elbow, ripping through skin and muscle. Ailish screamed, the hot agony unbearable. Dizziness assaulted her, sweat coated her body, and her chakras shut down completely. With as much breath as she could get, she said, "Get Dee in the car and get out of here." It was the only hope of Dee and Kyle living through this.

"Can't leave you!" Kyle said, but he was breathing hard, as though he were moving something heavy.

"Go!" It was hard to think, but she guessed her magic had reached Kyle, healing him enough to move Dee. She just hoped he and Dee could escape.

The rogue yanked her off the car, picked her up, threw her over his shoulder, and began to run. He jumped over something in his path. Hanging upside down over his back, she could just make out the shape of the other rogue dead or dying on the ground. Vaguely, she realized that unleashing her voice power had driven them both mad; they'd fought each other, and the winner got her.

She heard Dee's car start up and take off. *Please let Kyle and Dee get to safety.*

The rogue stopped running and yanked open a vehicle door. He threw Ailish in. She landed on her arm, and fireworks burst in her head, then all went black.

Phoenix stood up and walked to the wet bar to grab a water bottle. He hated being powerless and manipulated by some force he couldn't fight. The curse was bad enough, fighting the compulsion for witch blood was part of his code, his refusal to give in and be controlled.

But this . . . He twisted off the cap, drank some water. It all kept circling in his mind. Ailish really did have a voice of a siren; it was real. He'd felt its strength. Which meant she was enhancing magic every time. . . .

"Quinn Young knows." He set his water down, prowling the room. "Tully's words, *Won't die. Won't. Young swore the witch blood was enhanced. . . .*" Fury and disgust brewed violently. "The biggest fear of any rogue is dying. They don't have their souls, so they'll spend eternity as a shade. Young has told them that if they kill off all the earth witches, Asmodeus will have the power to grant them immortality and they'll rule the earth with him."

Key came out of the kitchen holding a full coffeepot

and several mugs. "Dumb shits never seem to realize that Asmodeus was behind the curse that stripped our immortality in the first place."

Axel said, "If Asmodeus succeeds in eliminating all witches and turning all hunters rogue, Wing Slayer will have no power on earth. There will be nothing to stand between the demon and earth. Asmodeus will probably get enough power to grant them immortality, just like Wing Slayer had enough power to make us immortal before the curse."

Key said, "Wing Slayer has regained enough power to grant soul mirrors immortality, so Asmodeus has to fight harder." He shifted his gaze to Phoenix. "He needs Ailish to become his demon witch. Then he'll control her siren power, using it to enhance the blood of earth witches to make his rogues stronger, as well as the dark magic of his demon witches."

Carla cleared her throat. "The Circle Witches are very concerned about that. We can't let Ailish turn into a demon witch."

"She's fighting to get the handfast off." Phoenix wanted to believe her. "Asmodeus is torturing her." He remembered her trapped in that dream. She'd sung once to wake up, but the second time she'd refused. He could still see that single tear running down her face, still smell the burnt scent of her pain. Unable to stand still, he paced between the back of the couch and the wet bar. It hit him that Asmodeus hadn't just been punishing her. "He had been trying to make her sing, to enhance the blood of more witches, and whatever else they might be—"

Her voice exploded in his head. He stumbled, catching himself on the bar. The words pulsed with pain, fear, and determination. He recognized the voice instantly. "Ailish!" The curse woke up in his veins as her voice resonated in his head and throughout his body. He could hear the desperation in each note. The bird-and-fire tattoo on his biceps grew hot, then burned like a branding iron.

A scream pierced his brain.

"I feel that," Carla said.

"I do, too," Darcy added. "She's enhancing magic."

Phoenix heard them from a distance. His entire being focused on that voice. What if Asmodeus had her? Any number of possibilities tumbled through his head. A lung-squeezing desperation to get to her slammed into him.

Fighting for control of his own body, he pulled out his BlackBerry. She wasn't home!

"Where are you going?" Axel asked.

Phoenix was surprised to see he was at the door, Black-Berry in one hand, doorknob in the other. He said the first thing that hit his brain: "We can't let Ailish become a demon witch." Then he opened the door and left.

He studied the GPS tracking on his screen while running to his bike. What the hell was she doing? She'd said she wouldn't use her power, so something had to have happened. He fired up the bike and roared out of the garage. Bending low over the handlebars, he broke every speed limit he could, passing anything that was between him and Ailish.

Finally, he found the bunch of condominiums and apartments mixed with small houses that were within walking distance of the beach. He roared down the street and spotted the dead rogue lying on the sidewalk.

Then he saw the white Suburban tear away from the curb.

Phoenix swore he heard the screech of a bird, and his biceps burned with rage. He didn't need the GPS tracking to know Ailish was in that vehicle; he could feel the weak thread of her magic and smell the stronger co-conut scent of her blood. He raced after the SUV, catching it at the end of the road. Pulling up to the driver's side, he could see the soft feminine face on a massive neck and shoulders. *Rogue.* In the passenger seat, he could see the top of a crumpled woman.

Ailish. It shafted through his chest to see her hurt, crumpled, and being taken away from him. Maybe it was the curse, or the soul-mirror bond, or the siren-phoenix connection, that made his heart pound with possessiveness. He didn't care; all that mattered to him was getting her back.

But how did he stop the SUV? He could call for backup or—

A boot shot out from the passenger side in a powerful kick and slammed into the face of the rogue. Ailish! She was awake and fighting!

The rogue's head snapped around from the impact of her kick and smashed into the window. Spider cracks raced through the glass while the SUV careened to the right, hit the curb, and rammed into a light pole. The truck idled loudly.

The rogue lifted his head and shook it. Then he turned to Ailish.

Phoenix revved his bike and skidded to a stop right next to the door. Holding the powerful machine steady with his thighs, he wrapped his fingers tightly around his knife, then smashed his fist through the cracked window.

The rogue started to jerk his head around, but Phoenix raised the knife and stabbed him in the heart. The man bucked and tried to grab the knife. Phoenix twisted the blade, shredding the heart. The rogue's life drained away.

He yelled at Ailish, "Get out! On the bike, now!"

People were starting to come out of their homes, but they were pretty far up the street. Most people were at work this time of the morning, but Phoenix's luck was running out. He wanted to get Ailish out of there before more rogues showed up. He heard her open the door and drop to the ground, then run around the front of the truck.

The rich coconut scent of her blood hit him. His skin began to itch violently while his veins burned. Then he saw her and rage burst inside him. She was stumbling, trying to get around the truck while cradling her right arm against her stomach. She'd pulled off her shirt and had wrapped it around her upper arm, leaving her dressed in a black sports bra and jeans. The cut on her arm had to be bad, as the shirt was drenched with blood. He saw a red welt on her side that looked as though she'd healed it and a slice through her jeans on her thigh that might be healed, too. But she couldn't heal her arm?

She moved closer.

The bloodlust flamed higher. His hand tingled where he'd touched her blood two nights ago. Her warm, rich blood would cool the burn and give him that awesome rush of power.

No! he told himself.

He put his hands on the handlebars and fought for control as she stopped close to him. So close that he could almost feel the weakness overtaking her. He looked up into her face and saw strain and pain etched into the spidery scars around her eyes. Her normally full mouth was thin and bloodless. "Will you be able to get on behind me and hold on?" Her blood, the smell, was burning through him, his veins swelling until he thought they were going to pop out of his skin.

Then she let go of her injured arm and put her hand on his shoulder, her fingers on his vest, her palm touching the bare skin. Her hand was damp and icy cold, and her pain sent sharp waves through him. He didn't know how she was standing, let alone conscious. He might need to ditch the bike and take the rogue's truck if she couldn't—

"Hey! I called nine one one!" A man was running toward them.

Damn, no time. "Get on!"

She swung her leg over and mounted the bike.

"You can't leave the scene!" another man yelled.

Phoenix grabbed Ailish's hand from his shoulder and put it around his waist. He could feel her agony, but they had to book. "Hold on." He put the bike in gear and raced away. It was sunny and about seventy degrees, but the air was damp and he was hauling ass down the Pacific Coast Highway. She had her arm locked around him, and he could feel her shivering. After a couple miles, she leaned against his back. It was the oddest feeling, her body pressed to his, her thighs spread around him. The burning in his biceps vanished, and so did the bloodlust, but his wing tats were fluttering beneath his skin. The creature was coming to life, rising from the flames, and it wanted to touch her.

But she'd used her voice. He'd told her how dangerous it was, that she was hurting people. Even Carla and Darcy felt it this time. On the other hand, she had obviously been under attack and was trying to save her life. How could he fault her for that?

Christ, what did he do now? Ailish needed to heal. He couldn't take her to the condos over the club and warehouse, or she'd incite the bloodlust in the unbonded hunters. Just the thought of it made his blood boil. His house had a hell of a lot more security than hers, so he turned his bike and headed inland. What was the fallout of her voice power? What other magic did she enhance? He was sure Young knew about Ailish's power, and that slimy demon minion was finding a way to use it. For sure by harvesting the extra power in earth witch blood, but what else? Young had sacrificed his own soul mirror, Darcy's mother, to get that Immortal Death Dagger burned into his arm. The idea that he could be harnessing the power released from Ailish's voice was a massive worry.

Finally, Phoenix rode up the hill to his crest-top house that looked over a section of suburbia. Below his house lay a planned community with parks, a public pool, and a recreation room. The streets were laid out in a grid, everything screaming neighborhood and home. Exactly what he hadn't had growing up living hand-to-mouth on the streets.

He didn't exactly have it now. He was too . . . uncivilized to live within the confines of the actual planned community. Phoenix looked like the danger and menace that they built their fences to keep out. Instead he lived above them on the hill, and he kept an eye on the neighborhood.

Now he was bringing Ailish there. Right now, with her lying against his back, the curse was banked, the bloodlust barely an annoyance. But when he got her off the bike and he wasn't touching her any longer, when she was alone in his house with no one to help her, what would he do?

He opened the garage and pulled his bike in next to his black Mustang GT. He had a second Yamaha R6 under a cover in the corner of the garage as his backup bike. He turned off the engine.

Ailish lifted her head from his back. "Where are we?"

Her voice was thin, the words slow. Worry gnawed at him. He hadn't felt her magic at all, not one attempt to heal her arm on the ride. Bracing the bike with his thighs, he took hold of her arm around his waist and said, "My house. Can you get off the bike?"

She stood, lifted her leg over while he kept hold of her arm. He felt the gooseflesh and her shivers, but she got off and stood there holding her ripped-open arm across her waist.

He let go, and with his next breath when he inhaled her coconut-blood scent, the curse hit him, cramping his gut, the poisonous craving bulging his veins and sending the blinding flash of enraged need to his brain. He got off the motorcycle, put it on the kickstand. He turned to see her standing there, swaying. Her black shirt was around her arm, her jeans cut, her hair tangled, and her face so pale that the scars stood out. Shit. "Come on, let's get you inside. You have to heal yourself."

"Right. First . . . sit down." Her legs gave out.

Phoenix caught her, sliding his arms beneath her shoulders and knees and lifting her. Drops of her blood spattered on his chest, hand, and arm. He snapped his jaw and clenched his teeth against the whip of icy hot pleasure searing through him. He strode to the door, shifted her, and used his palm print to unlock it. Then he went inside. His kitchen had dark green granite countertops and a natural stone floor. Usually he liked walking in here, liked having a home—a place where he was in control.

Right now, his control was being tested by the animal craving beating at him. With his veins swelling and pulsing, he felt like the Incredible Hulk ready to explode. He walked past the half stairs that went up to his media room and turned right down the steps into his sunken living room. He put Ailish on the couch.

She groaned and opened her eyes, her body stiffening and her sightless eyes darting around, trying to focus.

He hated her panic. She was the toughest, scrappiest, most resourceful woman he'd met. She kickboxed blind, for crying out loud! Seeing her beaten and cut into this shivering, vulnerable state destroyed him, making his stomach twist in fury while his chest ached to ease her. Bending down, he said, "Ailish, you're in my house. You need to focus and heal." He reached for her shirt and unwrapped it from around her upper arm. "Ah, Christ." An enraged shriek sounded in his head as he stared at the wound. She was sliced from shoulder to elbow. . . .

"Can't. Used too much power." She passed out again.

Damn it. She was going to bleed to death. He could feel her heart slowing. He pulled out his BlackBerry. "Axel, I need Darcy or Carla ASAP." He explained while assessing the rest of Ailish. Her cheek and jaw were bruising where she'd had her face slammed into something. Her jeans had drying blood around a tear, but when he looked, the cut was healed, just a red line.

Axel said, "They can't come, they're taking care of Morgan. And it's too risky. I can ask Darcy—"

Phoenix sat back on his heels, feeling as if he'd been sucker-punched. "What the fuck, Axel! She's hurt, cut down to the bone, blood every-the-fuck-where. She needs help!" He looked at her face and saw that her eyes were open.

She squinted, clearly trying to focus on him as she said, "They won't help. Let me rest a minute and I'll do it."

Hadn't she already told him that they wouldn't help her? The Circle Witches hadn't helped her. Phoenix could not believe this bullshit. She was bleeding out right before his eyes.

Axel was talking in his ear, but he dropped the phone, grabbing her face to keep her with him. "Ailish, tell me what to do." Blood was all over her. Hell, he didn't know enough. But he knew he was not going to let her die.

She didn't answer, but another voice called out, "Phoenix."

He reached for his knife before the voice registered. But then recognition hit, and he realized Darcy was projecting her voice through his BlackBerry on the floor. Desperate, he grabbed it and said, "You'll help her?"

"I'll try. Carla's working on gathering more help from the Circle Witches. But we need to connect with Ailish's magic. Can you feel her power at all?"

He looked down at the witch bleeding all over his couch and floor. Her witch-shimmer was the color of dried mud, with ugly red holes from the pain. She had to be in agony. He felt only fading power. "Just residual magic from using her siren voice power, I guess."

"Trying," Ailish said, squeezing her eyes closed in concentration and fisting her hands. Then she hissed in pain and relaxed back into unconsciousness.

"Darcy! What do we do?" He fought down his impatience during the long seconds of silence. Darcy was very powerful, and Phoenix assumed she was assessing Ailish with her third eye.

Then Darcy spoke in a steady, confident voice: "Her chakras are closed. You're her soul mirror, you can help her open them. If you choose to do it."

The thought that he could just let her die and go back to his life as he knew it whispered in his mind. No more feeling the chains of the past, the cage of caring too damned much, of having to worry every second about someone else.

He looked at her pale face, her dark eyelashes lying against the fine scars. She groaned, starting to surface again, and shivers began racking her body. It was terrible to see, her arm torn open, blood everywhere, her tight body shivering. He couldn't stand it. His biceps began burning, and he knew it wasn't a choice at all. He never walked away from a woman in trouble, not as long as he had the power to help her.

Her eyelids fluttered, then opened, and her teeth chattered.

He wouldn't let her die, so he set down the phone where Darcy could still hear him, then reached out, laying his hand on Ailish's face. "I'll do whatever it takes. Tell me how to help her."

"Move her clothes so you can touch her from pelvis to heart."

"Whose voice?" Ailish asked through her chattering teeth.

"Darcy, a witch. She's on the phone and helping us."
He took his hand from her face and quickly undid her
pants. Spreading the sides, he glanced down and saw her
black panties against her olive skin. They were thin and
flush against her, clearly illustrating that she was perfectly
smooth beneath them. Bare. Hairless. His blood heated
while disgust at his reaction to an injured woman got him
focused. He turned his attention to her tight bra top.

He pulled out his knife and slid the tip beneath the
elastic bottom.

She flinched and sluggishly tried to grab the knife with
her left hand. "No."

He was hit by renewed urgency at her pathetic defense. This was the witch who had kicked him onto his
ass. He moved swiftly, shoving her hand away and slic-
ing the top. He spread the edges apart, exposing her
small, perfect breasts.

She started to shake with more violence. Hell with this.
He shoved his knife in the holster at his back, stood, and
moved to the back of the couch. Then he leaned down
and picked her up, holding her against him. Trying to
warm her. Moving back to the couch, he said, "Not going to hurt you. Won't let anyone hurt you." Her jeans
slid halfway down her hips, her top hung off her. He
didn't care, it was just them.

He sat down, and she turned her face into his leather
vest. "Won't be a demon witch if I die now."

He cradled her against him. There was no way she
could lie to him now, with her blood draining onto his
thighs, her body trembling, her skin so damned cold.
Whatever she'd done in the past, she didn't want to be a
demon witch now. He believed her. He laid her hips on his
thighs and her shoulders in the curve of his right arm. Her
right arm rested on his knees. "Ailish, stay with me now.
I need you awake."

Her eyes fluttered.

He put his hand on her pelvic bone to try to coax her chakras open.

Her stomach jumped, and his hand tingled. He felt a flash of hope and dragged his hand up and over the cold skin on her stomach, ignoring the sexy dips and ridges of her muscles. He drew his fingers up between her breasts. He tried not to notice the small swells with sweet puckered nipples. Instead, he spread his hand over her heart. "Come on, Ailish, open your chakras," he coaxed. He could feel something stirring to life inside her, some energy beginning to bubble.

"Trying," she said.

Damn it, he could feel her slipping. Feel her body tiring of the fight. "Darcy, anything?"

From the phone, she said, "Not yet. We're trying to send her more power, but we need her chakras open. She's running out of time. Push her, do anything to get her power to recognize you."

How? His gaze caught on her nipples. If he touched the sensitive tips, would it jog her chakras open? He wanted to save her, not molest her. No time for moral debates! He slid his fingers around the base to cup her breast gently, then touched the pad of his thumb to her nipple.

She hissed, her stomach tightened, and her hips jerked. Then her magic washed over him in a misty spray, weak and evaporating almost as soon as it touched him. "You're doing it. Focus." He willed her to fight, moving his hand down to her panties and back up. He could feel the answering quiver of her magic.

Startled, he realized her powers were responding to him. Following him.

"Okay, I feel her magic. Three of us are circling our magic, trying to help her," Darcy said.

Ailish had her eyes closed in concentration, obviously

trying to capture the power and focus the healing energy to the wound on her arm. Her skin was sweaty, her shimmer still filled with pain holes. He had to help her direct her magic to where she needed it.

Now that he was committed to saving her, he refused to fail. Determined to win this battle, he lifted his hand, then settled it carefully over her wound. He sucked in his breath, her blood coating his palm, followed by the power rush. It tore through his veins and hit his brain like a sledgehammer. Her magic was pouring into him, and his head buzzed. Clarity of thought was a sunburst in his mind.

More. More blood, more power, take it all! Own it. Cut and don't stop until—

"Phoenix!" Darcy shouted. "What did you do?"

He shook his head hard, trying to dislodge the darkly seductive thoughts. "Pull back your powers!" he told Ailish.

"Can't get control," she groaned.

Fuck. He was getting too much; her powers were racing past her wounds in some elemental attempt to get to him, to bind with him. They were soaking into his cells and pickling his brain. He'd seen a witch hunter blooded before and knew the insanity would take hold. Panting, he yanked his hand off her wound. "Darcy, I touched her blood."

Ailish lay limp; even her witch-shimmer was weaker. The sight made his gut twist, and the skin of his biceps began to burn again.

"Phoenix, listen to me!" Darcy said, her voice urgent as she projected it through the phone. "It's the soul-mirror bond. It requires the blood exchange. Her power felt you and is trying to finish the bond. It's seeking your blood. Give her your blood."

He reached back and pulled out his knife. The lights

bounced off the silver blade. This act would bind them tighter. Both the soul-mirror and probably the siren-phoenix connection.

But he looked down at her face. He thought of her telling him that no witches would help her. Everyone had been afraid of the consequences. He hadn't fully believed her, not until now. No one was willing to go up against a demon to fight for this witch.

"Until now," Phoenix said. He lifted his palm and sliced it. The flash of pain was nothing to him. But as he watched the blood well up, he thought about what he was doing—binding them tighter. Going one step closer to becoming true soul mirrors.

Her protector. She would come to rely on him, and then there would come a moment when he didn't get there in time. She'd need him and he'd fail her. Even without the handfast, Ailish was blind! So many things could happen to her. If he grew to care about her, and then she died . . .

She was dying now! Pulling back from his dark thoughts, he reached across her to lay his bleeding palm on her massive cut.

9

The utterly cold darkness of death terrified Ailish. She could feel her life force draining from her.

Where would she go? Would the Ancestors accept her? How could they? She was promised to a demon. She had tried to learn what an earth witch was and then tried to live as one. She had searched and searched for ways to break the handfast, but she had failed.

The Ancestors wouldn't want her.

The crushing terror and darkness pulled her down and down, sinking like a rock into nothingness. She heard Phoenix calling her, but she couldn't answer. She had a spark of power, but then even that left her, flowing out of her with her blood.

The icy horror made even her bones shiver. Would this be her eternity? Dark, cold nothingness?

Then a bloom of life-giving heat spread from her arm inward. Sweeping through her to reach all her muscles and bones, going down to her very cells. It fed something in her, a hunger that had been gnawing silently at her since birth, suddenly satiated. A vibrant energy flowed into her chakras, filling them with power. Not her power, but that of other witches.

Earth witches.

She felt her body arch under the waves of healing magic, and she reached up to grab on to the warm arm.

"Breathe," Phoenix said, his voice an anchor in the maelstrom of swirling magic and the pain of healing muscles, veins, and skin. Her body kept filling, and she became vividly aware of Phoenix. The scent of leather, soap, and musk, his arm beneath her shoulders holding her against his chest. His powerful thighs under her butt and back.

Then the sensation of magic from other witches faded away.

"Ailish," he said in a low, gentle voice. "You're healing. The cut's nearly closed, your witch-shimmer is warming to dazzling gold."

The pain was draining off, and she was filled with an incredible well-being, a sense of wonderment. "I felt them. I still feel you." Opening her eyes, she saw his shadow over her. "Is this real?"

He brushed her hair back. "What?"

It was leaving now, but she felt it. "Witches really helped me? You helped me?" She had felt their magic, and it was wondrous.

"It's real. The witches have left now, but they helped."

She saw his shadow closing in on her, his deeply masculine scent covering her, then his kiss. The damp heat of his mouth ignited her magic into a frenzy of sparkles from her pelvis to her chest. Phoenix tasted like a rich tea with a hint of dark spices. She couldn't get enough, and she lifted her head into the kiss, tasting him. Her magic rushed, her skin tingled, and her entire being felt as if it were reaching, seeking, trying to absorb him into her.

Phoenix made a noise deep in his chest, and his kiss grew deeper, fiercer. He dragged his hand from her healed arm to stroke his palm back and forth over her nipple.

Bright, hot sensations swelled in her breast and mixed with her magic. Her body arched, desperate for more of his touch, to feel him closer. Desire thickened, urgency and need mounted, and it felt damned good. He had saved her, helped her.

Phoenix broke the kiss. Covering her breast with his

large hand, he squeezed gently. "Damn, you're sexy, a beautiful siren." He released her breast and drew his fingers down her belly.

Her magic chased after his touch until her womb felt swollen and a deep ache rooted between her legs.

"I want to see all of you, touch all of you." His fingers slid to the top of her panties. "Even if I can't get inside you the way I'm desperate to, we can—"

Desperate. Inside her. Sex. Cold fear jump-started in her stomach. She hadn't had sex since Kyle, had avoided sex. Sex and her feelings for him had set the whole handfast thing in motion. And Phoenix didn't really want her, didn't choose her; he was being compelled. He'd told her how much that pissed him off. He thought of her as some kind of burden. His words from last night filled her head: *leashed to a blind witch who is handfasted to a demon.*

She grabbed his wrist. "Stop." He didn't want this, it was just lust for him. He wasn't possessed, but he was like those men who had their will forced down and were controlled by a demon. They were soul mirrors, but he didn't want that bond, didn't want to have sex and complete the bond.

The stain of loneliness spread in her. She was alone. That made her think of the cold darkness of nothingness she had felt as she'd been dying. Summerland was the place of rest for witch-souls between reincarnations or for the souls that had completed their journey and stayed in Summerland as Ancestors, the old souls who guided the witches. It was supposed to be a place of beauty and peace, not that cold nothing absence of existence she'd felt. A shudder ripped through her.

"Ailish? What's wrong?"

His voice stirred up the ashes of her previous warm desire, but she resisted. "It's not real." Enough of this. She had to focus on getting the handfast off, on making the right choices, not the easy or lust-induced ones. And she had to stop her mother and the coven. She sat up and scrambled off Phoenix's lap, used magic to seal the edges of her bra top, and pulled up her pants.

He rose, his body so tight that she could practically hear his muscles popping. He stood toe-to-toe with her. "You're denying your desire for me is real?"

"You told me it's the soul-mirror bond. Not your choice, remember?"

He sucked in a breath. "I chose to save you, to give you my blood."

"But not your soul," she said softly, the deep crux of that slamming her in her heart. Even her magic cringed at that rejection. But could she blame him, when even the Ancestors, those revered old soul earth witches, rejected her? No surprise that he didn't trust her enough to bind his soul with hers.

A frustrated breath spilled out of him. "Our souls will bind, Ailish. Forever. If you give in and become a demon witch, my soul will be gone." He touched her arm. "I've fought since puberty to resist the curse and keep my soul."

She pulled her arm back. "Then we're not having sex. I'm not having sex anyway. Sex is just a way for Asmodeus to control me."

"I'm not trying to control you," he said.

"You told me not to use my voice, not to sing to try and break the handfast." Why was she debating this with him?

He stepped back, his shadow shifting as though he were crossing his arms. "But you did sing again. Yanking me to you. So who is controlling who?"

"I didn't sing to call you, I was trying to save . . ." The memories slammed into her, and her chest tightened painfully. "Dee and Kyle! A rogue cut Dee's throat, and they dragged me away from her when I was trying to heal her. She was dying! I sang to send my power to her. Kyle got her in the car, I think." Her mind was jumping, the memories rushing at her. "I heard a car start up and drive away. They must have escaped. I need a phone. I think I left my phone in the car. I can call my number and see if they answer." Her heart was pounding. They had to be okay.

Phoenix moved, scooping something off the ground. "You left your phone in the car?"

She wrapped her arms around her stomach in relief. "Yes. The number is—"

"Don't need it. I put a GPS tracking device in it yesterday."

She was just too tired, too overwhelmed, to be upset. "Can you see the location of the phone? Where it is?" It was a pain in the ass to be so dependent.

"Your house. They must be waiting there to see if you show up."

So was Dee alive? She thought fast. "Call my phone. Kyle can't be out in the open where the coven can get him."

"Coven of demon witches?" His voice went mean, his hatred of demon witches riding each word.

Bouncing on her toes, she said, "Yes. They want Kyle to force me into the Claiming Rite. That's why I went there. Here, just give me the phone!" She grabbed his arm and took the phone from him and dialed. Three rings later, she got a "Hello."

"Dee!" Thank the Ancestors! "Are you and Kyle all right?"

Dee answered, "I'm fine, just a red mark on my neck and a lot of dried blood. Kyle says you're a witch."

"I am." The woman deserved the truth. "But you two need to get someplace safe until I can reach you. I guess maybe a hotel or—"

"They'll come here," Phoenix said, and gave her directions.

Ailish repeated the directions, then hung up. "Thanks, that makes the most sense." She held out his phone to him. "It'll give me a few minutes to figure out where we should go. Dee's a target now that—"

She heard him move, then he put his hands on either side of her face. "Have to touch you. Bloodlust."

Her senses were pinging from his touch, but she realized what he meant. "Oh."

"And I want to touch you." He brushed his thumbs over her cheekbones.

The desire moved rich and thick through her, filling up her breasts, rolling down her belly, and swelling her between her legs. "Phoenix, don't."

"This is more than a compulsion. I chose to save you, Ailish, chose to give you my blood. There's something about you." He touched the scars around her eyes. "Little starbursts surrounding the silvery blue of your eyes."

A shudder of soft, tempting pleasure washed through her. "They used to be a dark blue." She had no idea what her eyes looked like now. But it had to be ugly.

His breath feathered her face. "They are so light in color, almost silver. Very striking."

She stood there, his BlackBerry in her hand, letting him caress her face. Basking in the contact, in the way his touch and words seemed to fill empty places in her. He slid his fingers into her hair, sending more sensual feelings cascading down her back.

"How did it happen, Ailish? How did you lose your sight?"

The words flowed out of her. "Witch karma."

His hands froze in her hair. "Who did you hurt?"

It was almost as if he'd pulled the plug on all those lovely sensations traveling her nerve endings. Lifting her chin, she said, "My mother." Once she said that much, the rest tumbled out. "She's the high witch of the Deus'Donovan coven."

"You're the daughter of a demon witch." His voice was rigid with hatred and shock. He pulled his fingers from her hair. "What changed your mind? What made you decide not to go into the family business?"

His anger was palpable. But so was hers. Hadn't she paid the price of being naïve and stupid? For being desperate? For making the wrong choice? Shoving Phoenix's BlackBerry into his midsection, she said, "Probably when she tricked me into handfasting with a demon."

Phoenix felt her words like a kick in the stomach. Doubt and suspicion weighed down his chest. All witches were born earth witches, they had to choose to become a demon witch. "How? You knew she was a demon witch, so how could she trick you?"

Ailish sucked in a breath. Her golden witch-shimmer darkened. "Because she was my mother. I trusted her."

Part of him wanted to believe her, and part of him whispered that she was lying to him, tricking him, and that he should pull out his knife and cut her until he had absorbed every ounce of her powerful blood. He knew it was the curse getting stronger, fed by her blood. He could feel the kick of it in his body, that luscious power singing through him, winding its way to his brain, and poisoning him with the addiction. But he wasn't a rogue. Not yet, not ever. Keeping a tight rein on himself, he said, "Let's go to the kitchen." He walked away, concentrating on breathing. He went around the couch, up the three steps to the main hallway, and headed left into the dining room.

He heard a soft thump and then Ailish's indrawn hiss.

Shit, he'd forgotten! He turned back to see her face set in grim lines as she put her hands on the couch and went around it. Then she took a few steps.

He could feel a small amount of her magic sweeping in front of her. He watched, frozen to the spot, as the light teasing of her magic caressed him and goaded his blood-lust. She kept moving, then must have sensed the rise in front of her and thought it was furniture. She stepped to the left, frowned, and stepped right, then probably realized it was a step. She lifted her foot, caught the edge of the step with the toe of her boot, and pitched forward.

The sight of her vulnerability snapped him out of the freeze, and he got to her in less than a second. Catching her arms, he stopped her fall and—

What? What was he going to do? Kill her? His hands burned for the feel of his cool knife. Then his biceps seared at the idea of hurting her. He could feel the wings struggling, rising, trying to get to her, to the witch they wanted to bind with.

Her head snapped up. "What?"

"You almost fell." The realization, the cold fact of her dark world, cooled the burn of his curse. He didn't want to hurt her, he wanted to protect her. He had walked away from her, leaving her to stumble blindly through his house. He wanted to pull her up against his body and swear he would never do that again. Never.

She brushed off his hands. "I have to find my own way. That's how I remember."

He hated that, but the fact was that she knew how to live in the dark. "Okay." He dropped his hands to his sides. If she could endure her burden of blindness, then he could deal with his bloodlust. "There are three steps up. That leads to a main hallway that runs down the middle of my house. The house is multilevel. We're going left." He turned and walked ahead, his back itching with the feel of her behind him. His tats burned with the urge to help her, guide her. He went straight to the fridge, opened it, and pulled out two ice-cold beers. Then he turned, watching Ailish make her way toward him.

She was a vision. Dark, choppy hair, strong face, and that long, sleek body that honest to God made his mouth water. "Want a beer?"

She cocked her head slightly, getting a fix on his voice, and moved past the split stairs leading up to the media room or down to the gym. Her right hip caught on a chair at the edge of his big kitchen table. She worked her way closer.

He remembered to draw in a breath as she was finally almost to the bar. "There's a granite counter two steps in front of you, bar stools you can sit on."

She inclined her head and slid onto the bar stool. "Where's that beer?"

Damn, the witch amazed the shit out of him. He twisted off the top and set the beer down for her. "Twelve o'clock." Then he twisted the cap off his and drank half of it down in a long, much needed swallow. Her blood still sang through him, and he burned for more, but she, the woman herself, was touching him deep in his chest. A place he'd closed off ten years ago, the day he'd found his mom. He didn't do relationships with women. He never let himself care, never gave them the power to destroy him by getting hurt or dying. That feeling in his chest better damn well be indigestion. Caring for Ailish, the woman who could give in to the demon or die? That was emotional suicide.

"I was sixteen and in love with Kyle."

Her words jerked Phoenix from his thoughts. He lowered his beer and had to force himself to stay still while the curse hissed, *She was his! Belonged to him! Kill Kyle!* Curling his hand around the bottle, he struggled to be reasonable. "The Kyle that's on his way here?"

"Yes."

"Do you still love him? Desire him?" His voice grew harder with each word. She'd evidently gone racing over there to save this Kyle. Hot rage stewed and bubbled, and swear to God, he realized his knife was in his hand. He stared at the blade and knew that if Kyle walked into his house that second, he would kill him. He forced the knife back to his holster and looked at the witch who was driving him insane. He needed an answer. Now. "Ailish?"

"No. Not anymore, not in nearly eight years." Her eyes were unfocused and moving, drifting left the way she did when she was thinking, remembering. "But back then in high school, I did love him. He was so normal, so . . . what I wanted to be."

His gut-searing, possessive jealousy calmed as he understood exactly what she meant. He'd wanted to be normal, have a home, a place he belonged. But more than anything, he'd wanted to not have to fight the voices for his mother's attention. Softening his tone, he asked, "What did you want to be?"

"Not a witch. Just a girl. I hated the coven business that was secretive and took my mother away from me. I was never allowed to see what they did, or where they went. My mother always left me at home."

Phoenix watched her face. What was she thinking? "By yourself?"

She nodded. "The house was heavily warded so no one could get through, but I hated it. Hated being alone in the dark. I would always turn on all the lights." She pulled her mouth tight, then said, "I didn't like all the secrets. I could never tell anyone what my mother did. It was . . ."

"Lonely?"

She looked to the left. "Maybe. Anyway, I dated Kyle, hung out with his friends, had dinner with his folks a couple times, and I was happy."

Yeah, he related to what it felt like to be on the outside of those warm-looking families in all those homes that lined the streets and wanting to be a part of it. But did she still feel that way about Kyle? She said no, yet she was try-ing to save the bastard. *Careful,* he warned himself, *don't lose control.* "Sounds like you still care for him."

She lifted her beer and took a sip. "I am trying to right a wrong with Kyle. I asked my mom to make Kyle love me again. I . . . knew what she was and I still did it. Even though my chakras cringed, I agreed to the hand-fast she suggested. My mom told me it was an old tradi-tion that would show Kyle how much I cared for him. I believed her, I wanted to believe her." She clenched her jaw, and her fingers clutching the beer bottle turned white. "Part of me knew it was wrong, but I ignored that. I wanted him to love me more than I wanted to do the right thing."

He could feel her struggle with the memories. Sixteen and in love . . . how many heartbreaks and disasters started that way? "What happened?"

"That night, when I realized it wasn't Kyle I was hand-fasting with, but a demon in his body, I freaked. I used my power to banish Asmodeus. But I had no control over my magic, and it went wild, somehow freezing the coven witches in place, creating windstorms . . . I don't remem-ber what else because . . ." She paused, using her finger-nail to pick at the label on the bottle. Finally she said, "I ran. I heard Kyle call out my name, but I ran. And kept running. Leaving him at the mercy of the coven."

"Where did you go?"

She snorted. "I ran until I got to a park, where I hid in the bathrooms. God, I was so stupid . . . what was I thinking, hiding in the bathrooms?"

It made him sick. He knew the streets and knew the dangers to a sixteen-year-old girl. "What happened?"

"I didn't know where to go. Hell, I didn't know how to survive. Once my fury at my mother wore off, I was sick and scared. I found out about this homeless shelter and made my way there. I met Haley and—"

Phoenix jerked with the impact of the name. "Haley? Haley Ryan?" Of course it was her, who else could it be?

She shifted on the bar stool. "You know her?"

"Hell, yeah." It shocked him. Haley had shown him who he was—a witch hunter. They were still friends, and Phoenix contributed to the shelter.

Ailish's silvery eyes caught the golden witch-shimmer on her skin. "You were in the homeless shelter?"

"Off and on, yeah. Grew up on the streets. No way in hell Haley let you stay in the shelter. She looked for witch hunter kids to bring in there. The curse would drive the witch hunters mad." It boggled his mind that they both knew Haley. Another thought occurred to him. "Did she know your mother was a demon witch?"

"Yes. I told her. I was desperate for help. I still didn't realize what demon witches did . . . until Haley told me." Her voice was thick with disgust.

Remembering how she'd claimed the Circle Witches wouldn't help her, he assumed she blamed Haley, too. "You can't blame her, Ailish. She's seen what they did to the street kids they snatched. Sometimes we could get them back before their minds were shattered or they were killed. They used the kids in sacrifices, summoned the demon into the boys, and gave the girls to them to rape. Haley couldn't take a chance on you."

She was silent for a few seconds and absently rubbed the healed wound on her arm. Her magic had removed all traces of blood, leaving her skin a smooth olive color with a brilliant golden shimmer. "You're wrong. Haley took a chance on me and paid for it. You're right that she wouldn't let me stay at the shelter. Instead she took me to her house. And that's where my mother found us. Haley grabbed me and we ran for her car. We made it inside the vehicle before my mother's magic hit, pinning Haley behind the driver's seat and choking the air from her." Ailish dropped her hands to the counter and fisted them, as if the memory still enraged her. "My mother told me she'd let Haley live if I submitted to the Claiming Rite. Her dark magic was so powerful, and my earth magic was sketchy! I panicked and began to sing to enhance my power. The car windows all exploded outward. . . ." She shuddered.

"Hitting your mother in the eyes?"

"The bitch deserved it." Her voice was hard, bitter with old rage. "The last thing I saw was the shock, fear, and pain on her face before the witch karma hit me."

And took her sight. How the fuck was that fair when she was just trying to save Haley? A strange brittle cry rang in his ears, while his biceps burned. Phoenix looked at one arm.

More of the bird showed. Two-thirds of the wing was out, and the flames were filling in. "The phoenix is rising." From giving her his blood? Maybe.

Ailish leaned forward, a stillness in the air between them. "Your tattoo?" She whispered the words.

He looked at her, and it hit him then how Asmodeus had known what she was. Why her mother had bargained her. "The witches discovered a legend about us. The siren and the phoenix." He told her as much as he knew.

"So my mother saw you when I was born, the phoenix fly over and burst into flames. And she bargained me to Asmodeus so she could become the high witch of the coven." Her voice was flat. "Yeah, it fits. All the secrets they never wanted me to know or the earth witches to find out." She looked up, finding him with surprising accuracy. "Why I wasn't allowed to sing."

"Because," he explained, "your voice calls me. Carla said your siren magic is powerful, going out in waves for miles, trying to find the phoenix and call him back to life. The coven had to prevent that as your familiar would try to protect you from their plans to give you to Asmodeus.

That's why I've been hearing your voice in my head when you sing with your magic. And trust me, the compulsion to go to you is strong and getting stronger each time."

"And enhancing all other magic, doing God knows what," she said softly. "I just wanted to get the handfast off."

He started to reach across the counter, needing to touch her, when he heard the car turn onto the road leading to his house. He jerked his hand back. What was he doing? He needed to let her go, get her out of his house before he gave in to the bloodlust. Right now, he could feel each and every vein in his body pulsing. But if he touched her, the bloodlust would vanish under the primal, bone-deep urge to mate with her.

His soul, tied to the daughter of a demon witch, handfasted to a demon, with only twelve days to live.

He drained his beer, then said, "Your friends are here."

Ailish had felt him reach toward her, then jerk back. She was still reeling from the fight with the rogues, losing so much blood, the massive power surge, and learning about the siren-phoenix legend. All of it left her tired and lethargic.

And Phoenix saving her life confused her. He could have let her die and his problems would have been solved.

She stood up off the bar stool. Whatever his reasons, he'd done it. "Thank you for helping me. Which way is the door?" She didn't have a good layout of his house in her mind. Didn't matter, though, she was leaving.

"Stay here, I'll go let them in." He walked away.

Ailish caught sight of his shadow and followed him. "We need to leave now. I—" Her quick reflexes allowed her to stop before slamming into him. "What?"

"I can't let you go. Can't. Shit, I'm— Ah, fuck it." He

reached for her, his hands coming down on her arms and pulling her to him. He crushed her to his chest.

Ailish inhaled his scent, the leather vest, soap, and his skin. It swelled inside of her until her magic bloomed hot and pressed against her chakras, begging for release, begging to touch him. He lifted one hand to stroke the bare skin of her back. Her powers began shivering, and her body heated with need. Her jeans irritated her skin, while her top constricted her breath. She was desperate to be skin-to-skin with Phoenix.

"Better," he said into her hair. "No bloodlust when I touch you. Just a blue-balled hard-on."

She felt his erection pressed against her stomach, while her hands slid beneath his vest to roam over his back. Powerful muscles and hot skin—she'd never get enough. She wanted to feel him all over, know all of him.

"Ailish, you're killing me. Every touch makes me hotter to have you. Need you." He slid his hand into her hair and tugged her head back. Then he went to work on her mouth.

A shiver raced through her as Phoenix opened his mouth over hers, taking her lips, then sliding deep inside. More sensations rolled through her, until her body felt soft and ready. Needy. It wasn't forced, it was real.

Trust. That was it—she could trust Phoenix. He didn't force her body, but instead her body went willingly where he took it. She went up on her toes, using her tongue to taste him, feeling his mouth, his—

He growled deep in his chest, his hand sliding down to caress her butt through her jeans. Finally, he moved his mouth to her ear. "Trust me, my siren witch. Let me bring us both pleasure. I'll start by stripping those jeans and panties off of you and—"

A knock at the door interrupted him.

Ailish felt her magic surge, wanting to shove away anything that tried to get between her and Phoenix.

"Shit!" His arms tightened around her.

"It's Dee and Kyle, I—"

"Hush."

She felt the weight of his gaze on her, the strength of his arms holding her, the sweep of feathers caressing her arms. She tilted her head up to listen to him.

There was a second knock on the door, but they both ignored it.

"When I stop touching you, the curse is going to hit me. Hard. So here's what's going to happen. I'm going to open the door, and those two are going to come in. You're all staying in my house. Do not step outside the house, Ailish. You're safe here."

"What about you? The curse?"

"I'm leaving. Here's my BlackBerry—" He reached in his pocket, pulled it out, and put the device in her hand. "I'll get another one at the warehouse."

She frowned. "The what?"

"It's our headquarters. I'll call you and give you the number where you can reach me. There's food here, plenty of rooms. Get some rest."

"But—"

He kissed her, rumbled a groan, then dragged his mouth away. "If you leave this house, I'll know. And I'll find you. I won't be able to stop myself, I'll come after you."

The curse. She finally understood. "My blood, you got too much."

"Not enough. Not nearly enough. Now I want, need, all of you." He dragged in a breath. "I won't hurt you. I won't. But I have to go."

She nodded. He had fought to save her life. That meant something to her, and she knew it had cost him, knew it bound them tighter. She could feel his torment now, as if his body were being torn apart. "I'll stay. We'll stay."

Another knock echoed through the house. "Ailish?" It was Dee's voice.

"I'm here," she answered.

Phoenix took one hand off her to open the door. "Come in and stay here with Ailish." Then he took his hand off her back and headed out the front door.

Her throat went tight with the sudden, intense urge to sing and call him back to her.

10

Phoenix was sweating, his left eye was swollen, his right hand looked like ground meat, and he was still ready to rumble. "Get up," he growled at Linc Dillinger.

Linc's gold eyes narrowed . . . well, one narrowed, the other one was ballooned shut. He rolled to his feet, then held up a hand. "I'm done."

Phoenix bounced on the balls of his feet. "Who's next?" He glanced at Key and Ram, both sporting cuts and bruises. Sutton had a laptop on his massive thighs. He set it aside and rose. The man was a tank with a bald head, an eagle earring, and the ability to crush small cars.

Perfect.

Sutton had just stripped off his shirt when the sounds of boots striding across the warehouse caused them all to turn. Phoenix forgot about Sutton, his rage spiking. *Axel.* The man who refused to help Ailish. That memory surged through him.

Axel said, "This isn't your fight, Sutton."

Sutton's shoulders dropped in disappointment. As a bonded witch hunter, he had even more strength. Maybe enough to put Phoenix on his ass and keep him there. Which was what Phoenix wanted, needed. Anything to make the pain stop. Sutton sighed. "He just got warmed up."

"Rain check," Phoenix said to Sutton. These men were helping him vent, helping him cope with the bloodlust.

Axel said, "I had no choice but to refuse to bring Darcy to the witch. Ailish is handfasted to a demon. I couldn't let Darcy or Carla get near her. What if she turns?"

Phoenix could barely contain his fury. "She was tricked into the handfast and has resisted for almost eight years. I saw her fighting Asmodeus in a mortal's body. I saw her tortured in her sleep." Barefoot and wearing only a pair of shorts, he stepped toward Axel. "She's an earth witch. The Circle Witches refused to help her, and now we refused her. You were going to let an earth witch die from a rogue's blade. How the hell does that jibe with our vow?"

Axel reached behind his neck and grabbed a handful of shirt, yanked it off. "Have you looked at your biceps? More of the phoenix is rising, and there's more flames. Has it occurred to you that she could call her phoenix, then become a demon witch and you'd be her familiar?" He pulled out his knife and tossed it.

Sutton caught the hilt.

Phoenix had seen his biceps, but it was Ailish who kept backing away from sex, not him. He'd said he wouldn't slide his cock into her, but the truth was . . . he couldn't be sure he'd control himself. The more he was with her, the harder it was to hold back. "So you would have let her die." The words made his chest hurt again.

Axel pulled off his boots. That left him wearing jeans and the hawk tattoo on his back that marked him as the chosen leader of the Wing Slayer Hunters. He moved to the middle of the blue mats. The workout area was a large square with treadmills, weights, and room for sparring. He fixed his green eyes on Phoenix. "Choice between Darcy's safety from Asmodeus and healing Ailish? You know the answer."

He'd let her die. It ripped through him with blinding speed, the need to strike and destroy. He bent over, put his 240 pounds into tackling his hawk. They flew to the ground, and Phoenix slammed his forearm against Axel's neck and pressed.

Axel flipped him over his head.

Phoenix rolled to his feet and spun into a roundhouse kick, catching Axel in the side.

Axel grunted, grabbed his foot, and jerked him onto his back. He was on Phoenix in a flash, delivering a punch to his ribs and his face.

Phoenix slammed his elbow into Axel's ribs and heard a satisfying crack.

The only sounds in the warehouse were the vicious grunts and thuds of flesh hitting flesh. Finally, Axel roundhouse kicked Phoenix into a wall, and Phoenix went down to his ass and stayed there. He held out his right hand. "Broken finger. Probably did it on your face."

Axel sank down against the wall and held out a bottle of water. "Ribs hurt like a mother. If I punctured a lung, you'd better run like hell when Darcy finds out."

Phoenix opened the bottle with his unbroken hand. "Hiding behind your witch?"

Axel snorted. "How's the bloodlust?"

"Laying low." Finally, he could draw a breath without feeling the poisonous craving. Now he just felt pain. He flexed his right hand. The right index finger was dislocated. Wincing, he set down the water, got hold of the finger, and yanked. He felt a flash of hot agony, then it faded away. "Much better." The rest of the bones and joints were in place. He healed fast, so no big deal.

Axel pointed out, "Yesterday you'd never have been able to drop me."

Phoenix leaned his head back and closed his eyes. "Her blood is powerful."

"And you got a hell of a lot of it, judging by your strength."

"Too much. Her powers wouldn't heal her, but poured into me. I gave her my blood to save her."

"Shit, Phoenix. You're binding yourself tighter to her. This isn't one of your hit-and-run rescues."

He opened his eyes, saw the other hunters standing around, their gazes riveted. He'd made no secret of his choices. He'd rescue women, hunt down the men hurting them, and fix the problem. Instant hero and then he was gone. He didn't want to be in a cage again, growing to care about someone so much that fear for her ruled his life. It made his goddamn chest hurt worrying that when the next crisis came, he might not get there in time. Might find her . . . He shook it off.

Ailish was different. She was fighting, and not just for herself. She'd saved her friends, too. Phoenix turned his head, looked at the man who had his respect even if they didn't always agree. "I'm not running this time, I'm sticking." The words surprised him, but they pleased the phoenix on his biceps. "Darcy or Carla found out anything more on breaking the handfast?"

"Don't think so, but you can ask Darcy yourself. She's upstairs in the condo."

He nodded his thanks, ran a hand through his hair, wiping away blood and sweat. "I need a shower first. Sutton, you got the cameras working on the outside of my house?"

"Yes, all set up."

Phoenix nodded. "Thanks." The cameras had already been in place but not activated. Sutton did his computer shit, whatever that was, and now they could all keep an eye on the house.

He climbed to his feet. "I'll grab a shower and check on Joe and Morgan—" His new BlackBerry rang from where he'd left it on the weight bench. He hurried over to it. After looking at the screen, he put it to his ear and said, "Haley, thanks for the tag back."

"I only have a couple minutes, but it sounded important."

"It's about Ailish Donovan. Do you know her?"

"She's a witch, Phoenix. You need to stay away from her."

He almost smiled at her orders. "Too late. I need to know more about her. Obviously you know her, what's her story?"

"Why? What's happened?"

He recognized the caution in her voice that she got whenever she was trying to protect someone. His only choice was to tell her the truth. "She's my soul mirror, Haley."

She drew in a breath of pure shock. "She's handfasted to a demon."

He hated that. "I know. But is she on the level? She says her mother tricked her into the handfast. And that her mother tried to kill you to force her—"

"It's true. She was only sixteen! And God, so freaking naïve and clueless. Ailish saved my life and paid for it with her sight."

He felt his wings expanding in relief as Haley backed up Ailish's story. But his gut churned at the knowledge of what Ailish had suffered. In spite of the multiple poundings he'd taken from the other hunters, his muscles twitched with the urge to hurry home to Ailish. "Why didn't you tell me, us, that Ailish was in town?" If he'd known this stuff from the beginning . . .

"Yeah, right. Tell the cursed witch hunter where the vulnerable witch is," she said dryly. "I've spent years trying to keep you *out* of trouble." She sighed, then said, "Maybe I should come back?"

Her last sentence caught his attention. Haley was decisive and took action. She didn't dither like this. He'd known her a long time, and only one thing made her unsure of herself. "Who's the guy?"

Silence.

His radar was pinging. "Haley."

"I have to go. Be careful, Phoenix." She hung up.

Phoenix looked up at the other hunters watching him. "Good news, Ailish was telling the truth." He zeroed in on Key. "Bad news, Haley's hooked up with another loser." She'd disappear until she got this one out of her system.

Phoenix had talked with the witches, but they needed to know more about Ailish's handfast. Axel wanted information on her mother—if demon witches were in Glassbreakers, the bonded hunters, Sutton and Axel, had to find and kill them. They'd come up with a plan to have a phone conference with Ailish after getting some sleep.

It was pre-dawn when he stopped at his house, planning just to check on Ailish, then leave before the bloodlust or sex lust turned him inside out. He'd sleep at the condo. But when he walked in, he could feel her unease and smell a lingering burnt butter scent.

Shit, she'd been having nightmares. It was the same scent he'd smelled two nights ago in her house. He tracked her scent and the sound of music down the stairs to the gym. It was the size of a three-car garage. Across from the entrance, he had a treadmill, an elliptic, and two stationary bikes facing a TV that dropped from the ceiling. The left side had all his weights and a rowing machine. The center was open, with blue mats for sparring, and the right side had the heavy bags. The stereo blasted out some head-banging music, and Ailish was working one of the bags.

She knew what she was doing. For a minute he watched, transfixed. Her punches were good, but her power was in her legs. Stepping crescent kick, flying side kick, jump spinning hook kick—they were all fast and brutal. Witch hunters had the speed and strength of several men, but a witch . . . she was pretty much a mortal physically, except for the chakras where her magic lived. Ailish had trained her body into a tool to banish demons.

Damn, she was beautiful. Dressed only in a shirt and panties and completely uninhibited and comfortable in her body. Working out her pain. "Ailish."

"Not now. Go away." She worked a few more kicks.

Her scent filled the room. Slight coconut of her blood, the heady scent of mango and sweat. But the burnt butter smell was still there. He knew what she was doing, trying to work off the pain, the endless frustration. She was leery of being touched. Didn't know how to trust herself or a man with sex. But fighting? That she knew. He stripped off his boots and socks, then walked across the mat. "Want a—"

She spun with a side kick and caught him right beneath his ribs.

He grunted, twisting enough to slide the kick off him.

She jumped back, hands up and in a staggered stance. "Don't touch me."

His blood went hot. There was no other way to describe it. The bloodlust crouched down in his veins, ready to spring. But there was something else, something darkly sexual and erotic that wanted her to not back down. To come at him with everything she had. Her arms were tight with tension, the muscles in her thighs were ready to pounce, and she was so damned sexy that he could barely breathe. "What are you going to do to stop me?"

She bounced on her feet.

Her breasts moved beneath that shirt, and his brain stuttered.

Ailish hopped and in a smooth movement lifted her knee and snapped her leg up, then brought her heel down in a path right for his face.

He ducked back just in time. Damn, she played rough. "Not bad. For a girl." He purposely goaded her, testing her control, seeing how she fought. "Got anything else, or—"

She slammed her fist into his jaw.

Phoenix caught her wrist and felt a spray of her lust-pain. She was clever and had followed the sound of his voice with her fist. But she needed more, more relief and more trust. He jerked her forward. "You're going to have to do better, little boxer. You want to fight with me, you'd better bring your A game. I'm not a girl, baby-cakes. And I'm not a mortal man. I can put you down on this mat and keep you there without breaking a sweat." He knew this was dangerous, but Ailish needed relief and she needed to learn to trust him. He just had to keep the bloodlust under control.

She drooped a bit and sighed. "You're right."

He let go of her wrist, telling himself that he wasn't disappointed. He was a witch hunter; he could hurt her, damn it. She was being smart. Hell, she wasn't going to goad the curse in him. He turned toward a small refrigerator where he kept bottled water. "I'll get a couple—"

She hit him in the back of the knees, buckling his legs. He dropped to the mat and rolled before her next kick caught him in the head. Phoenix snapped up to his feet, closed his mouth, and watched his prey. She was crouched, her arms up for protection, head tilted as she tracked his moves. Her face glowed, her witch-shimmer sparkled. The witch was having fun. She liked fighting. She wanted to fight, he'd give her a fight. He moved, his feet barely touching the mat as he circled her.

She caught his movement, turning with him, keeping him in front of her.

No way in hell was he going to risk hitting her. Instead he dropped to a crouch, swung a leg out, and caught her in the ankles.

Her feet flew out from under her. She hit the mat on her back and rolled, putting distance between them to recover. Phoenix didn't give her the chance. He leaped, caught her around the waist, and threw her back to the mat. His mistake was slapping his hands onto the ground so he didn't land on her.

Ailish drew up her knees and kicked him off her.

They were both on their feet, circling.

"You're holding back, hunter."

"You're going down, witch." And she was, just as soon as he figured out how to get her down without hurting her. Not that he wanted this to end. He was having too much fun. She was good. Nowhere near as good as him, but good. Strong and sexy. It was a hell of a turn-on.

"I'm sure I will, but I'm going to kick your ass before that happens." She spun around, and he braced for her kick.

Instead, she cracked him in the face with her elbow.

The blow rang in his head. Damn it, she was smart. He'd been looking for the kick, ready to grab her leg and dump her on that delicious satin-covered ass. Okay, maybe he'd been thinking that he'd have her legs spread, and he'd be able to see her—

She kicked him in the solar plexus, driving the air from his lungs.

Phoenix blinked once, then pulled his head out of his ass. Her face was set, but he could see the grin teasing her full mouth. If her golden shimmer were any brighter, she'd be able to flag down airplanes. Proud of herself, was she? "Ever heard of Chuck Norris?"

Her hands dropped a fraction. "Who?"

He aimed carefully and spun into a roundhouse. At the last second, he pulled his kick to keep from really hurting her and caught her in the shoulder. She flew a few feet across the mat.

She landed and he was right there, dropping down on

top of her, pinning her on her back. He locked her wrists in one hand, trapped her legs between his. He could feel her breasts pressing against his chest as she panted. With his free hand, he checked her shoulder where he'd kicked her. "Chuck Norris. The supermortal whose solution to every problem is a roundhouse kick. Now admit defeat, baby, I have you pinned." Her shoulder was fine.

"Admit defeat?" She laughed in his face.

God, she was hot. And shit, her scent was changing. The acrid burn was gone, replaced by the rich, buttery scent of arousal. His dick got hard and heavy, growing against her belly. "You're a bad little witch. Fighting makes you horny."

She started to struggle, warm pink staining her face. "Let go and I'll show you—"

He leaned down, brushing his cheek against hers. "It's sexy as hell," he whispered in her ear. "I've never met a woman like you. So strong, hard-assed, and willing to back it up with action."

She stopped fighting him. He could feel her pulse jump. "I wanted to sing. Even once I was awake, the more the lust beat at me, the more I wanted to sing."

The bird ruffled on his biceps, as if begging her to sing, to free him so he could touch her, be with her. He felt the same way, a deep longing wrapped around his hot desire. Pulling back, he looked at her face. "If you didn't sing, how did you get out of the dream?"

"Dug my fingernails into my thighs."

With her pinned beneath him, he couldn't look at her thighs, but he hadn't smelled her blood or seen any marks earlier. Putting his forehead against hers, he said, "So you came down here trying to work off the pain. Why didn't you just relieve yourself?"

Her body went tight, coiling with frustration. "I can't. I've tried, but . . . I can't."

He knew damn well she wasn't squeamish about touching her own body. "Can't how?"

She closed her eyes. "Come. Somehow the demon keeps me from that."

His biceps started to burn, while a roar raced through his head and enraged his blood. She'd been suffering like this for almost eight fucking years? And he'd kept pushing her, kissing her . . . *then leaving her to suffer more*! He shoved off her, keeping hold of one hand, and pulled her to her feet against his chest. "I'm taking you to my bed, where it's going to be just you and me. You can come as many times as you want, as many times as you need."

She raised her left hand. "The handfast—"

He swore he heard a crackle of flames, similar to the way a lion would roar. "The phoenix will keep the demon out." He turned, tugging her behind him. "Stairs." He led them up, wound through his house.

She stopped in the hallway before his bedroom. "Your soul . . . I'm barely holding on to mine, I can't be responsible for yours."

He turned and swept her up in his arms. "There are other ways to bring us both pleasure," he said as he walked into the room and kicked the door closed. He laid her on his thick comforter and stood between her legs hanging off the edge. Drawing his hand down her belly, he fingered the edge of her panties. "I've been imagining what's beneath these. You're bare there, aren't you? All that soft skin, swollen and wet . . ." He looked down at the black satin stretched over her mound. His heart pounded, his mouth watered. "Your mouth tastes like warm mango, what will you taste like here?" He drew his finger along the material to the heat between her legs.

She arched, a soft sound building in her throat. "Phoenix . . ."

Her raw voice, the wet heat pulsing against his finger, went through him. Right fucking through him. He drew his finger away, then rested his hands on her spread thighs. "Show me, Ailish. Show me what you look like naked." He needed this from her, needed her trust.

Her tank top and panties vanished. So did his clothes, but all he saw was Ailish spread out before him. Her breasts were exactly as he remembered them, small and proud, just like his witch. Her belly rippled with tense muscles. He felt her strong thigh muscles as he spread her legs more.

He wanted her to know what he saw. "You have velvety olive skin and glistening pink folds. You're swelling as I watch. Damn—" He had to swallow, then force his voice out. "Your clit is ripe and ready for me to kiss, and lick and suck." Her scent was filling his nostrils and making his cock so damned hard . . . "Ailish?"

Her hands fisted at her sides. "Hmm."

"I'm going to come just from licking you."

She tilted her head back, her body bowing.

He drew one hand up the inside of her thigh, lightly tracing the lips of her sex. "You're going to come, too, aren't you, baby?"

Her breasts jerked and bounced as she panted. "Yes, do it!"

Her magic was rising; he could feel it swirling everywhere he touched. He had never wanted a woman like this, never needed her pleasure like this. He dropped to his knees, leaned in, and, using his thumbs to part her, drew his tongue along her folds.

Her flavor filled his mouth, and his control shattered. Holding her hips, he lifted her, tonguing her clit, dipping into her, drawing in all of Ailish . . . her body, her magic, and her sheer essence.

She tasted like paradise.

* * *

Ailish's power surged, going wild with Phoenix kneeling between her legs, lapping at her. Sinking her fingers into his hair, she just . . . held on.

Trusted him.

The sensations built, her magic pulsed, her body sang, and she felt tears burn her eyes. So much pleasure. Then he moved, holding her hips in one hand, his finger circling her entrance, rasping gently over the skin. She curled her toes.

He growled, actually growled, against her clit and filled her with one finger. Her body clenched. Then he added a second and thrust in and out until all she felt was his mouth on her and his sensual stroking deep inside of her. The pleasure spiraled higher and higher . . .

A whisper of fear . . . she couldn't . . .

Feathers stroked her arms with such caring reassurance, she arched and cried out as hot pleasure exploded. Seconds later, strong arms dragged her off the bed and put her on his lap, her back to his chest, her legs spread wide.

His cock, so hot and hard, slid along her folds, but not inside her. Phoenix put his mouth to her ear. "Again, Ailish. With me . . ." He canted his hips so the head of his cock slid against her oversensitive clit. He palmed her breasts, tweaked her nipples. "I can feel your hot juices on my cock." He thrust again, rubbing himself deep between her folds.

Her magic began to pulse and rush, going deeper and deeper between her thighs, trying to reach him, to pull him into her body. The need took her breath away. If she couldn't have him all the way inside her, then she could touch him. She reached down and brushed her fingers over the head of his dick.

He groaned, thrusting harder and faster toward her fingers while kissing her ear, her neck, her jaw. He clamped one hand on her hip. "Have to hold you, stop from slamming up inside you." He shuddered. "Your magic is calling me, begging me, trying to draw me into you." He kissed her shoulder. "The drive to seal our souls . . ." He sucked in a breath, his hips pushing his cock against her.

Ailish turned her head and caught his mouth in a deep kiss. All the sensations crested—his cock stroking her folds, his hand on her breasts, their tongues tangled; she was surrounded by Phoenix. Her orgasm started as small shudders and she rocked against his cock frantically.

"Oh hell, yeah!" Phoenix said against her mouth, his hand on her hip anchoring her as they both exploded.

Her pleasure went wild, cries erupting from her throat. Feeling his hot seed spurting onto her thighs sent her into another round of spasms until she could barely breathe. "Too much," she finally whispered. He brought out too much in her, too much pleasure, too much emotion. He exposed her very soul and made her yearn for more and more. Even now, tremors of aftershocks kept erupting.

"I've got you." Phoenix pulled her back to rest against his chest and gently stroked her stomach, as if to ease the muscles there. Her thighs were boneless. A warm contentment she had never felt, never experienced, settled with a gentle mist.

He moved his hand down to the hip he'd grasped earlier. "Did I hurt you?"

"God, no."

He laughed and kissed her shoulder. "I wanted to be inside you so badly, I almost couldn't control it." He sucked in a breath.

Her peace fractured. "This was a bad idea. . . ."

"This was the best fucking idea ever." He turned her head and tilted her chin up. She saw his shadow, but she felt his gaze on her.

"I'm not losing you, Ailish," he told her. "We're going to fight this handfast and break it. I've already talked to

Darcy. She's consulted the Ancestors, and they said there's a price, we just need to figure out what it is and pay the demon. She thinks the answer is in the handfasting ceremony. We'll set up a phone conference tomorrow so she can find out more from you."

Shocked, she said, "They'll talk to me?"

He laced his hand in hers over her belly and answered, "By phone conference."

Sure, she got it. She didn't belong close to those gentle earth witches. But she was actually going to talk to them. She'd tried to learn all she could about being an earth witch, but there was so much she still didn't know. Could she ask them questions? But then she had to wonder. "Why are you going to all this trouble?" Where did he see this going?

He rested his chin on her head. "To give us a chance. And because I can't let you die."

She closed her eyes, trying to get control of her feelings. "Then you need to know the truth. There is no future for us."

His chest, stomach, and thigh muscles tightened beneath her. "Why the hell not?"

"Because if I die from not fulfilling the handfast, my mother and her coven dies with me. If I break the handfast . . ." She felt the cold invade her. And that invoked her memory of the dark nothingness when she'd nearly died. If she wanted to get into Summerland, she had to make the right decisions. "I'm going to kill them. I'll use my power to do it, and witch karma will kill me."

11

Phoenix ignored the bird scratching and burning him. He understood just how the creature felt. He pushed Ailish up to her feet, keeping his hand on her, not daring to let go. When she tried to pull her hand free, he got in her face. "Don't stop touching me. Your little announcement has me wired to kill, and if we let the bloodlust free, I'll lose it."

She put her hand on his chest, hurrying to get it all out. "I should have told you. I came home to die. The only question is will I get into Summerland when I do." She jerked her wrist up. "I need this off to even have a chance. If I do get it off and destroy the coven, then maybe they will accept me. Maybe I'll be good enough."

The damn witch might as well have kneed him in the balls. Her soul was in limbo, with a dark claim on it by Asmodeus. She had a reason to be afraid the Ancestors might not be able to allow her in while she had that binding on, marking her as handfasted to a demon. He grabbed her hand and pulled her with him into the large bathroom. The travertine tile beneath his feet just added to the cold, burning feeling deep in his chest.

He had feared caring about her, seeing it as another long-term burden, like she'd constantly need him to fix her problems, need him to keep her going. He wanted to laugh at himself, except he was too pissed off. Ailish didn't ask anyone to fix her problems, she did it herself.

She actually thought he'd let her go after demon witches? Alone? Unprotected?

Not while he was breathing.

Yeah, that feeling in his chest for Ailish, that warm, terrifying mix of tenderness and pride, scared the ever-lovin' shit out of him. But letting go? Walking away from her?

That felt like razor blades to his heart.

Keeping hold of her, he turned on the water and jets in the tub, grabbed a washcloth, and got it wet. He turned and dragged it across her thighs.

She jumped.

"Wiping off my semen." The semen that should be inside her. His cock jumped and started to fill, more than willing to do the job right this time. "Step in, about knee-high," he told her.

She hesitated, then she raised her leg, got in the tub, and sank into the hot, bubbling water.

Phoenix sat behind her and took hold of her shoulders to pull her back.

She resisted.

"Please, Ailish," he coaxed. Holding her made it all easier. Everything.

She reclined, fitting her back to his chest.

Wrapping his arms around her, he knew he was falling and falling hard. She was the other half of his soul. She'd been his to protect since birth. The enormity of that unfolded in his mind—he and Ailish, they had always been connected. Always needed each other, always found each other. He told her, "I think I was around four when you were born. I kept having this dream that I was flying, heard a baby cry, and then burst into flames." He told her what the nightmare felt like.

She put her hands over his on her waist. "You were only a child! To be pulled out of your body and experience that!" A shiver went through her, then her magic poured through her hand. "Did you tell anyone? You must have been terrified to go to sleep."

She was comforting him! The warm energy swirled and caressed him. The bird tattoos shuffled and seemed to try to pull his wings farther from the flames to catch her magic. "It was just me and my mom." He rubbed his thumb back and forth, stroking her. "She was . . . sick."

"You said you grew up on the streets?"

He hesitated out of sheer habit, but he wanted to tell her. "My mom heard voices from the time I was very young, right before kindergarten, so I must have been around four." He did the math in his head. "She would have been about twenty-six, about right for schizophrenia in women. It tends to show earlier in boys from what I read. Anyway, we ended up on the streets partly because she was running from something the voices told her was after her, but she could never define what it was. And partly because she couldn't hold down a job."

She stroked his hand and arm as though she were petting him. "What about her family or your father?"

Phoenix blamed his father. "Her family knew there was something odd about my father. Then she got pregnant and they disowned her. They refused to have anything to do with her if she kept me. Then my father died before I was born." How could a man do that to a woman? Separate her from her family, then leave her defenseless? "She managed for a few years, but then . . . the voices started."

"You took care of her." Her voice was firm and sure.

The way she kept touching him went straight to his balls. It wasn't sexual, it was warm and sensual and sincere. "She kept me and lost her family, her support. Even on the streets when she could barely figure out how to eat, she kept Social Services from taking me away from her. And later, when I met Key, she kind of adopted him, too." He wanted to get across to her that his mom was more than a crazy street bum. She'd had a huge heart, too.

"Isn't that what mothers are supposed to do? Try to take care of you and protect you?"

Her question made his chest ache. Her mother hadn't loved her, and she'd never experienced what real love felt like. His mother had loved him, and even now, years after her death, that love stayed with him. That's what made it so damned hard, so heart-stabbingly painful, to know he had turned his back on her. "I failed her. When she needed me, I wasn't there. I was eighteen, working a construction job in another town and staying there during the week. I chose to work the long-distance jobs, I wanted my freedom." The guilt nearly choked him. "Then she called, told me the voices were coming to get her." Sick shame and anger burst up inside him, then calmed.

He knew it was her magic easing his guilt and grief. He didn't deserve that, though he craved it, needed it. He meant to explain that he just wanted a break. But the truth was ugly, and it spilled out of him. "I was sick of being her caretaker and never having a life. For the first time, I had my own life, going to bars with friends, getting laid. I figured I'd earned this break from worrying about her. My paycheck got us off the streets and into a small apartment. She was safe. So I told her to lock the doors, she'd be fine." He could still remember his resentment of her desperate call, the sensation that he just couldn't get a break, that she was suffocating him.

Ailish tilted her head back, her sightless eyes drifting heavenward. The bathroom filled with the sounds of the bubbling water, the steam wafting up and curling the ends of her hair. "What happened?"

The banked rage erupted. "Damn it, she should have done what I told her! Listened to me instead of the fucking voices! I loved her, I goddamned loved her." He clamped his jaw so hard, his ears popped. "She knew I wouldn't abandon her, not forever, not like her family. I just wanted a break. Just a break."

"Instead you got a lifetime of guilt," she said softly.

"I got what I deserved." He lifted his free hand to finger the damp ends of her hair. "When I got home she was gone. Took me hours to find her. She had places she hid on the streets when the voices got too bad. She was in one of them, dead. She'd used a beer bottle and cut herself. She finally stopped the voices."

Ailish dropped a hand to the outside of his thigh. "She fought the best she knew how. Just like you fought the best you knew how. The cold truth is that we don't win the fight every time."

Thick emotion gripped him, and he closed his eyes. She wasn't talking just about him, she was talking about her battle, the one for her life and her soul. "Ailish . . ."

She sat forward. "I'm another fight you can't win. You were right—you can't trust me with your soul." She stood up.

Her lean body glistened as the water sluiced down, sliding over her breasts, down her belly, dipping between her legs. He reached for her.

She sensed it and jerked her hand back. "I won't become a demon witch, but I will make sure the coven dies. If I can't get the binding off, then they die with me on my birthday. But I'm going to try like hell to do the right thing, to break the handfast so I have a chance of getting into Summerland when I die. Then I'll use my siren voice and kill them. It'll kill me, too, and if we've bonded souls, that would shatter you. I won't do that. I can't."

She turned to get out. To walk away. Phoenix made her weak, made her long for what she couldn't have. She'd learned her lesson with Kyle . . . she couldn't be influenced by desperate longings and needs, she had to do the right thing. Make the right choice.

He rose and caught her up in his arms before she'd finished stepping out of the tub.

"Put me down!"

"No." Part of him thought about tossing her on the bed, parting her thighs, and pressing so deep inside her, she'd never try to walk away from him again. His cock throbbed with the need. Her coconut magic rose off her skin, trying to entice him to do that. Assuring him that he could seduce her in seconds.

What stopped him was the hideous handfast bracelet on her wrist. Not because he didn't trust her, but because she'd been forced into that bond. He wouldn't force her into the soul-mirror bond.

"We're not done, Ailish. I've only begun learning the best ways to make you come. But if you refuse to let me touch you like that, then you'll sleep with me, in my arms where the phoenix can keep you safe from the demon." She was his. Had been his. He remembered the sweet call of her first cry as a baby that killed him. So he hadn't been there all those years to protect her.

Not until she'd called his phoenix to life.

He was here now. And he was going to fight for her, fight the demon, her mother's coven, and Ailish herself.

Days Remaining on Handfast Contract: Eleven

When Ailish woke up, she knew instantly that Phoenix was gone from the bed. The room felt empty. She must have slept for hours, but she had no idea what time it was. Feeling disoriented and very much alone, she tried to get her bearings. She stretched out on the bed and her hand hit something plastic.

Her cell phone. And next to that were a couple of bags. What the hell? She sat up, pulled the bags to her, and reached in. Clothes, her clothes, she recognized them. The second bag had all kinds of stuff from her hairbrush to her laptop.

Phoenix had gone and gotten her things from her house? She pulled her knees up to her chin and wrapped her arms around them, trying to squeeze out the feeling in her chest. The spot that had always felt empty and alone. Dear Ancestors, now that spot felt as if it were full of gently moving wings.

She'd been alone for so long. She didn't know how to do this, how to deal with it.

Early this morning, after getting out of the bath, he had put her in his bed, then kissed her as though she were something to be treasured. He'd started at her eyes, moved down her mouth, over her jaw, taking his sweet time with her breasts . . .

"Shit." Damn tricky hunter was trying to make her . . . care. She wouldn't care. Not like that, not in the way that would make her lose sight of her goals. She cared that her mother had tried to kill Haley, that she'd used Kyle, then caused him to get in an accident. She cared that she'd dragged Kyle into a handfasting ceremony.

She cared about her soul.

She would not care about Phoenix. When she was gone, he'd be relieved. He'd never wanted to be leashed to her. She was blind and came from demon witches. Talk about a bad deal in a soul mirror. But she needed him to keep Dee and Kyle safe and to get the witches to help her break the handfast.

She took a shower and got dressed, then made her way into the kitchen, zeroing in on the delicious coffee smell. Normally she drank tea, but this coffee smelled so rich and enticing. She heard the sound of a paper turning at the table—newspaper? Was it Phoenix?

"Ailish, you're up," Dee said. "Do you want coffee? Phoenix made it. Some special blend he grinds up."

That's why the aroma was so strong, he ground his own beans. "Uh, I'll get it." She had it fixed in her head where most things were. She found the coffeemaker, and the cups in the cupboard just above. After getting one down, she felt for the handle of the coffeepot and poured herself a cup. "Where's Phoenix?"

"He said there was something he had to deal with and he'll give you a call when they're ready for the phone conference." Dee's voice was close by in the kitchen.

"What are you doing?" She heard dishes, smelled toast.

"Getting you breakfast, and don't fuss at me. Just go sit down."

Ailish sighed and carried her coffee to the long table on the other side of the bar. "You're bossy for an employee."

"Yeah, well, I'm putting in for hazard pay."

And she'd pay it. "You're lucky I don't charge you for my healing services." The chair across the table looked empty. Where was Kyle?

Dee set something in front of her. "Scrambled eggs and toast." Taking the seat at the end of the table, she added, "Thank you for saving my life. Those men just came out of nowhere, then the shock, the pain, my blood everywhere . . . that scared the hell out of me. I felt my life slipping away until your magic pulled me back."

Ailish said, "Don't thank me. It's my fault you were attacked. I'm not going to let it happen again."

Dee reached out and touched her arm. "Eat, Ailish. We're safe enough here. Phoenix seems very . . . capable."

She picked up her toast and took a bite. Toast was easier to manage than scrambled eggs.

"And in case you were wondering," Dee added, "he looks as dangerous as you thought. Very sexy."

Oh damn. She had said that when she'd been in the

car with Dee on the way to Kyle's house. But what really surprised her was the stabbing hot anger in her chest that Dee got to see Phoenix and she didn't. Oh God, she was jealous! Jealous!

Her phone rang. She snatched it up and answered, "Yeah?"

"Morning . . ." Phoenix's voice reached through the phone and shivered inside her chest.

"Ah, sure. Morning. Where are you?"

"At the condos."

"Your condos?"

"Axel owns them, along with the club and the warehouse. It's like a headquarters for us."

"Okay . . ." She felt Dee watching her. Did she look like a woman who woke up alone in a man's bed, confused? Lonely? Hurt. Not hurt, she was not hurt.

"Ailish, I had to leave this morning. Morgan's not doing well. She and Joe are friends of mine. She's seven months pregnant and in danger of losing the baby. Joe is beside himself."

"Joe's a witch hunter? Is Morgan a witch?"

"Mortal, they are both mortal, but the baby is a witch hunter boy. . . ."

She listened as he caught her up. "The earth witches can't help?" A longing to be one of those witches made her chakras ache, but she felt the weight of the handfast binding on her wrist.

She would never be the one to save a woman's baby.

"They've been with her since early this morning. Anyway, they're here with me now. I'm going to put you on speaker."

Her nerves stretched tight. She felt Dee moving around her, picking up her plate and taking it to the sink, then returning to refill her coffee. "Stop that," she snapped. "I don't need you babying me."

"Tough." Dee walked back into the coffeemaker.

She reached out and touched the fresh hot cup of coffee. It felt oddly comforting.

"Ailish, can you hear me?" Phoenix asked.

"Yes."

"Axel and Darcy are here. Axel is the leader of the Wing Slayer Hunters, and Darcy is his mate. Also here are Sutton and his mate, Carla."

She shifted on her seat, holding the phone tightly. "Hello. Darcy and Carla, thank you for helping me heal from the knife wounds." She would never forget what their healing magic felt like.

"This is Darcy, and you're welcome." Her voice was slightly smoky.

"I'm Carla," said a soft, clear voice. "Both Darcy and I have talked to the Ancestors, and they've told us that the handfast binding is always issued for a term with a price to break it."

Ailish fought a wave of shame. While these witches didn't sound judgmental or disgusted, how could they not be? The few witches she'd found turned from her as if she were dog shit. "Okay."

"If you could walk us through the handfast ceremony," Carla went on, "how it happened and what was said, we should be able to find the price."

She had the urge to defend herself, to say, *I was only sixteen! I thought I was in love! And that my mom was helping. . . .* But what good would that do? None. It was done. Instead, she said, "The ceremony was held at the Infernal Grounds."

"Where is that?" asked a male voice. Had to be Axel or Sutton.

"It's like a coven church where they do all their ceremonies and magic. I've only seen it once." She shifted uneasily beneath the memories. "There's an old chapel on the grounds that was the site of a mass murder. So many murders created ley lines." Before she could stop herself, she asked, "Do earth witches use ley lines? I mean, I know demon witches use them to summon Asmodeus from the Underworld. . . ." She clenched her free hand on the table.

"Yes," Carla said gently. "Ley lines are naturally occurring power sources where two forces meet. Like where water meets the earth, so the ocean shores are rich with them. Graveyards, too, from life meeting death. For us, ley lines enhance our earth magic, but it takes high magic and a familiar to control that much power."

She absorbed the information gratefully.

"That place, the Infernal Grounds, sounds like Screaming Chapel, where the massacre happened nearly seventy years ago," Phoenix said. "All kids know about that place. Rumor was that the empty church is haunted by those women. Kids say they hear screams if they get close."

"That's the place," Ailish said. She'd heard the story, too, how the town's new preacher had called a meeting, at which he'd separated the men and women. He had the men meeting outside and the women in the chapel. When he went to talk with the women, he locked the doors and began screaming about witchcraft plaguing the town. He pulled out two guns and started shooting. He killed seventeen women before the men broke down the doors and killed him.

"They did hear screams. That's the wards. They capture the screams of the murdered souls, and it's protected by hellhounds, too. So is my mother's house." She didn't want to think about the hellhounds. "What else do you want to know?"

Carla said, "Can you show us the ceremony? Project your memory onto the screen of the phone?"

She hesitated, not wanting to show these witches exactly how stupid she'd been. How she'd nearly traded away her soul and chakras for . . .

A hand settled on her shoulder.

Dee touching her. She couldn't get used to the way the woman invaded her space. And yet that touch made her feel stronger. "I'll do it."

Opening her chakras, Ailish summoned the memory and then projected it to the phone, just as she'd done when she'd projected it to Kyle's TV. She showed them the Infernal Grounds, standing at the altar together with Kyle, facing her mother with the coven witches behind them. She drank from the Goblet of Choice, then it vanished and . . .

The wine was sweet and tangy, and she began to feel strange, sluggish when she spoke the required words: "I have chosen."

"So be it," the coven said as one.

Maeve, wearing a fitted black robe, held out her hands, and the cord snaked from the altar to stretch out across her upturned palms. "Ailish, do you reject all others before now to accept this binding and all it entails?"

Her chakras cramped as they always did when she was near dark magic. But she was doing this for her and Kyle! It was okay, she thought, feeling a little dizzy. She fought the light-headedness to stand straight and proud in her little black robe. This was an important ceremony that would reveal how she loved Kyle with her whole heart. She turned to look at him, seeing the boy she loved through a kind of haze.

"Say the words, Ailish, so that I can make you mine."

Kyle's voice almost seemed to have an echo or vibration, as though he were as excited as she was. She sighed with a swell of love for him, discounting the warning cringe of her magic. Her powers probably didn't like the wine or the odd, thick feeling in her head. She lifted her left wrist toward her mother and said, "I accept."

"So be it," the coven chorused.

The cord snapped out and curled around her wrist. It

felt heavy and binding. But she was binding her heart and soul to Kyle, so that made sense.

Maeve Donovan turned and said, "Kyle, do you find Ailish Donovan, daughter of the high witch of the Deus'Donovan coven, worthy?"

"Yes."

"So be it," the witches chanted.

The cord looped around Kyle's left wrist. Then her mother lifted a jewel-handled knife.

Ailish was supposed to do something now. What? Oh! She raised her right hand, watching as it moved slowly, and held it out.

Maeve sliced the flesh part of Ailish's palm.

She watched the blood well up in a straight line, noticing that it burned in a kind of disconnected way.

"Lay your hand over the cord on Kyle's wrist and recite the words," her mom said.

She did as she was told, trying to remember the words that came next. "My soul is offered in blood and sealed in the Claiming Rite." She stared as her blood glistened on the cord and the skin of his arm and then vanished completely. A strange, profound sadness weighed down on her.

Maeve lifted the knife, the moonlight flashing off the black blade. "Fed by the blood of a willing witch, the binding is made for a term of eight years." She sliced her finger and said, "The blood pact is absolute, broken only by death. As this witch goes, so do the Deus'Donovan coven." She touched her blood to the rope binding between them.

"So be it."

Thunder rumbled beneath the ground, and smoke exploded from the candles and incense pots.

The rope spawned to life, shifting, moving . . . coiling round and round Ailish's wrist. She gasped as each loop cut deep inside her until she felt a horrible wrenching, as if she were being shredded from her pelvis to her heart.

Clutching her stomach and bending over, she cried, "It hurts!" Her chakras! It felt as though they were dying! "Oh no!" Ailish screamed, stumbling toward her mother and falling to her knees. What had she done?

Maeve didn't even look at her, she simply stared at the others in the coven. "Prepare her."

Ailish lifted her head, panting in fear and pain, then said, "Sulfur. Oh God!"

Kyle leaned down, grabbed her shoulders, and yanked her to her feet. "Shut up." He shoved her back toward the altar.

The dawning horror was worse than her pain. Her mother had betrayed her! She was giving her own daughter to a demon in Kyle's body! Looking at her mother, she demanded, "Why?"

Without a change of expression, Maeve said, "You were bargained from the day of your birth when we discovered you had the voice power. He has given me tremendous power in exchange for you. I am the high witch, and you will submit."

"So be it," the coven said as they surrounded her.

The panic that exploded within her tore something free in her mind. Words she hadn't known sprang up from her very soul:

Breath of life
In my cry

From the flames
Wings shall rise

"Stop her!" Maeve screamed.

It hurt her to open her chakras and feed her powers through her voice. The flow of words coming from her brain stopped. But never had anything been so clear to Ailish as the fact that she wanted desperately to save her

*chakras. She sang out her vital need, pouring all she had
into her voice:*

"Hold the darkness where it stands! Cage or banish
all that threatens the magic born of earth!"

*The ground burst up, the flames of the candles ex-
ploded into massive fires, hurricane winds blew, and tor-
rential rains pounded. Then a horrible stench erupted,
and Kyle crumpled to the ground.*

*Ailish turned and ran, the dark fear and heartsick be-
trayal fueling her flight.*

Breaking the memory video, Ailish said, "That was
the first time I sang that song, 'Breath of Life' . . .
I never knew where that came from."

"It's your Siren's Song," Carla said. "The legend says
only the siren and the phoenix know it. It's somehow
imprinted on both of you."

"But my mother realized what I was doing." She sat
there with the memories heavy on her heart. "And
stopped me." Because her mother had wanted Ailish only
for more power.

12

Phoenix watched Ailish's memory on the big screen in Axel's condo office. She looked so young, her hair hanging down over her shoulders, her lean figure not yet carved from the baby softness. The little black satin robe alone sickened and enraged him.

Her mother had given her daughter to a demon. Offered her daughter's innocent young body, had been going to let the demon kill her chakras and take her soul.

Oh yeah, he was going to kill her mother. He'd never looked forward to murder as much as he did right now.

He stayed silent as the whole scene played out, but he paced the room, hating that he couldn't be with her now. Touch her, somehow make the pain of this old memory bearable for her.

The phoenix on his arms was burning and pecking the shit out of him, trying to get free to save his siren. Just the partial song she'd showed them had caused a visceral reaction in him.

When the image memories finally ended, he whirled around. Axel and Darcy sat behind the massive desk, while Carla and Sutton sat in chairs moved to the side. "How do we break the handfast?" He had to free her from the demon.

Then make her his.

The urgency rode through him, pounding, pulsing, eating him from the inside out.

Carla stood up, her long hair pulled back in a braid,

her gaze troubled. "There are two things. First, Ailish, you denounced the Ancestors when you rejected all others before the binding."

"She didn't know!" Phoenix yelled. "She was sixteen! A baby!"

Carla put her hand on his arm. "Yes, I saw that. I understand that this was a horrible trick played on a young woman in love. But she has some responsibility here, too."

"She didn't know!" Didn't they see that?

"She's right." Ailish's flat voice broke through his building ire. "I knew what my mother was, and I begged her to help." Her voice dropped, as though she were ashamed. "I wanted him to love me, and I knew my mother was a very powerful demon witch. And at the ceremony, I felt the protest in my chakras, but I ignored it. Still, I didn't think . . . I didn't realize she was handfasting me to Asmodeus. That never even occurred to me."

Phoenix's chest seized with the agony in her voice. She made a mistake! And she was being punished harshly.

Carla took her hand from Phoenix and said, "Ailish, we're not judging you, we're trying to help."

"Thank you. What's the second thing?" Ailish asked, her voice tight.

Phoenix hated having to do this over a phone. But he couldn't be near her without touching her. This morning, once he'd let go of her, the bloodlust had seared him, damn near cooking him from the acid in his veins. When he'd taken her things back in the room and caught her warm scent with that edge of coconut power, he'd been frozen with dual urges. He wanted to strip down to his skin, get into that bed, wake her, and, while she was drowsy, slide deep into her body and seal her to him forever.

The other urge made him picture her blood all over his bed and his skin. Soaking in it, feeling the luscious power seeping into his pores . . . He'd gotten the hell out of there.

Carla's voice caught his attention. "The words *The blood pact is absolute, broken only by death. As this witch goes, so do the Deus'Donovan coven.* That's where the coven sealed their fate to yours."

Darcy said, "Damn Asmodeus and his sneaky contracts. He structured the contract so the only way to break the pact is by your death. He literally condemned you to death if you don't become a demon witch by the time the term of eight years is up."

"Yes," Ailish said, "and he made his coven agree in the contract to die with me if I don't become a demon witch, so they are desperate to force me into it as well. Of course, I thought I was handfasting to Kyle. My mother said it was done that way all the time, and I believed her."

Then her mother had betrayed her. Phoenix couldn't help but compare their mothers, and his mother came off like Betty fucking Crocker. That thought almost made him smile. She'd have laughed at that. Even when they'd had a place to live, she couldn't cook. Never could. But he needed to stay on point. Looking at Carla, he said, "How do we break the handfast without killing Ailish?"

She stood in the middle of the room, her gaze fixed on the blank big screen. "We have to outsmart the demon. This contract with the death clause, it's tight, but I think there's a loophole."

Hope eased his chest. "What?"

"Maeve. She performed the ceremony, added her blood to the binding on Ailish's arm to seal the coven's fate to Ailish's. Her blood and Ailish's blood are on that binding." Carla turned and faced him, her eyes full of green, brown, and yellow. "The death to break the contract, I think it can be Ailish or Maeve."

It was so simple! "Like when Axel killed the demon witch that cursed his sister, it freed Hannah of the death curse."

Axel frowned. "Unless it kills Ailish, too. If her mother dies when she does, why wouldn't she die when they do?"

Darcy answered, "Because the coven sealed their fate to Ailish: *As this witch goes, so do the Deus'Donovan coven*. But they didn't seal Ailish's fate to them. Yes, I think it'd work."

The relief was intense.

Axel added, "We need to go after them anyway. It'd be best to catch them at their Infernal Grounds where they all gather." He turned and looked at Phoenix. "But only the mated hunters."

He opened his mouth, but Ailish jumped in.

"You won't get through their wards. They are deep and horrible."

Sutton said, "How do we break them? Can earth witches do it? Or can you do it?"

Phoenix snarled, "Hell, no. She's not going near that place."

"Yeah, I am. This is my battle, my soul. I have to make this right. You heard Carla. It's not just the price to break the handfast, but I have to make reparation to the Ancestors for renouncing them. I can't do that by hiding while you do all the work, take all the risks."

Silence fell except for the static of the phone connection, the ticking of a clock, and the sounds of breathing. His heart twisted in his chest. Everything inside him screamed out in agony. Finally, he said, "Is it true?"

"Yes," both Darcy and Carla answered.

Then Carla said, "Being an earth witch is a tremendous gift. We reincarnate over and over to learn and gain more power. But with that gift, that power, comes responsibility. There are consequences when we make poor choices."

Ailish added, "I nearly let Asmodeus get hold of my siren magic. Why should the Ancestors trust me when I die, and allow me to go to Summerland and reincarnate with that same power?"

He got that there were consequences, but, "That doesn't mean you have to die." He knew that's what she was thinking, she'd told him that last night. The bird started panicking, fighting to get out. It was stretching his skin until it felt as though his biceps were going to rupture like an overripe watermelon. But he fought for logic, to make her, all of them, understand. "We'll kill your mother and that will break the handfast. Then you'll have the rest of your life to show the Ancestors that you are worthy."

He heard her breathing through the phone. "I—"

Joe burst into the room. "Darcy! Morgan's having contractions!"

Phoenix set a sandwich in front of Joe. "Eat it." The condo was a mess from people traipsing in and out. Cups set down randomly, herbs and candles all over the small kitchen table, jackets and sweatshirts tossed, a blanket on the couch from when Morgan had rested there.

Joe ate. The man had been in Special Forces, he knew the value of keeping up his strength. Phoenix watched him methodically work through the ham and cheese and doubted he tasted a bite. His eyes kept darting toward the bedroom.

"I'll go check." Phoenix shoved off the counter he was leaning against and went into the room. The king-size bed dominated the room. Morgan lay on her left side, a pillow between her legs, eyes closed. The room was sweet with candle wax, herbs, and heavy magic. Darcy's hair was stuck to her neck, her brown gaze furious. She sat on the bed, her hand on Morgan's belly. "Carla, I can't hold the baby!"

Carla sat on the other side of Morgan, holding her hand. "Okay, we're back," she said, her voice soothing.

On the bed next to Carla was a laptop. Carla's mom, Chandra, was on-screen. "We need more witches."

Phoenix said, "It didn't work?"

"Is the baby okay?" Morgan said.

"He's fine," Darcy said gently. "He just didn't want you pulling your spirit from his. He loves you. You're his world."

Carla picked up the laptop and scooted off the bed. "Morgan, try to sleep. Let your baby feel you there with him." She walked out of the room to where Joe was just finishing his last bite.

He stood up. "Carla?"

"They're okay, but it's not working. The baby panics when I try to draw Morgan's spirit away from her body. I can't help her until I get her in the astral plane. I need her there, in her doppelgänger body where she won't feel stress and fear." She sank into a chair. "That bastard buried a suggestion in her brain. I never saw it when we worked together, never realized . . ."

Phoenix put his hand on her shoulder. "You couldn't have known."

She looked up. "But it's there. Because Eric wanted that baby if it was a boy, I am almost a hundred percent positive he buried a command to find him when she hit about seven months in her pregnancy. That way he'd have control of her."

Phoenix went into the kitchen, poured the water simmering on the stove over a teabag in a mug, and returned to set it in front of her. "But she's not trying to find him, she's acting like he's trying to find her."

Carla nodded. "That's because Morgan's own brain is

fighting the suggestion. She knows Eric is a danger, so she's trying to protect her baby from him. In essence, she's fighting her own brain. That woman is tough."

Phoenix saw why Carla was so good at helping to treat brainwashing in mortals. She had a deep empathy that allowed her to understand people and their actions and reactions.

Joe said, "Carla, if she loses this baby, it'll break her."

And it'll destroy Joe, Phoenix thought. He loved Morgan. They all knew that Morgan's pregnancy gave her the will to fight back against Eric and the brain damage he'd inflicted on her.

"Phoenix, we just don't have enough power to hold this baby while I take Morgan to the astral plane. I was thinking . . . Ailish could use her power to enhance Darcy's magic and help hold the baby. Make him feel safe."

Joe jerked his head up. "Will she do it?"

Phoenix wasn't sure. "How dangerous will it be? She'll be enhancing all magic, not just your magic. Young knows about her ability to enhance magic. He might harness it if he can."

Her hazel eyes filled with yellow. "They've been getting more earth witches lately. Too many are dying, slaughtered. . . ." Carla looked at Joe, then at Phoenix, and her shoulders drooped. "It may be our only hope for this baby. We're only going to be able to stop the contractions for a while. Morgan's just under too much stress trying to fight this suggestion." She dunked her teabag, her forehead crinkling in thought. "You're her familiar, and you've exchanged blood. If you're nearby, that might help her keep the power more focused."

He wasn't sure. "How does that work? The siren-phoenix thing, I mean."

She walked into the kitchen and dumped her teabag in the trash while answering. "The siren witch only enhances all magic while calling for her familiar to rise from the flames. Once he has risen, and she performs the ceremony of impressing her familiar on a silver item to keep close to her body, the siren gains full control of her power. With her phoenix's help, she then enhances only the magic she is directly involved with . . . like if several witches were casting a spell together and the siren was there, she would enhance only that spell magic." Carla sank into a chair.

"If I made love to Ailish and sealed our bond, it would do the same thing, right? Make my bird her familiar and give her full control over her siren magic?" He forgot Joe was sitting there, but he wasn't doing the macho kiss-and-tell shit, he was trying to understand.

"Yes. But I'm not asking you to finish your bond and risk your soul. Just to use the connection you already have to help focus and contain her power." She warmed her hands around her mug. "This child, he deserves a chance. If a child isn't worth the risk of Ailish using her siren magic for just a few minutes, then who is?"

Carla's compassion made the answer clear. He started to reach for his phone, saying, "I'll call her and—" The alarm on his phone sounded. He yanked it out, thumbed to the screens showing the outside of his house, and saw Kyle Whaling walking from the door to a cab.

He speed-dialed Ailish.

Ailish worked with Dee, creating maps of the Infernal Grounds, where she thought the wards were, trying to remember as much as she could. She listed all the names of the demon witches she knew, with her mother, Maeve Donovan, at the top. Dee was her eyes, telling her what the map looked like, making changes Ailish told her, writing in notations . . . It was different working with someone like this. They were also working with Sutton, sending him all the info she had, and he was doing his own version of magic with the computer. He had Google maps of the Infernal Grounds. Her mother had moved since Ailish left, but Sutton was fairly sure he'd found her residence.

Finding the other witches was proving to be nearly impossible; Ailish knew only their first names.

Darcy and Carla were checking in when they could, but they were busy trying to help Morgan.

"Ailish."

She jumped at Kyle's voice. "Yeah?" She looked up and saw his shadow. It was shorter and thinner than Phoenix's.

"I'm leaving. A cab is out front to take me to the airport. I just can't stay here."

Ailish stood up and began walking toward his voice. "Kyle, it's too dangerous." She put her hand on his arm.

He jerked back. "Don't!"

She dropped her hand.

"You aren't who I thought you were. You dragged me into some freak show. Look—" He sucked in a breath. "I know you didn't mean to, I know you're like a good witch, or whatever. But this isn't my world. Not my reality."

"At least let me call Phoenix and—"

"I'm leaving." He turned and walked away. Then he paused. "For what it's worth, I should never have treated you like that in high school. Sleeping with you, then ignoring you. I regret that." Then he opened the door and set off the piercing alarm.

Ailish's phone rang before she could get to the door. She put it to her ear, and Phoenix yelled, "What the fuck is Kyle doing?"

She stood in the opened doorway. "He's going to the airport. I have to stop him, the coven—"

"Screw him. Get back in that house and close the damned door!"

She was really getting tired of his orders. "I won't let them hurt or kill him!"

"Ailish, please." The plea sounded real, and thankfully, the screaming alarm shut off. He added, "I'll send someone to make sure he gets to the airport, but I'm more worried about you and about Morgan."

"Morgan?" His friend. "Is she worse?"

"Go back inside and close the door. Once I rearm the system, I'll tell you about it. Trust me, I'll make sure Kyle's okay."

She turned and went in, shutting the door behind her. The reality was that Kyle wanted to get away from her. "I'm in. Can't the witches stop the contractions for Morgan?"

Ailish walked back into the kitchen as she listened to Phoenix explain. "Would you be willing to use your voice to help Darcy hold the baby while Carla takes Morgan to the astral plane?"

Her chakras swelled and pulsed with the desire. She'd be doing real earth witch magic, healing and helping a mortal and her baby. But would she be doing harm? "I don't have control over the power. What if I do harm?"

"The baby isn't going to make it, Ailish. We have to try."

Feeling a part of something special, she said, "I'll do it."

"We'll bring her tonight. Darcy and Carla want to force her to rest for a few hours before trying it again."

Phoenix moved quietly through the dark backyard of the ranch house set on well over an acre of land. Maeve Donovan's house was next door. Sutton approached from where the house backed up to woods. Axel flew overhead, circling, checking things out.

They needed to find and kill all the demon witches in the coven, but they wanted to start with the most powerful of them and cut off their leadership. They hoped to find the names and locations of the rest inside.

Axel had ordered him to stand down and stay at the warehouse.

Phoenix had said absolutely, just as long as he stood down next time Darcy was threatened.

Sutton had pulled them apart.

A low growl yanked him back from his thoughts. The backyard had a pool, swing set, trampoline, and . . . a huge German shepherd standing tall, his fur ruffling as he recognized the threat of an intruder in his territory. Though the dog was twenty feet away, unable to see Phoenix as he was shielding, he could scent him. Phoenix materialized and stared at the dog in concentration. He couldn't memory-shift an animal, but he reached through the optic nerve and disrupted his instincts.

The dog whined and sat down, confused.

Shielding again, he turned and ran silently. The dog would recover unharmed. He made it to the six-foot block wall, put his hand on it, leaped over, and slammed into a spiked shield. He fell straight to his ass. Blood welled up on his forehead and arm where he'd hit some kind of magical shield.

The dog whined again, still not recovered, but he knew something wasn't right. Phoenix got up and ran down the side of the house to the front, caught the edge of the fence, and hoped like hell a shield wasn't there.

He sailed over, landed in a crouch, and ran to the street. Keeping his shield around him, he said into his headpiece, "Hit a shield of some kind."

"Me, too," Sutton said.

"There's a force field shooting off electrical bolts at twelve feet." Axel's voice settled next to him.

Phoenix felt the movement of his wings but didn't see him. "Thought it was spikes." He wiped blood out of his eye, hoping his invisibility shield held. "We're supposed to be immune to most demon magic."

Axel nearly growled, "But not all. She's creating real force fields, we're not immune to that. We've always needed witches to bring down wards."

Sutton's voice moved up to them. "She probably can't shield the front with that force field. She wants to blend in, not be noticed."

Phoenix looked at the dingy white house with the posts and front rail covered in vines. The side of the house along the walkway had a trellis covered in more of that vine. Weepy trees covered the yard. "I'll go up and see if I can get to the door."

He headed up the driveway, stepped on the sidewalk, and immediately dread filled his chest. He took another step. The dread radiated down his arms. Another step and it spread so thickly that it was a struggle to move air in his lungs.

Another step, and his head began to ring.

He focused on the plain brown door, forcing another step, and sweat broke out on his lip, armpits, and back. Five more steps.

The ringing bellowed in his head.

Then images of blood, death . . . his dead mother.

He heard weird clicks and pops and shuttling from inside the house. Low growls of something . . . horrible.

Saw his mother dead.

The ringing in his head exploded.

His knees buckled, but he caught himself.

"Phoenix"—Axel's voice knifed through it all—"get your ass over here!"

He turned and hurried away, then caught a light pole, bent over, and vomited. He shuddered.

Quietly, Axel said, "Your shield dropped by the third step. If she's in there, she saw you."

Wiping his mouth, he said, "There has to be a way in. A way to get that bitch." Although Maeve had moved, Phoenix realized that Ailish had lived in a house like this until she was sixteen. That enraged him.

"I'll try." Sutton walked up the neighbor's side, then tried to cross over to the window to at least see in. Six feet from the window, his shield dropped. They could see the sweat coating his body. Three feet away, his legs buckled.

Axel flew over, trying to lower himself to the front door or window. He puked while still flying.

After another futile and utterly miserable hour, Axel said, "We need the witches to figure out how to break the wards."

Phoenix opened his mouth to argue . . .

Axel roared at him, "Either walk to the SUV or swear to Wing Slayer, I'll tranquilize you and shove your ass in there."

Phoenix fumed but told himself this wasn't failure. He'd find a way to kill Maeve Donovan and free Ailish.

After showering and eating, Sutton and Axel stood with their arms crossed, their faces set, as Darcy, Carla, and Joe helped Morgan. She'd had another bout of contractions, but they'd stopped them. They'd debated back and forth about the wisdom of taking her to Phoenix's house and attempting to heal her.

Morgan put an end to it. She insisted on going.

It was late, close to three A.M. It'd been a long night. Key, Linc, and Ram had been out hunting. They'd made kills but were still no closer to finding Young or where the Rogue Cadre's headquarters were in Glassbreakers.

Using his BlackBerry, he called Ailish to wake her up and let her know they were coming. But she sounded awake when she answered. "Didn't you go to sleep?" He liked the idea of her sleeping in his bed.

"No. Watching TV."

He heard the sounds of a movie playing in the background. She couldn't see it, so how did she watch it? It hurt his chest to think of her sitting there . . . what? Imagining what was happening? "What are you watching?"

"Chuck Norris. He doesn't talk much, does he?"

He closed his eyes and rubbed a spot between his ribs. He'd told her about Chuck Norris when they were sparring in his gym. But she'd never be able to see what he'd been talking about. And yet she was trying. Like she was trying to get to know him. He said roughly, "Norris's movies are mostly action. Why didn't you get some sleep?"

"I slept late after you left and I didn't want to get trapped in a dream. Plus . . ."

"What?"

"The urge to sing for you, it's getting stronger."

A longing built in both his biceps and that spot between his ribs. He wanted her to sing, to call him to her. "We're leaving now. Be there soon."

"Wait, do you know if Kyle made it to Arizona okay?"

Shit, he'd forgotten to tell her. "Yes, he got on the plane with no problems. Sutton checked, and his plane landed fine."

"That's good. Thanks. See you when you get here."

He stowed his phone, trying to banish the thought of Ailish sitting alone attempting to watch a movie she couldn't see. "Let's roll."

Ten minutes later, Phoenix took the lead on his motorcycle. Axel and Darcy were in the SUV with Joe and Morgan. And Sutton brought up the rear with Carla in his truck.

It was just after three o'clock in the morning and few people were out on the roads, yet as they pulled out of the garage, the skin on his neck and arms itched. He looked around and saw a motorcycle race out of an alley. "Shit, may have had a spy. I'm going after him!" he said in the headset while riding.

"Stand down, Phoenix," Axel commanded. "I'm calling it in to Ram, we need you on protection. If that was a spy, he'll call for backup. Let's move fast."

Shit. He could have gotten Ailish here faster, safer, except that the unbonded hunters would have been driven crazy by her witch blood. But Axel, Sutton, Darcy, and Carla were immortal, strong . . . He thought about it all as he wound through the industrial buildings. He scanned the roads as he passed by a gas station and an all-night convenience store. "Clear so far," he said into his headset.

"Clear in back," Sutton answered.

"Keep moving," Axel said.

They traveled farther inland. Phoenix had had enough of living around the beach as a homeless kid. He turned onto a long road that ran between the houses of the planned community he lived above and a school, park, and soccer field. This road was usually barren at this time of morning, so he gunned the bike up to sixty miles an hour. They had just passed the school when he saw a black Hummer skid out from the soccer field over the curb and onto the road, blocking them.

"Trouble!" Phoenix said. "Hummer ahead, blocking road."

"Hummer coming up behind," Sutton snarled.

"Setup," Axel said. "Get Morgan on the floor. Joe, ready to fire."

Phoenix could get his bike around the Hummer, but the SUV and truck couldn't. He wouldn't leave them. Six rogues poured out of the Hummer, taking aim with guns. The SUV and truck were bulletproof. Phoenix wasn't, so he swerved the bike into a 180 while bullets whizzed past his head and grazed his arms. "Shit!" He had one choice. "Jumping, Sutton. Hold steady." He passed the SUV and saw the Hummer picking up speed to ram the truck. Bastards. He slowed the bike. Bracing his feet, he stood, crouched, then jumped off the bike and into the bed of the truck. He hit the bottom at the same time he heard his beloved Yamaha R6 crash into the Hummer.

He had a second one at home in his garage, but damn, he was pissed. He popped up over the tailgate and fired into the faces of the driver and the passenger as they ran over his bike. The crunching metal rang in his head.

Axel, Sutton, and Joe stormed out of the vehicles, slamming doors to keep the women inside. Axel snapped his wings out, taking to the air and heading into a dive bomb toward the rogues up front. Sutton picked off rogues trying to get to the SUV. Phoenix slithered over the side of the truck and onto the street. He ran to the Hummer behind him. The two men in the front were dead, but more poured out the back. He fought doubly hard, pissed to the core that they'd been set up by the spy on the bike, teed off that he'd had to sacrifice his R6. In one fluid movement, he whipped his chain off his belt and snapped it around the neck of one rogue while killing another with his knife.

Joe came around the other side, firing two guns.

After twisting his knife in the heart of the rogue on his left, Phoenix got his knife out and then yanked the other one on the end of his chain right into his blade. He jerked out his knife and threw the dead man off his chain, then whipped around to see that Joe had killed one and was struggling with another.

The rogue stabbed Joe in the side. "Fuck!" Phoenix leaped up on the hood and over, jumping onto the copper-smelling bastard and slamming his face into the ground. Shoving his knee into the rogue's back, he grabbed the man's head and twisted until he'd severed the spine.

Joe was leaning against the front of the Hummer, guns up, eyes sharp, and blood pouring from his side. Phoenix grabbed his arm and jerked him to Sutton's truck.

Carla shoved open the door.

He threw Joe in and slammed the door, confident that Carla would heal him. He drew in a sharp breath when he felt the change in the atmosphere. As if lightning had infused electricity into the air. He could smell sulfur and burnt skin.

Quinn Young. His skin went cold and his heart hammered. He stepped back from the truck, fiery adrenaline washing through him. Phoenix looked around, trying to find Young. He spotted him coming from behind the Hummer. He must have been in the back of the vehicle. Young stood four inches over six feet, wore dark slacks, a collared short-sleeved pullover, and a shiny black dagger burned into his right forearm. The thing writhed and pulled on his skin as if it were dancing in excitement.

The sight of that hideous Immortal Death Dagger snapped Phoenix into action. He wrenched open the door to the truck, reached in, and grabbed Carla's arm. She was bent over Joe, but he yanked her out of the truck. "In the SUV," he told her urgently. Then he pulled Joe out and heaved him over his shoulder. He was moving at hyperspeed. He passed Carla running and grabbed her up with his free arm. They'd all be safer in one vehicle.

He glanced up ahead. Sutton was running toward them, his gaze fixed on Carla.

Axel was in the air after chasing down a couple of runners.

Phoenix took all this in while racing flat out toward the SUV.

Darcy threw open the back door. Phoenix shoved Joe in, then pushed Carla in after him. Sutton was only twenty feet away. He'd make it, they'd get away! He had just reached for the driver's door when something blew past him so fast that it scorched across his back.

The smell of sulfur and burnt skin filled his lungs. He whipped his head to the left and saw the Immortal Death Dagger slam into Sutton's chest.

Everything snapped into slow motion. Phoenix heard more screams. Sutton ran two additional steps, then toppled over like a tree.

Axel swooped down from the sky. "Get him and get out of here!" His bellow of fury was so violent, the air shook as he flew by.

Phoenix had begun to gallop toward Sutton when the hunter was suddenly flipped over onto his back, as if unseen hands had picked him up and turned him. The slimy, shuddering black dagger pulled out of his chest with a pop and hovered over him. The wound spurted blood, and Sutton lay still.

Phoenix reached him, his eye on the dagger.

It jerked toward him.

Axel dived down, and the dagger shot up after the hawk.

Phoenix scooped up Sutton, ran to the SUV, and climbed in the back. Darcy sat in the driver's seat. She peeled out before Phoenix had Sutton's legs in. The SUV bounced up over the curb and onto the schoolyard.

"Axel said go!" Darcy said.

Carla was grabbing Sutton off his lap. She had to be using magic to move him. "Knife!" she screamed.

Phoenix handed her his knife. He glanced out the window. Axel was in the sky, darting one way and then the other to avoid the Death Dagger. He'd drawn it away to keep it from killing Phoenix.

Quinn Young stood and watched, his arm held out and somehow controlling the dagger's movements in an effort to kill Axel. The only antidote for a cut to the heart from the Immortal Death Dagger was the blood of a soul mirror.

Young moved his arm, and Phoenix caught a glimpse of a black mark or tattoo over the biceps. A chill ran down his spine, then the mark vanished beneath the sleeve. Blinking, he said, "I should do something. If that dagger gets Axel—"

"It won't!" Darcy bounced in the seat. She drove up over the field, over bodies of dead rogues, around the Hummer, and then floored it the rest of the way up the road.

Carla was chanting. She sliced the knife across her palm and shoved it into the bleeding wound of Sutton. Her mate. She said, "Wing Slayer, I give him blood, please give him life. Ancestors, I beg you, please help him!" Tears ran down her face. Her magic filled the SUV.

Joe and Morgan were up front. All was silent but for Carla's chanting, breathing, and the sound of the road.

Phoenix offered his own silent prayers to Wing Slayer. For Sutton and Axel.

"Carly . . ." Sutton moved, his fingers closing around Carla's wrist where her hand was pressed to his chest. "I won't leave you, baby." He reached up and pulled her down to him, his arms folding around her. "I'm okay. Just let me catch my breath," he said.

Phoenix turned away, relieved and yet feeling like an intruder. "Darcy, how's Axel?" He knew they could communicate through the soul-mirror bond.

"Quinn Young has called back his knife and is leaving." She turned onto the lonely road that led up to his house. "Axel's going to circle around, make sure there's no more trouble, then he'll meet us at your house."

"Joe?" Phoenix asked.

He had Morgan in the seat with him. He turned and looked over at Phoenix. "Carla stopped the bleeding before you yanked her out like a sack of potatoes."

"Thanks," Phoenix said dryly, sure that Sutton was going to kick his ass now. Sutton shifted Carla, sitting up without letting go of her. Phoenix explained to the big man, "I was rough with her, but—"

Sutton's blue eyes met his. "I saw you saving her, keeping her out of Young's clutches. Saw you pick her up as you ran. Thank you."

Embarrassed, he shrugged as Darcy pulled up the circular driveway as close to the house as possible. Axel landed and they moved quickly inside the house. Once Phoenix had rearmed the system, he turned to Morgan. "How you doing, Blondie?"

The strain around her eyes and mouth were evident, and she had her arms wrapped around her belly. "I kept telling myself it wasn't Eric. That he's dead and my baby is safe." She blinked once and added, "That bastard isn't going to win. I won't let him make me crazy or hurt my baby."

Joe pulled her closer into his side, his eyes hot with anger. "Damn right."

Phoenix said, "Why don't you two go downstairs. We'll do this in the gym area." That should give the witches enough space to work, and they wouldn't wake up Dee in the guest room.

Joe took Morgan to get her settled. Darcy and Carla followed.

Axel had his phone out, on speaker. "Ram, anything?"

"Lost the trail of the rogue on the motorcycle. I'm on my way to the site of the attack, but they will be gone." The man's voice was tight.

Phoenix said, "He obviously called in to the Rogue Cadre that we were on the move."

Sutton rubbed his chest where the dagger had stabbed him. "They are organized, more organized than ever to move that fast. Looks like Young has taken up residence here."

Ram added, "It'll be a well-protected hideout. I'm hoping to get a lead, some trail to follow from the attack site."

"Careful," Axel said. "Young got Sutton with the Immortal Death Dagger."

"Either he's a dead man talking, or Carla got to him in time," Ram said.

The memory of seeing that dagger hit Sutton gave him heartburn. If Carla hadn't been there . . . He didn't even want to go there. They had to find a way to get past that dagger and kill Young by stabbing him in the heart, then send the dagger back to the Underworld.

13

Ailish hung back by the small fridge on the door side of the gym, just standing there, feeling out of place.

"You okay?" Phoenix came downstairs with Axel and Sutton.

"Yes." The other two witches fascinated her. She could feel them in the room, feel their chakras, their magic. From their conversation, she knew they had Morgan on the mat with pillows. Now they were checking on the baby, talking between themselves. "What do they look like?" she asked Phoenix.

"Who?"

"The witches." She felt like a little girl back when her mom and the coven met and talked. They always made her go in the other room. She'd sneak and try to watch, but she hadn't been able to hear what they were saying.

"Darcy is a little taller than you, an inch or so. She has auburn hair, brown eyes, and a silvery witch-shimmer. She's pretty and curvy, and she wears a necklace of silver hawk wings—that's her witch book."

She'd thought about this. "Silver conducts magic, so I guess that's where she stores all her magic?"

"Passed down from her mother," Phoenix answered, and went on with, "Carla's witch book is a pair of eagle wings in a band around her biceps. She's just a little shorter than you, very smart, she has a PhD in psychology. Hazel eyes, long white blond hair, and clumsy as hell outside. Which is always amusing since Sutton is a huge outdoorsman."

She nodded and kept her mouth shut so she didn't ask any more stupid questions. What did it matter what they looked like? Or if they had witch books passed down in their families? They were powerful earth witches, while Ailish was barely holding on to her soul. She shifted, her chakras bubbling with Phoenix so close by. Or maybe it was the witches.

"They are coming over here."

Phoenix's voice caught her attention. She took a breath.

"Ailish," Darcy said, "are you ready?"

She hoped she had her game face on. "You want me to touch Morgan and sing while you two do the actual work."

Carla said, "Actually, from the research I've done, the baby should respond to your siren voice, possibly be enthralled by it, and it will keep him calm. So you'll be doing that and enhancing our magic. Between you and Darcy, the baby should feel safe and secure so he doesn't try to leave the womb and find his mother. And it'll help me work with Morgan on the astral plane. But it also gives Asmodeus access to Morgan."

That worried her. "I'll be enhancing dark magic, too. It could give Asmodeus a boost to harm Morgan or anything else he's doing with his rogues and demon witches."

Phoenix stiffened next to her. "Young. He's up to something and obviously close by since he attacked tonight."

Alarm raced through her, and she snapped her head to her left. "When?"

"On the way over. Everyone's okay now." Phoenix shifted, and she saw the shadowy movement of him dragging his hand through his hair. "But we believe he's been taking advantage of your siren voice. He has his rogues killing more and more witches for the spiked power in their blood after you sing."

"Then why are we doing this?" Frustration hardened her voice. "My power is too dangerous."

Carla said, "Because otherwise the baby will be born too early and he'll die. If we don't use our power to save innocents like a baby, we have no business being witches."

That struck Ailish bone-deep. It was exactly what she wanted to do—be an earth witch.

"We're going to be as careful as we can," Darcy added. "We can't set a circle due to the handfast on you, it would push you out. So we're going to need to work fast and limit the damage of your siren voice enhancing other magic. If the demon does try something, Axel and Sutton will be able to keep him away from us, but you'll be vulnerable."

Ailish waved that away. "I'm used to the things he does, the pain or torment, it won't close my chakras. Plus from what you're saying, he's not going to want to stop me. He wants me to use the power."

"I'll be here," Phoenix said. "The blood exchange has given me the ability to block the demon from her dreams. It should be the same here." He touched her shoulder and leaned closer. "I won't let him hurt you."

She felt the determination coming from him. She saw the burden of trying to protect her and keep her from harm now that he had told her about his mom, his guilt about failing her because he made one choice. One decision to ignore her call. He hadn't ever wanted to be dragged back into a relationship where so much burden fell on him. Aside from Ailish's handfast, there was her blindness, which Phoenix had to see as a weakness. Yet he wouldn't walk away, couldn't. That experience had hardwired Phoenix to be the hero. Gently, she said, "I don't need a babysitter. I've trained for pain, and I don't break." She wouldn't crack under the strain like his mother and take the easy way out. Nor did she expect Phoenix to rescue her every time she got into trouble. She'd spent years learning to take care of herself.

His hand slid from her shoulder to her nape. "I didn't mean—"

Carla broke in, "Ailish, since you've begun the soul-mirror bond, and Phoenix's bird is your familiar, we think he might help focus your power. You won't have complete control like you would if you had finished the soul-mirror bond, but it should help limit the excess power going out into the atmosphere and enhancing other magic."

She listened, thrilled by the possibility of being able to fully control her power. Then reality took hold with the insistent urge rushing up her diaphragm. She shook her head. The intimacy of his hand, that single solid touch, nearly weakened her. But she couldn't risk it. "I have to do this alone. If you touch me, like you're touching me now, and I sing . . . I'll call you. I'll find a way to . . ." She clamped her mouth shut, the need tickling her throat.

"Phoenix," Carla said, "why don't we compromise. You stay across the room, but you'll be able to reach her if something happens. You should be close enough to try to help her control her voice power."

His hand flexed with tension on her neck. She turned her head up, wishing she could see his face. "Please. Do it this way. It's going to be hard enough when you hear me sing. And hard enough for me not to sing the Siren's Song to call your phoenix." If she did, they'd both lose control and seal their souls. She knew it.

He lowered his face to her, brushed his mouth over hers, and said, "We're getting this handfast off and then you're mine." Then he let her go.

Damn it, the words wanted to burst free from her throat. But she couldn't bind with him, couldn't risk his soul. While she was determined not to become a demon witch, she couldn't be sure the coven and Asmodeus wouldn't find a way to force her. If they were bonded, Phoenix would lose his soul, too. She couldn't risk it. Wouldn't. She had to make the right decisions.

If she was bonded to Phoenix and died, it would destroy him. He'd believe he'd failed again.

She walked between Carla and Darcy. Carla said, "Right here is good, Ailish. Morgan is on her side, supported by pillows, and facing you. She's as comfortable as we can make her. I'm going to stay on this side, and Darcy will go to Axel on the other side. Joe will wait by Phoenix across the room."

She nodded, heard Joe lean down and say something to Morgan, then move off. Ailish dropped to her knees. She had on her usual jeans and shirt, and her feet were bare. She could feel the woman in front of her. "Hi, Morgan."

"Thank you for doing this, Ailish." A hand wrapped around hers.

She was startled by the warm touch. "You're welcome. I just hope it works." Without causing more trouble by enhancing dark magic or inciting rogues to kill more earth witches for the increased power in their blood.

Morgan tugged on Ailish's hand and laid it flat over her hard, rounded belly. "He's kicking. Feel him? Feel how much he wants to live? We've fought so hard, this baby and me."

Ailish felt the bumps and ripples in the woman's stomach. Her breath caught in her throat, and her heart skipped a beat. There was a child in there, a vigorous little life. What did he look like? She could clearly feel Morgan's deep love, the love of a mother willing to do anything to give her child a chance. It felt thick, protective, and determined. In that moment, she knew she was experiencing real maternal love.

"I need to be strong and sane to help this baby grow into a Wing Slayer Hunter, not a rogue. We need you to succeed."

The baby kicked right into Ailish's hand, as if adding his plea. This mother loved her baby and was willing to fight to save him, and she believed that her love would keep him from turning into the rogue his father had been. Ailish felt an alliance with Morgan and her baby. This mother would never trick her child into a handfast with a demon. . . .

She shook that off. "I'll do everything I can to help."

"I know. I have faith in you, Darcy, and Carla."

Ailish thought she had a nice voice, like that of a television journalist. She kept her hand on Morgan's stomach. "Ready."

Darcy placed her hand next to Ailish's, then Carla said, "Morgan, I'm going to help you to sleep with my magic. You'll feel the warmth spreading through you, relaxing your muscles. Just let yourself go. . . ."

Ailish felt Carla's magic bloom around them, pure and white, like the warmth of the sun.

"Okay," Carla said, "she's in a relaxed hypnotic state. Darcy, how's the baby?"

"He's fine. Heartbeat is steady, no signs of stress."

"Good. Ailish, if you'll sing."

Ailish began opening her chakras. They popped open and her powers began swirling, rising so fast that it took her breath away. The power raced up her spine and then back down. She was astonished but soon realized her powers sensed Phoenix and churned in frustration because they couldn't quite reach him. There was a blood link, but their souls were not fully joined. The words pressed from her chest and up her throat:

Breath of life . . .

She fought the urge to sing the Siren's Song. Instead she concentrated on directing her energy up through her voice box and sang:

Earth, air, water, and flames
Flow from the earth to my voice
Bring the light of the Ancestors
To heal, to strengthen, to live.

Ailish felt her powers beginning to spin so fast, she couldn't keep the energy funneling. Her vocal cords strained, wanting to reshape the words into the Siren's Song. Her head throbbed. She thought of Morgan's baby, picturing tiny fingers and toes, soft skin, and a powdery smell, and she kept repeating the four lines. There were creaks and clunks of machines and weights trembling from the voice power spillover. It wasn't as violent as it had been in the past, and she had a feeling that was due to the bond she was forming with Phoenix. Her power could find him, so it didn't go totally wild.

She kept singing. Her chest grew warm with the knowledge that this was what she was supposed to do, this was her purpose! To help mortals and stand between them and demons.

Then she heard a hiss, like a furious snake, deep in her head. Dark energy began threading into her like curls of smoke. She ignored it, focusing on letting her voice soar with magic, wanting to reach the baby and assure him he was safe.

"Something's wrong," Phoenix said.

The handfast heated, and spikes of painful lust shot through her. Her nipples hardened against her will, but it felt as though long, thick nails were being driven into them. Her womb cramped, and she bent into the pain. Between her legs she grew damp, but it burned her delicate skin there.

She struggled to breathe and sing, breathe and sing.

Don't show the pain!

"Her scent is changing!" Phoenix's voice was more urgent. "Ailish, you need to stop."

No! She could do this, she could do earth magic. She forced herself to accept the pain Asmodeus threw at her, to keep her chakras open. Her chest grew heavy with the dark magic smoldering as though it were gathering.

She sang, trying to increase her power, hoping to push the demon magic out of her. But something else was there, pervading her mind. So close she could smell the cloying incense and sulfur. Then a familiar voice exploded in her head.

You think to defy me?

Her mother! Ailish lost all control. Dark magic erupted in her face like a firecracker. She felt the skin around her eyes burst open. The searing, unbearable agony ripped through her. She bit down on her lip to keep from crying out. She felt the hot blood running down her cheeks. Felt the shards of glass embedded in her eyes. She couldn't sing, her chakras cringed, her power thinned and shuddered, breaking apart.

Blood poured from her face. She was frozen in pain and shock, on her knees, when all hell broke loose around her.

"Stop! Ailish! Oh Christ!" Phoenix yelled.

"Grab him!" Axel ordered. "There's too much blood. Don't let Phoenix touch her!"

"Let me go!" Phoenix bellowed. "Ailish!"

It was her nightmare. She'd woken up screaming with this dream, and now she was living it. Her face burned, as though dozens of knives were stabbing around and into her eyes. Blood poured from her. Anguish and humiliation roiled violently in her stomach.

They were seeing her reduced to this helpless, pathetic creature by her mother. The very thing she'd trained so hard against.

Maeve had somehow used demon magic to reenact the witch karma that had blinded her. All these thoughts were flashing through her mind at the speed of light.

"Ailish . . ." Morgan woke from her hypnotic state and grabbed her arm. "You're bleeding! Lie down, let me help you!"

Morgan's touch snapped her shock. "No! Don't touch me!" She yanked her hands away before her mother did something hideous to the woman and her unborn baby. Oh God, had she gotten her blood on Morgan? It could create a blood link between the woman and her mother! She had to get away! Protect them all. The pain was so intense, the mat slippery with her blood. She crawled, hurried until she could get her feet under her. *Have to get away.* Covering her torn eyes and skin with her hands, she was hit with a wave of hot nausea, and she stumbled. *Please, please don't let me fall to my knees and vomit.*

Someone caught her and lifted her in his arms.

She knew it wasn't Phoenix. Didn't feel like him or smell like him. Had to be one of the others. "No!" She struggled, but he was too strong.

"Ailish, quit fighting. We have to stop the bleeding," Axel said, his voice calm while Phoenix was bellowing from across the room. Threatening to kill Sutton and Joe if they didn't let him go.

Axel held her tight against him, trapping her arms. She wanted to scream in frustration. "My mother did this! She can reach you with her magic if you touch me!"

"Let the bitch try," Axel said.

His flat, cold voice shocked her still. "But . . . what?"

"She's not going to hurt me. But we're going to find her and kill her. Doing this to her own daughter, that kind of shit pisses me off."

She was pretty sure pissing him off was a bad idea.

"Ailish," Darcy said, "stay still. Your blood is inciting the curse in Phoenix. We can't let him get near you, and they are barely holding him. Carla's standing right here, too." Then they touched her, their hands gentle as they drew their fingers over the torn skin around her eyes.

"The blood link!" They had to know her blood could link them to her mother.

They kept right on healing. Carla said, "We're shielding, but it doesn't matter. We won't let you suffer like this."

They were helping her! Earth witches were touching her, not recoiling in disgust. They murmured soft chants, their voices blending, and gradually her chakras unsealed as her magic responded and then rose to mix with theirs. The twining of power swirled through her, streaming over her face in a warm mist. The pain began to fade. Her stomach settled. The relief was so great, she unclenched her jaw. "It's better. Thank you."

"We can only heal you from the attack tonight," Carla said in a tight voice. "We can't reverse the witch karma that originally blinded you. If we'd gotten to you when it happened, before the cuts healed, we might have been able to save your sight."

Yeah, well, she'd asked, begged, the witches she'd found. Ailish stopped herself. These two were helping her now while Axel held her. They were probably doing it to keep Phoenix from losing control and killing her, but at least they were helping. The pain had narrowed down to just a tightness where the scars closed up. Trying to keep her voice normal, she said, "I'm fine now, I can walk. I'll go to the other side of the house, away from Phoenix." Dear Ancestors, she didn't want him to see her like this. So weak, so broken . . .

"You won't get two feet," Axel said. "Darcy, you have maybe one minute before he breaks free."

"Almost done, just getting all the blood off," Darcy said. She directed her next words to Ailish: "We didn't listen to Phoenix. He told us something was wrong. But Carla had located the memory and was magically healing it. We thought just a few more seconds . . ." Darcy's voice dropped. "I'm sorry, Ailish."

"Not your fault." It was her mother's fault. "What about Morgan?"

Carla said, "I was able to erase the buried command and replace it with calming energy. The baby is fine, your voice helped keep him calm while giving Darcy and me the power boost we needed." She stepped back from Ailish. "Blood's gone."

She didn't know what to make of these people. Their kindness was genuine, but she was afraid to trust it. She was a loner; she had to be, or her mother would use people she cared about. Separating herself mentally from them, she said to the big man holding her, "You can put me down."

He lowered her legs to the ground while steadying her with his arm. "We tried to get to your mother tonight, but couldn't get through her wards. We will find a way and we will kill her. You belong to us now, and we're going to get you free."

More conflicting feelings exploded within her. They had tried to get near her mother? Fear for them made her legs tremble. She had just felt her mother's rage and power! But Axel's *You belong to us* left her completely off balance.

"Shit," Sutton snarled. "He's loose!"

Before Ailish could react, someone grabbed her upper arms and yanked Axel's hand from her shoulder. She sucked in a breath and recognized the scent of Phoenix. He dragged her off her feet, his arms going around her and holding her against him.

She buried her face in his warm neck. Her vocal cords ached with the pressure of the words that would call him now.

"Goddammit, Ailish," he growled while his hand stroked her hair. "You didn't listen to me!"

Her weakness, this strange need to hold on to him for strength, frightened her. She was afraid for him, for all of them. She pushed back against his hand, wishing she could see his face, not just the formless shadow. He was going to get killed trying to protect her or be destroyed by her in some other fashion. "You tried to kill my mother? Do you know what she can do to you?" She pounded her fist on his chest.

Wrapping his hand in her hair, he lowered his face. "I saw what that bitch did to you! You have no idea, Ailish. Something exploded in me when I saw your face. . . ." He shuddered. "My brain was screaming to get to you and make it stop, the bird was screeching, and the blood-lust roared over it all. I had my knife in my hand. If I had lost control of the blood craving and killed you . . ." He clamped his mouth shut.

She was destroying him. That hurt her worse than anything the demon or her mother did to her. She had to end this now. Lifting her chin, she pushed on his shoulders in an attempt to stand on her own. "I'm handfasted to a demon," she said. "It's time you accept that, realize that there's no happy ending here. Not with me."

His arm remained locked around her waist, and she could feel his gaze burning into her. "I'm going to get through those wards and kill your mother. You're my happy ending, Ailish, and I'll fight Asmodeus and his entire coven for it. It's time you accept *that*."

God, he was stubborn! "You can't save me! Don't you get it? My siren voice enhanced my mother's power to enable her to do this to me. If it enhanced my mother's power, it enhanced other magic, too!" It tore her apart to realize what she was doing. She'd tried to do something good, something right.

Dual shrill squeaks made her jump in his arms. "What?"

"Darcy's and Carla's phones. That's their alarm for the Circle Witches. It means a witch is missing."

Darcy said, "Four witches snatched in four different

places." She sucked in a breath. "We should have stopped when Phoenix told us to. Too much siren power got out."

Oh God, this was the fallout, more power in witches' blood, which incited the rogues to find and slaughter them for it.

"That fast?" Sutton snarled. "It's only been, what, fifteen minutes since doing the magic with Morgan?"

Phoenix went stiff with rage. "As soon as Asmodeus knew she was using her voice, that rat bastard demon told his minion Young. Young had the rogues out hunting in anticipation of the power spike in witch blood."

"That's what I'm thinking, too," Axel said, his voice low and deadly.

"I'm sorry," Ailish said, wishing she knew how to fix this. She shoved at Phoenix's chest to break his hold on her.

He lifted her higher, his warm hand cupping her face. Putting his mouth close to hers, he said, "You saved the baby. That was your job. Our job is to go out and save the witches." He slid her to her feet. "Joe, you stay here with the women."

Axel said, "Darcy, send the info to the three of us, and Linc." Then to Sutton and Phoenix, he ordered, "Let's go."

"Wait," Ailish said, trying to catch up. "Isn't it dangerous for them to be around me?"

Darcy touched her arm. "No. The demon already knows we've helped you. But you're not going to sing or invite him in the house, and neither are we. Phoenix's house is secure, we're safe here."

Phoenix took hold of her chin, kissed her quickly, and said, "Sleep in my bed. Be there when I get back." Then he was gone.

Ailish stood there, hearing the hunters pounding up the stairs, hearing Joe go up after them, muttering about checking security. The fine hairs on her arms stood up as the truth hit her.

They trusted her. Even after her voice power was causing more horrors. They still believed in her.

Phoenix had taken his second R6 and sped off looking for the witch he'd been assigned, but he'd had zero luck finding her or the rogue that snatched her.

He'd been thinking about it for the last twenty minutes as he rode around. The rogues were being driven into a frenzy by the enhanced witch blood. Ailish sang tonight—he couldn't think about her scars exploding open or he'd lose his fucking mind—but the rogues had to be even more out of control. The bloodlust savaged their brains until they lived only for their next fix, and trying to stay alive so they wouldn't turn into shades.

Two rogues had fought over a witch at the chapel. He guessed that they had her and were on their way to a secure place when they lost control. Couldn't wait. Like smelling French fries in the car all the way home from a fast-food joint, they smelled the witch blood and had to have it. So they stopped on the way . . . the empty church.

He rode back to that church, got off his bike, and scouted the grounds and the chapel. Nothing; he had zero. Furious, he got back on his R6 and gunned it past the cemetery. Everything was quiet in the pre-dawn, but he noticed the storage business, one of those places that has rented units stacked together like apartment garages and was surrounded by heavy-duty chain-link fences with a trailer at the front. The trailer appeared empty, the gates locked by padlocks. Could the rogues be head-quartered here?

He was so frustrated, so hyped up for Ailish's blood, from seeing her face savaged, he needed to find the rogue-den and kill. Venting his rage helped, then he'd go back to the house and make love to Ailish.

Would he be able to keep from taking her completely, sliding his cock into her warm body? He shivered with hot desire in the cold, damp morning. Logic and life experience told him not to do it, not until they broke the handfast. He knew how hard Ailish was fighting to stay an earth witch, but Phoenix also knew her fear.

That the Ancestors in Summerland wouldn't accept her. And if they didn't, her soul would either die off or drift forever in the between-worlds.

What if she couldn't get the handfast off, couldn't make amends, and her fear of death took hold? What if she figured she was better off as a demon witch? What if, he thought in that gloomy, painful place in his mind, he wasn't enough to keep her with him? In addition to his own guilt, Phoenix also blamed his father. He was the man who got Sheri pregnant, pulled her away from all her family and support, then died without even telling her what he was. What her child, Phoenix, was.

Sheri had learned from Haley just as Phoenix had.

Then Phoenix had tried, every day of his life; he'd fought the voices for her, trying to yell over them, to keep her with him. But it hadn't been enough.

Now he was trying to fight a demon for Ailish. What if he still wasn't enough? What if he failed her? Like tonight—she hadn't listened when he'd told her to stop the magic!

The wings on his biceps bulged and shoved, trying to get free probably to beat the cowardice out of him. The wings, the bird, loved Ailish, were desperate for her to sing and sing until the two of them sealed the soul bond and freed the bird to be her familiar. The bird wasn't hesitant.

Sitting there in the damp fog, he knew the truth. He wanted that handfast off first so he didn't have to fight the demon for Ailish. So he didn't have to put his heart and soul on the line. So he didn't have to risk the worst failure of all . . . fighting for the other half of his soul, the whole of his heart, and losing.

The bird was telling him he was a damned coward.

A truck raced by, jerking him from his thoughts. He snapped his head around and heard a half cry, half scream from inside. Inhaling, he got a small whiff of witch blood.

A witch was in that truck! He gunned his bike after it, staying back just far enough to avoid detection. Quickly he called in his position to the other hunters, feeling real hope that this would lead to the cadre bat cave.

He blew past some kind of treatment plant that smelled of slimy Dumpster contents, hit a dirt road, and fought to keep from dumping the bike. His enhanced vision helped him to see well enough to get around rocks and shit in the road. Finally, he saw the truck stop up ahead.

Towering antennas surrounded a building. Phoenix knew it used to be a small independent radio station, but it'd been bought out and the property sold. There were several vehicles. The truck stopped and the passenger got out, dragging a crying and chanting witch.

Her blood scent hit him hard, and his veins swelled with it. They'd cut her to disable her powers. He got off the bike and started toward them, shielding himself. If he could focus his pain and lust on killing the rogues, then he could keep from killing the witch, rescue her, and get her to help. He broke into a run. The rogues had the witch between them and were hauling her toward the building. When he was three feet away, Phoenix palmed his knife, then ripped his chain off his belt hook and snapped it around the arm of one rogue, jerking hard enough to yank him off his feet and slam him to the ground.

The other rogue threw the witch toward the building, and by the time he turned, Phoenix roundhouse kicked him in the face, knocking him fifteen feet.

The first rogue got up and came at him. Phoenix leaped into him, knocking him to the ground and stabbing straight through to his heart. He twisted hard, making sure he was dead.

The smell of burnt skin set off warning bells in his head. He threw himself off the rogue and rolled.

He felt something fly by his shoulder but miss, leaving the stink of sulfur.

He rolled to his feet and whipped around, trying to find it. Was Quinn Young here with his Immortal Death Dagger? He heard the sound of a truck barreling up the road, but he focused on that smell.

Something tugged at his brain, some memory.

Then he saw the small knife, no bigger than his hand but black as sin, flying toward him. What the fuck? That wasn't the Immortal Death Dagger from Young's arm! He dived, and it missed. Dirt filled his nose and mouth, but adrenaline pumped like cheap beer. He jumped to his feet, turned around, and *oh fuck,* now there were two of those mini-daggers reeking of burnt skin and sulfur!

He snapped his chain, knocking both knives to the ground. They bounced off, shot back up, and came at him again.

The truck was closer. He darted a quick look as he evaded the two knives once more. Key's truck, he realized as he worked his way toward it, still evading the two knives.

A sharp pain arrowed into his back, right into his kidney. Instant, blinding agony boiled through him. Two thoughts exploded in his mind—there had been a third mini-dagger . . . and that mark he'd seen on Young?

Young was somehow making mini–Death Daggers.

Darkness closed in as he heard the truck squeal to a stop.

His final thought was of Ailish, his siren. Now she'd never sing for him. *Wing Slayer,* he called out in his mind, *protect her.*

14

Ailish heard all the noise and jumped up out of Phoenix's bed. Morgan and Joe were in the second guest room. Carla and Darcy had taken Phoenix's office. Her first thought was that Morgan was in trouble. She jerked on a pair of sweatpants and ran out.

The noise was coming from the front of the house. The alarm wasn't blaring, so the men must be back. She heard Axel's and Sutton's voices, and another man she didn't recognize. Where was Phoenix?

She hurried out to the living room.

"Where do we put him?"

"Who?" Ailish's voice came out a bellow. Fear snaked up her throat. Her heart beat fast.

"His room," Axel said, then his hands were on her arms. "Ailish, Phoenix has been hit. We don't know what the hell happened! It's just a stab, but he's bad."

Ailish heard men moving past her, carrying Phoenix. The entire house was up. She felt a wave of magic ripple through her. Darcy and Carla?

Phoenix was hurt. *Bad*. The word burst through her head, and she jerked her arms from Axel's hold, turned, and ran back into the bedroom. The magic was building, thickening. Her chakras bounced and pinged, then shot open, rushing from her pelvis to her throat. She stopped halfway into the room. The witches were chanting. She tried to see.

A hand came down on her shoulder. "Two women are standing at the edge of the bed on this side." Dee's voice anchored her. "Other men are in the room. Phoenix is on the bed, lying on his right side. His back is bloody about here"—she touched Ailish behind her left kidney—"and it looks serious. He's hardly breathing, almost gray in color."

Hot tears filled her eyes, her powers surged until her skin hurt, her throat spasmed. She couldn't say anything, instead she let herself be led to him. Dee pushed her between the nightstand and Carla. "How bad?"

"I see it with my third eye," Carla said, then she gasped. "It's the Immortal Death Dagger. A little one, some kind of clone, hit him. Oh no! He's dying!"

Darcy yelled, "We're losing him! His spirit is leaving!"

"No!" Ailish reached out and laid her hand on his face. His skin was cool and strange. "No! He can't die!" He'd saved her life, given her his blood. Held her, fought for her. He'd called her his happy ending.

"Save him!" a male voice filled with furious grief bellowed behind her. "Ailish, you're his soul mirror, save him!"

"Key, they aren't bonded," Carla said in a choked voice. "Her blood won't do it."

"Try!" Key demanded.

The force of his pain mixed with hers. Why hadn't she bonded with him? Then her blood could save him!

Because she'd been a coward. Afraid to be responsible for his soul. Now his soul was leaving. Bone-cracking shudders rolled up through her chakras in a desperate plea. As the room shrouded in gut-wrenching grief, Ailish refused to lose.

She'd fight.

She scrambled over his limp body, grabbed his knife, and cut her hand. The hot slash of pain only fed her urgency. Kneeling by his hips, she slapped her bleeding hand on Phoenix's wound. The she lifted her chest, sucked in a breath, and released the song of her soul:

Breath of life
In my cry

From the flames
Wings shall rise

"What's she doing?"
Darcy answered, "It's her Siren's Song, Key. She's trying to call the phoenix from the ashes of death."
"Sing, Ailish," Key said in a raw prayer.
Her voice rose as she poured every scrap of power into it.

Aching in beauty
Tears of healing

More power joined hers, flowing through Ailish with love and warmth. Dropping his knife, she put her other hand on his tattoo. Movement! She felt the feathers stir!

Wings of my soul
Soar to my call

Pausing only to draw more air into her lungs, she went on:

Breath of life
In my cry

"The wings are rising!" Carla cried out. "The flames are fully colored, and the wing is lifting out!"

From the flames
Wings shall rise

Aching in beauty
Tears of healing

Phoenix opened his eyes, and a blinding gold light seared his retinas. "Christ—" He squeezed his eyes shut. Was this what a hangover felt like?

"No, Wing Slayer."

He snapped his eyes open and sat up. "Huh?" He turned from the searing gold spotlight and looked right. "A bridge?" It shimmered, as if not quite there. Looked rickety as hell, too. Where the hell was he?

"To Summerland. Hasn't taken shape yet."

He couldn't process what that meant and stared at the wavy image, trying to bring it into focus. Was he dreaming? His memory was kind of vague. Giving up on the flickering bridge, he slowly shifted his gaze. At first he saw nothing but emptiness, and then . . .

There was no mistaking what he saw. "Wing Slayer." At over seven feet tall, the being was huge. His massive arms were wrapped in bronze bands stamped with wings, the wings of all his hunters. His face was cut strong and square, with a straight nose. The toga getup was weird as hell, but with all the muscles rippling everywhere on the god, it was doubtful anyone hassled him.

But his wings . . . Phoenix shaded his eyes, trying to see them. His wingspan had to be fourteen feet, and the arc at the top went as high as twelve feet. The tightly woven gold feathers gave off enough light to illuminate deep space. No wonder the dude popped so much muscle, those wings had to take some strength. "So what's the deal here, did I croak?"

A furious rumble shook . . . Phoenix looked down and quickly closed his eyes. There was nothing beneath him. He was just . . . floating. He hated heights. The shaking continued. "Keep that up and I'm gonna puke."

The air settled, but Wing Slayer's voice blasted him. "You wouldn't be in this situation, hunter, if you'd done your job."

Oh shit. He was getting reamed by his god. What had happened? He'd gone after that witch, found the rogue hideout, and . . . It all came back. Those freaky mini–Death Daggers. "I was trying to rescue the witch, but a dagger thing got me first."

"Not that job. Ailish. You're her phoenix, her familiar. She can't control that power until you bond with her. The fallout of her siren voice has given Young the ability to harvest the enhanced power in witch blood and use it to create clone daggers. They protect his lair. They only last a few hours, then he has to recharge them."

The god's voice was so huge and powerful, it rumbled every cell in his body. That seemed to jar his memory even more, so that he recalled the pain of that dagger and the way it had drained all his strength until there was nothing but blackness. And then there was what he saw when the rogues attacked him. "I saw a burn mark on Young's arm. He's growing them on his body, probably spawned by the original Immortal Death Dagger and a lot of witch blood." He'd known Young was up to something.

Wing Slayer narrowed his eyes into gold beams. "You're smart enough to figure this out, but not to see that you were given the privilege of a soul mirror, of being the legendary phoenix to the siren witch? You and Ailish have been together century after century. Never before did you think she wasn't good enough!"

The roar of those last words blew him back a dozen

feet, and he landed on his ass as if there were a floor beneath him instead of nothing but black air. "I was a bird those times! Not a man!" He ran his hand over his face and discovered he was sweating. Calming down, he said reasonably, "She's handfasted to a demon."

"She's not your problem now, is she? She's down there alone."

He jumped to his feet, finding a solid surface somehow. "Ailish!" He fought down the panic and forced himself to think. He'd screwed up, he acknowledged that. Letting the handfast scare him off because he was worried he couldn't win the fight for Ailish against a demon. It shamed him, but could he fix it? "Am I dead? Can I get back to her?"

"You are nearly dead. I met your spirit and we took a detour." He crossed his arms—two slabs of rippled concrete covered with deep golden brown skin. "Asmodeus is not the only one who can play with the rules." His wings twitched, similar to a panther twitching its tail right before it strikes and kills.

Fear wasn't something he felt often, but this deity gave off vibes. Killer vibes. "So . . . ?"

He sucked in a breath. "I'm waiting. I believe the siren witch will show what she's made of and call you. As long as I haven't taken you over the bridge—which is only symbolic, but you get the idea—you can go back."

"You're outsmarting the demon!"

He rose higher and looked down. "It would be easier if my hunters did their jobs. When Ailish is fully bonded to you, the two of you together will control her siren power. The residue that is giving Asmodeus, the rogues, and demon witches this boost will die off." The being swelled, growing even bigger as he added, "These witches, they are the key to booting the demon off Earth entirely. It's the one thing Asmodeus will never understand, the witches and their core of love."

Phoenix felt the sincerity of the god's words vibrate in his chest. "Why do you? Understand, I mean." Axel had told him that Wing Slayer had strong feelings about the witches. But now he was seeing it, feeling it. How did that happen? "You're half demon, you grew up in the Underworld."

His light eyes took on red, the gold light in his wings darkened, and things beneath his skin began to shift. Phoenix was stunned when he saw two protrusions pushing at the top of his forehead. Horns? His deep bass voice snarled, "Think I need a history lesson from you, hunter?"

His skin pebbled, his hair stood up, his heart tried to escape his chest. Phoenix was seeing the demon side of the god struggling to get out. For the first time in his life, he shut the fuck up.

"Wise," Wing Slayer said in approval, going fully back to his god form. Then he added, "I met a witch when I was on Earth centuries ago. Asmodeus was furious and—" He stopped talking, his wings brightening. "Ah. She's calling you."

Ailish's voice washed over him, her notes powerful as they reached into his head, heart, and blood to take root. He'd never felt anything as sensual and compelling. Already he sensed himself moving. . . . "Wait, how do we break the handfast?"

"Fight for her, die for her, whatever it takes. Don't let Asmodeus win!"

Ailish's voice took dominance, and everything else faded away. There was nothing but her voice guiding him, drawing him, and then he felt her tears on his arm. Her fingers stroked his tat while her voice filled the room, reaching, seeking . . .

Wings of my soul
Soar to my call

Energy flooded his body; he opened his eyes and saw her.

His Ailish. Wearing black sweats, another of her little tanks, her chest lifted high, her head tilted back, as she sang with such force, such tremendous magic, it made the bed itself shudder. A glass shattered somewhere, and things fell to the floor. Yet she never stopped, never paused. Her coconut-scented power wound deep inside him. He was on his side with his back to the doorway of the room. He rolled onto his back and swept his gaze around in a protective reflex to make sure she was safe.

His bedroom was in shambles—his closet spilled out, drawers tossed, books, keys, and assorted items littering the ground. Even the paint on the walls cracked and dripped. Ailish's siren voice had demolished his room. Six people stood around the bed: Axel, Sutton, Key, Darcy, Carla, and Dee. He could feel Darcy and Carla's magic, see the ravaged faces of his friends.

None of that mattered.

Only Ailish, his siren witch, the glory of her voice second only to the beauty of her. He reached up to her face, cupping her strong jaw. "Ailish, my siren."

"Out," Axel ordered.

Phoenix heard them all leave the room, heard the door shut tightly. He was alone with the woman who had the power to call him back from death.

He pulled her down into a kiss. Her taste flooded through him.

His god had commanded he fight for her. In that moment, he knew a profound truth: He would give his soul for her.

Cradling her face, he tugged his mouth from hers, then he flipped her beneath him. Her lips were swollen and wet, and he groaned. With his elbows braced on the bed, he used his thumbs to caress her scars and said, "You're mine. You have always been mine. I heard your birth cry . . . and I heard you call me back from death. I will always hear your call, my beauty, and I will always rise for you."

She reached up and skimmed her fingers over his jaw, his cheeks, his eyes. "My voice is yours. All this time I thought the power was mine. I fought to keep the demon from getting it, and I thought it was for me." Tears welled in her eyes. "But it's for you, it's to bring you to the world that needs you. I had to sing, had to call you back, my hunter, my phoenix."

Jesus, her feathery touches over his face rocketed through him, while her words made him sound important, not just another street rat. The need for her, the yearning of his soul to touch her soul, took hold of him. Her magic was caressing him everywhere her body touched his. She needed this as much as he did. "Ailish, you feel it, too. We belong together." He swept his hand down her side and tugged up her little tank.

She lifted her arms. "I ache for you. Only you."

Her honesty ripped away his last shred of control. He tossed her shirt and looked down. Her breasts were swollen, the dark nipples distended. Her magic still purred through her. He leaned down and suckled, drawing in the coconut essence that flavored her. At the same time, he slipped his hand beneath her sweats and panties, over the smooth, hot skin of her mound.

She parted her legs for him while making small frantic noises in her throat.

He knew the magic, the Siren's Song, pulsed in her. He licked and sucked one nipple, then the other, while pressing one finger into her hot channel.

Her walls rippled with the magic, and he shuddered. Her need was as great as his. He lifted his head and pushed up to her ear, while adding a second finger and stroking her in the most intimate way possible. She arched, a moan of pure desire slipping from her mouth. "You need me to fill you. I feel your hunger." He was hard and desperate to be inside her.

Her fingers dug into his tats while her hips pumped against him, seeking relief from the overwhelming mix of magic and desire building in her. "Yes." Turning her head until she was mouth-to-mouth with him, she said, "I called you back to me, and now I can't let you go. Even my magic cries out to you."

He kissed her.

Ailish couldn't bear anything between them. Even as his fingers filled her, his tongue mating with hers, his body covering her, surrounding her . . .

She needed more. Never had she felt as powerful as when she'd freed her voice to call him to her. She ran her hand down his side, feeling his leathers, and breathed a cry into his hot mouth.

She used her powers to strip them.

He licked and kissed along her jaw to her oh-so-sensitive ear. Sliding his fingers from her, he said, "Open for me wider, sweetheart." She parted her thighs as he fitted himself against her. "Like that," he whispered.

His broad head pressed against her entrance. Magic sparked and pulsed from her breasts down to where he was poised. He pressed an inch into her and then another inch. She lifted her hips, trying to take more, trying to ease the torture of not having him inside her.

Phoenix reared back, locking one hand around her hip, pinning her to the bed. "Easy, I'm trying to go easy. Not hurt you."

Heat was rising from his skin, his scent going dark and so sexy that she wanted to suck the flavor from him. She grabbed his wrist, trying to pull his hand from her. "Please!" The demand began to scream inside her. Her powers rushed and spun, her skin was so sensitive that every touch made her shiver, and deep in her first chakra, that place between her hip bones, yawned with emptiness.

Phoenix kept hold, pushing inside her at a maddeningly slow rate. "You're so fucking tight . . . clenching me . . ."

She heard him clamp his jaw, felt him fighting to go easy, and it hit her—he was protecting her. She'd told him she'd had sex only that one time . . . and he'd torture himself before he hurt her. He was huge, but she needed all of him.

A shudder ripped through him, but still he eased in, slow . . . careful . . . so that even his skin burned with the agony of holding back.

She began to sing softly, words that were only for him: "The flames stole you, the flames returned you."

His muscles went rigid, he was only halfway in her, and he swelled, his cock stretching her. "Ailish! No!"

She touched the feathers with one hand and Phoenix's tightly coiled back with the other. "My body burns, my magic weeps. For you."

She almost heard the chains of his control snap. Phoenix broke free, his hand on her hip slid beneath her bottom and lifted her. He pushed up on his other arm, made a deep growling noise, and thrust deep and true.

He filled her up, bowed her back as her entire being opened and took him. He touched her where no one else had, no one else ever could. She felt herself surrendering to him, wanting to be consumed by him. "More," she cried softly.

He pulled out and slammed back in, the sensations breaking loose. Dropping to his elbows, he said in a husky voice, "My siren . . ." Then he ravished her mouth while filling her over and over. His kiss hot, his thrusts deep, her breasts rubbing his chest, it was twining and building to a tremendous force. Energy gathered, pleasure thickened, every thrust added more. She tore her mouth from his, gasping with the intensity of it driving her higher and higher, reaching . . . almost . . .

"Ailish, call him. He's . . . ," he groaned, shoving hard into her. "Bring us home."

She arched back, her powers splitting, half rushing up her throat, bursting from her in a mating cry: "My light, my color, my phoenix!" Her remaining powers rushed down, circling their hips and fusing as their fierce pleasure broke free.

She closed her eyes, helpless beneath the waves of hot, pulsing release . . . and saw a burst of light. Her gray, shadowy world suddenly fractured, then filled with flashes of color—vivid blues and purples surrounded by crackling red, sun-bright yellow, and autumn gold. She could see and feel the colors weaving her and this hunter closer, tighter, forever. Her body shuddered in the ecstasy while her mind basked in the colors.

Phoenix thrust in deeper, throwing back his head and roaring as he came, pumping and filling her, sending her into another thrall of sensations as the spiraling, twisting colors took shape.

She saw the phoenix. He lifted his wings, free of the flames, and reached for her. Breathtaking magnificence. Her entire being responded as her hunter held her safe while giving her soul-binding pleasure.

Finally her body quieted, her magic settled, and the image faded.

She sighed, fulfilled, satiated . . . whole.

Phoenix pulled free and rolled to his side, drawing her into his arms. "You felt it?" His voice was quietly rough.

Surrounded by the warmth and safety of Phoenix, she knew he meant more than pleasure. He meant that they had joined. "I saw it," she said. Her world dimmed back to gray shadows, but with his arms around her, immersed in his dark, intense sexual scent, she was okay. "First I saw the amazing blue and purple colors, and fiery red and gold. Just the colors." She took a breath, the joy almost too much for her to endure. "Then I saw the phoenix. He lifted his wings, telling me he's home." She sounded stupid, but she was so overwhelmed that she couldn't stop telling him. "It's been so long since I've seen colors."

He spread his hand on her back. "What are you seeing now?"

"Nothing, just shadows. But I saw him, I can remember those colors." It was such a tremendous gift, a shiver went through her.

Phoenix pressed her back, lifting her chin until she felt the weight of his stare. "When did you see him?"

She felt silly and strange saying it, yet she wanted to tell him the truth. "I think it was when our souls joined."

He slid his hand up to cup her breast. Gently, he brushed the nipple, and his voice went low and husky. "When we orgasmed with me deep inside you." He shuddered. "Our souls are joined. Let's see if we can bring him back for you."

"Wait—" She held on to his wrist. "What about my siren magic? Is it causing more harm?" She'd unleashed everything she had calling him. She wouldn't do it again, but—

He brushed his mouth over hers. "Not anymore. If you can see the phoenix, you have your familiar. I saw the Wing Slayer, Ailish."

Hot chills thrilled through her. "Your god? Oh, Phoenix . . ." She put her hand on his face, trying to feel the joy he must have experienced. She wished she could see his eyes, but this was enough.

He turned his face to kiss her palm. "He said once we're bonded, we'll fully control your power and all the residue in the atmosphere will die off."

Relief and happiness filled her, but before she could ask more questions, Phoenix leaned down to her ear.

"Let me show you the phoenix. As many times as you wish to see him."

Phoenix walked into the condo and stopped. The furniture was all shoved back, and drawings were spread out on the floor. Key wore jeans, his tattoo, and the scent of rage. "I can't find it."

Three cans of Dr Pepper were on the coffee table, along with several empty wrappers of Kit Kat bars. Sketchbooks, pencils, markers, and charcoal littered the floor on the outside of the square.

Key was on a manic high, fueled by sugar, bloodlust, and a ferocious anger.

Axel and the others had returned to the condos in late morning, and then Axel had called him, told him to get over here. Phoenix had left Ailish with Dee.

"Key, you're spinning."

"No, it's here. The answer is here." He walked the perfect square. "Liam's hand, Liam's knife, Liam's scar, and then this . . ." He nudged a drawing with his toe.

Phoenix crossed his arms and looked down. "A few strands of red hair?"

"And this . . ." Key nudged another picture.

Phoenix saw the intriguing curve of a woman's shoulder. The lines were sensual and so female that he wished he could see the woman it belonged to. But what made it so disturbing was that Key's drawings were usually stark with violence. Not something this romantic and deeply feminine.

"This . . . ," Key said, pointing to the next drawing. "Does it go on the shoulder?"

Phoenix frowned. "What is it?" It looked like an abstract of a woman, her arms raised over her head in a circle, breasts full, hips rounded and then tapering to a point, no legs. "A mermaid?"

"No. It's her."

He looked up, seeing the lines etched around the man's mouth, the steely-colored agony smoldering in his eyes. "Who?"

Ignoring the question, Key said, "Look at this!"

The next picture screamed of brutality and pain. A woman's flat belly, drawn in soft charcoal, then the bloody wound gaping like a blood-soaked mouth silently screaming. Chills ran up his spine. Phoenix knew the depth of Key's talent, but when he saw shit like this, it was . . . harsh. Most of the time, Key's art kept him sane, but other times, like now, it had a stranglehold on him and tried to drag him into a world of charcoal and blood.

"Liam did it."

It always circled back to his brother. Did Key really have some art-psychic connection with his rogue brother, or was this guilt-and-rage insanity?

"Can't save her if I can't figure out who she is." He just stared down, his hand twitching at his side. And more astonishing, the huge dragon tattooed across his chest appeared to stare down at it, too.

He had to stop this now. Phoenix bent over and started gathering up the pages. "You won't find him if you give in to this craziness! You're going to lose control and go rogue."

"Stop! I have to see what he's doing!" Key tried to grab his hand.

Phoenix shoved him away. "Goddammit, Key! You're letting him win when you let the guilt control you." He was going to shove some protein down his throat and get him a willing woman to help. He picked up the last paper and set it on the shelf. "Liam's gone, and you—"

Key slammed into him.

Phoenix hit the floor, rolled, and it was on. Key needed to vent his violence, and Phoenix was happy to give him the opportunity. The two of them circled, striking, fighting. Key caught him with a punch that threw him over the couch.

Phoenix heaved him into the wall.

Finally, panting and hurting from his knees to his neck, Phoenix pinned Key. The sweating, bleeding hunter laughed, the gray menace sliding back in his gaze to reveal a bit of blue. "Damn, Phoenix, did you have Wheaties for breakfast?"

Relief eased the stone on his chest. "I could always kick your ass." He rolled off him and lay on his back. "Shit . . ." He reached under his back and pulled out a piece of glass. "We broke the table."

Key wiped his hand over his eyes. "And one of the legs off the chair."

He looked over at Key. "Ailish's magic set this off?"

"Seeing you nearly dead. Her magic just added fuel."

Phoenix knew Key was getting closer and closer to the curse winning over. He couldn't lose the only brother he'd ever had. They might not share DNA, but they shared a bond of growing up and surviving. Phoenix would kill Key before he'd let him go rogue.

"She still handfasted?"

The urgent worry rose. "Yes. She can't die. I have to free her."

"Her voice . . . holy shit, I could not believe it. It made the curse burn like a motherfucker, but I couldn't leave. She fought for you with her magic. It had to hurt her the way her power exploded out. But she never stopped singing."

His chest felt strange. He hurt everywhere, but his chest felt hot. "We're bonded now. Soul mirrors."

"Yeah. Smell her on you. You're getting stronger and faster. Not as good as me, but—"

Phoenix laughed and rolled to his feet. "That's an artist for you, always dreaming."

Key rose and put his hand on Phoenix's shoulder. "What about the handfast? She's got a death sentence on her wrist."

Those words hurt more than any punch Key had thrown. "I'm going to kill her mother and free her." He rubbed his chest. "I can't lose her."

"Phoenix, she might not be savable."

"I saw Wing Slayer before Ailish called me back. He told me to fight for her. I'm getting a second chance to be the man my father wasn't, the man I failed to be when my mother needed me." He remembered his witch in his arms last night, the way it felt to join his body, and his soul, with her. Ailish became more vital to him with every breath he took. If he let her die . . . if he had to watch her die . . . it would destroy him. "She's my second chance."

Phoenix and Key went down to the warehouse after they cleaned up the condo and Key ate real food. Sutton, Axel, Ram, and Linc were looking at a Google map on the big screen.

Axel glanced over. "Do much damage?"

Phoenix got out a bottle of water. "Fixed the chair. Coffee table needs witchcraft or a Dumpster."

The hawk shifted to Key. "You solid?"

"As a rock." He poured out some coffee and added, "Phoenix hangs out with Wing Slayer these days."

Everyone turned to him.

Phoenix should have hit Key harder. "He was stalling my soul, keeping me from making it to Summerland so Ailish could call me back."

"Knife?" Linc shoved up out of the chair and walked toward him, his gold eyes narrowing.

"Smooth silver, no wings." He pulled out his knife and tossed it to the other hunter.

Linc caught the blade, examined it, then threw it back. Holstering his knife, he ignored the bird getting restless.

The creature didn't like being away from Ailish. But he was still a hunter, and he had a job to do. Perching his ass on the edge of the pool table, he described what happened when he followed that truck and tried to rescue the witch. For the first time, he thought to ask, "What happened to her?"

"She helped me get you in the truck," Key said. "Got her out of there. Joe met us and took her to some witches. She's all right."

Phoenix took in just how much witch blood and magic Key had been exposed to last night. No wonder he was on edge. Looked fine now, though.

"Where'd those mini–Death Daggers come from?" Sutton asked. "Carly said you were dying from it."

Phoenix had to remember to thank the witches for helping Ailish save him. He told them what he knew: "Wing Slayer said Young is creating clone daggers to guard his lair. Apparently witch blood, and Ailish's siren voice, was enough to do it. They need to be recharged every few hours." He sipped some water, then added, "When Young attacked us, I saw a black mark here"—he gestured to his upper arm—"but I didn't know what it was."

Axel went still as stone, anger cut into every line. "He's growing those miniature Immortal Death Daggers on his body. What the fuck is he?"

Ram turned his gaze to Axel. "We don't know. He was a rogue witch hunter, but now . . . he's some kind of demon minion."

"Can he still be killed?" Linc asked.

Axel took a breath. "Yes. He still protects his heart, I saw that." He relaxed the line of his jaw and gestured to the screen. "Sutton and I flew around the Rogue Cadre hideout once we knew Phoenix would live."

That reminded Phoenix. "Thanks for getting the R6 for me."

Axel threw him a grin. "You were busy."

Snickers cracked the tension.

As long as they didn't make a comment about Ailish, he'd let them live.

Ram said, "Look at all those vehicles parked around that one-story building. There's a lot of rogues there. It's maybe a twelve-hundred-foot space. They aren't all in that building."

Sutton looked over at Ram. "Exactly what I thought. That's why I pulled this map up." He flicked on his laser pen. "Look at this." He pointed to a metal plate the size of a barn door.

"Tank of some kind?" Linc moved closer to study the image.

Ram's whole face tightened. "Underground bunker. That's what Young's been doing all this time. He had the rogues building a stronghold here in Glassbreakers." He looked around at all of them. "Between this bunker and his guard of mini–Death Daggers, he's going to be impossible to get at there."

Phoenix wouldn't soon forget what it felt like to get hit by one of those daggers. "I know this is important," he said as the bird fidgeted with his urgency. "But Ailish only has ten days." The resulting silence made his jaw clench.

Sutton pushed his chair back to the console and began typing. "Ailish, with Dee's help, showed me where the wards are at the Infernal Grounds."

The screen they'd been watching shifted to a view of the Infernal Grounds. There was the old chapel where the women had been massacred, accused of being witches by the town preacher. He could see the stone altar. The wards started in a circle from outside the chapel and continued around the altar and farther out to the wilderness area. The wards, according to the marks, were strongest on the chapel side.

"Ailish said the wards are very real, formed from the screams and terror of the murdered people. The dread and sick feelings are from them. The demon witches burn hallucinogenic herbs to enhance the effect. Ailish guessed that hellhounds patrol when the witches are not there. She said they are raised through a blood spell, pulling dead creatures from the earth."

Phoenix ran his hand over his face. "What do you want to bet they killed animals right there to use later?"

Linc made a furious noise in his chest. "There's a reason animals instinctively hate and fear demon witches."

Phoenix hoped Ailish never brought home a stray kitten or dog when she was growing up, but he had to stay focused. "We need to get through those wards."

Axel said, "Darcy and Carla are working with Ailish. This fight with Young and the rogues, it's long-term. We know that. But Ailish"—he turned to Phoenix—"is our priority. You, me, and Sutton will go tonight, under the cover of darkness, to check out the coven grounds and test the witches' spell to bring down the wards."

His chest eased. Ten days left to free Ailish.

"I don't think it'll work." Ailish was afraid. She was losing control. Her world had been so simple—break the handfast, kill her mother and the coven, and then the witch karma would kill her.

Hopefully, then, she'd get into Summerland. She'd get another chance to reincarnate and be a better witch. Do more good.

Simple. Only her life, and her soul, at stake.

But now? *Phoenix.* She was responsible for his soul.

"You opened your communication chakra last night," Carla said from the laptop. She and Darcy were projecting their voices through the machine from their homes. "You had to in order to call Phoenix with your Siren's Song. That's all you need to project your magic through the cell phone."

"I should be at the coven grounds." Ailish sat in

Phoenix's chair in his home office, working with the two witches to design a spell to bring down the wards. She leaned forward, trying to make them understand. "My mother can do devastating things with her magic. I have to be there, my siren power can stop her." Look what she'd done to Kyle, to Haley. She had to get these two women to grasp it. Had to make them understand. "I asked my mother once why she was different from me, a demon witch instead of an earth witch."

"Did she tell you?" Carla asked.

"She said it's because she's strong and powerful. Earth witches were cowards who scurried in dark corners, hiding like cockroaches. They are butchered by rogues because they are too weak to defend themselves. She might have been born an earth witch, but she wouldn't scurry in the shadows. She began trying to raise Asmodeus at sixteen and succeeded when she was nineteen. Because she wanted more and more power. She bragged about this, like she had done something really important so young. My mother will stop at nothing to achieve her goals." She took a breath. "I think I was born a siren because my power can win against her. I screwed up, though. I let her handfast me to a demon. I have to fix that. I have to be at the coven grounds." Not in the condos with Carla and Darcy.

"If that's true, you need to practice," Darcy said. "We're just testing tonight. Axel, Sutton, and Phoenix want to see what the wards feel like at the Infernal Grounds. And we're going to see what happens when we project a spell through the cell phone from the condos."

"We don't even know if the coven will be there," Carla added. "We're gathering information. And it'll give us a chance to see how your ability to enhance magic works now that you have a familiar."

There was another problem. "You saw what happened when I used my voice power." She ran her finger over the edge of the desk. It was nice wood, sanded smooth and stained. Probably dark; dark suited Phoenix.

"That was your Siren's Song, your magic reaching out to find Phoenix. The power was incredible." Carla's voice floated with sincerity. "There were waves flowing outward, but both Darcy and I felt the instant you bonded. All those excess waves of magic began to dissipate."

It felt strange to realize they had felt that very intimate, special moment with Phoenix. This was one of those moments when being blind worked for her . . . she couldn't see their expressions. She cleared her throat and said, "That's what Wing Slayer told Phoenix, too." But he'd only seen Wing Slayer because of those mini–Death Daggers that her unbounded voice power had helped create.

"Ailish," Carla said, "believe it. You're not causing harm any longer."

"Okay, yeah." She fidgeted, opening the long drawer and fiddling with pens, pencils, paper clips. Bonding with Phoenix gave her control of her power. She wouldn't accidentally enhance her mother's magic while trying to stop her. But she didn't believe it was going to be easy. They weren't going to be able to cast some spell through a phone, bring down the wards, and have the other hunters kill her mother and the coven.

Ailish had been given the gift of this power to stop her mother. It was going to have to be her.

And the witch-karma backlash would kill her.

Don't go there, Ailish warned herself. *Just believe that if you do the right thing, you'll get into Summerland.* She couldn't get weak now. Phoenix had given her everything. He'd brought color to her gray world, held her when she'd been afraid to let anyone touch her, and merged their bodies and souls. He'd pulled her out of a vast loneliness into a world of friends willing to fight for one another. He'd given her hope that she could be better.

In her next life.

And he would help her get stronger magically as her familiar through the soul-mirror bond.

It was up to her to be strong emotionally. Up to her to make sure she made the right choices, protected Phoenix's soul and his heart.

"What is it, Ailish?" Carla asked gently.

She looked up, saw the blurry gray blob that was the laptop. "Nothing. I'll do my part. I'll learn the spell and—"

"I know. What I don't know is what is worrying you."

That she'd fail. Grow weak. Do something desperate and foolish, like she'd done when she was sixteen and asked her mom to help her with Kyle. Try to find a way to live a happily-ever-after and end up hurting more people. Or that the coven would get her and torture her and somehow force her to turn. But they didn't need to know that, so she told them another concern. "Asmodeus and the coven aren't going to accept me having a soul mirror and familiar. They're going to do something—"

"Our familiars warn and protect us," Darcy broke in. "But with your handfast link, Asmodeus might be able to cause you pain."

She waved her hand. "I can handle that."

"You don't have to," Darcy told her. "Phoenix can take the pain so it won't interrupt your magic."

No! This was what really terrified her. She couldn't rely on him, not like that. She had to be able to take pain to resist if Asmodeus and his coven got hold of her. And besides . . . "I won't be dependent on him for things I can handle."

"Because you're blind?" Carla asked in a nonjudgmental voice. "It doesn't seem to bother Phoenix."

The woman was trying to be kind, Ailish got that. Phoenix had told her that Carla was a psychologist and helped people. But Ailish remembered his words to her in her house the night he'd broken in to check on her. *You think I want this? Suddenly leashed to a blind witch who is handfasted to a demon?* And then later he'd said, *Then I was compelled to come here, had to check to make sure you were okay, like I'm a fucking babysitter.* No, he hadn't wanted this, it had been forced on him.

Evidently time after time.

Ignoring the question about her blindness, she said, "We've been doing this century after century, haven't we? The siren is born, the phoenix burns to ash, then she calls him to life. He has no choice." No wonder Phoenix had resented her so strongly from the first. On some cellular memory level, he had to know she'd done this to him over and over.

"Before this, the phoenix wasn't a hunter but an actual bird," Carla said carefully. "And Phoenix can reject you. The hunter can always reject the witch."

Ailish shook her head, wondering how they could say that about Phoenix. "He couldn't. He tried, but he can't walk away from a woman in trouble." So Ailish had to be the one to push him back. Keep a reasonable distance between them. They had to work together with her magic, but they didn't have to build the personal connection any more than it was. Give Phoenix a chance to step back and see that he couldn't win this battle. But she was just vain enough to want to leave him with the memory of her as strong and that she did the right thing. The way an earth witch should. "If I die, Phoenix will be okay, right? I mean, nothing happens to him?"

The silence made her chakras ache. He had to be okay.

Finally, Darcy said, "The bird will die off, but Phoenix will live on. The bloodlust won't ever return as the curse is broken for both of you."

In other words, he'd be free.

15

Phoenix found Ailish up in his media room. He knew she'd done a long workout in his gym. Her hair was still damp from her shower. Now she had a sandwich and some iced tea and was eating while listening to the show.

He noticed she seemed to like the big suede couch that faced the TV and ignored the two recliners on either side. She wore her usual jeans and black shirt and had her feet up on the coffee table.

On the TV was one of the judge shows. The case seemed to be a dude who didn't believe he owed his ex-girlfriend the bail money she had paid to get him out of jail.

Ailish took a sip of her tea and said, "Stupid chick, putting his bail on your credit card. He can't have been that good in bed."

He walked into the room. "Would you put up bail for me?"

She jerked her head around. "Didn't hear you. Where's Dee?"

He sat next to her, leaned over, and took a bite of her sandwich. "Peanut butter and jelly?"

She shrugged. "Easy to eat."

Shit, she was killing him. Sitting here listening to a show she couldn't see, eating something because it was easier to manage. "Let me make you—"

"No, this is fine." She took another bite with obvious determination. "Dee?"

There was probably something wrong with his chest, he decided. He leaned back and stretched his arm out along the back of the couch. Her damp hair brushed his arm, and he fiddled with a heavy lock of it. "I had one of the hunters take her to pack up some things at her house and buy her whatever else she needed. Get her out of the house for a while."

"She's not coming back?" Ailish sounded lost.

Damn, his chest ached. "Of course she's coming back. The truth is I wanted some privacy for us." He was an idiot, taking her friend away from her like that. It hadn't occurred to him that Ailish would think Dee was abandoning her. He pulled his arm away and said, "I'll call her. You can talk to her and—"

"No. She's free to go where she likes as long as it's safe. She doesn't have to tell me or anything."

Jesus. He'd packed her off with Linc before giving her a chance to say goodbye to Ailish. What the fuck was wrong with him? "My fault. I said I'd tell you, but I should have had her check with you."

She shrugged.

"I'm sorry, Ailish. I'm used to doing things my way." He put his arm back behind her head and fingered her hair, watching as the TV lights played over her face. He wanted to tease from her the tension, the hurt she was hiding. "So would you bail me out like the chick on the show?"

She lifted one shoulder. "Who's going to put you in a cell?"

He grinned at that. "Good point. So what's the dog's excuse for not paying his girlfriend back the bail money?"

"Said it was her choice to bail him out. He didn't hold a gun to her head."

Phoenix watched Ailish's face. She loved this stuff. "Asswipe."

"Shh!" She leaned forward as the judge gave her ruling in the woman's favor, then lectured the winner about picking better boyfriends.

Ailish smiled. "You tell her, Judge! What the hell was she thinking bailing him out?"

"Hormones?"

"Always trouble," she responded, and reached for her sandwich.

Phoenix couldn't stand it, he grabbed the plate. He'd had enough sandwiches from shelters and soup kitchens growing up, and he guessed she'd probably had, too. "You're not eating this." He stood up and said, "I'm barbecuing steaks. Come give me a hand." He turned and walked out.

He'd just reached the stairs when her magic lit up his stomach and chest, then the plate disappeared from his hand.

He whipped around to see her standing there, between the couch and the chair, the plate in one hand, sandwich in the other. She took a bite.

He crossed the room in a second, wrapped his hand around the back of her neck, and tugged her forward.

She let him.

"You are so damned hot. No one pushes you around." It was amazing, freeing, to be able to be himself and know that when he crossed her line, she'd let him know. Fight back. Stand up for herself. He pulled her to his mouth, the plate getting smashed between them. She tasted like peanut butter, sweet jelly, and Ailish. Her magic felt like pure energy, vibrant, sizzling, and he didn't feel the curse at all. No bloodlust. He lifted his head and said, "I bought steaks on the way home. Thought we'd barbecue, and then we'll work on your powers."

Ailish hooked her bare foot over the rung of the chair. Phoenix had barbecued steaks while she made baked potatoes and corn. She'd used only as much magic as she'd needed.

She was going to show him that she wasn't dependent, wasn't a burden. He didn't need to worry about her or take care of her. She'd taken care of herself since she'd been sixteen.

He put the plate in front of her. "Wine at two o'clock," he said, then sat on her left at the head of the table.

He kept giving her directions. *Chair on your left. Glass on the right side of the sink. Three steps up.* Just casually telling her what she needed to know to navigate. It made her stomach clench with frustration. *Because you're blind?* Carla had asked. Did even his friends pity him? Stuck with a blind witch who was handfasted to a demon?

Refusing to dwell on it, she picked up her silverware. Using the fork, she figured out the steak was at six o'clock, potato at nine, and corn at three. Easy enough. Beginning with the steak, she carefully cut a piece and ate it.

This was the hard way, but she kept at it, determined to prove that she could do this, like a sighted woman or witch. Like Carla and Darcy. Besides, how she looked, the way she ate, it all mattered to her when it hadn't before.

Phoenix mattered.

The idea of him seeing her as a burden when she saw him as huge, virile, and capable really pissed her off. She cut a piece of steak, put it in her mouth, then tried not to choke.

It wasn't steak, but the end of the potato—dry, with skin on it. She chewed it up and swallowed, trying not to make a face.

"What are you doing?"

She flushed. Had he noticed? Or was there food on her mouth? Spilled into her lap? Had she knocked something over? "What?"

"You cut a piece of potato off the end and ate it."

"So?" She knew she was being stupid, stubborn, prideful.

"Unbuttered?"

She lifted her chin. "Maybe I like it that way."

He caught hold of her left hand. "You're so tense, you're going to bend the fork and knife. You're not enjoying your food."

Her stomach started to knot. "This is how it is for me."

"No, it's not. You have magic to help you, or me." He used his thumb to rub her sweaty palm. "What the hell were you going to do when you got to the corn?"

She admitted, "Slip in a little magic to make it stick to the fork."

He kept rubbing her palm. "I've seen you eat before. Why are you so worried now?"

Because she'd never been embarrassed about her blindness before, never felt so inadequate. She hated this. "I don't need you to be my eyes," she snapped. "I functioned perfectly fine. Alone." She lifted her face, looking at his shadow.

The silence was like a slap. His thumb stopped stroking her palm.

She sat there feeling the hot humiliation stain her face, neck, and chest, but she couldn't back down.

"So it's okay if I need you, if I was going to die without you. I needed you to sing, use all your power to call me back to life. Then I needed you to spread your legs and trust me to fuck you, and not hurt you, when a goddamned demon has been torturing you with lust for eight years? That's okay, but I can't do something as easy as buttering your potato?"

The fury pouring off him stunned her. It all jumbled together in her head. "I knew you wouldn't hurt me." No, no, no! Not what she should have said.

"I'm thinking about hurting you right now," he said, his thumb brushing across her palm once more.

It was so much easier when it was just her! "I don't know how to do this." His hand anchored her as she tried to find her way through all these new feelings and fears. She wanted to protect him, protect herself, and at the same time, she craved his approval, *craved him*. She could only see his shadow, but the feel of his hand wrapped around hers, his thumb skimming along her palm, made her feel safe. "It's always been just me I had to worry about. Now . . ."

"Yeah. We have so much more to lose."

He knew. He got it. Words just tumbled out of her mouth. "You are trusting me with your soul." That was monumental.

"Then I guess you'd better trust me to be your eyes."

"Damn it."

"Hate losing the argument?" he asked with amusement.

He reached inside her and brought out the truth. "Well, yeah, but I was going to distance myself from you, not let you matter so much."

He leaned in and kissed her. "Good luck with that, baby, because you are inside me now. Your magic lives inside me, and I'm going to get inside you every chance I can." He leaned back and said, "Use your magic to eat." He kept stroking her hand with his thumb. "But don't make me watch you struggle. You want something cut up or buttered, or just need to know where the hell it is on the table, speak up."

"In my old life, no one gave me grief like this. And if they did, I kicked their ass," she muttered, proving she was a sore loser. Taking her hand from him, she used her magic to cut up the steak, then butter and mash the potato. Then she created a magnetic field between the fork and the food. And ate. Damn him.

"Be a good little witch and I'll let you try to kick my ass later."

She liked the sound of that. "I'm a successful kick-boxer, hunter. I even had a few endorsements. I'm not some delicate witch you can cower with your trash talk and big, flashy muscles."

"You and cower don't even belong in the same state," he said dryly. "How did you get into kickboxing?" Then he added, "Buttered roll at twelve o'clock on your plate. Don't bite me."

She couldn't help but grin at that. "Thank you," she said, taking a stab at being gracious. Then she lifted her head toward his shadow. "I was weak and easy prey on the streets. My magic helped, but I didn't really know how to use it. I had to get stronger."

"Easy prey." The soft words had a Rottweiler bite behind them. "What happened to you?"

"The usual. Got food stolen, little knocked around—"

He clinked his silverware down on his plate. "Raped?"

"No. Couple drunks protected me a bit." She took a bite of her roll.

"I thought Haley got you help?"

"She did. She got me into a shelter in another part of Los Angeles." Pausing, she sipped her wine. It was a nice Merlot, smooth and rich. "But they gave me painkillers and I had an allergic reaction."

"Witches can't tolerate most synthetic medications. Magic or natural remedies work, but synthetic drugs can kill you. Didn't you know that?"

She shook her head. It wasn't as though her mother had taught her this stuff. "No. After that, the people at the shelter didn't know how to help me. I didn't sleep much." She drank more wine to wash down the memories of how weak, scared, and pathetic she'd been. "And when I did sleep, I often woke screaming. They finally asked me to leave."

"You were sixteen! They threw you out on the streets?"

She set down her glass. Heard him refill it. "You said you grew up on the streets. You know the drill. Can't save everyone. They knew there was something strange about me. I made them uneasy."

He took hold of her hand. "Why didn't you contact Haley? She would have helped you."

The memories eased with his touch, proving he was reaching deep inside her. "My mother almost killed her. Haley would have helped me and died for it. I have purposely kept my contact with her minimal so the coven will leave her alone."

"So what did you do?"

"I almost went home, went back to my mother." She remembered how easy it would have been. Call her mom and say, *Come get me*.

"What stopped you?"

The moment was still clear in her mind. "Seeing my mother's face when she was using magic to strangle Haley. It was nothing but a means to an end to her. She hadn't cared. She was hurting a woman to get me to do what she wanted—and I realized then that she had never loved me. At all. I was just a tool to acquire more and more dark magic." She forced herself to eat another bite of potato. Then she said, "I didn't want to be her, and I set out trying to survive and learn how to be an earth witch."

She heard him reach for another roll, then butter it. "If you didn't go home, what did you do?" he asked.

His movements were smooth and economical. Some people constantly shuffled and twitched. Phoenix had a stillness about him, as though he didn't have to fidget to remind people that he was there. "My eyes healed. I stole, lied, cheated, used my magic to get what I needed. I contacted Haley on other people's cell phones, and she helped me learn what she knew about being an earth witch. Much of it was trial and error. I did fortune-telling and crap like that to make money. I lived at a YWCA, and they had a kickboxing self-defense class. Got my ass kicked pretty good there for a while."

Phoenix took her hand again. "But you stuck with it."

"I was stubborn." She smiled in his direction. "And I noticed something interesting. The more I worked at it, the more I connected with my power."

He kept hold of her hand. "So you built yourself into the blind kickboxer, and made your mark. Aren't people wondering where you are now? You must have friends who know where you lived?"

"No, I cut all my ties before coming back here. I had an apartment, but I let that go. I retired from the kickboxing association. I put all my affairs in order. Most of the money is going to Haley's homeless shelter." She took in a breath, realizing how much she wanted to live and be with Phoenix.

"You're not going to die."

His determination bled through every word, alarming her. She had never known anything like this . . . connection . . . growing between them. But with that came a rush of feelings she didn't know how to deal with, like desperately wanting him to be happy and whole. Not broken by her. "Don't do this, Phoenix. Don't set yourself up to fail. We need each other. You know what I am."

"Have faith, Ailish. Wing Slayer told me to fight for you."

His voice, hardened by life, took on a glow when he talked about his near death experience and meeting his god. "Perhaps it's your test to achieve your immortality." She wanted him to be loved and accepted by his god, maybe even more than she wanted her Ancestors to accept her and give her a chance to reincarnate and be a better witch.

Phoenix slammed down his wineglass. "I won't fail.

I've spent the last decade rescuing women and hunting down the men who hurt them. I don't fail, Ailish. Ever." More wine splashed into their glasses. "Wing Slayer had some personal vendetta with Asmodeus and a notorious soft spot for witches. If I fail you, he'll eat my liver while I watch."

"But no pressure," she said softly, feeling the stress mount. She'd been passive for too long, ever since the rogues attacked her. Now she had to train for this battle. This time, her weapon was going to be her magic.

He lifted his wineglass. "Have you learned nothing from Chuck Norris? Failure is not in our language," he said in a mock serious tone. "Chuck Norris does not hunt, because the word *hunting* infers the possibility of failure. Chuck Norris goes killing."

Ailish picked up her glass and grinned. "So you're bilingual?"

"What?"

"Obviously you speak the language of Chuck. That roundhouse kick you took me down with spoke volumes."

Phoenix laughed so hard that he dropped his elbows on the table. Finally, he recovered and said, "Been doing some research?"

She sipped her wine and answered, "Internet. I found a whole slew of Chuck jokes and found his TV show. There are entire websites filled with them." She used her magic to have the computer read her anything she found. She'd spent an entire hour trying to figure out who this Chuck Norris was and why Phoenix identified with him so much.

"I'd see him on TVs in stores. Or sometimes in houses if I could get close enough without the people knowing I was there. Chuck Norris was a hero. A problem solver. He fought for the people who couldn't fight for themselves."

Ailish set down her glass and listened to him. "You wanted to be like him?"

He caught her fingers in his warm hand. "Better than being like my father."

"I doubt he meant to die," she said softly.

His hand tensed in hers. "He left my mother pregnant with a witch hunter baby, Ailish. She didn't know what he was. Her family disowned her because of him."

Oh hell, she got it, and it cut right to her soul. Phoenix had wished Chuck Norris would rescue him and his mother. But no Chuck Norris ever showed up, so Phoenix turned himself into a hero who didn't fail. She squeezed his hand, then let go. "So bounty hunting. How'd that start?"

"A woman came to Haley's homeless shelter desperate to hide from an abusive husband. Haley's shelter isn't set up for that, but Haley . . ."

Ailish knew. "She couldn't turn her away."

He let go of her hand, stood up, and started clearing the table. "She called me, I went and picked up the woman, got her story . . . she had a restraining order against the man, but the cops hadn't been able to do much."

She picked up her dishes and followed. "So you did." She went back to the table and cleared the wineglasses and butter dish.

"I didn't kill him. I don't kill mortals unless I have to. Too easy."

She heard him rinsing stuff, loading it in the dishwasher. Going back into the kitchen, she asked, "How many of his bones did you break?"

"Enough. Then I dumped him with the cops. They weren't real concerned about his injuries, either."

A mixture of pride and something else, something . . . bitter . . . surprised her. She liked that he helped this woman, but she also . . . "You had a relationship with her?" She wanted to bite off the words as soon as she said them.

Phoenix rinsed the glasses. "I don't do relationships. Ever. Not until you."

Standing by the refrigerator, she studied his shadow. "Why?"

"I'm short-term. Get in, save the woman, and get out. Before I . . ."

She heard her own heartbeat. "Before you what?"

He shut off the water. "Find out if I can break them. Like my father did my mother."

"The voices," she said. He blamed his father for that and himself for her death.

"She cracked. Maybe from the strain of trying to survive alone and raise a kid, or my father used his hunter ability to shift her memories and weakened her brain. Too much of that shit causes permanent damage. Who the fuck knows."

Holding the butter in her hand, she said, "You're not him." She wasn't stupid; she knew he'd been with a lot of women. Witch hunters used sex to control the bloodlust. Her powers bubbled up and tickled along her spine. To cover her reactions, she turned and opened the fridge. Where did he keep the butter? On a door shelf? She felt around and finally just set the dish in the first flat spot she found. "Women trust you." There was something about him. He felt dangerous, yet when he was near her, she felt safer. He wouldn't break a woman.

"Probably the pheromones, but yeah. And I like women." She heard him shut the dishwasher.

Like she needed that bit of info. She closed the fridge and decided to shift the topic. "How'd you go from bounty hunting to hooking up with the Wing Slayer Hunters?"

He started the dishwasher. "I did bounty hunting for a few years, made some money taking on dangerous jobs.

Then one day I tracked a target into a nightclub. He was a rogue and extremely dangerous. Axel and Sutton were running security on the club. Sometimes security can be meatheads, all muscles and ego without much brain. These two were witch hunters, and they quickly assessed the situation and let me do my job. We became friends. Then we decided to take the wings and commit to Wing Slayer."

Ailish leaned back against the counter, listening to him as he moved back and forth, putting stuff away. He took up a lot of space in the kitchen. Here in his home, he was wearing jeans and a short-sleeved shirt. Casual and relaxed. He stopped in front of her. It popped into her head—how many other women had he brought here? All kinds of insecurities sprang to life inside her. Deep, ugly feelings. *How many women had he slept with? Were they beautiful? Probably not scarred and—*

He put his hands on her shoulders and lowered his face to hers. "You're beautiful. Sexy."

She stiffened. "I wasn't talking out loud!"

His fingers tightened on her shoulders. "You must have. I heard you." He took one hand from her shoulder and stroked the delicate scarred skin around her eyes. "You got this fighting to save a woman's life. Not ugly, Ailish. And your eyes, they are so pale blue that they look silver. Very pretty. Delicate in your otherwise strong face."

She couldn't get her breath. *He liked her face? He seemed to like her body.*

"Okay, that time your mouth didn't move. I was watching."

"What?" She tilted her head up to his face.

He stroked her bottom lip with his thumb. "You have a very sexy mouth. I was looking at it when I heard you say that about me liking your face and your body. But your mouth didn't move."

He knew what she'd been thinking. "How—"

"Put your hand on my mouth. See if you can hear me and if I move my lips." He took hold of her wrist and lifted her hand to his mouth. His lips were full and firm and his breath warm against her skin. Then he sucked in a finger, his tongue caressing the digit. *The answer is hell, yes, I like your body. You're lean and strong, like a sleek car or fast bike.*

He was stroking her finger with his tongue. No words came from his mouth. "What's happening?" She tugged her finger out, fear and excitement skittering over her.

Phoenix pressed up against her, putting his hands on the counter to bracket her body. "It's a mind link. I've seen Darcy and Axel, and Carla and Sutton do it." His erection pushed against her stomach through his jeans. "Doing it with you, feeling your thoughts brush through my head—it's a turn on." *Tell me why you're hairless between your legs.*

Her breath caught in her throat, and heat flooded through her. The feel of him inside her head fired her nerve endings and made her breasts and deep core ache. *It was just easier. I do it with magic.* She had so little time left. An urgent, wild need began to build in her. It was nothing like the handfast but instead was all Phoenix. She wanted to yank his shirt off over his head, shove his pants down, and feel him. Touch, stroke, lick . . .

He leaned down, sliding his face across hers until his mouth was at her ear. His warm breath tingled. "I can hear you, my very bad, very sexy witch."

His words tumbled through her. She knew what she wanted. "Well then? What are you waiting for?"

His dark chuckle nearly made her beg. Then he grabbed her hand and pulled her along. He made an unexpected left. "Downstairs."

"The gym?" she said, navigating the stairs with no trouble.

"Private. I have monitors that will let me know if anyone is moving around the property."

Alone. In the gym. With him. Naked.

He closed the door to the gym and then, standing at the edge of the mat, said, "One second." He let go of her hand.

Then she heard the soft rustle of the shirt leaving his body. Boots off. Pants. Her heart started to hammer. She held perfectly still, trying to breathe. Then she felt the absence of him next to her.

"You want to explore?"

"Shit." She jumped. He was suddenly behind her, his mouth at her ear. And that ramped up her excitement more. She knew Phoenix wasn't a threat to her, knew it was just the two of them down here. He was playing.

He said, "If you can get me down, I'll concede. I'll let you touch and explore all you want."

Oh God. The thrills danced up her spine as if he were touching her with more than just his words, his challenge.

"No holds barred, babycakes. I'm stronger and faster than you, so you're going to need to up the stakes. You're going to need all the magic you can handle."

He was helping her practice her magic, too, and that just made it more arousing. She resisted the urge to lean back into that sexy voice. In answer, she unsnapped her pants.

"What are you doing?" His voice thickened.

"Don't want anything in my way. Got a problem with that, hunter?" She bent over, wiggled her hips, and shimmied the pants off. She was already barefoot. That left her in a clinging T-shirt and panties. Free to kick him to the ground.

"You fight dirty," he said, then melted away from her without a sound.

She kicked her pants to the wall and stood. She had walked the entire gym, memorized it. She knew exactly how to use the magic in her first four chakras for fighting. Opening them now, she swept the air and felt the warm mass of Phoenix standing very still, dead ahead on the mat. She knew he was right: It would take more to beat him. More magic and more cunning.

She began walking toward him, and with her air chakra open, she felt the second he moved. He was lightning fast, even faster than she remembered, literally moving quicker than her chakra could track.

It was almost funny—she had a hot, naked man at her mercy, if she could just catch him. Blind.

Magic. Use it. The words whispered in her mind, making her nipples tighten into sensitive little buds. Her stomach clenched. Her chakras swirled with more power than she'd ever felt before. But could she control it? That's what worried her; she didn't want to lose control of her power and hurt him, then maybe kill herself in the process. The fear seeded between her rib bones. . . .

A whispery soft touch of wings brushed her face. The fear vanished. She had a familiar, she just had to learn to use him. Trust him to control and focus all her magic, including her siren voice power, to enhance only what she chose. Ailish caught her rushing magic and began funneling it along her spine, faster, stronger. The power stream raced up and then tingled around her throat. She'd felt the same thing when she'd sung to call the phoenix last night. The pressure grew for a few seconds, then her fifth chakra sprang open. Communication with other realms, this was where her siren power lived.

But what did she do with it? She swept the room with air, trying to see what Phoenix was doing. The gym was quiet, no sound. Ailish concentrated, closing her eyes and listening for any movement or noise . . .

Twin images appeared, and she gasped. It was like making love last night: Every time she'd orgasmed with him deep inside her, she'd seen the bird. But now she saw two halves of the bird, with nearly the width of a doorway between them. She was seeing the tattoos on his arms! She didn't have to turn her head to see the bird; it was a connection between her and the phoenix that allowed her to track him anywhere in the gym. Long practice in the ring kept her game face in place while her mind whirled over strategies. She could see him, but how did she get him onto the ground?

She had to bring him to her. He'd told her to use magic, but part of her still shied away from losing control of her siren power.

But the bigger part of her wanted to win!

Tracking the birds, she saw Phoenix circling her, moving silently around the edges of the mat. She could feel the danger, feel the way he was coiling his muscles, ready to spring. Dangerous. Hot. Hers.

She shot out a fast kick.

He evaded her without any effort. "I'll go watch a movie while you learn to fight." He turned and walked to the stairs.

All she could see were the bird tats moving away from her. Her magic surged, trying to reach him. Her throat ached, and her competitive instinct burst free. She lifted both hands, focused everything she had on those twin tattoos, and sang, "The wings are mine! I claim them now!" The power rolled up in a huge wave, and she fought to control it.

Then she felt the wings sweeping fast and determined, corralling her magic into the path she chose.

Excited, thrilled, she struggled to stand still as her magic shot out.

"Holy shit," he said, and before the words were out, he was in front of her. "Your voice caught me and pulled me right to you!"

She lifted her hands, magically wrapping the pants she'd taken off around his ankles.

"Hey!"

She put both hands on his chest and shoved. His massive shadow went over and she heard the thump when he fell. "I win!" She danced in a circle. Then paused. "You're not hurt, are you?"

His shadow rose as he sat up and jerked the pants off his ankles. Then he snapped up to his full six-foot-four height of pure menace. "Impressive . . ." His voice rang with pride, then slid to challenge. "Come here, Ailish. Claim your prize. Unless you're afraid when I'm not tied up?"

"Be good, or I will tie you up," she taunted as she reached up and touched his biceps. The bird nuzzled his head in her palms. She dragged her palms over his shoulders, measuring the width of them. Then she traced down his chest, over his pectorals, and touched a nipple.

He jerked, and his nipple hardened. "I'll be good, only because I'm going to need my hands free to touch you," he said in his sex-growl voice.

She used her fingers to mark the path down his ribs, feeling the way he narrowed. So much strength. Even his bones felt brawny. Then his tapered-in waist. She stepped closer, until she felt his erection brushing her T-shirt. Her entire body was focused in her hands, in the sensation of Phoenix as she outlined his back. His strength was tightly packed into sensual muscle. No wonder he could heft her hundred and thirty pounds so effortlessly.

Her greedy magic poured through her fingers as she found that dip in his back just above his butt. There was no stopping. She leaned closer and pressed her mouth to his chest, brushed her lips over the hot skin as she filled her palms with his round butt cheeks.

"Your magic," he panted. "Everywhere."

She licked up and caught his nipple.

He palmed the back of her head. "Kiss me."

Lifting her head, she met his fiercely hungry, open-mouthed kiss. She rubbed up against him, feeling his erection slide up her stomach while she shaped and squeezed his backside.

He reached around, caught her wrists to pull her hands off his butt, and brought them to his stomach.

He growled into her mouth, pushing her hands down, the sparse hair on his lower stomach grazing her palms. Then the hair grew thicker, more wiry, until he wrapped both her hands around his dick.

Her heart leaped and hammered. Her magic reached through her stroking, tasting, drawing him to her. Everything swelled and ached as he filled her hands. Big, hot, stretched skin over a hard shaft. She circled the swollen head, brushed the slit, and he shuddered.

Mine . . . He filled her head with the statement. He broke the kiss, stripped off her shirt. Knelt down, tugged at her panties. The yawning, deep need broke free in her. Wild magic swayed and pulsed. She couldn't catch it, couldn't control it.

Phoenix swept an arm under her legs. *Catch you.*

Didn't even think. Trust. Fell into his arms.

He caught her, laid her on the mat, covered her with his massive body. Shimmering magic popped and raced between them. She could feel it lighting up all over her, more alluring than the flickering TV lights. It touched her skin and filled her dark world. "Phoenix . . ."

"Open for me, beauty."

She could feel his gaze on her face as she lay beneath him, and she wrapped her legs around him.

Phoenix drove home inside her. One long, deep stroke that caused all her magic to sigh. Then he began to thrust. Harder, faster.

She reached out and held on to the bird, opening her body, her chakras, her mind, taking what Phoenix gave her. Each thrust drove her higher.

"Ailish, you're inside me. Look, baby. See what I see!" he said in a voice filled with more than sex.

She opened her eyes, trying to see him.

But instead her vision filled with herself. A woman with a swollen mouth, strong face, scars, and incredibly silver eyes. And as she came apart for him, as the pleasure shattered her, she saw her witch-shimmer light up to a fierce, golden-bronzed glow.

My God, she was seeing herself as Phoenix saw her.

"My beauty," Phoenix roared as he came inside of her.

16

Ailish was so deep in his mind, another massive shudder of pleasure ripped through him. Her magic had him by the balls. It circled and caressed and squeezed. It milked his cock deep inside her, while her essence, her very presence, was in his mind, joined so perfectly that she could see with him.

That sent him over the edge, and he exploded inside her, spurting deep into her magic. The moment strung out, the two of them immersed in soul-deep pleasure.

Settling against her, feeling her body beneath his, smelling the commingled scent, feeling the very beat of her heart behind her breasts, he knew: She was ripping open his heart and making him too damned vulnerable.

And there wasn't a thing he could do about it.

He stroked her hair and laid his face next to hers, cheek-to-cheek. She needed touch, this witch of his. She was a heart-wrenching combination of tough and vulnerable. She'd suffered and survived, making herself stronger and able to defend herself.

He knew what drew him to her. Beyond the magic and souls and games of the gods and demons, he knew what it was. Ailish wouldn't break.

It was up to him to make sure she didn't die.

Ailish drew him away from his thoughts as she said, "I haven't seen what I look like in almost eight years."

He smiled, so damned proud that he'd been able to

show her. And her magic, Jesus, her power was huge. Too much for one small witch. But with his phoenix, she could control it. It was humbling.

He pulled away from her body, rolled to his side, and scooped her into his arms. "Told you, you're my beauty."

She put her hand on his chest. "I look different. Face is more angular, hard, I guess."

He leaned her back and traced her face. Touching the scars, her cheekbone, her jaw. "Not hard, strong. You were just a child when you lost your sight. The baby softness gave way to a woman's strength."

"Thank you for showing me." *For giving me this new definition of myself.*

He heard that mind whisper, but he didn't think she'd projected that to him. That meant she was starting to trust him on an unconscious level that made his chest swell. Noticing that her body was cooling, he threw a leg over her hips to warm her with his. "Your power is growing, and so is your control. I can't believe how you all but forced me to you."

She tensed. "Will it work tonight without you next to me? What if we can't control my siren magic that way and accidentally enhance demon magic?"

"Even Wing Slayer said you'll have full control once mated, Ailish." He kissed her again, trying to ease her worry, then added, "It's just an experiment. Axel, Sutton, and I want to see how much resistance we have against the wards, the witches want to try their spell, and we'll see how much your voice can enhance their magic."

Phoenix looked down at her left wrist, at the hated handfast binding. If tonight didn't work, he'd find another way to get her free of that demon.

Phoenix drove a black four-wheel-drive Xterra up the old road to Screaming Chapel. The whole area had been abandoned after the massacre more than seven decades ago. As soon as he got within half a mile of the chapel, he began to feel uneasy.

"See anything, Axel?" he said into his earpiece.

"Soon as I get near enough overhead, I hear screams and smell something bad. Too close, and it makes me dizzy. Don't really want to fall thirty feet to the ground."

Sutton said, "Ailish was right, there's some kind of hallucinogenic effect going on. When I get close enough, I remember the time Carly died in my arms."

Phoenix said, "I saw my dead mother when we were at the house. The drug has to be woven with dark magic to go after our worst memory, or . . ."

The SUV sputtered, lurched, then stopped dead. Even the lights went out. The scent of sulfur drifted around him. "Shit, they know we're here. Demon magic killed the electrical system in the car. Even the lights are gone."

He sat in the vehicle and searched the area. It took only a few seconds for his vision to adjust to the moon-lit night. He didn't see anyone skulking around on the road. "Either they have some force field to drain the car battery, or they have cameras watching the area, or spies, and used magic to cut the power."

Sutton said, "I don't see anyone around your vehicle. Get out and meet us a quarter mile ahead. That will put us close enough to let the witches try their spell."

Phoenix stayed alert, grabbed a flashlight and the keys, then got out. "Maybe the witches can help me restart the SUV when we leave. Not hoofing it all the way back."

"We could drop you someplace," Axel said dryly.

"I'd rather walk." He hated flying in airplanes, something all the hunters knew and teased him about. Men with wings carrying him? Not a chance. His own memory of flying had ended in flames. Phoenix went as far as he could before the wards made his ears ring, a feeling of pressure built in his chest, and his unease made him sweat.

The other two hunters landed in front of him. They were close enough now to see the glow of torches and shadows moving. "At least some of them are here," Phoenix said in a whisper. He checked his weapons, two knives, a gun, and his chain. Just in case they could break the wards and get in there.

Axel looked grim. "Time's running out for them. They must be doing everything they can to get Ailish to turn, especially now that they can no longer harness her siren power to enhance their magic."

He looked around again, seeing the dim shape of the chapel and feeling a strong sense of déjà vu. He'd never come up here as a kid; in fact, it always made him uneasy even to talk about it. "I think this is where Ailish was born, and where I died in the phoenix form."

Axel had his phone in his hand, but he jerked his gaze up. "You remember it?"

He shuddered. "Makes me think of burning. The memory is more real now than any time before." He could almost smell the scorched feathers. He hated the idea of Ailish being born out here, surrounded by viper witches and valued only for her worth in trade to a demon.

Axel nodded, then said to both of them, "Be ready. Phoenix, you're not immortal, remember that."

He wasn't going to let her mother kill him. Axel quickly talked to Darcy, then held up the phone while the witches directed their spell.

Even from the miles separating them, Phoenix felt Ailish's magic bloom in his guts. He could feel the bird lift his wings and help her. It was surreal, powerful, and made him so damned proud.

Ailish sat on the floor in a circle with the two other witches in Darcy's condo.

"I'm placing a white candle in a black bowl, sprinkling it with dirt of the earth . . ." Darcy paused in her explanations, then said, "And pouring in water to the top." The sound of water splashing into a bowl filled the room.

Carla was on Ailish's left. "We use white candles to break through dark magic and replace it with the magic of the earth."

Ailish's chakras already bubbled in excitement. She was going to do spell magic with earth witches. For eight years, this was what she'd wanted, to be a real earth witch.

"Okay," Darcy said. "We can't use a salt circle, so we're going to keep this simple, using only our first five chakras. The communication with other realms will help us push our power through the phone that Carla and I are holding between us. Let's join hands and form the circle."

Ailish's hands felt heavy in her lap. All those years she'd kept people from touching her. But they just reached out and took her hands as if it were normal. Natural. Ailish relaxed a little.

"Carla and I will begin the chant and light the flame. You'll feel our power circling through you. When that happens, add your voice power. If anyone feels a dark threat of any kind, break the circle by dropping hands. Got it?"

"Yes," Ailish said.

They began to chant:

Earth, air, water, and flames,
Circle and grow into
An army of light to
Bring down darkness!

Ailish felt the other witches' power begin to move through her. Her chakras made her a natural conduit;

now it was time to use her voice power. As they chanted, she began to sing:

> *Bury it with earth;*
> *Scatter it with air;*
> *Drown it with water;*
> *Burn it with fire!*

Ailish heard the flame on the candle surge. She kept her power flowing, absolutely thrilled at the bright magic churning in her, joining with the other two witches. It felt strong and good. She pushed more and more magic through her voice, which went through the circle. Her skin warmed, her nipples hurt, even her womb ached as her magic thrummed up from her very core. She began to feel the power drenching her, growing too thick, too much . . . and then the bird cooed softly, and she felt his wings sweeping the power, keeping it focused.

It was freeing and powerful . . . and she went with it, singing and singing, letting it build and build. Her joy in being a real earth witch and circling her powers with other witches, being part of something good, made her heart swell. Suddenly, she heard the bird screech. Terrible pressure filled her head and shoved between her eyes. Ailish snatched her hands away from Carla and Darcy just as she felt something break open on her forehead, and her spirit yanked out through the hole.

She tumbled down, like falling down a mine shaft, falling and falling, and she couldn't touch or see or feel anything. Then the scent of sulfur and incense slowed her descent. She saw shadows and flickering lights surrounded by fog, and then it began to clear.

A tall nude woman, hair cascading over her shoulders, stood at a stone altar.

Recognition exploded—she was seeing her mother! At

the coven grounds. She couldn't turn and look, but she sensed the rest of the coven witches spread out behind Maeve.

What was happening?

Black candles flickered on the altar, surrounding a gray rectangular box, like a small document safe, but the top had a jagged hole. Her mother clutched a black knife in her hand and looked up, her blue eyes zeroing in on Ailish. "You provided the blood link. Now I can kill the mother and baby."

Cold dread dripped down her spine. *Morgan! Her blood got on Morgan when Maeve caused Ailish's scars to burn open.* Hot rage and nausea choked her, but she could do nothing, only stare as her mother moved the knife to her flat stomach and sliced. Blood welled up in a shallow cut.

Then she cut again. And again. All the while whispering, "Morgan, I've come to kill your baby. Cut off his toes. His feet. His fingers . . ."

"So be it!" the other witches chanted.

Her mother held up the knife dripping with blood and returned her gaze to Ailish. "Submit or they die. If you still refuse, I'll kill the phoenix."

No! Ailish felt sick panic grip her.

Maeve said, "I saw him burn, knew you were a siren. We couldn't let you ever find out and call your familiar, so we gathered up his ashes and locked them in this safe."

Ailish's vision moved to the gray box with the hole in the top. The phoenix had risen, she realized, blowing out of the hole. But what did it all mean?

Her vision went back to her mother. "We used a bit of the ash to track him, but his witch hunter blood made him immune to our demon magic. Instead we found his mother. Pity she didn't kill him, although we told her to over and over. But now that your soul is bound with his, we can get to him through you."

Ailish's voice broke free and she screamed, "No! No!" The vision spun away as she was propelled back. Her head felt like there was a spike between her eyes, she was shaking, and nausea made her mouth water.

"Ailish, answer me!" Darcy yelled.

"Darcy!" Joe yelled, running in. "It's Morgan! She's bleeding!"

Phoenix felt the pressure on his chest ease, the ringing and screams in his ears begin to fade. Damn, the witches were doing it. He palmed his knife and wrapped his chain around his hand, ready to spring through once the wards were down enough and Axel gave the command.

He was so close to success. Kill Ailish's mother and free her from the handfast! He'd have Ailish, his soul mirror, to care for and protect, to help her with her magic.

The bird screeched, then went into a frenzy, clawing, pecking, the flames blistering his skin. "What?" he whispered to it. Something was wrong! Ailish's power shifted and scattered, as though she and the bird had lost control.

Darcy's voice came through the phone Axel held. "Ailish broke the circle and she's not answering us. She won't let me touch her to try to pull her out. Axel, she's in trouble."

Rage roared through him as Axel said, "We're coming back now. Be careful."

"Wait, Axel!" Darcy yelled. "It's Morgan. She's bleeding from cuts all over her stomach. It's demon magic. Hurry, I need your help!"

Axel's green eyes turned deadly, and his wings sprang from his back. "I'm coming now. So is Sutton."

Sutton's wings burst out, and the two of them took off.

Phoenix spun around and ran for the SUV at the speed of a panther. He got to the vehicle, jumped in, jammed the keys into the ignition, and turned.

Nothing. Dead.

Urgency ripped up his spine, the bone-crunching need to get to Ailish. He shoved out of the vehicle and broke into a run down the road. His boots churned up dust as he leaped over potholes and rocks.

Not fast enough! Ailish was in trouble! What happened? Was the demon hurting her? He had to get there. He pushed harder, his heart pumping, his muscles straining, his chest and back burning.

He could feel Ailish's distress, her emotional turmoil, her sweaty cold fear and regret.

A sudden flash of heat, and a weight burst from his back in a loud *whoosh*.

He stumbled but fought to stay on his feet and keep running. Faster, harder . . . as his muscles burned. He leaped over another rock and—

"Oh, hell." He was rising off the ground. Phoenix looked to the right. Blue-and-purple feathers shimmered in the moonlight over a powerful wing that stretched out five or six feet.

He jerked his head left and saw the same thing.

Wings. Flying. Just like before, almost twenty-four years ago when Ailish had been born. His muscles knew what to do, how to pump the wings and take him into the air.

He hoped he didn't burn up this time, but his need to get to Ailish overrode that. He soared high over the skies of Glassbreakers, into the industrial area, and down into the back of the club. He used his palm print to open the garage, ran to the elevator, opened it, and got halfway in when he realized he had a problem.

His wings wouldn't fit.

He'd seen Axel and Sutton do this. They just sort of shrugged, and the wings lifted and then folded and disappeared back into the tattoos. He glanced down at one of his biceps; the tat was gone. Then he lifted his shoulders. "Fold up."

The wings ruffled, as if they were hurrying him. He snapped, "I get can't upstairs to Ailish with the wings out!"

The wings lifted, curled, and vanished.

He hurried into the elevator and pushed the button. As the doors closed, he check his biceps. The tattoo of the phoenix rising from the flames was there. Same with the other arm. The bird looked impatient, but it was there.

The doors opened and Phoenix ran into Axel's condo. Morgan lay on the couch. Darcy and Carla leaned over her, while Axel and Sutton both touched their witches to help funnel their magic. Joe hovered. "Where's Ailish?" he asked.

Axel looked at him. "How did you . . . Wings?"

"Yes. Where is she?" He looked around and didn't see her. Fear and worry erupted inside him. Good Christ, she hadn't left, maybe run away or—

"In your condo."

Slightly relieved, he asked, "How's Morgan?" He looked between Carla's and Darcy's hands to see shallow cuts all over Morgan's swollen stomach. The dark magic had opened the healed scars from when Eric had cut her. Then he caught sight of the two witches' hands. Thick dark lines were crawling up their fingers and over the backs of their hands before fading away. They were pulling out the demon magic, and both their witch-shimmers had pain holes in them. Sutton and Axel were siphoning off the pain, but it was not enough.

"What the hell happened?"

Axel answered, "Ailish said that when her mother tore open her scars, her blood got on Morgan, establishing a blood link."

He reasoned it out. "Maeve has a blood link to Ailish through their mother-daughter relationship."

"And Maeve deepened the link with her daughter by

adding her blood to the handfast contract," Axel reminded him.

He ground his jaw. "Ailish's blood got on Morgan, linking her mother." That shit didn't work with witch hunters, which was why Axel hadn't been worried when he'd picked Ailish up. "Trying to force Ailish to finish the handfast by hurting Morgan and her baby. Just like that bitch tried to kill Haley." It made his head ring with rage.

Carla lifted her head, and Sutton pulled her long blond hair out of her way so she could look at Phoenix. "Go see her, Phoenix. She was upset, her witch-shimmer a sick color. She wouldn't let us touch her. This wasn't her fault. She was helping, trying so hard." Carla shuddered, either from pain or frustration. "Go see her. Take care of her."

Phoenix looked at Joe, crouched down by Morgan's head, his back bunched with rage-filled muscles as he gently stroked Morgan's sweaty face.

There was nothing he could do here, so he pulled the door closed and strode down to his condo. Opening the door, he spotted Ailish sitting in the corner of the leather couch, the room dark except for the flashing lights of the TV. No sound. It tore at his chest to see her sitting there, arms wrapped around her bent knees, staring. She looked so alone.

He shut the door.

She didn't move. Just sat there, eyes wide and fixed on the TV that she couldn't see. "Why don't you have the sound on?" He sank next to her on the couch.

"I like the lights. They move over my skin and change the shadows. It doesn't feel so dark."

A sharp pain hit his chest. "Ailish, it wasn't your fault." He wrapped his arm around her shoulders. She was stiff, and he didn't feel any of her magic.

She lifted her head from her knees and turned to look

at him. "I infected Morgan and her baby with demon magic. I saw my mother tonight. She told me she'll kill Morgan and the baby, kill you, kill everyone until I submit."

He could feel her desolation. "She can't kill me, can't get to the rest of us. She had to go after the mortal." He slid his hand beneath her hair to her nape. "We'll work together. . . ."

She let go of her legs and with her stealthy grace stood up and walked to where the TV was mounted on the wall. Tilting her head back so the lights bathed her face, she said, "We can't. I have to kill my mother to break her link to Morgan. Alone."

Protective adrenaline surged through him, driving him to his feet. "You're not alone."

She turned, facing him. "Maybe the handfast will break before the witch karma kills me. Maybe that will be enough for the Ancestors."

He sucked in air, trying to get control of the absolute furious need to protect her, keep her safe, keep her with him. Her fear of the darkness, of spending eternity in cold nothingness, was so acute, he experienced her dread filling his stomach. She was standing in the lights of the TV, trying to absorb them, trying to chase out the cold darkness she so feared. "I'm not going to let you die."

"Yes, you are."

He closed the distance between them, wrapped his arms around her, feeling all her muscles packed into her tight frame, and tried to fill her with his warmth. She stood motionless, arms at her side. She was slipping away, and he tried to pull her back. "We're going to do this together. You'll get strong enough to magically fight your mother off, and use your magic to break down the wards. I'll kill her." He pressed his face into her hair.

"She has your ashes." Her voice was hopeless.

A strange echo pinged in his head and through his body. Slowly, he let her go and took a step back. "What ashes?"

"The ashes of the phoenix that burned at my birth. My mother gathered them, and used them to try to kill you."

His gut tightened, and he watched the TV lights play off her face and silvery eyes. "I'm immune to magic like that. All witch hunters are. Wing Slayer made us that way, leaving only our mortal relatives vulnerable. Before the curse, the earth witches would protect or heal them if—" It slammed home so hard that it knocked him back another step. "My mother."

"They tried to make her kill you. They still have the ashes and will use our soul bond to find a way to destroy you."

Murderous anger exploded behind his eyes, filling his vision with a red fog. In his head he saw the image of his mother, her body nearly empty of blood, cold and pitiful in that alley behind the Dumpster. The broken beer bottle in her lax hand, caked with her dried blood. She'd cut and cut, her wrists, her neck, even her thigh . . . to stop the voices.

It hadn't been his father's fault for getting her pregnant and dying. Not her family's fault for abandoning her when she was pregnant.

No, it had been *his* fault. For being a familiar to a siren witch, flying and burning, letting the vipers get his ashes. For being this creature . . . and yet his mother had loved him and never once hurt him. Ever. Instead she'd gone deeper and deeper into herself, tried to hurt herself.

Eventually she'd killed herself.

Suffocating with the guilt, rage, the memories, he stormed out. Away.

17

Phoenix knew Key was there, standing silently behind him. The other hunter had shown up about ten minutes ago. But right now, his head was filled with his mother. He stared at the headstone. It said only her name, *Sheri Torq*. He wasn't a poet; he hadn't known how to capture his mother's life in a single phrase.

His head pounded. The anger drained off, and it began to make more sense. He remembered bits and pieces of their life before the voices. She'd held down a job as a nurse. The days she was off, they'd get up, have breakfast, do chores, then go to the park or library, read together, watch videos. It had all changed so fast.

Around the time he'd begun having the dream of flying across the sky, hearing the baby cry, and burning. He'd been four, and his mother had been twenty-six. It fit.

Sheri had thought she had schizophrenia. She'd taught Phoenix that word in one of her better times, even explained that she'd read somewhere the average age of onset was twenty-five for women. She had tried medications, but they'd always failed.

Finally, he said, "I thought she was weak, that she'd been broken by my father. Turns out she was stronger than most. She never tried to hurt me."

Moving up to stand next to Phoenix, Key said, "Ailish tracked me down on the cell phone and told me what happened."

Ailish. Christ, the way he'd hauled ass out of there, what did she think? What if she left? He turned to Key. "Where is she?"

"In the condo. She wanted to leave, but I convinced her to stay, told her that her mother is trying to drive her to the streets where they can get her. Sutton has a camera watching the door, she won't get out without someone knowing."

Relieved that she was safe, he rubbed his forehead and looked down at his mom's grave.

"Sheri saved me," Key said. "Stopped me from becoming a murdering animal like the rest of my family. Especially after . . ."

"Yeah." Phoenix knew. His mother had loved Key. "Remember that time she caught you drawing pictures of naked women and selling them to the boys?"

Key snorted. "She asked me how I'd feel about those boys looking at naked pictures of her. Or Haley. Made me feel like a real shit."

"You were a shit. Still are."

"I'm not the one who stole the communion wine from the church," Key pointed out.

A smile cracked his face. Sheri had marched his butt to the church and made him confess. He could still feel the burn of that humiliation. She'd told him stealing food to survive was one thing, but stealing the symbolic blood of Christ? Not cool. "Funny how she never asked where the Hershey's Kisses we stole for her came from."

Key laughed. "Or the books. She loved to read."

"Still miss her," he said, unable to admit that to anyone else. "I wanted to give her the life she never had."

Key turned his gray eyes on him. "She wanted to give you a chance at life. She succeeded. Don't take that away from her, Phoenix. She succeeded. She fought the demon witches the only way she could. Sheri won, and she can rest now."

It still hurt to have failed her, to have caused her so much pain. But Key was right: She'd loved him and fought for him. He would honor that. "Now it's my turn to fight them."

Could he be as strong as his mother and free Ailish?

Ailish knew it was a dream because she could see. She was little, maybe six years old. Wearing her pink night-gown with the puffy little cap sleeves and white flowers with yellow centers and green leaves growing out of the stems.

It was deep night and the house blazed with lights. But the light by her bed had gone out.

Her room was filled with shadows. Thick shadows that moved with creepy clicks and pops, as though the pieces didn't fit right. Hellhounds. Assembled from dead animals, the parts never fit right.

They were charged with protecting her and keeping her in the house. The malice in them made her spine cringe. At the time, she hadn't understood chakras or earth magic. But every cell in her body knew the hellhounds were wrong. Evil. Unnatural.

They'd rip her apart if they weren't under orders from her mother to keep her unharmed.

They were in her room. Skulking in the shadows, sensing her. Ailish didn't know if they saw or smelled or what. Some had eyes, some didn't. . . .

She'd woken terrified. Her heart pounding in her chest, her skin itchy with cold sweat, her stomach roiling.

She had to get to the light. The hallway light was on. It flooded the doorway to her room. The hellhounds didn't like the light. She had to make herself push back the blanket and run for that bright glow.

Click. Pop. Skuttle.

A sob worked up her throat. She wished her mother were home! Oh God.

Pop.

It was closer. She tried to peer into the darkness of her room. She could see her dresser, was that something next to it?

Click, click.

"Stay back!" she shouted, her voice floating into the darkness. Her nose clogged with unshed tears. Her throat ached. Her fingers hurt where she clutched the blanket.

Pop, skuttle.

She hated not knowing what was in the dark! Hated the dark! Hated being so scared. She jerked back the covers and scooted to the edge of the bed. Put her feet on the floor.

Something touched her ankle.

Ailish screamed so hard, her throat burned. She shoved off the bed and ran. . . .

"Ailish, wake up."

She tried to listen to the voice, but all she could hear were the scuttles, pops, and clicks. The terror pounded through her. She needed a light, needed—

"Sweetheart, what is that? You're showing me something."

She startled awake, cradled in Phoenix's lap, his arms around her, his scent and warmth chasing away the nightmare. Her magic was flowing through her, reaching for him.

"Is that your nightmare I'm seeing?"

She couldn't stop it! She was projecting her terror to him through their mind link, she guessed. "Sorry, umm, hellhounds. I was dreaming and—"

"That's you," he said softly. "The little girl." He spread his hand out on her back and rubbed gently. Her residual terror began to melt away, and her heart started to calm down. His scent, the leather, soap, and musk, sank through her skin to her blood. Ailish knew she was acting like a one-woman freak show. She closed her eyes to get control and gasped. *I see something.* It was a room. There was very little light, yet she could see perfectly. There was the door, the dresser, the wood floor. She could see into dark corners! No hellhounds!

He slid his hand beneath her shirt to the skin on her back. *Keep your eyes closed and look with me. See? No hellhounds. It was just a nightmare.*

She felt him shift, turning his body slightly. She saw the room across from the bed. The long, light green wall with the TV mounted on it. At the right edge of the wall was a doorway. She knew that led to the bathroom and closet.

Phoenix stood up while holding her and turned. Now she saw the bed with the rumpled covers. The comforter had big squares of brown and green. The sheets were green. She could see the other side of the room. *How?*

Your magic. It reached out and pulled me in even while you slept. I could see your nightmare. See you as a little girl, afraid of the dark and the hellhounds. Could see the terror and tears in your huge blue eyes. His hand on her back stiffened.

She could feel his fury. For her. He cared enough about her to bring light to her shadows. Her throat ached, but she swallowed it down as the memories of everything else came back. Seeing her mother with her third eye, learning what she'd done with Phoenix's ashes, and Maeve hurting Morgan. "What are you doing here?" She thought he'd go back to his house.

"I'm here for you." He put his hand on her face. "Ailish, I was shocked, upset, but I don't blame you for your mother."

Her throat tightened. Didn't he get it? She had to make him understand. Pushing against his chest, she dropped her legs to the ground and stood. Stepping back, she felt the chill of the room without his warmth. "I infected Morgan. My mother will use our soul-mirror bond to infect you. I'm the disease, don't you see? This is why I've always stayed away from people. I have to do this alone." She thought he understood that. He had walked out, leaving her alone. Why the hell had he come back?

He stepped forward.

She moved back, desperately fighting to keep the shredded bits of her defenses in place. "I only wanted to be an earth witch. When I helped Darcy and Carla heal Morgan, I thought I was. And then tonight, I thought I was helping earth witches fight demon witches."

He moved so fast, he nudged her back, slapped his hands against the wall on either side of her head, and lowered his face to hers. "When your mother trapped you in your third eye tonight, I knew something was wrong. Desperate to get back to you, I hurried to the car, but it wouldn't start."

Ailish froze against the wall, feeling the heat of him surround her, burning through her defenses.

"So I started to run, my urgency growing with every stride, until wings sprang from my back and I took to the air and flew back to you. Wings, Ailish."

Her mouth dropped open. "Like Axel and Sutton?"

"Exactly. You know what that means?" He didn't wait for an answer. "*You are an earth witch*. The bird only lives for you. You brought out his wings just like Darcy and Carla brought out their mates'."

Her body filled with a bright hope that scared the shit out of her. She wanted to believe him. "But I'm still handfasted, and—"

"Trust me. Like you did when you were asleep and showed me your nightmare. Ailish, I trusted you with my soul. Isn't it time you trust me with yours? Trust us together?"

This was the man who held her in her nightmare, understood her fear of hellhounds and darkness, and found a way to overcome her blindness to show her she was safe in the room. And in his arms. He judged her not by her mother's actions, but by her own. Ailish saw that as clearly as she'd seen the bedroom through his eyes. She reached up and sank her hands into his hair. "Yes." She brushed her mouth across his, dragging her hands down his face, once again trying to see him, just as he'd shown her her own face, and the bedroom . . .

She broke the kiss, holding his face between her hands. "Can you show me what you look like?"

He leaned his forehead against hers. "We can try. If I look at myself in a mirror, you should see what I see."

Her magic heated up and spread through her like liquid desire that was half sexual and half a longing so deep, she thought it came from the center of her heart. She pushed him back, grabbed his hand, and felt her way to the bathroom door. "Where's the mirror? Over the sink? Is there a full-length mirror?" She turned and said, "Oh! Can I see you naked?"

Phoenix laughed, his rich voice echoing in the bathroom. He shut the door and said, "Full-length mirror on the back of the door."

Ailish heard him take off his boots. Then his vest. She leaned against the counter, gripped the edges of the cool granite. She wanted to see him. It bothered her that other women saw Phoenix and she couldn't.

"Honey, you're thinking so loud I can hear you without touching you." His leather pants whispered as he stripped them off. He reached out and took her hand. "Other women may have seen me, but only you have brought my bird to life. Now come here."

He tugged her to his side and put his arm around her.

"I can feel your chakras, feel your excitement. Close your eyes."

The bathroom had overhead lighting. Ailish could see shadowy shapes, but it was all just shades of gray. She closed her eyes.

Phoenix leaned down. "Come inside me, take a look."

His low voice traveled through her chakras, and her powers poured out. The flow was fast but sensual, melding her and this man together. Was she flowing inside him? He in her? He began stroking her shoulder, and then . . . feathers stroked her, too. The bird, reassuring her that it was okay to let the magic sweep her away.

The image was sudden and clear. Ailish felt her breath catch and she lifted her hand, reaching out to touch the mirror. It was cold and hard. But reflecting in that surface was Phoenix. She stood next to him and saw herself wearing just a T-shirt.

Phoenix was naked and dark. Huge. Tall. She tried to take him in. Black hair the color of a raven's wings. It fell midway down his neck in an uneven cut. She looked at his dark eyes and saw both death and life. Now she knew why Dee had said he looked like an outlaw. His eyes told a story of a man who didn't care if he lived or died. Eyes that told of killing and making tough choices. He had high, hard cheekbones, a strong forehead and chin. Dark stubble ran over his beard line.

He wasn't smiling or frowning. Just looking at himself.

Even his neck was strong. His shoulders were huge— nearly the width of a door. His skin tone, she didn't know, maybe some Native American? Didn't care, except that it was Phoenix. She looked over his arms, the impossibly ripped bulges. "The tattoo."

He turned his right arm into the mirror.

There it was. The half of the brilliantly colored blue-and-purple phoenix rising from the furious flames, like life and death. The bird was life and the flames were death. Just like Phoenix.

"More," she said softly. He was looking straight ahead. She could see only to his stomach.

He looked down.

Ailish followed him, down the flat carved stomach, seeing the line of hair she traced with her fingers that led to the springier, coarser hair. Then his penis. Full, ridged, huge.

She reached for him, desperate to touch him, to trace the vivid blue lines, to circle the swollen head. She hit the cool mirror.

Without moving his gaze, Phoenix took her hand and put it on his cock. She saw him guide her hand to himself. Her panties went wet. Using just a finger, she traced the head, touched the slit.

Phoenix shuddered, his body jerking, but he held his gaze, letting her look and touch him. She traced the length of him. He was bigger than she'd realized.

"You take all of me. I can sink into you all the way up to my balls." He spread his legs wider, took her hand, and cupped his balls.

Ailish felt the most vulnerable part of this hard, dangerous hunter resting in her hand, the heavy sacs so fragile, and her heart clenched. A fighter never reveals his vulnerable spot to his opponent.

You're my lover.

He took his hand from hers, leaving her cupping his balls.

I trust you.

She'd never been that to anyone. Never. Not a trusted lover. She caressed him gently.

He groaned, his arm around her tightening. "I can show you what it looks like to enter you. How hot it is to slide into you. How your body and your magic take all of me."

She shivered with pleasure, with the sheer connection between them.

"Take off your shirt, beauty."

His gaze turned from himself to her. She saw herself enveloped in the shirt she'd found. It was black and hung almost to her knees. Phoenix was looking at her, showing her. She took her hand from him, got hold of the shirt, and pulled it off. It was weird—she watched herself pull off a shirt. She saw her legs, her thighs—they were lean and muscled. Saw her black panties. Her waist and breasts. She was as small breasted as she thought. But her stomach and arms were muscular. Her hair was getting long.

She hadn't realized she'd opened her eyes, but Phoenix was looking right at them. Silvery blue. Then his gaze dropped.

"Panties."

She saw herself as she bent to slide them down her thighs and kicked them off.

He turned, lifted her in his arms. He was looking at her face when he said, "Fast and hard now. Then we'll shower, and in bed, slow and lingering. I'm going to show you what it's like to spread your legs and kiss you until you come for me." His eyes closed and his mouth came down on hers.

Ailish forgot about seeing and thought only of Phoenix. His tongue in her mouth, her breasts against his chest. She wrapped her legs around his waist and shifted the kiss, sinking her tongue into him and rubbing herself against him.

Phoenix lifted his head with a growl, put his forehead against hers, and said, "Need to be inside you." With one arm he shifted her higher. "See with me, Ailish." He looked down as he took hold of his cock.

She saw him push against her. Felt the thick head of him penetrating. Then he went deeper, an inch at a time, the huge length of him disappearing inside of her.

Her body clenched hard.

"Oh yeah." He thrust and buried himself inside of her.

They were flush, his wiry pubic hair brushing her smooth skin. "Joined."

"Yes." He lifted her and then thrust.

Ailish watched as he thrust time and again, going harder and deeper until she was coated with sweat and need, until all she could feel was Phoenix filling her up and driving her to bright lights of pleasure. Just as her orgasm burst over her, he yelled out, wrapped his arms tightly around her so that she felt his pleasure rocketing through him and mixing deeply with hers.

DAYS REMAINING ON HANDFAST CONTRACT: NINE

Phoenix walked into the condo kitchen. Empty.

He looked in Key's room. The other hunter had come in with him this morning and slept here.

Empty.

Where the hell was she? The bird didn't like it, either; he started that burning shit with the flames. "Knock it off, I'll find her." He pulled out his BlackBerry and accessed the cameras. No alarm had gone off, so she hadn't gone far. Nothing in the hallway. Maybe Key showed her the club? He looked in there.

Nothing.

Next he tried the warehouse. She wasn't by the computers or in the sitting area, not playing pool—and he was pretty sure Ailish could use her magic to play pool—so where? Wait, the gym. Maybe Key had showed her the gym. He accessed that camera view and—

Shock gut-punched him.

Narrowing his gaze, he saw Key, wearing sweats, snap a full kick at Ailish's face.

The bird screeched in his head. "Shut up," he said, and watched on his BlackBerry while heading for the door.

Ailish ducked, then caught Key's other leg with a knee strike. Key went down on his ass.

The bird quieted, his feathers ruffling as if preening. The bird was as proud of their witch as he was, now that the creature understood Key wouldn't hurt Ailish. Since the witch was bonded to Phoenix, Ailish didn't incite Key's bloodlust.

They were simply sparring. He took the stairs down and went into the warehouse.

He passed the pool table and rounded the partition to the gym. "Basic self-defense for the witches," Ram said. "I think it's a good idea."

"Told you," Key said. "Ailish is using her magic to track her opponents, not hurt them. Then she takes them down solely with her mortal skills. No witch karma."

"It's a great idea. Ailish, would you be willing to train Carla and me?" Darcy asked.

Key laughed. "Carla?"

Phoenix leaned his shoulder against the partition and watched. Ailish stood in the center of the two hunters and Darcy. Her face glowed, not just the sweat and witch-shimmer, but something else.

Acceptance.

Darcy smacked Key on the arm. "Carla's not clumsy. You should see her dance. She just doesn't like hiking and stuff."

Ailish said, "If Carla wants to learn, I'm happy to teach her. And you. I'll teach you as much as I can in the next few days."

Silence fell like a rock. Phoenix fought the heavy feeling in his chest, the agony rolling off the bird. They couldn't lose her. Wouldn't. He walked in. "Ailish."

She lifted her head, her face turning toward him with unerring accuracy.

It kicked him right in the gut. Her beautiful eyes in her strong face, her faint scars bracketing those eyes. She looked straight at him when he knew she saw only a shadow. But she was so attuned to him now, so connected, she could find him in a crowd. He'd bet she knew he was standing there from the second he arrived. She looked like a warrior witch, wearing shorts and a tank, her muscles gleaming, and those scars . . . showing that she'd stand between a friend and death.

She'd been only sixteen years old.

But she'd done it.

He wouldn't lose her. He reached out and tugged her to him, kissed her, then said, "If kicking Key's ass is too easy, I'll spar with you."

She laughed. *Not a chance, hunter. You play dirty.*

She was in his head, and it took all he had not to shudder visibly at the pleasure of it. Of her. *You like it dirty.* He showed her dirty, forming a picture in his mind. A game of naked pool. He'd have to show her the table, he'd have to bend over her . . .

"Whatever you two are doing, knock that shit off," Key said. "It's creepy, makes me feel like a voyeur."

Phoenix shifted Ailish to his side. "Thought you liked to watch."

"Women, you moron. Not you doing some kind of kinky psychic sex stuff. You're throwing off enough pheromones to gag an elephant." He turned and stalked out of the gym area, still muttering, "Christ, now I'll never eat again."

"Your dragon's getting fat anyway."

"Is not."

Ailish frowned. "He has a dragon?"

"Tat on his chest." Phoenix looked down at her face, saw the curiosity roll through, and said, "No."

She put her hand on his chest. "But a dragon? That sounds really cool. Just a peek?"

Darcy said, "Phoenix, show her. The dragon is beautiful."

He glared at Darcy. "You women are all the same. Always fawning over Key."

Darcy grinned at him. "Yeah, if Key will have me, I'm going to dump Axel."

"Not. Funny," Axel said from the other room. "Key's a good hunter, now you're going to make me kill him."

"Kind of funny," Darcy shot back. "Ailish laughed."

"Ailish," Axel called out, "help a man out here, don't encourage Darcy."

She was glowing. Phoenix watched her as she considered what Axel said and as she absorbed the feeling of being included in simple teasing. "Want me to fight her to see which one of us gets Key?"

He heard Axel choke. Probably on coffee.

Key was roaring with laughter. Ram chuckled.

"Oh darlin', he will make you pay for that one," Phoenix said, then added, "So will I. Now let's go get some coffee."

Key touched her shoulder. "Going upstairs to get cleaned up. Later." He walked away.

Phoenix slid his arm off her shoulder, took hold of her hand, and walked with her. It was easy to find the connection between them and show her where they were going. He knew Ailish would commit the layout of the warehouse to memory, then she'd be able to move around freely.

She tightened her hand in his. "I can see."

It was so hard not to shift his gaze to her face, but keep it focused on where they were going. "Key's workstation. He does our tats, and he also has a drawing board."

"For his work. He told me," she said softly.

Phoenix was amazed. He'd been sleeping and Ailish had been making friends. He'd heard her slide quietly out of bed, but he knew she was safe in the condo, and Key was there. So he'd let himself sleep.

He explained what he was showing her. "Pool table. Sitting area, drinks in fridge, coffee there." He let her see the coffeepot. "Past that is the computer console, all the monitors, and basically, that's Sutton's baby." He showed her enough for her to get the gist of it.

"Coffee, Ailish?" Ram called out. "Cream? Sugar? Or we can make tea."

"Tea, thanks. Black is fine."

Ram walked over with tea for Ailish. "It's hot. Grab the handle with your right hand."

Phoenix watched, part of him twitching to guide Ailish's hand to the cup. But she did fine, reached out, felt the heat, and got hold of the handle. She had her bearings, she could handle herself. He turned and poured coffee, then walked over and sat on the arm of her chair.

Ram filled a cup for himself, then said, "Ailish, nice to meet you, and thanks for the demo." He turned to Axel. "A, going to check in on Eli and Ginny. He's restless and wants to know how he'll face his test while sitting on his ass in a safe house."

Phoenix looked down at Ailish. "Eli is the hunter the rogues were trying to force to turn. They dumped witch blood on him and hurt his sister in front of him." Then he shifted his gaze to Ram. "He has a point. Linc was fighting with us when he came face-to-face with his friend who had turned rogue."

Axel rolled his head to stretch his neck. "Fine, but he needs to get his tat or Wing Slayer won't test him, and Ginny needs protection. The rogues know she's his weakness. Make that happen."

"Eli wants a griffin, Key can do that soon. As for Ginny, I'm giving her a job here, and she can stay here or with one of us."

Axel sighed. "Why do you even ask me?"

"Makes you feel important." Ram turned and headed out the back.

Darcy laughed.

Axel walked over and sat next to her on the couch.

"Next time you need my blood to heal him, I'm not giving it to you."

She put her hand on his thigh. "Yeah, you will."

Axel intertwined his fingers with hers. "Fine, but I'll make him suffer first."

Phoenix used to wonder how a total hard-ass like Axel could be brought to his knees by a witch. It was only now that he realized that true courage was in opening yourself up to a woman and giving her the power to destroy you.

Ailish said, "Darcy, I know you said Morgan's better this morning, but for how long? How much time do we have?"

Phoenix felt her worry and guilt about Morgan.

Darcy answered, "Carla and I managed to pull out most of the dark magic. We can't break the blood link, but we set your mother back at least a couple days."

Phoenix saw her slight wince. "Your mother was manipulating you," he said. "Showing you that about my mother . . . that was to try to break us up. They failed in trying to get my mother to kill me—" He stopped. "So she told you to feed your guilt and scare you. Maybe hoping I'd blame you and reject you."

Darcy tilted her head to the side. "What's this about?"

Realizing Ailish must not have told them, he explained about the ashes of his phoenix and Maeve's threats.

Darcy leaned forward. "Let me see if I understand. The phoenix flew over at Ailish's birth, and burst into flames. Maeve and her coven saw it, and realized Ailish was a siren so they gathered the ashes. While the physical bird died, the soul went back to Phoenix. That created the link the demon witches needed to torment Phoenix's mother." Darcy took a sip of her tea, her gaze reflective.

Ailish said, "The coven thought they could keep the phoenix from rising because they'd locked the ashes in a fireproof safe."

Darcy smiled. "But you're much more powerful than your mother realized. When you called him back from the dead, the ashes blew out of the safe. The whole legend of the phoenix and the siren evolved to fit with the soul-mirror bond. We really shouldn't be surprised, since witches have always evolved, usually growing stronger as we reincarnate."

Ailish said, "But can she hurt Phoenix? She said she can use our soul-mirror link to destroy him."

Phoenix felt the bird shuffle and fret in his tat. Shifting his coffee to his other hand, he put an arm around her. The bird settled down, nuzzling against her shoulder. "Not if she's dead," he said. "The wards were weakening. It was slow, but it was working."

"He's right," Axel said.

"But Ailish's mother knew we were doing it and disrupted it by locking on to Ailish and getting her to stop the magic. Carla and I can't bring down those wards without her, probably not even if we were on-site."

"Which you won't be," Axel said firmly.

Darcy ignored him. "Ailish, the power in your voice was completely focused last night, there was no spillover. What broke our efforts was your mother."

Ailish grimaced. "She was hurting Morgan. I saw it and I couldn't stop it." Her hands fisted. "She said she'll kill Morgan if I don't submit."

Phoenix could feel her agitation. How was she supposed to make a choice like that? "We're going to get her, Ailish. We'll stop her."

She ignored him and said to Darcy, "I didn't want to infect you or Carla, either."

"Stop saying that, you're not a virus!" Phoenix snapped.

She turned toward his voice. "My blood infected Morgan with demon magic. What would you call it?"

"Ailish . . ." He ground out the word.

"No, it's not going to be that easy, Phoenix. Maybe we'll kill my mother, and maybe that will break the hand-fast . . ."

"It will!" It had to. Or Ailish would die. He would lose her. He would stand by helplessly and watch the witch given to him to protect die. His chest did that weird hurting shit again, as if his heart were being torn apart. He'd fail everyone: his witch, his god, and his heart. "I won't let you die."

Ailish sucked in a deep breath. "Phoenix, I screwed up, not you. I did this—" She lifted her left hand. "I went to my mother begging her to make Kyle love me. I knew she was a demon witch, yet I trusted her. I nearly got Kyle killed, then Haley, and then Dee. I'm trying to be an earth witch, I am. I'm trying to make amends, to prove to the Ancestors that I'm worth a second chance. But look what I did to Morgan."

With his arm around her shoulder, he pulled her cheek against his chest. The raw longing on her face tore his guts to shreds, and he knew Ailish wouldn't want the others to see that. "You are worthy," he said in a choked voice. "The Ancestors will see that." They had to. How could they not see her heart as he did? She was trying, risking herself to help people.

Yet he could almost feel her slipping away from him.

Ailish lifted her head, her expression turning hard. "Whatever happens, the coven must be destroyed." She turned back to Darcy. "What do I do?"

Phoenix saw that Darcy's brown eyes were filled with sympathy. But her voice was firm. "Practice opening your sixth chakra and getting control. Do it with Phoenix touching you. He should be able to feel it if your mother tries anything. He could pull you out, or even redirect you. But you have to let him in to do that. Don't try to push Phoenix away to protect him. With enough practice, you should be able to resist your mother derailing you. And if you focus hard enough, you might be able to see what she doesn't want you to."

Ailish's gaze drifted left as she thought, then she said, "I can find out if she can use our bond to hurt Phoenix."

"Your mother is very dangerous. Be careful, and trust Phoenix. He's your familiar, he can protect you or pull you out of the third-eye trance. Trust him."

He looked down at her. "You trust me, don't you?"

She flashed a smile that was so intimate, it made his breath catch. "Yes."

He wouldn't let her down.

18

"Want to drive?"

Ailish was behind Phoenix on the bike. He stopped and dropped his legs to balance the motorcycle. Was he teasing her? "I can't—"

"Chicken?"

She smacked his arm. He rode the bike with just his leathers, but he made her wear his thick jacket with long sleeves and a helmet. "Dude, they don't give blind people driver's licenses."

"Stop making excuses. You're not blind when you're with me. I can see for you."

She swore she felt her heart grow in her chest.

"Come on, sweetheart. Get in front of me."

Excitement danced through her. Holding on to his shoulder, she swung her leg over and stood beside him. Keeping the bike steady with his legs, he took hold of her waist and guided her onto the seat in front of him. His thighs closed around her hips. This was stupid. She knew it was. She had no idea how to—

He took hold of her hands and put them on the handlebars. "All you have to do is trust me. You're going to steer, I'll take care of the rest."

"At least I'm wearing a helmet. You're not."

He laughed. "I won't let anything happen to you." He put his hands next to hers as the bike rumbled beneath them. "Now lean back and move with me."

She sank back against him and closed her eyes, and a

second later, images filled her mind. The beach was on their right. Phoenix turned his head and she saw the ocean. It was late afternoon, the sun sparkled off the blue-and-gray water. It was so vast that it took her breath away. The waves swelled up in that slow-motion roll, then broke quickly into white froth. It was so beautiful, it almost hurt to see it.

I can show you anything you want to see. But I don't want to stay in one place too long since you're a breathing GPS device. We'll come back. He turned his gaze to the road. They were in a dirt patch on the shoulder. Phoenix looked at the highway and took in the cars moving by, then the bike revved beneath them and they were moving. *Steer left and take us onto the road.*

It was like being a kid and pretending to drive. Phoenix was so much stronger, he easily corrected any mistakes she made in steering. The road opened in front of her. They rode up on cars in front of them, then steered around them and passed. It was like playing a video game when she was young! There was so much to see!

With Phoenix giving her directions in her head, they got off the highway running along the beach and turned inland. They passed gas stations, convenience stores, fast-food places. Ailish recognized some things from her memories of the town, but eight years was a long time. And the people! She was trying to drink it all in, trying to impress every image on her memory. The colors and shapes of the cars, the blue sky, the road, and the buildings. The way shadows fell through the buildings and marked the payment.

Then she started noticing signs with words. At first she couldn't quite process them. She recognized the letters, but they didn't add up to anything. They wouldn't flow from images to words in her head. Mild panic and stinging regret tightened through her.

She had loved to read and had devoured books before

losing her sight. All those nights alone, so damned afraid of the hellhounds, she would huddle under the biggest light in the house and read. Usually romances. She'd loved the hope and happy endings. She'd clung to the idea that she was worthy of love.

Had she lost the ability to read?

We're passing the signs too fast for you to read them. I'll focus on the next sign longer. There, coming up on it now.

Ailish wasn't even pretending to drive now. She let herself lean back and just absorb what Phoenix was looking at. It was an advertisement on a large billboard, so far ahead that she couldn't believe she could see it.

Hunter vision, he said in her head.

Show-off. The letters were clear, and as she studied them, they began to form a familiar pattern. "Your wife called, she said it's okay to buy a boat!" Ailish read the words out loud, sure they were lost in the wind. She could still read! Not that it really mattered, but it felt good. She could read the details of the boat company below. She started reading all the signs she could find. Company names on buildings, street signs, everything.

Now who's the show-off? Phoenix laughed, then suddenly tensed. "Shit," he said aloud as a big black car swerved in front of them. *Trouble.* He swung the bike into a hard right onto another, smaller road. *Hold on.* He accelerated so fast that it made her dizzy, but she hung on to his sight. He leaned forward until he surrounded her body.

Ailish moved her hands down to hold on to the grooves of the fuel tank in front of her. Buildings, signs, and trees passed in a blur as he twisted and turned through a community.

Shots rang out. Phoenix pushed her lower over the gas tank with his body. *Two vehicles, stay down . . . Oh shit!*

Ailish saw the knife fly past them as Phoenix swung right, off the road entirely. Her heart pounded, fear roared in her ears. That knife had been glistening black. Phoenix looked back, and she saw it following them.

Immortal Death Dagger. Young's in one of those vehicles.

Her chakras cringed at the words, but Ailish was having none of that shit. That knife would kill Phoenix. *Maybe I can stop it.* She willed her chakras to open and called her magic. Pulling out of Phoenix's vision, she focused her air chakra on that thing. She reached back with one hand and snapped Phoenix's chain free of the hook on his belt.

They were climbing through hills, but Ailish ignored everything but the dagger. It followed every turn Phoenix made, coming closer and closer. Gathering the chain in her hand, she could feel the malevolence in the dagger as it homed in on his back. It was a dozen feet away and gaining fast when she silently communicated, *Behind you, turn left!*

Phoenix swung the bike into a hard turn. Ailish had one chance. Her right arm was bent, and she snapped her arm out, letting go of the chain and then using magic to push it into the knife. An unholy clanging and wet smacking chilled her spine. Sliding into Phoenix's vision, she saw the chain wrapping around the dagger and the knife undulating and shifting as it fought the chain. She'd bought them time, but . . .

We're going to jump, Phoenix warned in her head.

With him looking straight ahead, she saw they were barreling straight toward the edge of a cliff. She could see water farther out. Was he crazy?

Sing! Call out my wings! Now!

Her magic responded to him, rushing up to her throat. He'd trusted her to slow down that dagger. She trusted him and sang the only thing she could think of: "Wings of my soul, soar to my call!"

He gunned the engine. Terror spiked and she opened

her eyes, jerking out of his vision. She felt the bike sail
off the edge at the same time Phoenix wrapped his arms
around her waist. *Let go of the bike!*

Ailish unclenched her fingers from around the gas
tank, and the machine fell out from under them. Vertigo
and fear filled her lungs with a scream when she felt a
huge sweep of wings slide by her arms and side.

Below, she heard a splash.

The only thing that kept her from falling was Phoenix's
arms around her waist. *I've got you.* Then he flipped her
around and caught her. *Put your legs around me.*

He didn't have to tell her twice. She locked her legs
around his waist, used magic to get rid of the helmet, and
flattened herself against his body. She felt his chest muscles expand and contract in rhythmic movements as he
pumped his wings. *What happened to the Death Dagger?*

*It broke free of the chain just as we jumped, but it
couldn't keep up with us once we were flying. Young
must have called it back.*

Relief eased through her. *Phoenix?*

He stroked her hair. *What?*

*Don't you dare blame the motorcycle going into the
water on me. It wasn't my driving that did it!*

His chuckle was rich and vibrated in her head, flowed
down her spine, and curled through her pelvis. *It'll be all
your fault when I tell the story.*

This was the first time Ailish got to actually see what
Phoenix's house looked like. He landed outside on the
circular driveway. She saw a blue car with white stripes
sitting there, but she was much more interested in the
house. It was modern, wide, and multilevel to create a
building-block look. Like a beach house on the cliffs, except this one didn't overlook waves.

Phoenix turned his head, showing her his view—

hundreds of homes spread out below him. An entire community. She could see the school and soccer fields, more parks amid the houses, and a large swimming pool.

All the things he'd missed as a kid, now he could look at them every day. Phoenix had found his place, his home.

Setting her on her feet, he said, "Have to figure out how to put the wings away."

She reached up and stroked the feathers. He was looking at one wing, so she could see the feathers ranged in color from bright blue to deep purple. "They just popped out when I sang?"

"Yep." He caught her hand. "And they won't go back into the tattoo if you keep stroking them."

"It's like that with my magic. My chakras open and my powers rush out when you are near me." She saw the wing lift, bending closer to his body, then it vanished with a soft whisper of feathers against skin.

"Come on." He led her toward the garage on the kitchen side of the house and put his palm against some kind of plate. A whirring noise started, then the big door rolled up.

"That's your car?" A black, sleek-looking machine with two white stripes. It gleamed beneath the garage lights.

"Mustang GT," Phoenix said.

She pulled out of his grip to touch the edge of the car. It was cool and smooth. The images she was seeing disappeared, leaving her back in her gray, shadowy world, but she had seen what the car looked like. She noticed a mild headache, probably from trying to process so many images.

Phoenix caught her hand, tugging her with him, and said, "Keep your eyes open, and I don't think you'll see through me. Give your head a rest."

She paused, noticing the headache had faded. "You knew I had a headache? Why did it stop?"

He tugged her to him, putting a hand on her face. "I felt it start when we were flying home and you insisted you wanted to see my wings. I can siphon off the pain. It's what soul mirrors do."

"I've trained to function through pain. You don't have to do that."

He leaned his forehead against hers. "I want to. I need to." Threading his other hand in her hair, he said, "You were amazing today, Ailish. The way you used your magic and my chain to stall that Death Dagger impressed the hell out of me."

His praise sent tingles through her, and her powers danced and popped. Along with the way he'd trusted her when she'd told him to turn the bike so she could get at the dagger.

He leaned down and kissed her gently. "We're going to break the handfast together. You're mine, and I'm not going to lose you." He let go of her face and led her to the house.

Ailish had the visual of the garage in her mind and was able to easily move around the car. They walked inside to the smell of something warm and spicy. She stopped and inhaled.

"A half hour until dinner," Dee said.

A surge of happiness swelled behind her breastbone. "Dee, you came back!"

"Of course I did. Someone has to take care of you."

Normally, she'd snarl at a comment like that. But she was just too pleased to have Dee back. "What is that smell?" Ailish asked. "Whatever it is, I think I'm giving you a raise."

Dee was clinking glasses and moving around the kitchen. "Lasagna. I like to cook, and this kitchen is fabulous! Plus I had my own errand boy."

"Hey," a male voice protested.

Ailish jumped.

"It's just Linc," Phoenix said, squeezing her hand. "He's a witch hunter, the one I asked to take Dee to pack her stuff up and go shopping for whatever she needed. He stayed here last night to make sure she was safe."

"Just?" The voice moved closer. "Hi, Ailish, I'm Linc Dillinger."

His voice was smooth and rich, like melted gold. He stopped in front of her, standing an inch or two taller than Phoenix and slightly leaner. Ailish held out her hand. "Hi, Linc. I'm the witch causing all the trouble."

He enveloped her hand in both of his. "You don't look big enough to cause much trouble, sugar."

Phoenix put his arm around her. "She can drop you on your ass, Dillinger. Now give Ailish her hand back."

Linc laughed, a rich, fluid sound, and released Ailish's hand. "I heard you have some skills."

"Did you hear I kicked Phoenix to the ground when I met him?" Ailish asked sweetly.

That made Linc roar with laughter. "I'd have paid to see that."

"How much? I can do it again." She saw no reason to mention that she'd only succeeded the first time because she'd taken Phoenix by surprise.

"How about we make it interesting?" Linc rolled out the challenge in that smooth voice of his. "Set up a match, maybe get a little action going—"

Phoenix made a noise deep in his chest. "How about I cut out your heart and we'll take bets on how long it keeps beating?"

"Is that a no?"

Charm just rolled off this guy. It made her want to laugh. The only men who made the effort with her were usually possessed by demons. It was nice. Not that she thought it was real—

He's flirting with you because you're pretty, sexy, and clever. Phoenix squeezed her shoulders, then let go and said, "How's the headache?"

"Almost gone. Give me a minute."

Ailish shrugged off Phoenix's leather jacket and walked to his room. She made her way to the closet and called an empty hanger to her hand. Once done hanging up the jacket, she used the bathroom, then went to her bag of stuff in the corner of the room. Bending over, she found her hairbrush tucked just where she'd left it in the bag. She combed out her hair from the ride and helmet, then put the brush back. She walked out of the bedroom, passed the sunken living room on her left and the two staircases on her right, then stopped where the hallway opened into the dining room and kitchen to figure out where everyone was.

"No problems here. It was quiet. Dee and I went grocery shopping. The woman knows her way around food."

"Any problems with the card?" Phoenix asked.

It sounded like Phoenix and Linc were at the bar, probably sitting on the stools. What card was Phoenix asking Dee about?

"Nope," Dee answered. "Debit card worked fine with the PIN number you gave me."

Ailish automatically tracked Dee's voice as coming from the kitchen side of the bar. So Phoenix had given Dee a debit card. Ailish would reimburse the cost. She walked out, bypassing the table and bar to go into the kitchen. "Can I help, Dee?"

"Everything's pretty much done," Dee said, then pressed a mug into her hand. "Ginger tea for the headache."

Surprised, she said, "Thanks." Dee must have heard when Phoenix asked her about the headache. It was already fading. She took a sip, then asked, "You just happened to have ginger tea on hand?"

Dee was moving around again. "After Phoenix told me you can't take regular painkillers or medications, I did some research on natural remedies and stocked up."

Unsure how to respond to Dee and Phoenix doing all this, she changed the subject. "I can set the table or something."

"I already did it," Linc announced, clearly proud of himself. "I grated up cheese, smashed garlic, and put the pan in the oven."

"Now you can take the pan out of the oven," Dee said.

The smell of sizzling lasagna filled the kitchen as Linc took out the pan. "And," he continued, "I'm taking Dee out tonight to thank her for cooking dinner."

"Out where?" Ailish set her half-drunk tea on the counter and put her hand on her hip. Linc was a witch hunter, Dee was a mortal woman. She walked up to him. "Exactly where are you taking Dee?"

Linc rose to his full height. "Seriously?"

She tilted her head back. "I've never been more serious."

"Ailish . . ." Dee started.

"Do you know what this man is? He has pheromones to seduce you. And he's dangerous."

"Phoenix, little help here," Linc pleaded.

"Don't you even ask him for help," Ailish said. "You're talking to me."

"Damn, woman, you are harsh."

Ailish didn't react. "I'm waiting." She felt the movement when he crossed his arms over his chest. She guessed he was glaring at her.

"What are you going to do to stop me?"

She thought fast and vaguely remembered another car in the driveway. She'd been in Phoenix's vision, and he'd just glanced at it. Plus, she'd been too interested in the house to pay much attention. But she could use it now.

"I'm guessing you didn't fly here. Try starting your car with the wiring fried from witchcraft."

"My Viper!" Linc roared at her.

Phoenix jumped up.

Ailish whirled on him. "Not a word from you or your Mustang gets it, too. I can handle this."

"Ailish . . ." Dee put her hand on her arm. "I know he's a witch hunter. He told me. He's taking me to a club called Axel of Evil. It'll be fine." Then Dee hugged her, tight. "Thank you."

"For what?" She couldn't quite get her bearings. The hug from Dee felt kind of good.

Breaking the hug but holding Ailish's arms, she said, "For caring. I can't remember the last time someone cared that much. But I'll be fine. I'm just looking for fun. Nothing more."

Fun? Even Ailish could feel the heat coming off Linc. If Dee went out with him, they were going to . . . And what was wrong with that?

He won't hurt her. I swear, Ailish. Linc's a charmer and a gambler, but he sincerely likes women. Dee knows what she wants. Trust me, she wants Linc. He doesn't lie to women about sex—he always tells them there's no relationship.

Phoenix's voice was reassuring in her head. She wondered if she'd overreacted. *Do I look like an idiot?*

No. You look like a friend.

Cool. She liked that. "Fine, but if Dee comes home unhappy, say goodbye to your Viper."

Linc said, "Deal. More women should have friends like you."

That caught her by surprise. "You're just saying that so I don't zap your car."

He laughed, clinked some glassware and splashed some liquid, then put a glass in her hand. "Maybe some wine will mellow you."

She smiled at him. "Sure, get the witch drunk. How could that go wrong for you?"

Linc didn't seem too worried. "Bet you're bluffing about my Viper."

Ailish grinned. "Ask Phoenix what happened to his R6."

She felt Linc stiffen and turn from her. "What?"

Bad, bad witch, Phoenix teased her. Then he answered Linc, "Off a cliff and into the ocean. Second bike I've lost since I met her."

"Damn," Linc said.

Phoenix held Ailish's hand and showed her the back-yard as they walked out onto the wood deck off the kitchen and dining room. He let her see the barbecue, table, and chairs, then led her down the steps to the grassy slope that spread over a half acre or so. Lifting his gaze, he showed her the fence. Farther out in the distance were more homes.

The grass was cool and slightly damp. He wore only his jeans, and Ailish was in her sleep shorts and a tank so she could feel as much of the elements on her skin as possible. The trees dotting the grass swayed gently in the soft breeze; the moon was full and poured silvery light down on them.

Already he could feel Ailish responding, her chakras opening and reaching. Absorbing. She had needed this, probably craved it. He wanted to see her as he had the first night—deep in her magic under the night sky. Only this time he'd be with her, helping her to focus her power and protecting her.

To reassure her, he said, "There's a half mile of clear-ance around my property beyond the fence, I own it all. Very secure. No one can see us." Even with his hunter vision, the homes in the distance were just specks of scat-tered lights. Ailish could be free in her magic.

"Here should be good," she said. She had chosen a spot in the middle of the yard, where the shadows of trees didn't reach.

He spread out a blanket, took her hand, and sat across from her.

"I don't need to see any more." She pulled out of his vision.

He watched as she opened her eyes. The moonlight poured over her, gleaming off her dark, choppy hair and making her eyes look even more silver. She was already feeling the power; he could see it in the way her witch-shimmer glowed a brighter gold. "How many chakras are open?"

"Four. I didn't really do anything, they just wanted to open and feel the moon and air." She reached out and ran her hand over the blades of grass.

Her nipples puckered beneath her shirt, and he saw her squirm a little.

Oh yeah, the power was filling her. He inhaled, and her mango-and-coconut scent was rich with the warm butter of her desire.

Made him hotter than hell.

"Good. Ailish, you believe me that we're alone?"

"Yes," she said instantly.

Her fast answer pleased him and the bird. He was dancing all over Phoenix's biceps, trying to reach her, trying to brush his wings over her golden shimmer in the silvery light. Feeling the same way, Phoenix reached out and grasped the edge of her tank. "Take this off and feel the moon."

She didn't hesitate, she lifted her arms for him.

He caught his breath when the top was off. She had lithe, well-defined shoulders that sloped into her soft breasts with the dark, richly colored nipples. As he watched, she arched, leaning her head back and thrusting out her breasts like an offering. The nipples were so tight, yet the mounds were soft and lined with blue veins that carried her powerful witch blood.

His heart pounded the blood through him to swell his cock. "More, Ailish. You want to feel the moonlight everywhere. Lay down for me."

She was languid, as though every cell were sucking in all that power. "It's filling me."

He moved so he was at her side, then spoke into her ear. "It's okay. Let it fill you. I'm right here, the bird's right here."

Her whole body shuddered. Then, in a slow, fluid movement, she stretched out her long legs and lay down on the blanket.

His mouth dried up. Balancing on his knees, he reached for her little shorts and tugged them off.

She lifted her hips, helping him. Her trust was a gift, she was a gift. Setting the shorts aside, he looked at his witch, his Ailish. Stretched out on the brown blanket, her body glowed with a brilliant witch-shimmer as she bathed in the silvery light of the moon. Raking his gaze down her, he got to her bare skin at the vee of her hips and reached up to gently spread her legs.

Her scent hit him, making his mouth water. Her folds were damp, swollen, and so damned pretty. He dragged his gaze away. For now. He had one more thing to give her. She had let him see her, this stunning beauty bathed in the lights of magic, and he could give her this. Stretched out beside her, he slipped his arm under her shoulders and held her close to his side. "Close your eyes, beauty."

"The magic is getting too full."

Oh yeah, he'd seen. He rubbed his palm down her arm, determined to stay in control. "I want to show you something. Close your eyes and look with me." He gave her a second, keeping his own eyes closed. "Ready?"

"Yes."

He opened his eyes and looked at the full, brilliant moon.

She sucked in a breath. "It's gorgeous!" She stretched her arms over her head, her muscles elongating sensually. "I can feel it touching me, going through my skin and deeper. My power is gathering, beginning to spin."

He kept his gaze on the moon, holding her close to him, feeling her body roll with waves of that coconut-scented witchcraft. It surrounded him, embedding Ailish in his senses for eternity. Unable to resist, he turned to look at her.

She opened her eyes, breaking off their merged vision, and said, "I can see the bird."

The phoenix fluttered happily in the tattoo. The connection between the bird and Ailish was incredible, so strong that it surpassed her blindness and she could see him in real three-dimensionality when Phoenix could see him only in the tattoo. This was something so special, it made him struggle to get a breath. "He's yours, Ailish."

She smiled, and damn, it made him feel like a king to earn that from her.

There were no rules to this stuff, but every hunter who mated with his witch knew one thing—sex was its own magic.

Right now, he could feel the power in her building to an explosion, but she was holding back. Frightened. He couldn't blame her. For eight years she'd been tortured with lust and afraid to trust her own body, her own magic. And then her mother had managed to burst open her scars and lock her in her third eye. But Phoenix wouldn't let that happen this time. She'd trusted him up till now. He needed to teach her to trust him always.

"I'll help you," he said softly, then leaned down and closed his mouth over her nipple.

Her taste, her magic, hit the back of his throat, and he

suckled, drawing her in deeper. His thoughts shattered so only her safety and her pleasure remained. He reached down between her smooth legs to the soft, wet skin there.

A growl of need built in his throat. His jeans were strangling his dick, but tough shit. This was for her. His witch. He couldn't get enough and slid his fingers inside her swollen channel. Her body sucked at him, twitching with her magic, pulling on his fingers, trying to draw him in deeper. She bucked into his touch. He shifted so his palm pressed against her sensitive little clit, then put his mouth up to her ear and told her the truth: "You're my magic, Ailish."

She cried out, her magic cresting in a powerful eruption through his body, streaming, stoking, touching him intimately. He could feel the bird working, helping her control the magic.

Instinct had him draw her closer. Taking his hand away, he pulled her leg up over his hip and pressed his heavy thigh against her still pulsing core. "It's okay, Ailish. I have you."

Her witch-shimmer took on the colors of the phoenix.

19

Ailish felt the wings of the phoenix wrap around her as she traveled through a long tunnel. This was different, not the forced falling that had happened when her mother captured her in her third eye. This time, she and the bird flew together. Eventually, the pressure on her forehead consumed her, and then . . .

A window opened. It started as a white dot that spread bigger and bigger.

She saw the coven. They were at the Infernal Grounds, and the torches were burning, the smoke thick with incense. Candles flared. The witches were in their robes with long sleeves and hoods. They were circling and chanting something.

Control, she thought. She had to have control. The bird hovered next to her at the edge of her vision. As long as she saw him, she was safe. Concentrating, she moved higher over the scene.

Below her, the demon witches circled a patch of dirt and chanted, "Asmodeus, your name is power."

She fought down her revulsion and watched, trying to understand.

The witches all dropped their robes, their bodies gleaming with oils. They swayed and cried, "Asmodeus, your name is power!

"Lord of my loins!

"Master of my soul!

"Reveal your ley lines!"

The earth began to shake and tremble. Trails of dust rose.

Ailish watched and remembered that the ley lines were created by the mass murder on the grounds decades ago. They were power sources for earth witches and for demon witches. She could see the dark lines writhing and snaking below the earth.

Were they summoning the demon? She didn't think so; she didn't see a mortal he could possess.

Her mother moved to the center, and the chanting dropped to a hum. Maeve lifted a knife and cut her thigh.

A cry of life.
From my loins.
A gift to my master
In the ley lines.

After gathering the blood, she sprinkled it over the ley line writhing beneath the earth.

Release it now!
Set it free!
Cry of life!
Kill the bird!

All the coven witches cut their hands and dripped more blood.

The earth shuddered, then burst open, emitting the cry of a newborn. Then she saw her mother call the cry to her own lungs.

The vision changed, and she saw Phoenix flying. . . . He was glorious, his dark hair streaming out behind him, the powerful, richly colored wings pumping. Then her mother released the newborn cry, and her exquisite Phoenix, both the man and the bird, exploded into flames.

Horror, thick and terrible, choked her. "No," she cried,

understanding now how her mother planned to destroy Phoenix.

Maeve heard her and jerked her head around in surprise. Then she narrowed her eyes and looked right at Ailish. "You will submit, Ailish. I am the high witch of the Deus'Donovan coven, more powerful than you ever conceived."

The bird screeched and tried to pull her away. But Ailish was too angry. "I will never be you."

Maeve conjured a mirror and held it up. "Look at yourself. Ugly. Blind and helpless. A creature to be pitied."

Ailish saw herself as her mother did. Hard face, white, jagged scars around nearly colorless eyes. Doubt, insecurity, and shame spread in her like an oil slick.

"You think Phoenix wants to be stuck with that? He needed you to get rid of the curse, but he knows you'll die and he'll be free. All he has to do is keep you from assuming your rightful place as a demon witch, and he wins. Free of the curse and free of you."

She kept staring at that image of her in the mirror, nothing like Darcy and Carla. Phoenix had showed her what they looked like, pretty and soft with an inner quality that glowed in their witch-shimmers. While she was scarred and edgy. This was how her mother saw her: ugly and lacking.

Did Phoenix?

You're my siren, my beauty, Ailish. Come back. His voice chased out the cold nausea, while the image of her that he'd showed her in the gym right after they'd made love filled her head.

Her mother said, "Look, Ailish. Look at what you will be if you finish the bond." The mirror shifted, showing a sighted woman with blue eyes and no scars. "You'll have real power. . . ."

She didn't want to be that woman in the mirror, she wanted to be the woman Phoenix showed her. Worthy.

She forced her third eye closed, felt the brush of wings fold around her as she traveled back to her body.

Awareness came back in pieces. Phoenix's leather, soap, and musk scent. His arms around her, his thigh pressed between her legs.

His mouth gently kissing her scars.

That made her eyes burn. He saw her as something worthy enough to fight for. Could he be tricking her? Just keeping her from turning and taking his soul until she died? Yes. But did she think he was? No.

He lifted his head, his shadow looming over her. "I heard you. You reached right out to me and showed me that false image of yourself. Like you showed me your nightmare last night."

She'd showed him her weakness. It was appalling, and yet . . . she didn't feel weak, she felt strong and protected. Strong enough to refuse to acknowledge the insecurity her mother had pulled out in her. Instead, she told him, "I know what my mother is planning for you." She described what she saw.

"Figures. I hate fire," he said in an exasperated tone. "It's always been my nightmare to fly and burn."

She ran her fingers over his face. "I'm not going to let her burn you. Now that I know what she's up to, I'll find a way to stop her, but that means I have to be there. I'm going with you and the others to the Infernal Grounds." She held her breath, waiting for him to argue.

He rested his hand on her breast. She could feel the tension in his body. "You're making me crazy."

Softly she repeated, "I'm going."

"I know." He put his mouth to hers. "We fight together. We win together."

He gave in? "You aren't going to trick me?"

"No. I want to. Jesus, I want to lock you in the gym downstairs, but you'd just get out. Besides, you trusted me by telling me what you saw. You thought about sneaking off and trying to kill your mother yourself, didn't you?"

Of course she had. But Phoenix had blown apart her solitary way of doing things. They'd trusted each other when the rogues attacked them on the bike, and they had won. She was beginning to believe they were going to win here. Kill the coven, break the handfast, and maybe prove to the Ancestors that she was worthy. "We're stronger together." But she was still holding back. She wanted to give him more, to tell him the truth in her soul.

She had seen herself through his eyes, felt his deep caring, and she wanted him to know how she saw him. How she *felt* about him. Her mother, the cold, evil bitch, had clearly illustrated everything that love was not.

Then Phoenix had reached into her and revealed the depth of his caring by sharing his image of her. That gave her more courage than she'd had in her entire life. She hoped she wasn't going to have to die, but if she did, she would make sure he knew how she felt.

She struggled to form a picture in her mind, using the images he'd shown her. She built it one step at a time. First she pictured the gently sloping grassy yard bathed in the moonlight.

"Ailish," Phoenix said, "what are you showing me?"

"Wait." Now she pictured Phoenix naked, standing beneath the moonlight. His legs spread, his warrior build taking up space, and the phoenix rising from the flame tats.

Phoenix laid his hand on her face. "That's how you see me?"

"Yes." Her heart pounded with trepidation. This was all new to her. But she wouldn't back down. Not now. "And this is how I want to show you I love you." She pictured herself, kneeling, kissing him, then drawing him deep into her mouth.

He stiffened for a beat, then peeled away from her.

The cold air swept over the places he had warmed. Never in her life had she felt more naked or vulnerable.

Or stupid.

Maybe her mother had been right. Her magic cringed in shame, her throat tightened. She didn't know what to do. Get up and go in the house? She felt around for her clothes, not even sure where he—

He caught her hand. "The idea that someone would love me, rely on me, used to terrify me. I didn't want to fail someone who loved me and break them. It was easier just to be the short-term hero."

She couldn't talk. It was too much, the fear of rejection mixing with the desperate, painful hope. This was what she had avoided. She could handle physical pain, but not this. . . .

"But you, Ailish, you make me want to be more than a hero. I want to be the man worthy of you, a siren witch so special she's only born once in a century. I want to protect you, fight with you, and fill your world with light." He rolled over, covering her with his naked and very hard body. "I need to be inside you, touching your magic . . ." He spread her legs wide and thrust into her. "To tell you I love you. You're mine, Ailish."

His deep love poured through her and sent her over into an orgasm.

They were just inside the house when his phone rang. Ailish heard him dig into the pants he was carrying and pull it out. "It's Ram," he told her, then answered, "Yeah?"

She walked to the bedroom as he followed behind.

"Six witches," he said, his voice razor sharp.

Ailish went to her corner and fished around until she found her sweatpants. She put the shorts in the bag.

"I don't want to leave Ailish." Pause. "He is? Okay, I'll leave when Dee gets here." He hung up.

"Missing witches?" she asked.

"Yes. Linc's bringing Dee back here, then we'll both go out to find them."

She looked for her brush.

"What are you doing?"

She snapped up to her full height, startled that he was standing right behind her. "Going to take a shower."

"Your stuff is still in the bag I packed for you."

She turned, standing in front of it. "It's out of the way. You weren't using this corner." Years of not having a home, not having her own space, hell, of not having much to call her own, made her defensive. Protective. She wanted him to leave her space alone.

Phoenix moved away, and she forced herself to relax. He had brought her the stuff, he wasn't going to take it from her. Embarrassed, she turned back for her toothbrush.

Phoenix was opening and closing dresser drawers. "Now that we know where the rogue hideout is, we're going to try and cut them off and rescue the witches."

Holding her pile of clothes, she said, "You won't get too close to those mini-dagger things?"

"No, not until we figure out how to get around them."

She relaxed a little and noticed that his movements were edgy. The rogues were getting too much of a head start while he waited for Linc and Dee. "Go. You're wasting time."

"No. I want to save those witches, but I'm not leaving you."

Annoyed, she said, "The house is safe. I'm not going outside, and I sure as hell won't be inviting a demon inside. Linc is bringing Dee here, you said he can be trusted." The very idea of the witches being cut again and again until all their blood drained out, just so the copper-stinking rogue could get his power high, made her want to go out and hunt those bastards herself.

Phoenix walked back to her and touched her face. "You sure? It'll only be a few more minutes. Linc's fast in his Viper."

"Yes." She trusted Phoenix, loved Phoenix, but she also had to be able to stand on her own. She'd managed to take care of herself for eight years. This was important to her, vital. She wouldn't be the burden to him that his mother had been.

He leaned down and kissed her, then straightened. "Drawers on the right side of the dresser are yours. Take the right side of the closet. Put your stuff in the bathroom. I only use one drawer in there, you can use the others. We'll get the rest of your stuff later, or buy what you need."

The shift in subject caught her off guard. "I'm fine with—"

"You're not living out of bags stuffed into a corner like you're homeless," he said, shaking his head. "You have a home, a place where you belong. With me."

Warmth traveled through her. This was what love was, giving each other what they needed. She needed her own space, and Phoenix needed to save earth witches and hunt rogues. "Go. I'll put my stuff away and wait for Dee."

He took her hand and put her phone in it. "You need me, you call." One last kiss, then he strode out, moving at hunter speed.

She smiled, picturing him in that awesome Mustang. A minute or so later, she heard the alarm beep as he rearmed the house. She decided not to shower until Dee was safely in the house, so she pulled on her sweatpants and tank top, slipped the phone into her front pocket, and passed the time stowing her clothes in the dresser and hanging them in the closet. Next she put her laptop in the bottom drawer, then picked up the bag containing the rest of her stuff and walked toward the bathroom.

A high-pitched, pain-filled scream froze her in place.

Oh God, she recognized that sound! *Dee!* Ailish reached into the bag, fished around, and found her packets of silver crystals. She shoved them into her other pocket. Then she ran down the hallway to the front door.

"No—oh God!" Dee cried.

"Get out here, Ailish Donovan! You've got to the count of three or I'm pouring acid on her face. She'll be as blind and ugly as you. One!"

Male voice. Possessed? She didn't know! What should she do?

"Two!"

She had no choice. Quickly she reached into her pants and hit the speed dial for Phoenix, leaving the line open. She fisted the silver granules and opened the door.

The alarm blared. She smelled sulfur on her left. Reacting, she got ready to kick—

Something pressed against her neck and fired a big, hot jolt through her, shutting down her nerves, muscles, and chakras. The ground came up and smacked her. Her arms and legs twitched. Stun gun? She tried to think! Saw shadows moving around her.

"Bring the woman. We need her alive to keep the witch under control." Ailish heard the words, but her tongue was dead in her mouth. She was picked up and thrown in a vehicle.

Training took over. She forced her sluggish body to respond, shoving herself up on her arms and bringing her legs up to snap a kick into the shadow's head area.

But her body was slow and clumsy.

He grabbed her foot, twisted brutally, and snapped the bones. Vicious pain screamed through her, and she rolled to her side, gagging. He climbed in after her and whispered in a voice that echoed with demonic vibes, "Make it easy on yourself, witch. Agree. Or I'm going to make you scream until you'll beg me to fuck you while you call me master." He jammed something against her neck, and a jolt of hot pain went through her, then darkness.

Phoenix raced out of the community and turned left. The streets were pretty clear at midnight. Ten minutes later, he'd just made it to the empty church that was on the way to the rogue hideout when his phone vibrated. He hit the switch for his Bluetooth. "Yeah."

"Trouble," Ram said. "Linc and Dee attacked. They got Dee."

"Fuck!" Ailish! He spun the wheel of the Mustang, turning back when he heard the frantic beeping that signaled his home alarm had gone off. Then a signal for another call. He grabbed his phone from the center compartment and looked at the screen. A call from Ailish.

He switched to her line and said, "Ailish?"

All he heard in response was the blare of his house alarm and noises. Grunts, a pop that sounded like electricity, and then a male voice he didn't recognize say, "Bring the woman. We need her alive to keep the witch under control."

Fear for Ailish exploded. He pulled the car over to the side of the road and heard, "Make it easy on yourself, witch. Agree. Or I'm going to make you scream until you'll beg me to fuck you—"

Phoenix threw himself out of the car as his wings burst from his back. He called Axel and began to run. "The demon witches have Ailish. I'm going now." The male voice he heard had to be a man possessed by Asmodeus. It didn't take any leap of imagination to figure out they had used Dee to get Ailish out of the house.

"The wards," Axel reminded him.

His wings began pumping as he ran. "Ask Darcy and Carla to try to get them down or break them." He left the ground and began flying. "If they can't, I'll find another way through them." He hadn't forgotten that Maeve

Donovan had a plan to destroy him. He was going to rip out her throat before she got a chance to release the cry that would burn him to ash.

Failing that, he was going to dive-bomb Maeve and take that bitch down with him and free Ailish.

He wouldn't fail. Not this time.

A terrified sob tore through the deep gray fog. Surfacing, Ailish took stock. Her head hurt, spots on her neck burned, and her ankle was on fire. Full awareness came back swiftly. She was at the coven grounds, could feel the skin-crawling wards surrounding her. She smelled sulfur. Heard voices. She could feel that she was lying in the dirt. Reaching out with her hand, she felt only emptiness. "Dee?" Where was she? Had they left her behind?

A hand wrapped around her arm and jerked her to her feet. She landed on her right foot, but every movement sent agony through her shattered left ankle. She strained to focus her eyes, able to see the shadows of a group of demon witches to her left. The one in front had to be her mother. To her right, another witch, and something next to her, a shadowy crouched shape she couldn't make out. The handfast binding felt heavy and warm.

"Choose, witch. Submit to me. Accept me as your lord and master. Or we begin."

The possessed mortal's voice made her skin chill. It was a blending of the mortal and the demon in a sickening echo, driving home that she was in real trouble. For eight years, she'd trained for this moment.

The showdown.

She had to resist, force her chakras open and fight. And if she lost, she had to die an earth witch. With a dry mouth, she said, "No."

"Prod her."

Ailish steeled herself for more pain. She heard a sizzle, and every cell in her body tightened . . .

A horrible scream.

Dee! The cry came from her right, the crouched figure! She struggled to make her eyes work, but nothing more focused.

She heard a sob and gagging, then Dee vomiting.

Bile rose in her throat, her skin shrank back, but deep in her gut, rage took hold. "Stop!" She couldn't let Dee be tortured! As an earth witch, she was supposed to stand between mortals and demons!

Ailish, I'm here. Can you bring down the wards?

Phoenix! Her chakras quivered in response to him in her head. *They have Dee!* She formed the layout in her mind, trying to show him where Dee was.

A figure walked up to her. "You were given a great honor, and you humiliated me." Her mother lifted her hand from her side and slammed a force of magic into Ailish's left ankle.

The pain detonated, shooting up her leg, seizing her bladder. She doubled over, crumpling to the ground. She tasted her own blood, biting her tongue and lip to keep from screaming. Tears burned and streamed from her eyes.

Shit, I feel your pain! I can't get through the fucking wards! Phoenix's voice bellowed in her head.

Her chakras responded by bubbling a little harder, trying to get to Phoenix and the bird. They opened enough to allow a weak stream of power to rise like water from a hose. Having Phoenix close to her, the bird funneling her power, helped, but the stream was pale and anemic. The red-hot agony eased to a bearable throbbing. She realized that with her chakras partially opened, he was able to take some of her pain.

Can you sing?

His voice—oh God, it was like a lifeline. It gave her courage, made her determined. She tried to measure her power; she had only two chakras open. *Need more power,* she answered as two robed demon witches grabbed her shoulders and dragged her to her knees before the possessed mortal where he stood in front of the altar. From behind her, Maeve commanded, "Ready our demon lord."

The coven witches swarmed over the male, pulling off his clothes and touching him in ways that made Ailish grateful for her blindness. They fawned over him in sexual worshipping as the scent of sulfur grew thicker. Even the two witches holding her rushed forward, desperate to touch the vessel that held Asmodeus.

Within seconds, the handfast binding on her wrist sent out dozens of sparks along her nerve endings, forcing her body to respond in a sick kind of lust that made her nipples swell painfully and her core dampen. This was nothing like when Phoenix touched her; with Phoenix, her body responded with a natural beauty that made her magic rush and sing.

Darcy and Carla are trying to send more power to you. You should feel it.

As the witches were tearing off their robes, moaning and writhing, a warm sensation that felt a bit like a patch of sunlight on a cold day began swelling in her chakras. She recognized the feel of Darcy's and Carla's magic. The sounds of the coven and their demon slid further away from her as she focused on that energy, the joy of twining and circling magic.

She had to do four things: Bring down the wards, get between Dee and the witches, banish the demon, and stop her mother from releasing her birth cry once Phoenix was in sight.

From her pelvic floor, energy rose, bubbling up, opening her third fire chakra, her fourth air chakra, and straight up through her throat chakra. Kneeling on the ground, her ankle a sick throb, she put her left hand in her pocket and opened the packets of sliver. Fisting a handful, she said in her head, *Now.*

Funneling the magic upward, she felt the bird sweep with his powerful wings, helping her fuse in the power from the earth witches and control it all. Ailish took a breath to push the power through her voice and sang:

> *Earth, air, water, and flames,*
> *Circle and grow into—*

"Stop!" Her mother grabbed her hair and stomped down on Ailish's broken ankle.

The searing pain made her scream out the words:

> *An army of light to*
> *Bring down darkness!*

While singing the words, Ailish threw the silver over her shoulder toward her mother and flung herself to the left, rolling to where Dee lay, and she finished:

> *Bind it, bury it, choke it, burn it!*

She came up on her knees, aiming her power at the wards on the other side of Dee.

The ground trembled violently. The wards blew apart like a popped balloon, releasing screams and pressure.

Three loud screeches cut through the night like battle cries. She could feel Phoenix getting closer, feel the bird as if his wings beat in her own chest.

"Kill the woman, kill the bird!" Asmodeus's command throbbed in the blended voices of the demon and human.

A dark, cold energy blew across her skin as her mother began to turn, around and around.

Other witches swarmed toward Dee.

Behind her, Dee coughed and gasped, "Can't breathe!"

They were choking her with dark magic! Haley had described it as having oily rags stuffed down your throat while bands tightened around your chest. Ailish had to stop them!

If she used her magic to hurt them, the witch karma would kill her, and then they'd kill Dee. She struggled to think.

Her mother kept spinning like a top, pulling in energy while the other witches chanted, "No air, no breath, black death, black death." Dirt blew up from the ground, ringing Dee and pushing Ailish out.

The shadows in the sky grew larger.

Her mother stopped spinning.

Dee jerked and twitched, wheezing for air.

Whom did she choose? What did she do? Twenty-four years of frustration, betrayal, being unloved and used, exploded within her, and just as Maeve lifted her arms high and opened her mouth to utter the birth cry that would burn her beloved Phoenix, Ailish sprang, hitting her mother in the chest, knocking the air from her lungs, and slamming her to the ground. She wrapped one hand around her mother's neck—"Breath of life, in my cry . . ." She flung out her hand to Dee and sang, "Give life to another!"

Her mother gagged as the cry shot from her lungs, through Ailish, and out her hand. It hit the ring of dirt and witches, forced them to part like the Red Sea, and went straight into Dee.

Ailish heard her suck in a breath a second before her mother's furious magic hit her chest, lifted her up, and blasted her back onto the ground.

20

Phoenix landed just as Ailish was thrown off that bitch. She hit the ground hard, and the bird squawked in fury. He had his knife in his hand, cut his palm, and went to her.

Meanwhile, Axel dive-bombed the male, slamming him to the ground and knocking him out cold.

Sutton cut Dee free from the chair she was tied to and turned to face the demon witches.

Phoenix got on the other side of Ailish so he could watch while he tended to her ankle. The pain coming from her felt like pulverized bones. She wore sweats and no shoes, making it easy to see where the broken bone tore through the skin. Yet her chakras were open. Her resilience amazed the shit out of him. He laid his bloody hand on the wound. "Heal, baby. We've got work to do."

Her damaged eyes went to him. "Dee?"

"She's breathing." Her powers heated the wound, and a quick look showed him the healing light. "Can you stand? Banish Asmodeus?" Phoenix needed that demon out of the way before he killed her mother and freed his siren from the handfast. "Look with me." He felt her mind brush and meld with his, and he showed her the mortal man crumpled at the base of the altar. He was starting to rouse with a deep groan. It was a horrible sound of many voices forced through one. The demon was compelling the mortal to get up even though he was hurt.

Ailish saw it, too, and said, "Let me up."

Phoenix removed his hand and pulled her to her feet. She rushed to the man, held out her hands, and unleashed her magic.

Phoenix protected her back. The coven witches were firing flames and knives with their magic. The hunters edged forward, ready for the kill.

The ground shook, as if massive snakes writhed beneath them. Phoenix suspected it was the ley lines. The tremors grew as Ailish forced more of her earth magic into the mortal. Finally the ground split open, the smell of sulfur bloomed, then the ground sucked it up and closed. The mortal slumped down, unconscious.

The witches shrieked in rage as their demon was banished back to the Underworld.

Maeve Donovan shouted, "Dead and dismantled, a soul no longer. Bones and teeth and eyes and claws. No soul, no soul, my blood conceives you. My blood binds you. My blood commands you!"

The other witches joined the chant.

Ailish whipped around, her face going white. "Shit! They're raising hellhounds!"

Using Phoenix's vision, Ailish saw her mother had a knife and cut herself on her breast, her thigh, and her hand. The blood welled up, and she dipped her fingers in it to sprinkle the ground.

The rest of the coven cut themselves and chanted. Some had knives, others used their fingernails to tear their skin.

Sutton and Axel were trying to get through a wall of knives and flames.

The coven kept chanting and sprinkling their blood. The dirt was stirring, beginning to vomit up bones and other parts of dead animals.

"No!" Ailish sang out the word, and the wall of fire

and knives shattered. She sprang forward, hopped once, and snapped her foot into Maeve's stomach.

Her mother flew back into the rest of the coven, the knife dropping from her hands.

Unfortunately, the force of the kick caused Maeve's blood to spray out from the cuts.

Click. Pop.

Terror slid down her throat. Deep instinct forced her eyes open, and she lost her vision from Phoenix. All she saw were shadows rising from the earth and assembling.

Click. Pop. Skuttle. A low growl.

"How many!" she screamed. The sounds made her skin crawl. "Where are they!"

Phoenix shoved her back, his body filling her dim sight. Then he was moving so fast, she felt a breeze. Fighting. He was battling the hellhounds, keeping them from her, protecting her from the one thing he knew truly terrified her.

Axel and Sutton flanked Phoenix, and they fought the hellhounds and the coven. She was behind a wall of huge witch hunters with wings. She felt Dee's hand close around hers.

Rage rushed up over her panic. She squeezed her eyes shut and centered herself. Felt the wings of the bird brushing her as Phoenix kicked and stabbed and dis-membered those creatures.

But Ailish knew the coven magic would keep reassem-bling them. She squeezed Dee's hand, "Stay back," she told her, then let go and reached out to touch the wing of the phoenix.

Her heart calmed, her mind centered, and Phoenix's hunter-sharp vision filled her head.

The hellhounds ranged in size from that of a small dog to a wolf on steroids. They were put together wrong, a big head on a small body, with claws for feet. Some had teeth or claws in place of a nose or sticking out of their legs. Bones protruded through decaying fur or skin. Some had eyes, a few had noses. They stank of week-old corpses left in the sun.

They popped and clicked and scuttled.

Behind them, the coven witches kept spilling their blood to maintain the power to regenerate the hellhounds.

She had to put a stop to this and began summoning her power. Then she ducked below Phoenix's wing and shot between him and Axel. Jumping in front of them, she pushed her power through her voice and sang out:

> *Earth owns the body, time owns the soul.*
> *Bones and teeth and eyes and claws,*
> *Break free of the blood binding!*
> *Earth, reclaim your dead!*

She swept her hands back and forth in front of her, and her magic swirled up and down her spine, spun in her head, then shot out her hands. Just when she thought she'd never control it, the bird filled her mind with his electric-blue-and-purple beauty. Phoenix stepped closer, his hard body against her back, his arms on either side of her. She knew he kept his hands free to protect her.

Through his vision, she saw the earth tremble and the hellhounds broke apart with sickening clicks and pops. Winds ripped across the dirt. The pieces of the hellhounds vanished, and the winds calmed.

Her mother screamed her fury: "You worthless bitch, I should have drowned you at birth!"

Phoenix jerked behind her, a hand going to his throat. Ailish couldn't see him, but she felt the cold wave of dark magic wrap around his neck and squeeze, trying to choke him.

"Oh hell, no." She evaded Phoenix's hand as he tried to grab her and stormed over to Maeve. Somehow, she stayed in Phoenix's sight and he kept his eyes focused on what she needed to see, even while he fought the choking magic trying to kill him. Ailish approached the woman who had birthed her. Maeve stood naked, dirty, and streaked with drying blood, trying to kill the man she loved.

"Witch karma, there's nothing you—"

She whirled into a roundhouse kick, slammed her newly healed foot into the side of her mother's head, and sent her flying across the grounds. The dark magic trying to hurt Phoenix broke from the impact of the kick. "I don't use my powers to cause harm!"

"I'll kill you!" Maeve screamed.

Ailish followed Phoenix's line of vision to where her mother had landed by the stone altar and was now climbing to her feet. "You can try, but you'll never harm Phoenix!"

"I've got this," Phoenix said softly beside her, his wing caressing her shoulder. "Don't look." Then he moved away, and the images were suddenly blocked by the blue-and-purple phoenix. He filled her sight, his eyes shining with love, his chest puffed out, and his wings spread. He came to her, touching her mind with his love while Phoenix did what had to be done.

The earth rocked, followed by a powerful stench of sulfur and then a strange emptiness.

Your mother's gone. Asmodeus took her to the Underworld, Phoenix said in her mind, and the bird faded from view.

The coven began to scream in outraged fury and fear as they realized what had happened. Their high witch was dead and now in the Underworld. Her mother. *No, don't think about that now.*

Ailish closed her eyes, and Phoenix's vision opened in her mind once more. Their connection was strengthening to allow her to merge into his sight without touching him.

All hell broke loose. The coven witches attacked, using their powers to make missiles out of burning candles, rocks, knives, anything they could find. Ailish snapped into action, using her kickboxing skills to drop the witches.

The hunters killed them.

"Axel's wing is on fire," Phoenix said. As he ran past, he turned his head to look at Axel and thereby show her where to aim her magic. Ailish called for water and doused the fire. It was all happening so fast.

And then it was quiet. Ailish stood in the middle of the grounds, sweaty, tired, and unable to process that it was over.

Except she could still feel the binding on her left wrist. She was still handfasted. Her mother was dead, and the binding was still there.

"No!" Phoenix bellowed from several feet away. A second later, he reached her side, then took hold of her arm and raised her wrist.

"I'm sorry," she said softly, understanding that he'd heard her thoughts when she'd realized the handfast binding was still there.

He sucked in a shuddering breath, then rubbed his thumb over her skin and the hideous bracelet, as if he couldn't believe it was still there.

The other hunters were moving around, taking care of the mortal man who'd been possessed and Dee. But Ailish and Phoenix stood trapped in wretched, silent grief. They both knew the truth: Her mother's death hadn't broken the handfast binding.

Only Ailish's death would do it. They knew now that she had to die. She was the daughter of a demon witch, handfasted to a demon and she had to pay. With her life and maybe, her soul.

She'd be in darkness forever.

*   *   *

Phoenix soared across the night sky with Ailish in his arms. Her head was tucked against his chest. The bird made horrible little sounds of pain as he flew. The creature loved her.

Phoenix loved her.

How could they lose her?

She'd been so fierce out there. And when her mother tried to choke him with magic, Ailish had been magnificent, her dark hair flying, striding across the dirt in that bra top with her slim, honed muscles rippling, her sweats clinging to her . . . And that roundhouse?

Chuck Norris perfect.

And earlier, when her mother had been going to release the cry that would burn him—Ailish had fought to save him and Dee.

How could he fail her?

It shredded his guts, and his eyes started to burn.

The house came into view, and soon he landed on the grass of the sloping backyard, then strode up to the back deck. Using his palm, he undid the locks and then went inside. He strode with her to his room.

Their room.

He took her into the bathroom, leaned in, and turned on the shower jets. Then he set her on her feet and stripped her and then himself.

Lifting her, he stepped into the shower, then washed them both. Ailish tried to help, but he batted her hands away. He washed her, determined to get the blood, dirt, and painful memories off her. His cock ached from seeing her, touching her, from her scent, even her soft sighs. She was a very sensual woman. The feel of his soapy hands on her made her buttery scent of desire thicken until his mouth watered to lap at her very center.

Forcing himself to focus, he rinsed them both and then turned off the shower. He reached for a towel and began to dry her.

She tried to take the towel from him.

Taking hold of her face, he looked down into her eyes. It was uncanny the way she always looked back at him. With everyone else, she looked toward them. "I will fight for you until my last breath, and when I'm dead, you'll call me back to fight for you again. It's my duty, my right, and goddamn it, I need to do this, to take care of you right now." He couldn't look away from her. His beauty, so gifted that she could call him to life from ashes. If he lost her . . . He couldn't stop himself, he leaned down and kissed her, trying to taste her love.

It tasted like Ailish. So fucking perfect, his heart swelled. He tore his mouth away, flung the towel down, and picked her up. He strode from the steamy bathroom into the cooler bedroom. She shivered.

His wings sprang out. Surprised, he shifted to support the sudden weight protruding from his back. His wings curved around Ailish in his arms, warming her.

She was wearing nothing but his wings. His. The blue-and-purple feathers against her olive skin were so pretty. She lifted a hand and stroked the edges of the feathers as he walked to the bed.

It was pleasant, and mildly sexy, as if she were touching his arm.

She smiled, then moved her hand to the inside of his wing, stroking and petting.

The profoundly sensual touch froze him at the edge of the bed. His cock bobbed and his balls seized up as if she had stroked them. The wings were a deeply intricate part of him, and they had some hot spots.

It's like stroking your penis. So hard, with soft, velvety skin, or feathers. She whispered the words in his head, then reached up and dragged his mouth down to hers.

Heat and wild feelings of love, of pride in her, awe that

she loved him, too many feelings to identify, exploded inside him. He tore his mouth away, set her on her feet.

She put her hand on his chest. "I want to touch your wings. Feel them. Feel both of you. I need both of you." Her voice was raw, not quite with tears, but with real and honest feeling.

Feelings. They were overwhelming them both.

He kissed her, tasting her mouth, tasting her love. He broke away, turned her to face the bed, and tugged her back to his chest. "You have us both." He cupped her breasts, touched her nipples, and felt the throb of her desire pebbling them.

The wings bent around her, at an angle that should have made it impossible for them to caress her, but they did, feathering over her stomach, her legs. Ailish relaxed against him, content to let them, him and the bird, give her what she needed.

He leaned his face down to her ear. "We're going to make love to you. I'm going to fill you and he's going to hold you." He skimmed his hand down her stomach while lifting his wings and using the insides to rub against her nipples. The sensation of those pebbled peaks brushing against the tender lining of his wings shot straight to his groin. She arched into the touch and moaned softly.

He had to touch more of her and moved his hand lower to her bare, smooth mound. He slid his fingers between her legs and groaned against her ear. She was damp and swelling as he touched her and stroked her folds. His groan made her shudder more.

Ailish, his blind witch, needed him to fill her other senses.

He traced her ear with his tongue as he penetrated her soft channel with one finger, then two. He stroked her, feeling her hot magic begin to throb around him.

"Not yet," he said against her ear. "You can go higher, the wings have you." He was pushing her to the edge, then holding her there. He thrust in deep, but not deep enough.

She whimpered, tossing her head.

For Ailish to trust him enough to whimper, to let him know how badly she ached, was the sweetest sound he'd heard. He took his fingers from her.

She put her knee on the bed and started to crawl forward.

He saw her ass, those firm, muscular buttocks, then she moved and she was exposed to him. Wet, flushed, swollen, and so beautiful, he forgot to breathe. He bent over her, curled his arm around her waist, and touched the head of his cock to her entrance. Her magic surged, trying to pull him in. At the same time, his wings stroked her, touched her, and held her in a silent promise of forever. "Please." It was all he could say. He had to be inside her.

"Yes." Her voice came out laced with her power.

The magic spread around them as Phoenix thrust into her, but it wasn't enough. It would never be enough. He could feel her beneath him, feel her hot channel pulsing with magic, feel the wings holding her, and it wasn't enough!

He thrust and pumped and struggled to reach her soul, her life force, her very heart. So he could hold it safe. The pleasure of stroking into her raced through him as Ailish tightened. He held her closer, kissed her neck, fondled her nipples, fingered her clit, while the pleasure burned and tortured. . . .

Ailish shoved back, taking his cock all the way to her womb, and sang, "I love you, Phoenix." Her voice soared with magic, the wings cradled her tighter, and she shattered.

The feel of Ailish coming, surrounding his cock, lov-

ing him, and showering him with magic raced down his
spine and exploded. He pumped into her, filling her with
his seed, as if he could fill her with life.

Forever.

Never to die and leave him.

Phoenix clutched her tighter. "I can't lose you," he
said into the thick strands of her hair. "You're my very
soul."

21

Ailish sat on the grass in the deep night. The moon was waning, like her life. Watching Phoenix struggling to save her was tearing her apart. She had tried her voice power again and again. In desperation, Phoenix had tried every tool he could find. He'd hounded the witches, begged them to ask the Circle Witches, the Ancestors, to search their knowledge chakras time and again.

Nothing worked.

Ailish had to pay.

But each night, when Phoenix finally fell into an exhausted sleep, she slipped out of bed.

Tonight she made it outside without waking Phoenix. Sitting quietly, she felt her magic stir at her pelvis and begin to rise. The energy flowed up her spine.

Then she felt him behind her. He sat down, lifted her, and placed her on his lap. Every night the same thing. . . .

He knew what she searched for. She was trying to reach her knowledge chakra, trying to see if the Ancestors would find a way to accept her.

Or if she'd exist in blackness until she was no more, until she became nothing.

Ailish leaned back against his chest as her powers spun up and down her spine. Her fifth chakra opened, then her sixth. She pushed and pushed. Her body swelled with the magic, her nipples full, her core growing damp.

Her skin grew so sensitive that the slightest breeze felt sexual.

She felt Phoenix's body react, but he simply held her, supported her.

Until she cried out in frustration, her last chakra out of reach. They didn't know if it was the handfast blocking her, or fear of finding out that she wouldn't get into Summerland.

Then he'd make love to her, vowing he wouldn't let her go. He'd find a way, any way, to save her.

DAYS REMAINING ON HANDFAST CONTRACT: THREE

Ailish was worried about Phoenix. He was angry and blaming himself. Driven to discover a solution to save her.

Then today he'd grown quiet and told her he wanted to take her on a ride with his newest motorcycle. They'd gone to the cemetery, and he'd shown her his mother's grave. He'd told her stories about Sheri, and she could feel his love for the woman who'd fought so hard to save him.

They were sitting on the grass next to his mother's resting place. Holding her hand, he said, "While I'll always wish I'd come home when she called me, I understand now that she was protecting me. That my mother loved me enough to die for me. If I hadn't met you, I'd never have known that she wasn't crazy. They'd told her to hurt and kill me, yet she never did."

Her throat tightened and her chest burned. Phoenix was finally forgiving himself.

"She was strong. I know that now. She was . . ." He squeezed her hand. "I don't know how to say it."

"A loving and protective mother?" Ailish asked. Not the cold, ambitious, cruel creature her mother had been.

"Yes." He put his arm around her. "That was her."

She hated that she was doing this to him, that she'd

leave him. But she saw now what this was about. Phoenix was coming to terms with the truth—there wasn't going to be a happy ending. But just as he'd stopped blaming himself for failing his mother, he wasn't going to blame himself for Ailish.

She wore the handfast binding, not him. It was her mistake, her transgression, and she had to pay. Phoenix couldn't save her from that. But while they wouldn't get a happy ending, they'd had happy moments. She was grateful for those; she absorbed them and held them close.

She leaned against his side. "Your mother would be proud of you." How could she not be? Look how he'd grown, look at the good he did. Killing rogues, saving earth witches. Caring about people.

He dropped his face into her hair and said in a low voice thick with resolve, "I hope so."

She felt an uneasy shiver slide down her spine. But before she could put her finger on why, he pulled her to her feet and they rode home with Phoenix showing her the scenery. When they pulled into the garage, he told her that he felt her head starting to throb and she needed to open her eyes. She got off, he set the bike on the kickstand, put his arm around her, and they walked into the house together.

"Surprise!" a chorus of voices shouted.

Ailish jerked in shock. "What?"

"Look, sweetheart." He walked with her to the dining room table.

She closed her eyes and the images flooded her mind. The entire room had blue and purple streamers and balloons. In the middle of the table was a massive chocolate cake, surrounded by at least half a dozen gifts. The room itself was filled with people: Axel, Darcy, Sutton, Carla, Key, Ram, Linc, Joe, Morgan, and Dee. "A party?"

"Happy birthday," Phoenix said softly from her side.

"But it's not my birthday yet." She still had a couple more days with him. And that uneasy feeling came back.

"That's why it's a surprise," he teased her. "We've been planning this for days."

Her worry disappeared. He had planned a party for her. She'd never had a party, never had a cake. Never had this kind of feeling, so full and happy. She didn't know what to say.

"Happy birthday, Ailish."

She recognized that voice! "Haley?" Using Phoenix's sight, she looked at the woman she hadn't been able to see in eight years. Her thick blond hair was cut in soft layers, her blue eyes had faint lines around them, but they were still the same sharp bullshit detectors. In the next second, she saw and felt herself being hugged by the taller woman.

Haley stepped back. "Key tracked me down. He and Sutton flew me back for your birthday." She took her hand. "I should have been here sooner. I just . . . sometimes . . ."

Ailish knew Haley had her own demons. Most days, her entire life was one hundred percent invested in her shelter and runaways, but once a year or so, Phoenix had explained, she found a guy and disappeared. "Haley . . ." She squeezed her hand. "I told you to leave. I didn't want my mother to get a second chance to hurt or kill you. But over the years you have helped me. I always knew you were there. Always."

"Come and sit," Dee called out from the table. "We'll open presents, grill hamburgers, have cake and ice cream."

She walked to the chair Dee had pulled out, Phoenix by her side, and sank into it.

"Open mine first," Dee said, clearly excited. She was

living there in the house with them, taking care of all the mundane things that neither she nor Phoenix cared about. The woman put the gift into her hands.

Phoenix pulled a chair up next to her so he could show her the images. It was a big emerald green bag, with mountains of tissue paper. She put her hand in the bag and drew out something soft and square buried in more tissue paper. Suddenly she was desperate to see it and tore at the wrapping.

Phoenix laughed.

Ailish uncovered it. A pillow. Phoenix showed her the front of it. "Oh, Dee . . ." She couldn't believe it. She ran her fingers over the stitching of a phoenix rising from the flames. "Did you do this?" She was going to embarrass them all if she cried.

Dee shifted from foot to foot next to her. "Yes. I wanted you to always have your phoenix with you."

Oh God. Ailish jumped up and hugged her. Then she hugged her pillow. "I've never had a friend like you." She'd been so sure Dee would want to get as far away from her as possible after her experience with the coven.

"You do now," Dee said.

She opened the rest of the gifts, all of them sweet or funny. They had hamburgers, then they teased her that she'd never be able to blow out the candles on her cake. "Please," she told them, "I have magic." Silently, she wished for the one thing she wanted more than anything—that Phoenix would be all right. Dee had sworn she'd stay with him and take care of him. She just wanted his heart to heal and be happy. It was that deep love for him, not her magic, that helped her blow out every single candle.

She was exhausted. They were all sitting in a stupor around the demolished cake, sipping coffee or tea, when her phone rang, surprising her. She had no idea who it could be, since the people who usually called her were in the room with her. "Hello?"

"Ailish, it's Kyle."

Her stomach tightened with her old regret at involving him with her mother and putting him in extreme danger. "Kyle, what's wrong?" Her mother was dead, he should be safe.

"Nothing is wrong. One of your friends called me in Arizona to let me know it was safe to come home. I'm back to work and life feels normal again. It all seems like a bad memory."

She took a breath, trying to accept that she'd done the best she could, but to Kyle, the boy she had once loved, she'd always be a bad memory. "You'll be fine now. Safe. I'm sorry—"

"Ailish," he cut her off, "I called to tell you thank you. I was angry, scared, I had no control over what was happening, and I lashed out at you. You saved Dee's life at my house, and probably mine since I ran out there. You were trying to protect me. Thank you for that."

Her stomach eased. Phoenix's hand slid to her nape, caressing gently. He could hear the conversation. She answered, "You're welcome, Kyle. I hope you have a happy life."

"Good. You, too, Ailish. Bye."

She hung up the phone and set it on the table. While the others were talking, she said to Phoenix, "Did you ask him to call me?"

"No." He rubbed her neck. "He called because he wanted to. He was never good enough for you, and I still want to kill him on principle, but he's not a bad guy."

She knew he wasn't lying; he couldn't lie to her with their mind link. She smiled with relief that she'd made her peace with Kyle. He'd been important to her once, and she was glad that he knew she'd tried to make up for dragging him into a nightmare. She picked up her tea and turned to compliment Dee on the delicious cake.

Phoenix slipped his hand from her nape, got up, and walked out. A few minutes later, he came back into the dining room. "There's one more gift, Ailish. My gift to you."

She turned to him, seeing only shadows. "But you've given me everything," she said. She didn't need a gift from him.

He crouched by her chair and put the box in her hand. "Close your eyes so you can see. Open this."

The image formed. A black velvet box about the size of her hand. She touched the soft velvet, then gently pried open the lid.

Inside, nestled on more velvet, was a pair of silver phoenix wings curved into a bracelet. Her throat closed up.

Phoenix reached into the box, took the bracelet in his large fingers, and opened it with the hinge between the wings. Then he snapped it around her right wrist. "You're an earth witch, and you should have a witch book, like Darcy and Carla. Now wherever you go . . ." He trailed off, his voice rough. His fingers tightened around her arm. "The Ancestors will know you're an earth witch. My earth witch. Mine."

Days Remaining on Handfast Contract: Two

Phoenix watched as Morgan showed Ailish the baby's room. He stood at the door and looked at whatever Morgan pointed to so Ailish could see through him.

But he wasn't listening to their excited chatter. He was thinking. Praying. Begging. He couldn't lose her. He'd sworn to his god that he'd fight for her.

Die for her.

A soft hand on his shoulder. "I got an answer," Darcy said softly.

"Ailish, Morgan, I'm going to check in with Key."

They waved him off. Morgan had Ailish's hand on her belly as the baby kicked or hiccuped or something.

He turned and followed Darcy out to the hallway and down to the condo he used. They went inside.

Darcy's shoulders were tense, her brown eyes worried, and her silvery witch-shimmer dim. "Carla and I both opened our knowledge chakras and we confirmed with the Ancestors. Killing her mother wasn't enough to break the contract as we'd hoped. Only Ailish's death will break it."

"I know that part," he said, impatient. Ailish was his siren, his beauty. She'd called out his bird and claimed his heart. She'd told him she loved him with a courage that left him breathless. God, he loved her. She had healed him, taught him that love was more powerful than any other force.

Darcy touched his arm. "You are right. Since your souls are melded together as one, if you die for her, Asmodeus has to accept it. The handfast will break."

"How do I do it?" He wasn't going to screw this up. He had one chance, one opportunity, to free his witch, to give her the love she deserved.

Darcy's face paled, her witch-shimmer graying. "The eternal fires of hell."

He shuddered, the memory roaring over him of flames eating him. "Can you send me to the flames in the Underword?"

"No. I won't attempt to open a gateway. Earth witches banish demons, not open gateways in ley lines."

He wanted to slam his fist into the wall. "I'm saving her life, keeping her from the darkness! You don't know . . ." He thought of her struggling each night to open her knowledge chakra, but the fear . . . Jesus, it smelled like a dying flower, too sweet and slightly acerbic. Sometimes she woke from a dream, shaking, and he could slip into her mind to see her being chased through endless darkness by hellhounds. He'd pull her in his arms and vow to save her.

And he would. Wing Slayer had told him, *Fight for her, die for her, whatever it takes. . . .* That was real love. His mother had fought and died for him, and now, at this moment, he fully understood. She had loved him that much. He could do no less for the woman he loved. He hoped his mother would be as proud of him as he was of her.

He saw the tears running down Darcy's face and reached out, hugging her. "Don't cry. Thank you, Darcy. I know you didn't want to tell me." He held her tight, Axel's witch, who had brought them all the hope of a soul mirror. She had been their first ray of light.

"This isn't fair to either of you."

"Just don't burden her with it. Please. She's suffering and trying to hide it."

She didn't answer.

He knew Axel had slipped into the room, drawn by Darcy's pain. Pulling back from her, he looked down into her face. "Ailish filled my world with magic, Darcy. I was born to die for her. I have to free her now, so that in another time, another place, she can sing me back to life."

Axel reached out and tugged her back to his chest while looking up at Phoenix. "Darcy can't send you to the Underworld, but Wing Slayer is half demon. He grew up in the Underworld. As your god, he can take you there."

DAYS REMAINING ON HANDFAST CONTRACT: ONE

Phoenix made love to her again and again, trying to fill his soul.

Finally she slept, wearing only his wings wrapped around her wrist and that handfast binding.

His heart filled with lead as he left their room. Each step was painful, but he was resolved. For this, his wore his leathers, his boots, and his knife. In the backyard, he knelt in the wet grass and called out his wings.

They burst from his back, the bird as determined as Phoenix.

He took out his knife, sliced his hand, and watched the blood well up. Then he bowed his head and said, "A blood pact is absolute, broken only by death. Wing Slayer, I beg you. Let me die for Ailish."

The atmosphere changed, the scent of damp grass giving way to metal and flowers, the metal very masculine, almost harsh and unforgiving. The flowers . . . that was ethereal, as if the scent floated with him but wasn't his. Raising his head, he saw the waning moonlight gleam off Wing Slayer's massive wings. They were a darkened bronze, though, not the shimmering gold. Anger?

"You knew I had to die to free her."

"I hoped killing her mother would work, but I know Asmodeus weaves his contracts tightly." The god's voice thundered through him with a deep bass vibration. "This decision had to be yours and only yours."

What he was going to do would hurt Ailish. Her love for him was . . . infinite and humbling. "Can you make this easier on her? Help her accept that this is what I chose to do from love?" Ailish had never had that kind of love.

"I can impress your love on her, but I won't take away her feelings. Just as your mother deserved your grief, you deserve hers."

Overwhelming sorrow choked him. Separating from Ailish hurt, leaving her hurt. He wanted to ask his god if they'd find each other again, but he didn't. He needed to just believe that they would, believe he would hear her voice call him to life once more. He had to. It was the only way he could leave her. "Allow me to pay the price to break her handfast. Allow me to make reparations to her Ancestors. I belong to her, we share a soul, and I choose to give my life to free her."

The scent of metal heated until it smelled like a soldering iron. The air crackled with electricity. The grass wilted beneath him. "You'll burn in the eternal fires of hell, accepting the pain of a slow death. Because you are a witch hunter with extraordinary powers of healing, Asmodeus will stop the flames and revive you again and again, and try to get you to recant your willingness to die for Ailish."

His fear of burning was bone-deep. But his love for Ailish was timeless. He had only one question: "Will this work? Will it free her?"

Wing Slayer nodded, his gold eyes brightening. "Yes. With your souls joined, it fulfills the contract."

Relief mixed with his love and regret. "I won't recant." He looked at his god. "Ailish is worthy."

Wing Slayer reached out with his right hand and clasped Phoenix's cut hand. It was like being struck by lightning: A bolt raced through him, traveling his nerves, his arteries, and through the very marrow of his bones. Every cell in his body recognized his god and bowed to his will.

"My hunter. Your sacrifice is accepted." Holding up Phoenix's knife, he added, "Wear my wings on your blade. My mark of pride in my hunter." With his other hand, he passed the knife to Phoenix.

Taking the blade, he looked at the silver hilt imprinted with the wings of the phoenix. The centuries-old symbol of their god accepting them. Wing Slayer gave it to him now so he would know his soul was safe. So he would go into the flames with his god's approval and pride. He didn't know how to thank him, so he silently slid the knife into the holster at his back.

When Phoenix released the knife, his world shattered. He had been kneeling on the grass beneath the moonlight, talking to Wing Slayer.

In the next moment of awareness, he stood before a roaring wall of flames, easily reaching heights of twenty feet, and there seemed to be no end on either side. It sounded like a train. The heat blasted him. The smell of burning flesh and oily smoke stuffed his nose and gagged him. His leather pants were melting, burning him, his wings wilted, and he was still yards from the actual flames.

"Go on, hero," a snorting voice said.

Another voice added, "Ask his mother if he's a hero."

Skin-crawling laughter mixed with the raging sounds of the fire.

He turned to the right. There on a dais was a throne chair, all massive wood legs, red velvet cushions, and a hideous creature on it. Even sitting, the creature was massive, probably as tall as Wing Slayer. It had three heads: a ram, a bull, and a monster's head in the middle. Black wings spread out against the back of the chair, and a snake-like tail curled down and around one leg. Its cloven feet added to the horror. Asmodeus, the three-headed demon.

The monster's head said, "Heroes' screams are entertaining. They never think they'll scream."

Screams poured out from the flames. Gut-wrenching, agonizing screams that made Phoenix's teeth hurt. Sweat broke out and his guts churned.

The ram's head said, "Just say no, hero. The witch tricked you. She's done this to you over and over, time after time, calling you to life, then burning you to death." The heads all nodded.

The memory of flying over Ailish's birth, her first cry filling him with such aching glory that he couldn't contain the joy . . . then flames erupting. Sick fear and dread pressing in on him.

The hilt of the knife seared into his back, below the wings. Wing Slayer reminding him of his vow, his commitment to die for his witch. His blood filled with Ailish, with her siren's voice calling him . . . her scent filling his lungs, the way her touch ignited him, and the way her mind merged with his until she could see through his eyes. He could see her silvery eyes, bracketed by scars set into her strong face.

She'd had the courage to tell him she loved him first.

He'd have the courage to say it now. In the way that mattered.

Phoenix turned and walked into the flames. The first step ripped a scream from his bowels. The burning agony seared and made him long for death, for freedom from the unending pain. Each step after that, the fire melted his skin, ruined his muscles and bones, drank his blood.

Then stopped. He'd collapse on the cold ground, slick with his own sweat, and heal.

Then it started all over again, until, finally, death came and his earthly body broke apart and crumbled to black ash.

22

Ailish jerked awake when she heard a scream so terrible, her heart shuddered. Sitting up, she felt around the bed in desperation.

He was gone.

Her heart dropped to her stomach. The silver phoenix on her right wrist pulsed with a fierce heat. Something was wrong! With Phoenix! Fighting her panic, she opened her first five chakras. Then she reached for him, reached to feel the man or the bird.

She recoiled when all she felt was heat.

"Oh God, oh God." She jumped out of bed, dressed with magic, and grabbed the phone. "Darcy!" She projected her power through the phone to find the witch.

"Ailish . . ." Darcy's voice was thick and tangled. Not sleep, but maybe tears?

The panic climbed up her throat and came out in a bellow. "What has he done!"

"He loves you." Darcy's voice was kind but tear-filled. "He said he was born to die for you."

No, no, no! This was the thing she'd sensed that had made her so uneasy. Now she knew why he'd taken her to his mother's grave—so she would understand that Phoenix loved her enough to die for her, just as his mother had done for him. She began to shake. "How?" she demanded, and endured a second of silence, then begged, "Please! I have to . . ." She didn't know, but she had to find him, had to get to him. "I can't breathe without him!" She couldn't let him do this!

Ailish listened in horror as Darcy told her. She dropped the phone and, following where her chakras led her, ran through the house and out the back, down the stairs to the grass, to the last place she'd felt Phoenix's energy. She could smell his leather, soap, and musk scent. The grass was wilted. Dropping to her knees, she wrapped her fingers around the phoenix and forced open her sixth chakra. Her powers raced and spun up and down her spine.

Without the bird to help her, the power was filling and expanding until even her eyelashes hurt.

She pulled on her memories, each and every one of Phoenix. The way he made her feel strong, powerful, able, and worthy. The way he'd chased out her shadows, bringing light to her gray world. What he looked like in that heartbreakingly sensual way of his.

She had to open her seventh chakra, had to find the way to save him. She shoved aside her fear; her eternity didn't matter as much as saving Phoenix.

He was willing to die for her. For love.

Her gray world exploded in a violet-colored fog. The swirling was beautiful, loaded with patterns of symbols, pictures, writings . . . it was all churning in the violet-colored mist.

The churning fog kept revealing things: facts, data, formulas, and spells. There was so much knowledge—she'd done it, she was in her knowledge chakra!

She wanted to learn and study each droplet of fog that was bursting with things to discover. It was mesmerizing to watch the knowledge churn and spin in the incredible violet-colored glory. If she knew more, she—

No time! Have to find the answer to saving Phoenix! Focus, look for the answer. There was too much! Phoenix, siren, legend, soul mirror, handfast binding . . .

She couldn't find the answer, then suddenly she saw Phoenix. *Burning!* "Oh God, no!"

Everything wavered, and Ailish fought to hold on. She needed to know how to save him!

A creature appeared. Huge, with wings, bronzed bands wrapped around his massive biceps. "Wing Slayer," she breathed in reverence.

"Ailish, the siren witch. You found me."

His voice flowed with power. It was rich, with a tinge of thunderous command. That he would talk to her was a shock. She didn't waste time. "Take me to Phoenix. We have to save him."

"He's in the Underworld."

"I'll go anywhere, do anything. Please. He can't do this, he has died too many times for me! It's time to save him."

The god held out his hand.

Ailish didn't hesitate. Within her knowledge chakra, she put her hand in his. Immediately, the scent of metal and flowers filled her, while her blood raced with the touch of eternal power. The swirling fog of her seventh chakra vanished.

She had no idea if a second passed or a year.

The first thing she became aware of was the booming sounds of popping and snapping flames. The power of it sucked the air from her lungs, while her mind screamed, *Phoenix!*

"He's dead."

The voice made her chakras cringe. But her mind was focused on Phoenix and the flames. He couldn't be in there!

Wing Slayer held fast to her hand and said, "Release the witch from the handfast. The price has been paid."

Ailish felt the handfast binding fall free of her wrist. No! Suddenly, she wanted it back. If it was gone, that meant . . . No! Phoenix was dead!

The god spoke gently. "You're free, Ailish. Phoenix paid with his life. I will gather his soul from the ashes."

"Ashes?" *Dead*. Ailish's mind rebelled. Her chakras fought it, reaching for Phoenix.

A ripple raced from the god's hand through her to touch her eyes. Her vision cleared and she saw a neat pile of ashes at their feet. The flames roared to their left, and there was something she didn't want to look at beyond the ashes.

But all she could see . . . oh God . . . the ashes.

She ripped her hand from Wing Slayer's and fell to her knees. The huge hunter reduced to this pile. Her mind replayed what she'd seen in her knowledge chakra: Phoenix walking into those flames with his animal grace, his head held high, his shoulders back, and his wings spread wide even as the feathers wilted.

Her Phoenix. Her beloved. Burned to ash. Other images flashed:

The way he'd showed her what he looked like in the bathroom mirror after her nightmare.

The way he'd sparred with her in the gym.

When he'd taken her sandwich away, insisting on making her steak.

His laughter when she'd called him bilingual because she'd said he spoke "the language of Chuck."

The way they'd fought the rogues, Young, and his Immortal Death Dagger on the motorcycle together.

How he and the bird had blocked her from seeing him kill her mother.

His love washed over her, and his death shredded her heart. He had died for her! She held out her hands, and her grief ruptured through her chakras up her throat, the pain so furious that she sucked in a breath, closed her eyes, and sang:

Breath of life
In my cry

From the flames
Wings shall rise

Aching in beauty
Tears of healing

Wings of my soul
Soar to my call

She poured out all her love, all her soul-shattering grief, her utter desolation, into each word. She couldn't stop, even as tears burned her eyes and fell down her face, mixing with the ashes, she sang and sang. Even when her breath faltered and her throat bled, she sang.

She'd never stop. Never. If she kept singing, she could keep some little part of him with her. She sang.

And sang.

Her mouth grew so dry, she felt her lips crack and bleed.

Ailish forced more power into her voice, desperate to feel just one more touch, one more brush of wings, hear one more word, inhale his scent . . .

Her grief wouldn't let her stop. She sang with unending love, struggling to reach across death and time to touch him with her love once more.

Days Remaining on Handfast Contract: Zero

"Ailish, my siren, my beauty, I heard you."

Oh, Ancestors! She heard his voice! Had she cracked? Or maybe she'd died?

"Open your eyes," Wing Slayer commanded of her.

Ailish lifted her lids, expecting shadows.

Instead, she saw Phoenix. With her own eyes. He was magnificent, kneeling across from her. They were on the grass in the back of his house. Her eyes filled with hot tears and streamed down her face. "How? Are you really here?" His glorious wings spread out behind him in rich, vibrant blues and purples. His huge chest rippled with muscle and no burns.

His dark eyes fixed on her. "You called me from the ashes." He lifted his hand and brushed a finger across her bottom lip. "You're bleeding."

His touch shivered through her. And Ailish threw herself into his arms. "You died! I felt your suffering!" Fierce, raw tremors ripped through her.

Strong arms wrapped around her, holding her. "I thought it would be another century before you called me back. Another hundred years. But I heard you singing and singing."

She lifted her head, looking to the left, able to see Wing Slayer. "Is he really alive?"

The god inclined his head. "With your profound love for Phoenix, you were able to reach out to me in your knowledge chakra. Because you and Phoenix are soul mirrors, that makes me your god, too, and I could take you into the Underworld. Then you sang, you sang for an entire day. Your voice filled and soared, even when your lips bled, you wouldn't stop. Your knees were bruised and blistered. You wouldn't stop."

"I wanted to find him." Ailish looked up at Phoenix. "I needed to find you, show you that I loved you every bit as much. I'd have followed you into the flames, but Wing Slayer pulled your ashes out. I couldn't leave your ashes. So I tried to reach you, to tell you I love you. Always."

Phoenix leaned his mouth close to hers. "I heard you. I came back to you." He closed his hand around her bare left wrist. "Thank you, Wing Slayer."

Ailish turned to look at the god. She began to piece it together. "Did you know I could call him back to life?"

"Once I touched you and felt your love for Phoenix, I knew you could."

The god radiated power and a vibration of otherworld knowledge that was beyond them. She lowered her head. "Thank you." Then she lifted her head and added, "Please, don't let him ever do this again. This burning and dying for me. Please, I don't want him to suffer anymore." She hurt to her very soul that Phoenix had suffered and burned.

Phoenix stroked her arm. "You didn't make me, sweetheart. I chose to do it, and I would do it again. For you." He paused, then added, "It worked, you are free. Her Ancestors will accept her now, right?"

"They welcome you, Ailish. They have waited for you for a very long time. In the years since the handfast, you have proven your worth."

Her heart swelled so big, she could barely breathe. Looking at the majestic god, she said, "I am honored."

Wing Slayer looked into her eyes. "I am powerful, but even I can't restore your sight permanently. There are costs to power, and you used your power to cause harm."

Phoenix slipped inside her head. *I'm sorry, sweetheart. But you can see through me.*

I'm not sorry, Phoenix. I would do it again to save Haley.

He squeezed her hand. *I love you.*

Wing Slayer said, "Phoenix, hand me your knife."

She felt the jolt of pride in him when he pulled out his knife and showed her the hilt. *Wings. He marked my knife, accepting me as his hunter before casting me into the Underworld.*

Ailish looked at the silver hilt of his knife, stamped with wings that looked just like her bracelet. "They are perfect."

Wing Slayer took the knife. "Hold out your joined hands with your thumbs up."

Phoenix pulled their hands forward while he said to her, "Can you still see?"

"Yes." She saw the beautiful wings wrapped around her right wrist.

Wing Slayer announced, "Your Ancestors are here, witch, do you feel them?"

She quieted and felt their benevolent spirits flowing around them. They were stunning and filled with a peaceful radiance. "Yes."

The god moved, flashing the knife so quickly, it was just a streak. The twin rings appeared around the base of their thumbs. Then he wrapped his large hand around their joined thumbs. "As true soul mirrors, may the two of you reflect the faith, courage, honor, strength, and cunning to fight the curse and protect the innocent. We give you the gift of time to aid you." He focused on Ailish. "And grant your request that Phoenix not die in the flames over and over. With immortality, you'll stay together in life."

The touch of Wing Slayer traveled through her then like a bolt. It raced through her blood, seared through her chakras, found each and every cell or atom that had ever lived. He was creating a new force within her and Phoenix, and marking them both with some invisible touch. Even the hairs on her arms raised in response. But his words, his vow to rescue Phoenix from the repeated suffering of the flames, made her love this god with all her heart. "Thank you," she whispered.

Then Wing Slayer touched her beloved bracelet. "Look at Phoenix now. Take in the sight of him and the image will be in your bracelet for you to see any time you wish."

Ailish turned and saw Phoenix. The moonlight reflected off his dark hair, illuminating his outlaw face and his eyes glowing with love for her. She drank him in, the shape of his nose, the curve of his lips, the depths of his eyes, the lines of his jaw. She heard lightning and thunder, felt the dramatic rocking of the earth, felt the winds whipping around them as Wing Slayer left. But she looked only at Phoenix.

Finally she blinked.

And then he was gone. She saw only shadows and shapes.

She touched the bracelet with her hand, and there he was. Tears of gratitude filled her eyes. "You are the last thing I will ever see with my true sight."

"My gift. . . ." Wing Slayer's words floated around them, then faded away.

Then Phoenix took her in his arms and filled her with so much more.

Epilogue

TWO MONTHS LATER

Ailish heard the wails of the baby coming down the hallway outside the condo.

"Morgan went shopping," Phoenix said, his voice full of laughter. Ailish was on her laptop, Phoenix and Key were watching a movie.

Key got up and opened the door.

The screams nearly made the windows rattle.

"Ailish, can you try? Please?" Joe asked.

She set aside her laptop and held out her arms. The baby was two weeks old and very attached to his mother. He loved Joe and preferred falling asleep on Joe's chest. But he knew the second Morgan left the condo, and he voiced his opinion loud and long.

Joe settled the baby in her arms. She stood, amused when Joe put his hand under her elbow just in case she fell. That man might not be the biological father, but he was little Devlin's true daddy. Opening her chakras, she began to sing:

> *Child of magic,*
> *Born of love.*
>
> *Dry your tears,*
> *Still your grief.*

Your mama loves you,
Even from afar.

Feel her worship,
In your heart.

Dev's tears stopped, his rigid body relaxed, and he pressed his face against her chest, as if burrowing closer to her voice magic. Finally, he fell into a deep sleep. Ailish leaned down, inhaling his powder-and-milk scent just as Phoenix slid his arm around her shoulders. Seamlessly she slid into his head, able to see through his eyes.

They both looked down at the little guy sleeping peacefully now.

Deep happiness spread through Ailish. She had come home to Glassbreakers, blind and alone. She'd thought she would die that way. Now she had Phoenix, the man who brought light to her dark world and had sacrificed his life to free her from the handfast. She had never known that kind of love. And she had friends. Every day was a gift.

Seeing you like this makes me wish for a child of our own, Phoenix said in her mind.

They'd love him or her fiercely, and like Dev, the child would have more than just his parents; he'd have the Wing Slayer Hunters and their witches loving him as well. *You'd be a good father,* she told him.

"Can I hold him?"

Ailish had been so intent on the baby and Phoenix, she nearly jumped at Key's voice right in front of her. "Sure." She used Phoenix's vision to settle Devlin in the other hunter's arms.

Key cradled the sleeping boy in his arms, slipping his finger into the closed fist. "I hope I'm here to teach you how to fight the curse."

Ailish felt the wave of pain from Phoenix, and her stomach twisted.

The darkness in Key was getting a deep hook in him. They could all feel him withdrawing from them. He was having more manic episodes of drawing slaughtered witches and insisting his brother, Liam, had killed them. But Phoenix feared it was Key's bloodlust getting hold of him, and one day he would be sucked so deep into the vortex that he wouldn't just draw a witch kill, he'd actually go out and murder a witch. But baby Dev seemed to reach Key, calming the violence and bringing out the protective, caring, and funny side of the artistic hunter.

With their mind link, Ailish told Phoenix, *We fought a demon and won to break my handfast. We'll find a way to save Key, too.*

Phoenix pulled her tighter against him. *Together, we're unbeatable. I love you, Ailish.*

As she touched the silver wings around her wrist, the image of Phoenix filled her mind. *And I love you. Always.*